John Gruffydd was born and educated in Cardiff. He spent his working life as a lawyer in the North West of England. His first novel "In Search of Mr Lemon" was written under the pen name of John Graham while he was still practising as a barrister. Since retiring he divides his time between the Wirral and Andalucia.

TO MY GRANDCHILDREN.

John Gruffydd

A DEATH IN THE VALLEY

AUSTIN MACAULEY
PUBLISHERS LTD.

Copyright © John Gruffydd

The right of John Gruffydd to be identified as author of this work has been asserted by him in accordance with section 77 and 78 of the Copyright, Designs and Patents Act 1988.

All rights reserved. No part of this publication may be reproduced, stored in a retrieval system, or transmitted in any form or by any means, electronic, mechanical, photocopying, recording, or otherwise, without the prior permission of the publishers.

Any person who commits any unauthorized act in relation to this publication may be liable to criminal prosecution and civil claims for damages.

A CIP catalogue record for this title is available from the British Library.

ISBN 978 1 84963 922 4

www.austinmacauley.com

First Published (2015)
Austin Macauley Publishers Ltd.
25 Canada Square
Canary Wharf
London
E14 5LB

Printed and bound in Great Britain

The characters and events in this book are fictitious and are not intended to represent any real events or any persons living or dead.

I

IN THE BLEAK MIDWINTER

One

He left the car just off the road where it wouldn't be seen and approached the house on foot. He knew there would be little chance of coming across anyone else as he half walked and half stumbled down the slope. Even the sheep didn't bother with the patchy grass on that side. The ground underneath his feet was sticky and yielding from the unrelenting rain yet even that didn't prevent the sensation of crunching from the coal dust that had been mingling with the soil for generations.

He looked back at the emptiness around him. He couldn't deny that the rolling green landscape had a certain rugged beauty that reminded him of childhood holidays spent in peace and security with his grandparents. The hills were not as dramatic as those of his childhood and there was an unfamiliar and bone chilling dampness in the air but it was still strongly evocative of a time before he knew of sorrow or anger, or had seen death or poverty.

The man smiled as he remembered winter days spent playing for hours with his brothers in snow covered fields in the biting but bracing cold, confident that when they went inside there would always be a roaring fire, hot food and a loving family to welcome them. No sooner had that memory crossed his mind than he was consciously supressing it. He was here in this bleak and lonely place for a purpose and that purpose would not be served by lapses into nostalgia.

He looked up at the sky. The clouds were dark and low. There was no sign of the sun behind them nor any clue that there ever existed in nature such a phenomenon as a blue sky. Although it was still relatively early in the afternoon there was darkness in the air. That was good. Few if any people would brave the rain to venture out here and any that did wouldn't notice him in the gloom as he moved down the slope dressed as he was in dark clothing. Nevertheless he was careful. His head constantly moved from side to side checking the path at the bottom of the hill, ready to dive into the mud at the first sight of anyone walking on it. He dragged his feet deliberately as he walked. It was highly unlikely that anyone would be looking for footprints after he'd finished and left but, just in case they were, he wasn't going to leave clear impressions for them to find.

As he reached the path he crouched down behind the wall that was on the other side and formed the rear boundary of the property. He checked again. There was no one there. No one had any reason to be in this desolate spot, miles from town on a winter's afternoon – no one that is except him. He peeped over the wall and could see the house. It looked empty. There were no lights on and no indication of anyone moving inside. It was a large, solid old house. It looked as if it had once been a farmhouse. He wondered what on earth anyone could farm in conditions like this but then he reminded himself that his own grandparents had spent their lives scraping a living out of land that was not dissimilar. Once more he supressed the drift into nostalgia and concentrated on the task in hand.

The wall was no great barrier to him. It had been built as a territorial marker rather than for protection. It was barely more than waist high and he vaulted it with ease. He found himself in a garden. It was neat and carefully set out. He was instantly struck by how incongruous it looked in comparison to the puny and unkempt vegetation on the other side of the wall. He wondered what sort of person would spend his time meticulously planning such a slice of suburbia in these inappropriate surroundings and then fighting what must be a never ending battle to maintain it. If he wanted to live in the wilderness why did he not leave it to the forces of nature to shape the land around his home?

He stopped himself from thinking further on the subject. It does not do to visualise or empathise with those who are to become your victims. You must not make them human or give them the sort of feelings that in a happier time you once had. That would only deflect you from the matter in hand. These are not human beings like your long dead parents or brothers.

They are the means of putting clothes on your back and food on your table – no more and no less.

He walked across the cropped lawn to the back of the house and looked up at the alarm box. The light showed that it was set. The house would be empty. As he looked through one of the downstairs windows he could see the sensor in the corner of the room. He reckoned that the doors and windows would be alarmed but even if they weren't, the sensors would set the alarm off before he got halfway across the first room. He would not be able to knock out the control box before that happened. The alarm box was too high to get at from the outside.

He weighed up the odds in his mind. It would take him no more than five minutes to find the control box and immobilise it. He was, after all, a professional and every alarm system conceived by man can be neutralised by a professional. The chances were that if the alarm rang nobody would hear it in the time it took him to silence it. On the other hand, the system looked sophisticated. For all he knew it was connected directly to the police station. He could be going about his business in the house oblivious to the fact that the police were on the way. It made sense. The owner of the house was not someone to neglect detail. The state of the garden proved that if nothing else. He would know that an alarm that did nothing but sound a siren would be no deterrent in a location like this. Surely, if he took the trouble to install an expensive system he would take the extra step of connecting it to the police station. Maybe there were cameras as well.

No, he couldn't take the risk. He had no alternative but to wait until somebody returned to the house and switched off the alarm and only then would he enter. It wasn't an ideal situation. It was far easier and safer to go into an empty house but in this case that wasn't an option. He was experienced enough and confident enough to do it the hard way when necessary.

Carefully and expertly he examined each of the ground floor windows at the back and sides of the house. He made sure as he did so that he wasn't seen from the road. He needed to select a suitable one for entry when the time came. He would have to work fast as soon as the alarm was turned off. He would not have the time to choose a window then. After considering each one he made his decision. It was at the side near to the back of the house and, best of all, shielded from the road by a bush. He was able to see that there was no lock on the window and it wasn't alarmed. It didn't need to be. Directly facing it was the winking light of a sensor. Once the alarm was turned off he could have the window open in seconds and be through it. He pressed his face against the glass to look at the darkened room into which the window led. It looked like a spare one, maybe used as a study or for storage. There was a desk and chair against one wall and some ill matching cupboards against another. Roughly stacked boxes suggested that this was where junk was left while its long term fate was decided. He reasoned that nobody entering the house would go straight to that room. It was an ideal place for him to make his entry to and then wait in until the coast was clear for him to move to the room he was interested in.

Having made his plan he walked back across the lawn. He had to be patient now. Near the back wall was a garden shed where he could wait out of the drizzling rain until the time came to return to that window. First there was something he had to do. Better to do it now than after he had finished. He approached the tree and did what he needed. Then he turned his attention to the shed.

The padlock provided a barrier for seconds only and he opened the door and went in. Inside the walls were lined with shelving and racks on which were set out the paraphernalia of the obsessive gardener. There was no chair but there was sufficient space on the floor for him to sit down. Pulling the door behind him he squatted down, conscious of the smell of fertiliser and creosote but grateful to be dry and sheltered as he focussed on what he had to do and awaited the chance to do it.

It had been a frustrating morning for her. Shopping always was these days. It was no longer a matter of a daily visit to the

High Street to scan the array of goods that each of a street full of shops offered her, no longer a matter of passing the time of day with the familiar faces that she inevitably came across as she navigated from one shop doorway to the next. Now she had the questionable pleasure of a weekly visit to the supermarket on the other side of town. She hated every part of it. Trying to park a car that was far too big for her in a space that was too tight for comfort started her off on the wrong foot and it got no better. She was still old fashioned enough to want to walk into a shop and speak to a human being about what was on offer or whatever the hot gossip of the day was. That pleasure had been stolen from her by those modern day conquistadors of the supermarket industry who, like their forerunners, imposed their values on a defenceless population with promises of untold riches that proved to be illusory. Now she was condemned to follow the endless train of zombie-like shoppers pushing defiant trolleys along aisle after aisle never seeming to find what she was looking for. The alien invaders always assured her that they had brought her greater freedom of choice and in many ways that was right. She could see three or four brands of baked beans set out for her consideration with each brand seeking to outbid the others in the originality of its sauces and accompaniments. Maddeningly, however, they never seemed to have exactly what she wanted in the size or quantity that she wanted it in.

The clothing department was as irritating as the food department. As there were no clothes shops left in town she was forced to clothe herself from the acres of hangers that might as well be labelled "take it or leave it". There was not even so much as an assistant who could listen to her needs or offer opinions on what would suit her. There was plenty to choose from but nothing she could choose. When she found something she liked the supermarket would decree that she could only buy it in a colour that didn't suit her or a size that did not fit her. If she wanted summer clothes they offered winter clothes. If she wanted gloves the supermarket offered them to her in a matching set with a scarf she didn't want.

She wasn't one to ponder on the nature of capitalism or the corrosive effect of insatiably greedy and increasingly ruthless corporations on the time honoured conventions of fair trading. Those were concepts for others, without the responsibility of running a home that their husbands would be happy to return to each night, to grapple with. All she knew was that supermarkets were symptomatic of the way life was going these days; they all talk about giving her choice but in reality they give her what they want her to have. They kill off the opposition so they can be free to offer the kind of choice that suits them – buy what's on our shelves or go hungry and naked.

Today had been as bad as ever. She needed a new coat to cope with the cold that the next few months promised but the supermarket decided she would not have one. She had wanted to cook something special for her husband's dinner tonight but the ingredients were either absent or offered in such large quantities that they would feed a ravenous football team rather than the middle-aged couple that they were. She had to recast the menu three times before she got what she needed. The queues at the check out stretched halfway down the aisles and she managed to select the slowest one. The check out operator was surly and didn't mind who knew that she didn't want to be there. She even managed to load the head office directed *"thank you for shopping with us"* with so much menace that it sounded like a challenge to a fight.

When she finally wrestled the trolley to her car she found a people carrier the size of a tank parked so close to it that she had to struggle in through the passenger door and then reverse gingerly out waiting for the scraping noise that would add yet another scratch to the impressive array of war wounds that her bumpers proudly displayed. She was not therefore in the best of humours as she steered her car laboriously between the gateposts that led to the converted farmhouse in a lonely spot outside of town that she shared with her husband.

As she brought her car to a halt it made a crunching sound on the gravel of the drive. She saw instantly that her husband's car wasn't there. He was still at work. Although he had taken on a less demanding job since retiring from the force he still seemed to work the same long hours. He was rarely home before six even though his hours were supposed to be flexible. Sometimes in the summer he would get back a little earlier so that he could spend time working in his beloved garden but in winter he never did. She didn't mind that too much. At least in the winter he had no distractions once he was home. They could spend the dark evenings sitting together in front of the fire oblivious to the wind whistling over the emptiness around them. She loved the time they spent like that. Theirs was not what anyone could call a passionate relationship but on those winter nights when she was with him she always felt a warmth that wasn't entirely down to the fire in front of her.

She was well aware that some would look at her marriage and wonder what he saw in her. She had no illusions about being a great beauty and, in public at least, she tended to come over as quiet, withdrawn and, she had to accept, a little dull. He, by contrast, was a strong, charismatic character whom everybody seemed to know and like. She had seen the looks women sometimes gave him and the flirtatious way in which he responded. It didn't matter to her. He was her husband and he made her feel safe and comfortable. Alone with him she could show her true character. Away from the company of others they would talk for hours and without inhibition of their deepest feelings, their most profound experiences and their most closely kept secrets. They would explore the furthest corners of each other's minds with a frankness that she found to be as sensual as any physical contact. No other woman would share such intimacy with him. Those other women could flatter his ego as much as they wanted. He would flirt with them, revel in the attention but then return to her, his wife. She didn't feel threatened. She may not have the looks or the charm but what she did have was a good husband and that was all she asked for. Her life may seem humdrum to outsiders but she was quite happy to sacrifice the shallow pleasures of the outside world for what she had in her marriage.

She was now going into the house he had lovingly renovated for them and she was going to cook a dinner that they could share in their own world, shut away from the jealous women who coveted her husband and, for that matter, anyone else. They were miles from town, out of sight of other houses and with only the occasional sheep straying from the other side of the hill to remind them that they were not the only living creatures on the planet. Tonight, as every night, they would be completely alone.

She let herself in by the front door and disabled the alarm. As she punched in the code 1,9,2,7 she wondered how many other households here in South Wales used on their alarms the year the FA Cup came to Cardiff. She always wondered whether astute burglars were wise to it and always tried those digits first within a 30 mile radius of the city. They should change it really, just in case but they had never got round to it and, despite its location, there was something about this solid old house with its thick white walls that made her feel secure. Maybe it was the man who came home to it each night.

He had heard the car pulling up. He peeped out of the shed door and saw a light go on inside the house. It was time to move. Noiselessly he hurried to the window, peered in and listened. She was still moving about carrying her shopping to the kitchen from her car. He would have to wait for her to settle before entering the house. He could not afford to bump into her before he had done what he had come there for.

It took her three journeys to empty the car of shopping. Eventually, he heard her lock the car and slam shut the heavy oak front door. As he looked through the window across the room he could see her pass the door as she headed for the back of the house. Now he had to work quickly. With the expertise that came with years of practice he had the window open in an instant. Despite the smoothness of his movement it still made a noise as it slid up. He paused, holding his breath, straining for any sound that might signal that she had heard him. There was none. With the grace of a gymnast he levered himself in through the open window and dropped gently onto the wooden floor below. He was in. Once again he waited to ensure that she was not moving about before he headed for the door.

In the kitchen she had laid her ingredients methodically in front of her and was thumbing through the recipe book before starting to prepare them. She reached for the knife and as she did so she thought she heard a creaking noise from the study. It made her pause. No further noise followed. That's the trouble with these old houses. They seem to creak and groan randomly and spontaneously. When she first moved in she used to be a little frightened by the noises when alone at night but he had reassured her that it was natural and that the isolation of their location made them safer at night rather than more vulnerable. After all, he had told her, you won't find weak willed drunks or drugged up teenagers walking past the house on their way home at night and being tempted to chance their arms with a spur of the moment burglary. That made her feel better. He was an ex-policeman and should know about these things. Now the nocturnal noises simply made her pause momentarily before carrying on with the task in hand. She started chopping the vegetables making a rhythmic tapping on the board as she did so.

He heard the sound of chopping from the kitchen. She would be engrossed in the task in hand and he had the chance to move upstairs. He slid out of the study and, virtually on all fours to reduce the noise, he climbed the stairs. He passed the kitchen door as he rose. It was partly open and he could see her intent on making every piece of vegetable a uniform size. She would not look up. As he reached the landing he glanced around to get his bearings. He found what was obviously the main bedroom and pushed the door open. It was quite a small room and the bed took up most of it. The room was made smaller by the walk in wardrobe that had been built in. The householder's obviously into home improvement he thought but stopped before he found himself thinking of him as a human being again.

He moved to the cabinet by the side of the bed. There was what looked like a jewellery case on top of it. He reached over to it, just a little too quickly and too clumsily. His sleeve brushed against the bedside lamp and it started to topple off the cabinet. His reflex reaction would have been to grab hold of it but in that split second it was overridden by the acquired instinct of avoiding the noise that sudden movement can cause. He did not have time to rationalise or reconcile the two reactions before the lamp hit the floor and shattered. The noise made him freeze, afraid even to breathe.

Downstairs in the kitchen she heard the crash. That wasn't like the creaking noises she had grown used to. It couldn't be explained by movement of beams or joists. Something – or someone – had caused something to fall. She was now nervous. Her first thought was to ring her husband. He would know what to do and, with any luck he would hurry back to her earlier than usual. It was no good. The call went unanswered. He must be in court or interviewing a witness or something. Telling herself to stop being so pathetic she walked slowly up the stairs. She deliberately stepped heavily on them. She wanted to be heard. If anyone was up there she didn't want to surprise him, she wanted him to leave before she had to confront him. Mentally scolding herself for such foolishness she reached the top of the stairs, calmer now and confident of finding the aftermath of a gust of wind through a window that had been left open or some everyday object that had been left in a precarious position and had finally succumbed to gravity. There couldn't be a person there; she would have seen him going up.

He heard her footsteps on the stairs. He had to hide. His hiding place had to be in the bedroom. He couldn't risk going out of the door onto the landing. He slid open the door of the wardrobe and manoeuvred himself in behind a row of hangers containing clothes. There wasn't much room there but enough to keep him concealed. He slid the door until it was almost closed and flattened himself against the back of the wardrobe. He had to concentrate on his breathing now. He felt as if it could be heard all across the house and he had to slow it down and make it shallower. He would now have to wait until she went down again.

She checked the bathroom. That was the most obvious place for something to fall. She could find nothing to account for the noise. She moved across the landing to the bedroom. It was in darkness. She turned on the light and entered. Inside the wardrobe he was willing his heart to stop beating so prominently. She soon noticed the lamp lying in pieces on the floor. She had to smile. There she was imaging all kinds of evil creatures roaming around the house and the reality was that she had placed the lamp too near the edge and it had fallen off, as simple as that. She was an avid bedtime reader and had a habit of cramming the top of the cabinet with so many books and magazines that she wouldn't leave enough room for the bedside light. She put down the kitchen knife that she was still carrying and went over to survey the damage. Having done so she turned to go back down to fetch a brush and shovel so she could clear up the mess.

He saw the light go out and started to gently slide open the wardrobe door. At that moment the light went on again. She had left behind the kitchen knife and had returned for it. Gritting his teeth to prevent any sound emerging from his mouth, he braced himself for what might come next. He waited a few seconds. He'd got away with it. That was close. Another second and he would have been emerging from the wardrobe in full view of the woman who was now standing in the doorway.

She frowned as she looked at the wardrobe door. Was it her imagination or had it moved since she last saw it? Surely that was ridiculous. However, obsessive tidier that she was, she went over to close it.

As she touched it she felt a great weight crash into her. She was thrown back onto the bed. The weight was on top of her now. Her first thought was that the wall had collapsed on her but now she realised. What was pinning her down onto the bed wasn't made of bricks or plaster. It was a man, a big heavy dark clad man who was now squeezing the breath out of her.

She let out a desperate scream with what breath she had left. As she did so she realised that there was no one to hear that scream. No one that was apart from the man that was now on top of her grunting like an animal. All that this thought did was to make her scream again, even more desperately. The scream carried through the window, across the meticulous garden and into the wilderness beyond. It was all to no avail. The sheep must have heard it as they huddled together for shelter on the other side of the hill but it reached no human ears. It reached nobody who could save her from the force that had so suddenly and violently confronted her and which now, unrelentingly, was forcing the life out of her.

His face was almost touching hers, so close that the stench of onions and rotting teeth on his breath filled her nostrils making her baulk. Drops of his sweat fell on her cheek as they struggled. His grunting was almost rhythmic now and his eyes were bulging. The will to live began to ebb from her as fatigue spread through her flailing limbs, seducing her with the treacherous promise of peace and rest.

Then it was over. She let out a final scream, a marrow chilling soul piercing scream that drifted unheeded into the air. As the scream died the house fell into silence. Outside, the wind whistled through bare branches, the rain seeped into the gritty earth and the sheep continued to huddle together oblivious to what had occurred. Silently they chewed the sporadic tufts of wiry grass little knowing and little caring that they had been witnesses to a death in the valley.

Two

Nigel swore. "Oh bugger!" he cried as if invoking the spirit of a long dead Irish sex offender. "Sod it, damn it and bugger it!" It sounded like the name of a dubious firm of solicitors. It is true that he swore with the rounded vowels and perfect enunciation of one who had enjoyed an expensive and traditional education but, nevertheless, he swore with a vehemence that cut like a scalpel through the antiseptic silence that hung over the hospice as heavily as the winter fog outside.

It was enough to make the nun behind the desk jump in surprise. It was not the language that shocked her. She was well used to far worse from those patients who chose to face the inevitability of their ends by hurling vile curses as if the Angel of Death were so sensitive as to be deterred from his mission by obscenity. What shocked her was the complete lack of any obvious target for the abuse. All she could see in front of the well dressed and obviously angry visitor was the Christmas tree with an inoffensive fairy on top that had been brought in to lighten an atmosphere heavy with untimely death. What had that fairy done to provoke such anger in the hitherto impeccably mannered man who had come to see Mr Webster?

As he looked across at the nun's puzzled face Nigel realised that he had inadvertently, in his frustration, given voice to a reaction that he had intended to keep to himself. He mumbled an embarrassed apology and, hunching his shoulders against the biting cold, stepped out into the car park.

Sitting in the shelter of the Bentley Nigel gazed morosely at the wood and leather interior and reflected on what had passed. It had been a bad day. Acting, as he did, as the solicitor to the powerful and respectable had made him complacent and, he had to admit, a little smug. When your clients are the backbone of the establishment you expect them to get what they want from a legal system that the establishment created and the establishment runs. The police cases that he undertook were a perfect example.

Every so often some toe rag urged on by bleeding hearts and grasping lawyers would proclaim himself the victim of police brutality or corruption and some poor copper with years of public service behind him would find himself dragged through the mud. It was at such times that Nigel would be called upon to defend the honour of the forces of law and order and the pockets of their insurers.

His first approach would usually be to send an avuncular ex bobby along in the guise of an investigator. He would explain in an ever so friendly manner to all the witnesses how damaging this whole process would be to the poor policeman involved, a dedicated public servant whose career now hung in the balance. He would then explain in an equally friendly manner to the complainant how difficult life tended to become for those who complained against the police and how there was a lot to be said for letting sleeping dogs lie. In this way, and with a smile ever present on his face, the investigator would usually ensure that the complaint went no further. On those occasions when it did then the gloves came off and Nigel would defend the claim and in so doing attack the complainant with a ferocity worthy of a pit bull with inflamed piles.

Nigel saw no wrong in this. In his eyes it was no more than justice. Most of the claims were without foundation and even when they were not devoid of merit those that brought them were. As Nigel saw it the police were there to serve society and regularly put their bodies on the line to do so. Why should they be denied the unqualified gratitude of society because someone whose life has been dedicated to far less worthy aims takes umbrage at being frustrated by police action from achieving them? It was not so important to Nigel whether some breach of some impenetrably complex regulation had put a copper, acting in good faith, on the wrong side of laws designed to protect the wrongdoer. What mattered to him was who was on the side of good and who on the side of evil.

At first sight the case of Giuseppe Contemponi had seemed no different from all the others. A small time crook from

Naples he had come over to the Welsh valleys to take over the family café. No sooner had he done so than he had turned it into a front for the fencing of stolen goods, the sale of drugs and who knows what other criminal activities. Eventually, as all small time crooks do, he tried to move into the big time. He had tried to rob a post office in a neighbouring village at gunpoint. He had entered the living quarters above the post office at night and threatened the postmaster's wife. He had, however, reckoned without Tom Webster the postmaster who had given a perfect description of him and then picked him out on an identification parade. In that way the career of Giuseppe Contemponi the armed robber had ended as quickly as it had begun. He was sentenced to fifteen years but only served six months before falling to his death from the prison roof while waving a banner protesting his innocence.

That was twenty years ago but the legend of "Big Beppe" had lived on in the valleys. From time to time some misguided or self seeking local politician or journalist would mount a campaign for an inquiry and a pardon but such campaigns, whilst noisy and emotional, always fizzled out. They did so because emotion is no substitute for hard evidence and there wasn't any – until now.

It had been with mild irritation that Nigel had received the news that he had to travel to a God forsaken corner of South Wales in the week before Christmas to speak to a witness who claimed to have important new evidence in the case. Such new evidence, Nigel heard, had led to a claim being made against the local police force by Giuseppe Contemponi Junior, "Little Beppe" or "Beppo" as he was known to distinguish him from his father. This spawn of a career criminal was alleging perversion of the course of justice and seeking a pardon for his father and, more importantly from Nigel's point of view, damages from the police. Nigel knew that the ex-bobby would not do for the interview of the new witness who had caused the long dead case to be reopened. Nobody less than Nigel himself was required for the job. The new witness was none other than Tom Webster, the ex postmaster whose evidence had convicted Beppe in the first place. He would need careful handling and Nigel knew that this meant that, inconvenient as it was, a journey away from the comfort of his home and office into a cold and desolate Welsh valley town was inevitable.

A night in a smart hotel in Cardiff Bay had done much to ameliorate Nigel's displeasure. Suitably refreshed, he ventured out to the hospice where Tom Webster was to be found to persuade that man that any regret he may now belatedly feel for his contribution to the tragic turn that events had taken was misplaced. Nothing could alter the fact that Beppe Contemponi had been a merciless criminal who had brought onto himself the tragic end that he had suffered.

That at least was the intention, but it was not how matters turned out.

Nigel had been forced onto the back foot as soon as he entered Webster's room. He had a photograph of Webster on his file and expected to be meeting the same ruddy faced, wild haired man with what doctors always referred to as a well nourished physique. Instead, lying on the bed was a skeleton wrapped tightly in skin that was taut like a drum head, thin like tissue paper and bearing the yellow tinge that old documents acquire after about a century of storage. The hair was no more and every contour of the shrivelled skull was exposed. Cancer had taken away the Tom Webster in the picture and left in its place a shrunken apparition of impending death.

Nigel now realised why he had to speak to this man before Christmas. There wouldn't be a second chance. The pathetic figure in front of him would not see the New Year. He guessed that this was why Webster had suddenly decided to speak after all these years. He was clearing his conscience in preparation for the imminent meeting with his maker. What Nigel could not grasp was why Webster felt that the death of Beppe Contemponi was something that he should feel responsible for. Maybe it was a natural emotion to feel sympathy for a man who had lost his life so tragically but that was all it was, an emotion, and Nigel didn't do emotion. A public school education had taught him to treat emotion as a false friend and a career in the law had taught him that only facts could be trusted not to betray you. So far as he could see the death of Beppe Contemponi and the approaching death of Tom Webster could not alter the facts of the case.

Nigel felt himself freeze at the harrowing sight before him. He did not know how to speak to Webster. It seemed to him inappropriate to be friendly and informal with a corpse and he feared that an over authoritarian approach might finish the poor devil off. He retreated, therefore, into cold formality holding it as a shield to keep at bay the pitiful reality of Webster's situation. After a curt introduction he began by reading, without expression, from the transcript of the evidence that Tom Webster had given to the court in May, 1990. He repeated what Webster had said about being awoken in the early hours of 1st December, 1989 by banging on the door of the living quarters above the post office in Pentreglo. He included the account of a man with a scarf over his lower face pushing his way in, brandishing a gun when the door was opened.

There was no reaction from the bed as Nigel continued to read, coming on to the part where Webster had described a gun being held against his wife's head and being threatened that she would die in front of him if he did not open the safe. Webster simply listened with his sunken unblinking eyes focussed on Nigel as he read. As Nigel finished reading of how Webster had told the court of the scarf falling and of the close up and prolonged view he had had of the robber's face he paused and looked down at the cadaverous figure before him inviting an acknowledgement. There was none. Webster continued to fix Nigel with his eyes, concentrating all his efforts on dragging breath painfully into his body, savouring it like an unexpected treat and then releasing it with regret.

Nigel went on to read of how Webster had attended an identification parade at Pentreglo Police Station at 2 p.m. on December 18th 1989 and unhesitatingly picked out Giuseppe Contemponi as the man who had robbed the post office. He looked again at Webster. There was still no reaction, still the staring eyes, still the laboured breathing. No matter how reluctant he was to upset the poor man it was futile just sitting reading without receiving any reaction. He could have stayed in his office and done that. Gently he asked, "Is that right, Mr Webster?"

Tom Webster took a deep and painful breath, using it to fuel his whispered reply.

"Is that what I said in court?"

"This is the official transcript of the court proceedings," Nigel assured him.

Another deep breath and another whispered reply, "Then it's what I said in court."

Nigel made a conscious effort to contain his frustration.

"I am aware that it was what you said in court but what I want to know is whether it was true."

This time the whisper came more quickly. "It's true, I did pick him out..."

Nigel began to relax and was about to ask another question when Webster, having stolen another breath, finished his sentence.

"...but it wasn't him who robbed the post office." Webster gave a slight shake of his emaciated skull as he spoke.

Nigel was ready for that. He plucked another document from his file.

"I am aware," he said, injecting the slightest touch of coldness into his tone, "that you recently wrote a letter to Mr Contemponi's solicitors claiming that your identification was wrong. That's how this whole business began when they told his son. However, that does not alter the fact that you made a clear identification of Giuseppe Contemponi just seventeen days after the robbery."

Webster tried to speak but Nigel, warming to his task, spoke over him.

"...and not only did you pick out Mr Contemponi at the identification parade but you had given a description of the robber within twelve hours of the robbery and, based on the photographs I have seen, it fitted him like a glove."

"But it wasn't him," repeated Webster, this time with a new found firmness in his voice.

Nigel momentarily forgot the need for a gentle approach and replied with unrestrained sarcasm.

"What sort of coincidence is that? You give a description of the robber that matches Contemponi exactly even before you have seen him at the identification parade. Then when you are faced with a group of men all of whom could match that description you pick one at random and lo and behold it's Contemponi. How do you explain that if he wasn't the man?"

When Webster spoke it was with a clear and determined voice that threatened to exhaust his last reserves of strength. He fixed Nigel with his unrelenting stare and seemed to be forcibly propelling the words at him to ensure that they were fully absorbed.

"It was rigged, that's how I explain it. The identification parade, the statement, all rigged."

Nigel abandoned any last effort to conceal his mounting impatience.

"Tell me about this rigging," he said. The hostility in his voice could not be mistaken.

Webster closed his eyes as if sleeping. He breathed deeply a few times and then summoned all his strength to lift himself onto one puny elbow. Looking straight at Nigel he did as he was asked.

"It was about a week before Christmas, a Saturday night at about seven o'clock. I got an urgent call from the police station. They needed to see me about the robbery. I went there and a copper met me at the door. He told me he was going to show me the man who robbed the post office. I was taken to a corridor where there were cell doors. He took me to outside one of the cells and told me to look in through the spyhole that was in the door. There was a man sitting there. I had a good hard look at him but he wouldn't have known I was doing it. I'd never seen him before in my life but the copper told me he was the man who had robbed the post office. I said I didn't think it was but he said it was definitely the man. He told me to remember his face because I was likely to be called upon to identify him soon. The next evening I got a call from the police again. They said I had to attend an identification parade on the

Monday. I went along and they made me walk along a line of men. I didn't know any of them but the man I'd seen on the Saturday was among them. I shouldn't have done it but I remembered what I'd been told. I picked him out and told them he was the one I'd seen at the post office. It was a lie but that's what I told them. "

"What about the statement?" Nigel's tone had become less aggressive.

"I gave a statement the day after the robbery. I told the truth in it. I said I could not really describe the man. That's the statement I should have stuck with. As soon as I had been shown the man in the cell I was taken to an interview room and asked for another statement. I was asked to describe the man who'd robbed us. I did as he asked. The description I gave was pretty detailed. It had to be. I had only seen the poor bastard five minutes before. It's no wonder I got his description right but it was still all lies. "

Webster slumped down again onto the pillow. Nigel was lost for words. Webster took another effort-laden breath and broke the silence. His face, expressionless when Nigel had first entered the room, now seemed contorted with pain.

"Because of what I did I killed an innocent man. Now I'm on my way out. The nuns and the nurses tell me to be positive but I know that before very long it will be over. I don't know what I'll be facing but, whatever it is, I'm not going to face it with a man's death on my conscience."

Nigel realised that this was not going to be as easy a task as he had anticipated. He had to try a different tack. His voice was kind and reassuring as he leaned forward to speak quietly to Webster.

"You have nothing on your conscience to be ashamed of. You did your public duty. Nobody is going to judge you harshly for that, in this world or the next. Maybe the police took a few short cuts to achieve a conviction. I can't condone that, of course, but does that mean that you should feel responsible for what Mr Contemponi did?"

Nigel shook his head to illustrate his point. He found himself placing a brotherly hand on the sharp bony shoulder below him as he continued. "What happened to Mr Contemponi happened because *he* decided to rob you and *he* decided to carry out some suicidal rooftop protest rather than accept his guilt. You didn't do these things, *he* did. The Police may have got a conviction by the wrong route but isn't the most important thing that a guilty man was convicted? You should be content with that rather than torturing yourself about the way it was achieved."

Webster had been lying back with his eyes closed. They shot open as Nigel finished speaking.

"He was an innocent man not a guilty one." Webster seemed to growl the words. His voice, though feeble, contained a touch of anger.

Nigel's reaction was immediate. The suggestion that if a man could not be proved guilty he was automatically innocent was one that offended his sense of logic, tempered as that sense had been by his deep immersion in the establishment.

"Why are you so sure Contemponi was innocent?" he snapped tetchily.

Webster paused before replying, wishing to make sure that he had enough breath left to make his meaning clear.

"I am sure," he replied, "because that man could not have committed the robbery. I know that because there was no robbery. Neither he nor anyone else robbed that post office. The money was missing because I stole it."

This time the silence lasted even longer. Nigel quietly thought through the implications of what he had heard while Tom Webster, as if freed of a burden, sunk down into his pillow the anger melting away from his features.

When Nigel finally spoke all he could say was, "I suppose you can prove you stole it," as if the other man was claiming an inheritance instead of confessing to theft and perjury. It was a stupid question but Nigel was grasping at straws to avoid having to come to a conclusion that he dreaded reaching.

Webster made the slightest movement of his head towards the bedside locker.

"It's all in there," he said, "the bank records showing the money going in to an account in my name and...," there was the slightest hint of a wry smile as he continued, "... going out again almost as quickly. The money was taken out after I put it in and I never knew what happened to it. My wife said that a bent bank clerk skimmed it off knowing I couldn't complain. I believed her at the time but now I'm not so sure."

"Why?" was all that Nigel could say after he skimmed through the records.

As Webster prepared himself for his reply Nigel thought he saw tears forming in his eyes.

"Angela," was the one word reply before Webster explained further. "Why does a man do anything stupid?" he asked rhetorically before answering himself. "A woman. It's always a woman. From the first apple in the Garden of Eden it's always a woman. In my case that woman was Angela, my wife. I had been a widower for too long and I was lonely. She came along and she seemed the answer to my loneliness. Now I know she was too young for me but you don't notice things like that when you are besotted the way I was over Angela. I didn't dare hope that she would feel the same way but when she did I felt that I was so fortunate that I would have done anything to keep her. If that meant stealing so that I could buy her what made her happy then that was what I would do and what I did do. I only took small amounts at first which I covered up in the books. Then they got bigger and harder to cover up. The end of year audit was due and I knew I would be found out so I decided to go for broke. I emptied the safe of cash and reported a robbery. That way I didn't have to worry about the audit. I thought they'd get me sooner or later but I was going to worry about that when it happened, only it never did. I couldn't believe my luck when I was called into the police station that night. I didn't think about the poor wretch I was condemning. I just thought I was going to live happily ever after."

Webster started to breathe more rapidly and shallowly, making an unsettling squeaking sound as he did so. Nigel was concerned that the effort of talking for so long was about to finish him off but then he realised. The old man was crying.

After a few moments Webster took control of himself once more and continued. He was no longer talking to Nigel and did not seem even to be aware of his presence as he spoke sadly to the ceiling.

"It wasn't to be, of course. She was never going to be content as the wife of an ageing postmaster. As soon as the money ran out so did her pretence of loving me. That's all it was you know, a pretence. I've been in this place now for four months and in that time do you know how often she has visited me? Do you know how often she has written to me or called to see how I was?"

It was another rhetorical question. Webster did not look at Nigel. He didn't expect a reply. More shallow squeaking breaths and he answered it.

"None," he said. "Not once." He turned his head towards the wall but Nigel could see the tears flowing down his brittle features.

Nigel was finding it difficult to handle this open show of emotion. As a defence mechanism he shuffled his papers and then turned to a clean page in his notebook. His pen poised he prepared to take a formal statement from the retired postmaster. He needed a record of the damning confession he had just heard. He needed more details so he could investigate further, check out the truth of what he was told and identify the one who had brought disgrace to the institution he had dedicated a large part of his professional life to protect. Try as he might he could coax no more from Webster. The shrunken form of what had once been a vibrant human being lay there oblivious to his questions. He had said what he had to say and his conscience was as clear as he could make it. All that was left was to quietly await an end that would not be long in coming.

Nigel looked down at him. For Tom Webster there would be no future but Nigel knew that for him the next few months would be anything but easy. The sinking feeling in his gut told him that this was not a case that was going to go away. He would need to return here to Wales after Christmas and, following an investigation, he would have no alternative but to recommend that the claim by Giuseppe Contemponi junior be met. Worst of all he would have to report that, within the police force that he had represented so conscientiously there had been something the existence of which he had hitherto refused to accept – a bent copper.

"Sod it, damn it and bugger it!"

Three

Mervyn Jenkins, known to all as MJ, slid quietly out of the bed. She was still sleeping and he did not want to wake her. If he woke her he would have to talk to her and he really had nothing to say to her far less any interest in what she might have to say to him. He had often wondered over the years how he could reach such levels of intimacy with a woman and yet have no wish to speak to her. In truth he knew little of what interested her outside the bedroom. He knew her tastes in fashion or what she would choose from an expensive restaurant menu but was ignorant and disinterested in her deeper emotions, her politics, her religious beliefs or in what she truly wanted out of life.

It was so different with Iris. His bond with her went so much further than the physical. It was never hard to talk to her and, in talking, to open his soul and reveal its innermost secrets – all its secrets that is, apart from the existence of the figure whose sleeping form he was now looking at. Throughout their marriage MJ and Iris had shared their deepest hopes and fears, debated their opinions on every subject they encountered and pooled their knowledge and experience until they were as one harmonious mind. In all of that time there was only one subject of which Iris was ignorant, MJ's extra marital affairs.

MJ looked down at the bed. She was still so breathtakingly beautiful that even after all these years of their affair he was still excited by the thought that she was his. The affair had lasted far longer than he had ever expected but it was a relationship that was built purely on physical attraction. It had always been that way ever since they met when he was a young beat policeman looking for excitement and she was a young attractive woman stuck in a boring marriage. So great had the mutual attraction been that there had been no need for them to become particularly well acquainted before launching into a frenzied relationship. Even as they matured and the initial thrill diminished the passion remained strong allowing the relationship to endure for longer than many marriages. Even as the inevitable descent into routine gathered pace, the union survived to the extent that she was now an addiction for MJ. He needed her and depended on the continuation of their affair as an addict depends on his next fix. As with all addictions the need for her drove him to act as his rational mind told him he should not act and like all addictions that need carried with it the inevitability that it would not end without him and those close to him being damaged.

As he quietly showered and then dressed MJ reflected on the irony of his situation. His relationship with one woman was a perfect meeting of minds and his relationship with the other was a perfect meeting of bodies. If only he could have had the two together in one woman! Instead he had spent too much time forced into a double life and keeping a secret from the one with whom there was supposed to be no secrets. Perhaps many men would envy his position but it was not the way MJ wanted it. He hated the dishonesty of it all and knew that it had to stop. One of those women had to be removed from his life whatever it took to achieve it. He had already set the wheels in motion. It was too late to stop them now. All he could do was to brace himself and be prepared to ride out the consequences.

He was able to let himself out of the house without disturbing her. It was late afternoon and just beginning to go dark. A cold wind blew along the street carrying nerve numbing droplets of icy rain. A typical January day in South Wales. MJ needed to get back to Pentreglo to look in at the office. Working for a solicitor, sitting in on court hearings, attending to clients in custody and interviewing witnesses was ideal work for an ex copper and it gave MJ the freedom to pursue his affair without detection – just as long as he looked in at the office every day.

He took the mountain road towards Pentreglo which was in the next valley. In the half light it was difficult to make out which of the dark shapes around him were the work of nature and which the work of the Coal Board or the coal owners before them. Although the slag heaps were now landscaped they still stood out as a reminder of why places like Pentreglo ever existed.

The mining of coal, the coal that drove British industry and provided the steam to carry British adventurers to the far corners of empire, was the sole reason for the birth, the life and ultimately the death of Pentreglo and so many of the communities around it. Coal shaped its menfolk, bending their spines as they pursued its ever narrowing seams and filling their lungs with its dust. It shaped the womenfolk, providing the meagre wages that each week they would use to put food on the family table and clothes on the family's backs. It shaped the children, narrowing their dreams of the future down to a life in the pit or caring for those who went down the pit. All those who had lived in Pentreglo had known to listen in dread for the siren that threatened the prospect that the relentless search for coal had created another widow or more orphans. They had known the bitterness and division that came with the strikes and the lock outs that were an inevitable part of an industry that exploited men as much as it exploited the wealth of the land.

Those experiences had been ingrained in the people of Pentreglo for generations just as the dark coal dust was ingrained in the scars of the miners. They are past memories now. There is now no mine in Pentreglo. Whether the result of economic realities or political meanness of spirit, the closure of the pit had an instant and profound effect on the area. Men lost their self-respect, women their place in the family structure and children the security of their future. Of course, the people of Pentreglo had always enjoyed a love hate relationship with the coal industry but when it went it took with it the whole reason for the existence of the town whose very name, Pentreglo or "village of coal", bound it to that industry. When, by the decree of uncaring and distant powers that be, the coal industry was abandoned Pentreglo was left like a port without water or a body without a soul.

MJ remembered the dark days of the pit closure and the strike that preceded it just as he remembered the divided loyalties that he and so many of his fellow officers had felt. It was the one time when MJ had been ashamed to wear the uniform of a police officer as he was called upon to be complicit in the forcible grinding down of the spirit of brave and honourable men and women from his own area; men and women whose boots the spineless and vindictive characters whose bidding he was doing were not fit to lick.

As MJ started to descend into the valley he knew that he would soon reach the point from which, in daylight, he could see Ty Gwyn, the imposing white converted farmhouse outside Pentreglo where he and Iris had lived since his retirement from the force. It would probably be too dark to see it properly but he always glanced across as he reached that spot.

What was more likely was that he would see Sam Hopkins in his usual place. Sam was always there, rain or shine, for some part of the day, sitting on the bench that he and his wife had put there in memory of their daughter, staring solemnly at the spot where she had died. Every few days Sam would change the flowers around the makeshift shrine that he had created or polish the plaque that marked the spot. The rest of the time he would just sit and stare as if asking the very earth how it could be that somebody so beautiful and so loved could be taken away so suddenly before she had even had the chance to celebrate her seventeenth birthday.

MJ remembered Sam from before the accident. He had memories of an outgoing man with a friendly manner and a reassuring strength of character. He had been an electrician down the pit before it closed and an active trade unionist who had been well known and respected in the community. When the pit closed Sam had the good sense to invest his redundancy money in setting himself up as an electrical contractor. The business had been doing well until that December night when the death of his beloved Debbie had killed the old Sam Hopkins and left behind the silent, bitter man who could be seen every day staring from that bench.

From the moment that Debbie Hopkins first drew breath she was the centre of all that her father did. She was the reason why he worked, a recurring topic in every conversation he took part in and the focus of all that he dreamed of for the future. When she died he was left with nothing – nothing but a burning grief that time had not even begun to heal and a poisonous hatred of one man. The energy with which Sam Hopkins had loved his daughter fuelled the intensity with which he hated the man he held responsible for her death. To compound the tragedy Terry Driscoll had, before that terrible night, been like a son to Sam. When Debbie and Terry became teenage sweethearts Sam was quick to welcome the young man into his home. When Terry left school it was to commence an apprenticeship with Sam. The expectation of all was of a future partnership between Terry and the Hopkins family in work and also in life.

All that changed on the night when Terry Driscoll was at the wheel of the firm's van as it rolled off the mountain road and down the steep slope. Debbie Hopkins had entered that van that night as a passenger and when she left it she did so as a corpse. Sam Hopkins had spoken to Terry Driscoll just once since Debbie's death. It was at the hospital to where the body had been taken and Sam, his grief and shock boiling into a terrifying rage, had pinned a stunned and heartbroken Terry against a wall, squeezing his throat with such murderous intensity that it had taken two porters and a policeman to drag him away. As they struggled to restrain him his shouted threats could be heard drowning out the wailing of those who mourned his daughter.

"Mark my words, Driscoll, you'll die for this. I'll get you no matter how long it takes. They can't hold me for ever. I'll have you, Driscoll, I'll have you!"

MJ's colleagues had told him of how they had spoken to Sam Hopkins after the incident. They knew that his actions had been those of a man who had lost everything and was struggling to deal with his loss. They decided against further formal investigation, reasoning that criminal charges would only add unnecessarily to his grief and confining themselves to a friendly warning. What was disturbing, they told MJ, was that even as the rage subsided the hatred did not. MJ experienced it himself some months later when he came across Sam in the street and casually asked him how he was.

"If I see him, I'll kill him and if I don't see him I'll get someone else to kill him," Sam had replied in an eerily calm voice. "When he is dead like my Debbie then ask me how I am."

The police investigation of the accident was brief. The facts spoke for themselves. Terry faced no criminal charges. They tried to explain to Sam that, on a winter's night on an unlit mountain road with sheep liable to stray into the path of vehicles, even the most experienced of drivers could be unlucky and go over the side. Sam listened carefully, thanked the officers and quietly left them saying, "He killed my daughter and he will die for it. A life for a life. That's what the Bible says and it's not for me to question the Bible."

Sam never got the opportunity to carry out his threats. As soon as he was told that there would be no charges Terry left the village. He was not seen again. Sam, frustrated in his wish to have Terry prosecuted had to content himself with suing him in the civil courts. If he had hoped for a courtroom showdown he was disappointed. His own insurance company, who covered the use of the van, simply paid without comment the minimal damages that become payable on the death of a child and the case was in that way killed off as swiftly and as painfully for Sam as his beautiful Debbie had been.

Sure enough, Sam was there as MJ drove past. He didn't even look up as the car passed him. Instead he continued to stare and to wonder why.

Instinctively MJ glanced towards Ty Gwyn. It was too dark to see it properly but something seemed wrong. There was a light flashing against the white walls. It seemed like a blue light. Was it a fire engine? There was no sign of any flames and surely Iris would have rung if there had been a problem. MJ cursed as he remembered that he had left his phone on silent. He always did this when conducting his affair to avoid being disturbed by Iris while in the act of betraying her. This time he had been so concerned to slip away quietly that he had forgotten to switch it back.

Automatically he reached for it in his pocket and checked it while at the same time increasing his speed. In a split second the bend was upon him and he had to pull the wheel sharply to stay on the right side of the road. Not for the first time he realised that this bend, innocent enough in daylight and at modest speed, was dangerously deceptive and prone to punish momentary inattention.

There was a missed call from Iris on the phone. Alarmingly there was also a missed call from work and one from a number that MJ remembered as the number of Pentreglo Police Station. He didn't stop to listen to the messages that had been left but instead pressed the accelerator further and headed towards Ty Gwyn. As he approached, an ambulance passed going in the opposite direction with blue lights flashing. MJ increased his speed. Now he could see the police car, light still flashing, parked across the road. Policemen in fluorescent jackets were cordoning off the front of the house while others erected floodlights to illuminate the drive. Standing at the front door talking to a scene of crime officer was the familiar figure of Nev Powell, divisional head of the local CID. MJ knew him well. They had worked together when he was in the force. He stopped next to the police car and ran over to Nev.

"MJ," called Nev, "where the hell have you been? We've been ringing your office and your mobile."

MJ answered with a question. "Who's that in the ambulance? Is it Iris? Is she alright?"

Nev's eyes narrowed. "Did you get the message I left?" he asked.

"No. I didn't get the message. Now tell me, is Iris alright?"

"That's not Iris in the ambulance," said Nev. "She's not hurt."

"Well who is it?"

"Wish I knew," said Nev. "I was hoping Iris could tell me that but she says she doesn't know. We'll have to take a DNA sample from the body."

"The body? You mean someone's dead?"

Nev nodded and shuffled his feet awkwardly.

"Why don't you listen to the message we left, MJ, it explains it all."

MJ ignored the suggestion. "Where's Iris?" he asked. "You say she's alright, well where is she? Let me talk to her."

Nev looked even more awkward. "I didn't say she was alright," he said, "only that she wasn't hurt."

"So what's wrong with her? Where is she?"

Nev took a deep breath.

"I'm sorry about this, MJ," he began, studiously avoiding the other man's eyes, "but I don't suppose you'd say that Iris is alright at all. She's at the police station. We need to ask her some questions about the man whose body we've found in your house."

II

HUNTING THE VIPER

Four

If you ask me, I think Scrooge had it right the first time. Christmas is humbug! It's all right for kids of course but why should grown men and women get so excited about it? I don't. As the month of December progresses I just get depressed. As the streets and the shops get more crowded I get claustrophobic. When I am assaulted on all sides by gift ideas, sentimental TV adverts or over the top window displays a panic reaction sets in. Others may associate this time of year with joy and goodwill but I just think of being cold and hung over or stuffing myself with so much food that I feel sick and fit only for slumping uncomfortably in a chair farting in harmony with the Queen's speech.

I'm sitting in the departure lounge of Malaga Airport. It's Christmas Eve and I'm fed up. All I can see around me are corpulent ex pats with Santa Claus hats indulging in the kind of raucous vulgarity that they would call the spirit of Christmas. They've no right to be so happy. It's December. Nobody has any right to be happy in December, at least not in the Northern Hemisphere. It's the middle of winter, dark and miserable and all of us in the departure lounge are leaving a country that is mildly dark and miserable for one where darkness and misery are sewn into the national fabric.

That's why our forefathers started celebrating at this time of year in the centuries before the whole thing got hijacked by the Christians. By the time midwinter came around they would be pissed off and suicidal with the long nights and freezing weather so they'd all eat and drink themselves into a comatose state to help them bear it all. By the time they sobered up they could start looking forward to spring and all the random copulation that passed for religious rituals in those days.

It's the hypocrisy of it all that gets me; that and the subtle racism behind those who talk about "the true meaning of Christmas". People who would stab you in the back any other day of the year suddenly become your best friend as they drown you in a flood of fake bonhomie. Those whom you would never catch turning the other cheek or loving their neighbours suddenly apply their own interpretation to the Christian message by self-righteously looking down on all those who don't subscribe to it. For my part I'm a Jew, not a practising one of course, but ethnically that's what I am which gives me my excuse, if excuse be needed, to mark the winter solstice without over reliance on stables, wise men and insincere platitudes. So far as I am concerned if Christians want to celebrate their beliefs at the same time as the mid-winter over indulgence festival that's a sensible idea, like teachers having their annual conferences during the school holidays. However, that doesn't give them the right to treat those who mark the low point of the winter without reference to the symbols of Christianity as if they were fanatics, hell bent on tearing down the edifices of civilization. God save us from the once a year Christians!

It's half an hour to boarding and I am sitting at the departure gate. Sue always deposits me there in plenty of time so I don't go wandering off to get lost in a bar somewhere and miss the flight. Meanwhile, she has gone off to fulfil her mission of ensuring that there is nothing left on the shelves of the Duty Free shop by the time of our departure. As an act of kindness she doesn't take me with her on such occasions. She is well aware of the distress I feel as the credit card is surrendered in exchange for some glossily packed item that we don't need and she is too compassionate a person to subject me to the torture of seeing it for myself. It would be like forcing me to watch a much loved pet being put down.

Freed from the obligation of having to talk to my wife I can allow my mind to wander back over Christmases past. That's how Scrooge did it after all. What was it that made me such a disagreeable old sod whenever late December looms? I wonder if it all goes back to Christmas 1973?

It seems such a long time ago now. I was newly married and newly qualified as a solicitor. Sue and I were about to spend our first Christmas in our neat little semi on the outskirts of Cardiff, just a few minutes' walk from the bus stop from where each day I would catch the bus to Pentreglo there to further the cause of justice from the humble and somewhat shabby offices of Aneurin Stevenson and Co. solicitors to the hopeless and penniless.

It was the last working day before Christmas. Sue had spent the previous week in a frenzy of scrubbing, polishing, sweeping and tidying in preparation for the arrival of our first ever guests in our new home, Sue's fearsome and judgmental sister Sandra accompanied by her insipid husband Dennis and the indulged and irritating offspring of their union, Rupert.

"Don't forget, Gareth, I'll be late home from work tonight. We're taking presents to the Children's Home. I won't be back until about eight," Sue announced briskly as she headed for the front door. "Sandra and Dennis will be here at about seven so make sure you're here when they arrive, the house is clean and you're sober."

I nodded meekly.

"And don't forget the turkey," she added. "It's all paid for and put aside so all you have to do is collect it before six when they close."

It was all very well for Sue. She would have an easy day at work, an early finish and then a few mince pies and some sherry at the Children's Home before wishing everyone Happy Christmas and returning home in the right mood to enjoy the festive season despite the forbidding presence of Sandra.

My day was not nearly as attractive in prospect. I was about to make my debut as an advocate at Pentreglo Magistrates Court and to do so on the very day every advocate dreaded – the pre-Christmas bail applications. Before a bench of magistrates handpicked for their complete lack of any trace of the softer human emotions and spurred on by the entreaties, promises and sometimes threats of their clients and their families, a succession of solicitors, like contestants in a TV talent show, seek to persuade the court that decent citizens could still sleep soundly in their beds if the defendant they represented were allowed his liberty over the Christmas period.

The rules of this annual ritual were well established and rigorously followed like those of some ancient ceremony with its origins buried in the mists of time. The magistrates would be reminded with monotonous regularity that, however compelling the evidence, the defendant before them was innocent until proved guilty and had the same entitlement to breathe the fresh air of freedom as any other innocent resident of this green and pleasant land. Promises of restraint would be proffered and as a triumphant finale the court would be reminded, as it had been reminded by all who had gone before and would be reminded by all who followed, of its ability to calm any lingering fears by imposing conditions on any bail that it granted. The golden rule was never to mention what everyone understood to be the real purpose behind the charade; that it was Christmas and a man facing a long prison sentence on conviction wanted a last chance to get drunk before he started it. Surely in the spirit of the season Their Worships could turn a blind eye to the risk that, in drink and with nothing to lose, the man they freed might be tempted to help himself to a few extra Christmas presents or settle a few old scores for the sake of Auld Lang Syne.

The rules required the magistrates to listen in silent hostility to each set of identical clichés and platitudes on the conveyor belt for between five and ten minutes before a perfunctory consultation with the clerk and an equally perfunctory refusal of bail. If any advocate was naïve enough to go beyond ten minutes the rules ceased to apply and the magistrates were allowed to exhibit exaggerated signs of boredom and irritation like yawning ostentatiously, shaking their heads in unison or staring pointedly at the clock. With each successive application the tetchiness of the magistrates increased, the ten minute period became more truncated and the hostility became more overt.

At the end of the ritual the advocate would retire from the court with head bowed to face the tears and threats of the client's family before trudging heavy hearted to the cells to face a persistent and caustic critique of his courtroom techniques and parentage from the man whose virtues he had been emphasising only minutes before.

As the new boy I found my case relegated to the end of the list by the worldly wise and sadistic clerk. This gave me the opportunity to visit my client, Edwin "Hooky" Hughes, a celebrated local burglar prior to pleading his case. I had hoped that, being far more experienced in this sort of thing than I was, he would give me some tips as to what I could say in his favour.

"Where's my bleeding brief?" was the warm greeting that met me as I entered the cell. Hooky ignored me and addressed himself directly to the policeman who stood impassively behind me.

"I asked for a QC and they send me the sodding office boy," he protested. "Tell them to send me someone who's started shaving."

I thought I saw the policeman smirk as he stepped out of the cell leaving me alone with Hooky. My heart sank as I heard the door slam behind me.

"Good morning, Mr Hughes," I started nervously. "My name is Gareth Parry and I'm the solicitor representing you today." I had been dreaming for five years of saying to someone that I was his solicitor but somehow the moment wasn't quite what I had dreamt of. Hooky stared at me in disbelief as I continued, getting straight to the point and trying to sound professional.

"According to the Prosecution's summary you were caught inside a shop at three o'clock in the morning with a bag of housebreaking tools. Do you have anything to say about that?"

"Housebreaking tools?" Hooky's eyes widened in shock at the suggestion. "Those weren't housebreaking tools. They were the tools of my trade. I'm a joiner and I'd been doing a job that night hanging some doors for a bloke."

"At three o' clock in the morning?"

"Of course not." Hooky rolled his eyes in frustration. "I'd gone to the pub on the way home from the job and, well, I had a few more than I'd planned. You know how it is?"

I did indeed but I wasn't going to let my professional mask slip by admitting it. Instead I allowed Hooky to continue.

"So after I left the pub I was walking past this shop and I saw that the window was broken so I thought as I had my tools with me I had better fix it like, in case anyone tried to get in. So I climbed in and went to look for a bit of wood or something to nail over the hole but I was so pissed I must have fallen asleep and I was just waking up when the copper found me. It was all down to the drink see."

I smiled to myself in relief. I had found the theme of the application I was going to make.

"I suppose you would say that you have now seen the dangers of excessive drinking and you're going to give it up in future," I asked tentatively.

For a few moments Hooky pondered the alien concept of a life without alcohol. Eventually he nodded.

"Yes that's right. You tell them, son. I'm not going to touch another drop as long as I live. I'm on the wagon."

"Is there anything else you want me to say?" I asked.

Hooky considered the question carefully before replying.

"You can tell them about the work I do for the community, with the kids like. I coach the under nines at the rugby club."

"I didn't know you were involved in the rugby club," I said. "Did you play?"

Hooky's chest swelled with pride as he answered. "Had a trial with Cardiff once. They told me I was too small but I still played ten seasons with the village team. I was first choice hooker all that time."

"Hooker? Is that why they call you 'Hooky'?"

I took the grunt in response to be a confirmation and started to close my file ready to go up to court. Hooky took hold of my arm.

"Promise me you'll get me bail, son," he said. "I've got things to do. I've got to get out. I'll make it worth your while."

I graciously declined the bribe that I knew Hooky was in no position to pay in any event.

"I'm sorry," I said. "I can't make any promises but I can assure you that I will do my very best for you."

"That's not good enough," he snapped. "If you can't promise then put Stan Matthews in the witness box. He'll speak up for me."

"Stan Matthews?" I had a mental picture of a slightly built man with brylcreemed hair and football boots.

Hooky shook his head despairingly. "Stan Matthews. Detective Constable Matthews. He's the CID man here. I've given him some useful information in the past. He'll put a word in for me. He said he would."

I found Detective Constable Matthews leaning against the wall outside the courtroom. He was friendly enough if a little patronising as he welcomed the new "legal eagle" to Pentreglo.

"So you're Hooky's mouthpiece today," he said, "best of luck with it."

"Actually," I asked tentatively, "I was rather hoping you might be prepared to give evidence for him when I apply for bail."

D.C. Matthews seemed surprised by the request.

"Are you sure that's what he wants?" he asked.

I assured him that Hooky had been very clear in his request. D.C. Matthews smiled warmly and placed a hand on my shoulder.

"If that's what Hooky wants then that's what Hooky will get," he said. "He's not a bad bloke you know. He drinks a bit too much but when he's sober he's a perfect gent. No trouble at all."

Emboldened by those remarks I entered the courtroom and took my seat. The magistrates' patience had clearly been stretched by the unrelenting repetitive applications that had occupied the previous two hours. As I stood to address them I could see an intolerant twitch from the chairman and I spoke against a background of ill-disguised sighs and groans. The ten minute rule had clearly been abandoned under the weight of clichés from my predecessors. The intake of breath that accompanied my assertion that the case against Hooky was based on mere speculation was so forceful that I could almost feel the papers being sucked out of my hand. I repeated Hooky's promise to give up drink only to provoke on the bench a collective mutter of disbelief that was audible at the back of the court.

"Thank you, Mr Parry," said the chairman. He had clearly heard enough but in my youth and inexperience I failed to take the hint.

When I announced that I intended to call Detective Constable Matthews the gasps from the Bench could be heard in Cardiff.

The chairman had a stony expression on his face as he addressed me.

"Are you sure that's necessary?" he asked through lips that had begun to quiver with impatience. I assured him that it was.

The clerk gave me a look of undiluted menace before turning to advise the chairman that if I was unwise enough to call the officer as a witness it would not look good before an appeal court if they prevented me from doing so.

"And then can we remand him in custody?" I heard the chairman say before directing the usher through gritted teeth to call forward Detective Constable Matthews.

Stan smiled knowingly at the magistrates and they smiled back. Their smiles faded as they turned to listen to my first question. I launched straight into it without even asking the witness to identify himself.

"Do you know Edwin Hughes?" I asked a fairly safe opening question. The answer was equally safe.

"I certainly do," replied Stan though I could have done without the smirk. Now to the important bits.

"Would you say that he is someone who has assisted police officers in the past?"

"Well he's certainly helped keep us in our jobs." Not quite the answer I was looking for but I pressed on.

"On the night of his arrest he had certain implements with him."

"We've already heard that." The chairman's interjection was immediate and venomous. Ignoring it I continued with the question.

"Would you agree that these were the tools of his trade?"

Stan Matthews considered the question momentarily before agreeing with me. "First blood to me," I thought and then, before I could continue the chairman interjected again.

"What is his trade?" he barked.

"He's a burglar, sir," replied Stan with another smirk.

I decided to move on. "Is it correct that my client has a particular connection with the local rugby club?" I asked.

Stan had to trawl through his memory for that one but eventually agreed.

"What exactly is that connection?" I asked dramatically. Stan turned to look straight at the chairman.

"He stole all the lead off the roof last year I believe."

I thought I saw the corners of the chairman's mouth lift slightly in what, in a human being, would have been called a smile. This was most certainly not going to plan. I was in a hole but I refused to stop digging.

"That's not what I meant." I heard myself say.

"I'm sure it wasn't," was the response from the chairman who, at least, seemed to have conquered his anger. He now sounded positively amused and I suspected that he was treating this episode as an entertaining respite from the tedium of the previous couple of hours.

Attempting to steer Stan Matthews back onto the right track I asked, "Do you agree that my client is universally known by the name 'Hooky'?"

Matthews agreed.

"Can you tell their worships why he has that name?"

Matthews apparently could.

"It's because he's bent, your worships, like a hook."

"Bent?" The clerk of court wanted to ensure that the meaning was not lost.

"That's bent as in dishonest, your worships," added the detective helpfully, exchanging knowing looks with the chairman.

I turned round to see Hooky who was now sitting with his head in his hands. I decided to play my ace.

"Detective Constable Matthews," I began, fixing the witness with a firm stare, "would you say that, when not in drink, my client is a perfect gentleman?"

Detective Constable Matthews stared back at me. "Not at all, sir. I would describe him as a thoroughly dishonest character from whom the public need to be protected."

Hooky was not a happy man.

"I knew I should have got myself a QC," he said bitterly. "Stan Matthews really did for me and you let him. Why the hell did you put him in the witness box?"

I decided against the obvious response for fear of provoking Hooky further. With a mumbled expression of regret and an unappreciated and inappropriate seasonal greeting I turned to take my leave.

"Hey, Parry," said Hooky as I was stepping out of the cell, "you know what I said about giving up drinking?"

I was naïve enough to nod.

"Well it was all bullshit," he cried triumphantly. "I'm going straight down the pub as soon as I get a decent lawyer to get me out of here and I'm going to get rat arsed!"

Hooky must have felt that saying this would be a punishment to me for my incompetence because, as I walked along the cell corridor I heard him add, "You know what, Parry? Just for that I'm going to take up smoking again too!"

The memory of that day still makes me shudder but not so much for what went on in court. That was just the start of it. My reminiscences are cut short by the return of Sue, buckling at the knees under the weight of extravagant purchases. Perhaps when I am safely on the plane I can revisit that day when the Christmas spirit took its leave of me.

Five

According to the disturbingly juvenile-sounding pilot we are now at 35000 feet and about 50 miles south of Madrid. Why the hell does he bother telling us this? It's not as if anyone's contemplating jumping out for a quick bit of sightseeing or shopping in the capital. If there were such people then I agree it's worth telling them that it's a bloody long way down and a fair hike to Madrid when they hit the ground. Otherwise what's the point? Now he's telling us the outside temperature. That's even more pointless. Is he aiming it at those planning to nip out for a quick smoke on the wing so that they can remember to wrap up warm? He should concentrate on flying the plane and not bother us with information that cannot be of the slightest use to anyone on it.

I realise why he does it of course. It's to give us confidence that he knows what he's doing. "What a marvellous pilot!" they'll say. "He can read his instruments! With any luck he knows what all the knobs and levers do as well!" It also gives the frustrated pilots on the flight the opportunity to look wisely down at the route map in the inflight magazine and mutter approval. "Yes we're south of Madrid, he's taking the right route home and not going the long way. Now, if he'd have said we were approaching Helsinki…"

I know, I'm a miserable old sod complaining for the sake of it. That's just the way I am when December comes along. It's all to do with Christmas and the more I think about it the more I blame it on Christmas 1973. My humiliation in court was bad enough but the real problems didn't start until I got back to the office.

I was still visibly shaking when I walked in to see Lenny, paper hat on his head, dispensing sherry in plastic cups to the typists. Lenny was the senior partner's nephew. He was a couple of years younger than I and still training but he was being groomed to take over the firm in the fullness of time. It was already clear to old Mr Stevenson that Lenny wasn't going to challenge the giants of jurisprudence but he had a bright affable manner and was willing to share a drink with anyone. Mr Stevenson had learned enough about running a High Street solicitor's practice to know that these qualities were a far surer guarantee of success than legal knowledge. Meanwhile, with my reputation for being earnest and knowledgeable in matters legal, if sometimes a little boring, I was being prepared for a role as the man who would discreetly watch Lenny's back after his uncle became too old to do so for himself.

"Rough day at court?" asked Lenny putting on his best sympathetic face. I could only grunt in response. Lenny put down the sherry bottle disdainfully and reached into a filing cabinet from where he produced a bottle of whisky. After pouring a generous measure into a plastic cup he passed it to me assuring me that it was the perfect remedy for miserable magistrates. In my state of shock I found myself knocking it back in one go. Without a word Lenny refilled the cup and without pausing I knocked that back too.

The sensation was not an unpleasant one. I could no longer feel the anger and frustration that had gnawed at me since my miserable showing in court. In fact I realised that I couldn't feel very much at all. My head seemed to be positioned as usual at the regulation distance of just under six feet from the ground but below that there was nothing to acknowledge the existence of my arms, legs or body.

"I've had a word with Uncle Nye," Lenny seemed to be saying from a distance far greater than the two or three feet away from me where he was standing. "He says we can knock off early and go to the pub. You'll feel better for it."

Actually I felt fine insofar as I could feel anything and I heard myself agreeing in a voice that bore little resemblance to my own. I still remembered that I had to collect the turkey and greet Sandra and family but in those days when pubs closed for the afternoon I reckoned that, even though Lenny had never been known to leave a pub while it remained open, I would still have plenty of time for that. Anyway, I thought with the logic with which alcohol frequently endows us, a couple of beers and a sit down will be just the job to clear the fuzzy feeling that had taken up residence in my head.

The landlord was delighted to see Lenny enter the pub. He knew that wherever Lenny was a healthy stream of income would follow. For the next two hours he nurtured his favourite customer and his guest with admirable attentiveness delivering a steady stream of foaming pints into the appreciative hands of Lenny and the increasingly uncoordinated ones that apparently belonged to me.

By the time the landlord rang the bell for last orders I was feeling bloated, nauseous and incapable of controlling my limbs. The bell came as a relief to me. I could now take my leave of Lenny, go home for an hour's rest and then go to collect the turkey before awaiting the dubious pleasure of Sandra's arrival.

As Lenny began to stand up and I began to ponder how to do likewise the landlord rushed over with an anxious look on his face. It was Christmas and he didn't want to lose his best source of income so early.

"You're not leaving are you, boys?" he asked nervously. "Come along to the Function Room where my special customers go."

Flattered at being considered special and relieved that his seasonal festivities were not, as he had feared, going to be interrupted by the pedantry of the licensing laws Lenny accepted on my behalf. My brain had already resolved to decline the invitation but my tongue was too unresponsive to carry out the command. I found myself being propelled along a corridor and through the ornate doors of the Function Room. As we entered a mighty cheer rang out and my eyes were confronted by the sight of what seemed to be the whole of Glamorgan Constabulary from traffic officers to Chief Inspectors, some in full uniform, applauding our arrival. They were standing in groups laden with beer and whisky rubbing shoulders with the great and the good of Pentreglo. There was the chief clerk from the Magistrates Court chatting, glass in hand, with some of the magistrates plotting, no doubt, their latest atrocity against the cause of justice. Local councillors, lured as local politicians tend to be, by the thought of a free drink, passed through the room trawling for people to treat them. Even the mayor was there with his chain of office looking decidedly askew. In one corner I saw members of the local fire brigade. I assumed that they were the ones who were off duty over Christmas since, otherwise, they were at risk of exacerbating any fire they attended by breathing on it.

"Well if it isn't the legal eagle!" said a voice that I recognised only too well. I had last heard it destroying Hooky's chance of a Christmas drink, not to mention my professional reputation, from the witness box.

"No hard feelings eh?" said Stan Matthews thrusting a large whisky in my direction. "It's all a game after all."

Actually, I take exception to those who describe the solemn processes of our legal system as a game but by then I had insufficient command of my faculties to debate the issue with Stan Matthews or anyone else.

It seemed that the assembled guardians of law and order had hit upon a new form of entertainment – feeding drinks to the now dishevelled solicitor in their midst and collapsing into hysterical laughter as, before their eyes, he transformed himself into a hopeless drunk. They were particularly good at playing the game. No sooner did I finish one drink than a smiling policeman, urged on raucously by his mates forced another on me. I was now too far gone to resist and dutifully consumed every offering without even having any idea what I was drinking. I could feel my head dropping and my grip on reality loosening. The closer to comatose I became the louder the laughter seemed to be.

"Hang on! Perry Mason's been sick."

I heard those words somewhere in the recesses of my consciousness and didn't initially realise that they were referring to me. I had no recollection of having been sick but as I looked down and finally focussed my eyes I noticed the telltale deposit at my feet and, more disturbingly, all over my suit. Somewhere in the blurred distance I heard Stan's voice.

"Don't worry, Perry we'll sort some clothes out for you."

Moments later Stan was in front of me brandishing an oversized fluorescent red anorak and matching trousers that had been generously donated by the firefighters. Applauding vigorously the assembled members of the constabulary formed a circle around me to protect my dignity, not that there was much left to protect, while Stan, with a suspicious level of dexterity, removed my vomit stained suit and replaced it with the fetching fluorescent red outfit in which I was supposed to go home.

Stan stuffed my suit into a large carrier bag and handed it to me before calling out to the assembled throng for a volunteer to take me to the bus stop.

"O.K., Stan," replied a middle-aged uniformed officer. "We're on patrol at six. We'll see him onto the bus on the way."

As I was poured into the patrol car a nagging thought competed with the pounding ache in my head. There was something significant about six o'clock but I had to struggle to remember what it was. Suddenly it came to me through the mental fog. The turkey! I was going to be late picking it up and I would have to think of some way to get over that problem.

I had more pressing concerns during the bus journey – how to stay in my seat. I had always assumed that there was some principle of physics that kept a passenger secure in his seat as a bus rounded corners. It had to be a natural phenomenon because it did not require any conscious effort. I was wrong. I now know that it is a purely human reflex and a reflex, what's more, that deserts the body during periods of extreme intoxication. No matter how hard I concentrated, every turn of the bus sent me sprawling against the window or into the aisle. My fellow passengers loved it and took to shouting "ole" like a crowd at a bullfight every time they saw the helpless character with the rag doll body and the face contorted in concentration fly across the bus.

Eventually, I was able to roll off the bus at my stop and, with the hood of the anorak over my head and the bag of soiled clothing over my shoulder, I set off uncertainly but determinedly towards the butcher's shop. It was closed when I got there but my hopes rose when I saw that the lights were still on and people were moving around inside. I hammered, with hindsight maybe too vigorously, on the door but the violent movement proved too much for my delicate sense of balance and I slid to the pavement. As I made use of the drainpipe to regain my feet the door opened and I was confronted by a thickset man in a striped apron carrying what looked disturbingly like a large meat cleaver.

"Yes, what can I do for you?" he asked suspiciously. My mind formed the sentence perfectly.

"I have come to collect the turkey for Mrs Parry," was what my mind said but, sadly, my tongue was not equal to the task and what emerged was a series of guttural exclamations that had the butcher shaking his head with incomprehension. I tried again with no greater success. For the third attempt I injected what I intended to be a note of urgency into my voice but to the butcher it sounded like aggression. He backed into the shop and raised the cleaver.

"Clear off or I'll call the police," were his parting words, with not so much as a "Merry Christmas" to accompany them as he slammed the door shut.

"Right," I thought to myself as I stumbled homeward, "where can I get a turkey in Cardiff at this time? It can't be that difficult!" Applying my befuddled logic to the problem I soon saw the light or, to give it its full title "The Light of India Restaurant and Takeaway"; the malfunctioning neon sign of which now beckoned to me.

It's a strange thing. The butcher was born and bred in Cardiff and has spoken English all his life yet he could not understand a word I said to him. On the other hand Abdul, manager of the "Light of India", spoke only Bengali until he was twenty-one yet he understood me instantly. It's astonishing what a few years of feeding the closing time cravings of seriously drunk Welshmen can do for one's linguistic flexibility!

Abdul shrugged his shoulders as I made my request of him.

"I'm sorry, sir we don't sell turkeys," he said patiently.

I wasn't going to be fobbed off that easily. I looked up at the pictures that proudly advertised the gastronomic wonders on offer. One picture caught my eye as it danced in front of it, shifting in and out of focus.

"I'll have that," I said pointing at the picture with one hand whilst gripping the counter with the other to keep myself upright. Abdul followed the direction of the quivering digit.

"That's a tandoori chicken," he explained, still patient.

"O.K. I'll have it," I said. "They'll never know."

I tossed the bag containing the tandoori chicken into the carrier with my suit and slung it over my shoulder. Although the bag wasn't particularly heavy I found it upsetting my equilibrium. It seemed to be pushing me against walls and lampposts as I tried to walk the last twenty yards or so to my home. In a flash the solution to my problem presented itself. It was so obvious that I wondered why I had not thought of it before. I would continue the journey on all fours – genius! Watched by a curious, but fortunately not amorous, spaniel I covered the remaining distance on my hands and knees, only mildly inconvenienced by the puddles in the pavement.

It was as I reached my front door that the next obstacle confronted me. I couldn't get up. There was only one thing for it. I pulled up the hood, lay my bag beside me and resolved to lie there until a solution presented itself.

"Rupert, get away from him now!"

I must have dozed off but there was no mistaking the strident tones that woke me up. Sandra had arrived.

I heard an anguished wail in response.

"But, Mum, it's Father Christmas. He must have fallen off the roof. I think he's dead!"

I realised I was lying there with a hooded red coat and a bag beside me. What else was young Rupert to think? His mother's voice rose an octave.

"Rupert, I won't tell you again. Get away from him!"

Poor Rupert was so beside himself with grief that he did something that his father had never dared do in five years of marriage. He ignored a direct command from Sandra.

"Santa, Santa," cried a distraught Rupert tugging at my hood as I struggled to keep my face hidden rather than shatter a young child's illusions in the cruellest of ways, "are you alright?" Adding after a pause, "If you are alright don't forget the bike and the games I asked for."

"Dennis!" shrieked Sandra, unaccustomed to such defiance. "Get that boy away from there!"

Dennis gently ushered his near hysterical son away from me while Sandra bent down and moved my hood just enough to confirm her suspicions.

"Disgusting!" she snapped before commanding her ever obedient husband to find them a hotel for the night. I waited for a few moments until they were gone and then struggled to my feet, opened the front door at the third attempt, picked up my bag and went straight to bed.

When Sue resumed speaking to me, in mid-February as I recall, she filled me in on what happened next. Her day up to then had been idyllic. There had been carols and presents around a beautifully decorated tree as she beheld the happy and grateful faces of the children at the home. A few hot mince pies with sherry and peace, goodwill and all those warm emotions that go to make Christmas spirit, positively oozed from every pore as she made her way home. The strains of "Silent Night" still echoed in her ears as she entered the house.

She was surprised to see the lights out and even more surprised by the peculiar odour that greeted her. It was that seductive mixture of curry and alcohol-infused vomit that sometimes rises from the pavements of Cardiff city centre after a particularly busy Saturday night. She was still wondering where everyone was when the phone rang.

"Hello, Sue," said a disapproving voice at the other end. "I thought I had better ring to see how Gareth is, not that he deserves it. You poor thing!"

"Gareth?" Sue was puzzled. "Gareth's not here. I was just wondering where he and you might be. Aren't you together somewhere?"

"Not there?" said Sandra a little too quickly before composing herself. "Of course he's not there. How silly of me. Well, Happy Christmas."

Before Sue could respond Sandra had slammed the phone down. Her curiosity awakened, Sue decided to follow the beguiling smell. It took her to the bedroom. At first all she could see was a large husband shaped lump in the bed. She threw back the covers to reveal me, still fully clothed and shod albeit looking rather different from when she had last seen me. My fluorescent red trousers were stained at the knees with the dirt from the pavement. A badly soiled suit lay beside me and clutched to my bosom like a new born baby was the source of the lurid red stain that was expanding across the sheet – a tandoori chicken.

Yes that seemed a long time ago. In fact it was a long time ago. Since then I have become a father and then a grandfather. I have spent over thirty years practising as a solicitor in Pentreglo in partnership with Lenny until, last year, I retired to Spain. Now I am on my way back to Cardiff to spend Christmas with my son, Martin, his wife and, best of all, my grandson Jake. Miserable though I was I knew that spending time with Jake would cheer me up – at least until Sue took off to the January sales.

We have landed now and I have just switched my phone back on ready to ring Martin to pick us up. Before I have a chance to do so a text arrives from him. He is outside waiting for us to collect our cases. He also has a message to pass on to me. Lenny has been in touch and invited me to meet him in the pub after Christmas.

Six

I almost didn't recognise Lenny as I entered the pub. His above average bulk had been his trademark, a testament to his enduring love affair with beer. He would hold a pint of Brains in his hand as if in the presence of a holy relic and gaze into the foam topped pool of pleasure before him much as, in the imagination of Shakespeare, Romeo must have gazed into the eyes of Juliet. Beer was his comfort in times of stress, his consolation in times of sorrow and his reward in times of triumph. It was with a pint of beer in his hand that he did his best work for the partnership forging the kind of lifetime friendships that only beer can create with police officers, bank managers and anyone else who could guarantee a steady flow of new clients through the battered doors of our offices. If clients needed reassurance, deals needed to be closed or ruffled feathers needed to be smoothed then Lenny, the knight in beer-stained armour would be there, his trusty pint in his hand, to do what was needed. Lenny's great talent was his awe inspiring ability to consume elephantine quantities of his favourite liquid without his sobriety being noticeably affected. He was a heavy drinker but never a drunk. With each successive pint he would become more loquacious and amusing but, as those around him took leave of their powers of rational thought, Lenny retained his to the immense advantage of our practice.

Thus it was that on that liquid foundation was built the legal edifice of Stevenson and Parry and it was on that same foundation that it prospered until my retirement. The price I had to pay for being the beneficiary of Lenny's hop-inspired social skills was twofold. Firstly it meant that it fell to me to do the bulk of the actual running of the office, making the court appearances, managing the files, drafting the documents and all those other things that a solicitor is supposed to be doing in the time Lenny spent in the pub. Secondly there would be those nights, Christmas 1973 being an early example, when I would be unguarded enough to accompany Lenny on one of his "sessions" as he called them which would unerringly lead to me ending up being deposited comatose and dishevelled in the approximate vicinity of my front door.

As she became used to these lapses Sue became remarkably tolerant of them partly because Lenny was such a disarmingly likeable character and partly because, as a price to pay for a relatively successful career, the odd drunken night was infinitely preferable to selling my soul to Satan or, even worse, joining the Conservative Party.

It's not that Lenny escaped from paying a price for his tireless efforts on behalf of the firm. In his case it was about six inches on his waistline, six stone on his weight and six shades of red on his complexion.

As I had done so many times during my working life I scanned the pub for a rotund man with a florid complexion holding court with a pint in his hand. At first glance I could not see him. There was the usual mix, old men with flat caps and cardigans seeking refuge from the biting January cold, loud office workers trying to keep alive the spirit of the office party, students passing the time before returning to serious drinking at their universities and hen pecked husbands, resplendent in their Christmas jumpers awaiting the return of their loved ones from the sales. However, Lenny was nowhere to be seen.

Eventually my eyes alighted on a forlorn figure in the corner and after a second and third look I realised that it was Lenny. I was shocked by the change in his appearance. There seemed only half of him there such was the weight he had lost since last we met. The face that could have guided aeroplanes home on a foggy night now bore a disturbingly healthy hue. Most alarmingly he looked naked without his usual pint of beer in front of him. In its place was what looked suspiciously and surprisingly like a glass of mineral water.

"It's my doctor," he said glumly "The miserable sadist made me give up drink. He said I wouldn't see Christmas if I didn't."

"Well you did see Christmas didn't you?" I pointed out in trying to put a positive spin on what, for Lenny, was clearly a major tragedy.

Lenny shook his head sadly before replying with more than a trace of bitterness in his voice.

"I saw it alright and I didn't like what I saw. I never realised what a boring bloody time of year it is when you're sober. How do these teetotallers cope with life? That's what I want to know."

"Why are we meeting in a pub then?" I asked. "It must be torture watching everyone drinking around you."

Lenny shook his head again.

"Where else would we meet?" he asked. "I don't know anywhere else. Taking the beer away is bad but this..." He gazed round lovingly at the four walls of the pub. "This is like a home to me. They can't take that away too."

"We could have gone to a coffee shop."

Lenny seemed appalled at my suggestion. He responded with feeling.

"A coffee shop? I went to one of them once. Didn't like it. There were people there drinking coffee. Where's the pleasure in that? It's sad. That's what it is, sad. I've nothing against coffee in its place but you don't go out to drink coffee in public."

I thought he had finished and was about to speak when he resumed his lament with increased fervour.

"You go to one of those places and ask for a cup of coffee and they look at you funny. They want to know if you want it tall or skinny or latte or God knows what. You don't have that problem with beer; you ask for a pint of Brains and you get it. These people who work in the coffee shops though – they call them barristers you know. Those spotty faced kids who work at coffee shops, they call them barristers. They're not barristers. Barristers are pompous pricks who wear wigs and talk down to you. They don't serve coffee."

"I think they are called baristas," I said trying to be helpful and stressing the second syllable to emphasise the difference. I was wasting my time. Lenny was on his hobby horse and he was not ready to dismount. He continued glumly.

"No one smiles there you know."

"Where?"

"In coffee shops. No one smiles or talks to anyone else. They don't argue or tell jokes or anything normal like that. They just sit there drinking tall skinny lattes and tapping away at laptops. That's not living. It's not like being in a pub."

Lenny paused to drink some water with a look of distaste on his face. I decided to change the subject.

"How are things in the office?" I asked.

As he answered me Lenny instinctively took hold of his glass. It was a gesture I knew well although I had previously only seen him do it with glasses containing beer. It was what Lenny did when he wanted to persuade someone of something. It made him look sensible and friendly, the kind of person you wouldn't say no to.

"That was actually one of the reasons I thought we could meet," he admitted. "One of your old cases has raised its head again after twenty years. Do you remember Beppe Contemponi?"

Do I remember him? Beppe Contemponi is one of those clients whose memory I'll carry to my grave. I represented him since he first arrived from Italy. Of course he was a bit of a rogue but so were most of the people I represented in my career. Unlike many of them though, he always struck me as a decent bloke at heart. I remember him as a big, powerful man but with a gentle manner and always polite to me and my staff. I never saw him lose his temper or use his size to intimidate. What's more, when he wasn't selling stolen cigarettes or those containing something other than tobacco, he provided an essential and popular service in the form of the café he ran just along the valley from Pentreglo.

Surprise is an inadequate word to describe how I felt when I was told that Beppe had been charged with armed robbery. I simply didn't believe he had it in him. He was a bit of a chancer maybe and undoubtedly dishonest but as for violence I just couldn't see it. What changed my mind was the evidence I saw mounting against him. It wasn't simply the fact that he lied about his movements on the night of the robbery. Those who live their lives on the line between the legitimate and the crooked often have good reason to cover their tracks. It wasn't even the fibres from Beppe's scarf found at the post office. That piece of evidence bore all the hallmarks of being planted to bolster the case. The fibres were not found until a week after Beppe's arrest and the scarf had been in the possession of the police in the meantime. It would have been the easiest thing in the world to seize the scarf from Beppe's home, take it to the post office to waft around the furniture and then to suggest that the Scenes of Crimes Officer, who had found nothing on his first search, have another go at looking for clues.

No, if it had just been down to the fibres the case would never have got off the ground. What convinced me that my instincts about Beppe must have been wrong was the statement of Tom Webster, the level headed and impeccably honest Postmaster of Pentreglo. I read his description of a tall, heavily built man with a coffee coloured complexion, dark wavy hair and a nose bent to the left and in my mind I saw Beppe. Later that day I attended at an identification parade at which Nev Powell, the officer in charge of the investigation, had assembled an impressive array of Mediterranean types with bent noses and saw Tom Webster unerringly pick Beppe out from among them.

Despite the strength of the evidence Beppe was adamant in protesting his innocence. He became frustrated and distressed at his inability to prove that innocence. This was an unusual reaction from Beppe who in the past, like most habitual criminals, would accept overwhelming evidence with resignation and pragmatism. I told myself it must have been the seriousness of the charge that had prompted this change in Beppe.

The final straw came at the trial. His previous alibi having been discredited Beppe changed his story and insisted that he had been at home with his wife at the time of the robbery. Rita Contemponi was called as a witness to support her husband's account but, although she tried hard, she couldn't have been a worse witness if she had wanted him to be convicted. She contradicted almost every detail of Beppe's evidence and, whilst denying vehemently that she was lying to protect her husband, gave a clear impression to the contrary with every prolonged silence, every vague response and every unconvincing assertion of memory lapses with which she met the relentless and skilful cross examination.

Even after conviction Beppe stubbornly refused to accept his guilt. He insisted that he had been framed and the evidence rigged. To my shame I fobbed off every complaint. Now I was listening to Lenny telling me how Tom Webster, that most reliable of witnesses, had made a statement retracting his identification of Beppe. On his deathbed, I heard, he had confirmed that statement to a solicitor acting for the Police Authority adding allegations of police complicity. Although he had died the following day before he could make a more detailed statement, he had signed that solicitor's notes of the interview to confirm their accuracy. Lenny even went on to tell me how Tom had gone on to prove with bank statements that there had never been a robbery and that the missing money had gone into an offshore bank account from where it promptly disappeared.

"We became involved a couple of months ago," said Lenny. "A copy of Tom Webster's retraction statement was sent to Beppe's son Beppo who's been living in Italy with his grandparents and, needless to say, he was not a happy man when he read it. We were his dad's solicitors so he was straight on the phone to us screaming for justice. He says he wants compensation and he wants a full pardon but in reality what he really wants is vengeance, I suspect. He may be half Welsh but when it comes to family honour and vengeance he's very Italian."

"What about Beppe's widow, Rita?" I asked. "She's not Italian. She wouldn't have anything to do with blood feuds or anything like that. Shouldn't she be running the case?"

"Yes, if anyone could find her," agreed Lenny, "but she's off the radar. According to Beppo she fell out big style with

Beppe's family in Italy, left him with them and hasn't been seen since."

"What's the police attitude to this?" I asked.

Lenny grinned. "At first they sent us their standard response telling us to fuck off but after their solicitor spoke to Tom Webster they changed their tune. Off the record they've agreed that they'll pay compensation and support a posthumous pardon for Beppe but you know what senior police officers are like when anyone accuses one of their own of wrongdoing. They are insisting that there be a full investigation and they won't formally admit liability until the bent copper or coppers are identified and charged with perverting the course of justice. That suits Beppo although I think he's got something different in mind for that copper. He wants his balls on a plate!"

I remember how I felt when I heard of Beppe's death. I obviously felt bad but I never felt any personal responsibility for it. Bad things happen to solicitors' clients from time to time but if those solicitors react every time by questioning their own role they would never be able to do their jobs. Now, as I listened to Lenny I tried to justify to myself the scepticism with which I had met Beppe's claims of a frame up. Should I have listened with a more open mind? Could I have done anything differently? Would it have made any difference if I had? The trouble was that this was the 1980s, the early years of the Police and Criminal Evidence Act or PACE as it was universally known. The act had brought in a whole network of rules and codes of practice designed to render impossible the kind of questionable police practices that had led to so many unsafe convictions in the past. During the 1980s the police were, generally speaking, still in awe of the new safeguards and hadn't yet worked out ways of circumventing them. Police interviews of suspects had become bland and unchallenging as the interviewing officers feared having confessions thrown out of court for breach of one of the seemingly hundreds of rules about treating potential criminals as if they were your opponents in a village cricket match. Foul mouthed and thoroughly unpleasant detainees were suddenly being treated with a bureaucratic courtesy that contrasted favourably with their treatment at the local dole office or council housing department. It was inconceivable to solicitors like me in those days that an identification parade could be blatantly rigged so as to guarantee the identification of an innocent man.

One of the major changes brought in by PACE was the advent of the Custody Officer, an independent policeman whose job was to protect those in the police cells from illegitimate interference by detectives investigating them. It was impossible for a witness to be shown a detainee prior to an identification parade because it was the Custody Officer's job to keep the prisoners apart from the witnesses and, in the absence of good and documented reasons, the investigating officers. It couldn't happen because the Custody Officer wouldn't let it happen – unless…I realised Lenny's problem.

I asked the question I needed to in order to confirm what was now going through my head.

"The custody officer when all this is supposed to have taken place. It was MJ wasn't it?"

Lenny nodded. "That is precisely our problem," he said. "We have a client who has a pretty strong case of police malpractice to pursue and the chief perpetrator of that malpractice seems to be one of our own employees."

It had been Lenny's idea to employ Mervyn Jenkins, or MJ as he was known to all his colleagues, after his retirement from the police. Until now it had been an inspired idea. MJ knew everyone involved in the criminal process in our valley and beyond, from both sides of the law. He was vastly experienced and well respected. He could be trusted to look after the more mundane aspects of the firm's criminal practice leaving the solicitors to concentrate on presenting cases in court or, in Lenny's case, chatting up more contacts in the pub. All MJ asked in return was a modest salary to supplement his police pension and freedom from intrusive supervision. That freedom allowed him to disappear at times during the day on what, rumour had it, were illicit romantic liaisons but as long as he did his work we kept our noses out of his personal life.

Over the ten years or so when we worked together MJ and I were not just close colleagues. We became good friends and many were the times when I had good reason to be grateful for the help and support he had given me over and above the call of duty. He is a charismatic man with a quick wit and a worldly wisdom that makes him fascinating company. I enjoyed working with Mervyn Jenkins and, what's more, I would have trusted him with my life. Perhaps that only goes to show what a bad judge of character I am. Beppe Contemponi, whom I had down as a robber, was innocent while MJ, whom I regarded as totally trustworthy, must have been party to a deliberate miscarriage of justice that cost a man his life.

As I thought about it my mind rebelled against the very idea. Surely I can't be that green. Yes, MJ is a smooth talker who could sell sausages to a rabbi, yes he's a charmer who knows he can dismantle the defences of any man or woman (particularly woman) he wants to get closer to but I refuse to believe that I have misjudged him so drastically. He was an exemplary copper, straight and fair, and he carried the same qualities into his employment with us. A man like that wouldn't stoop so low as to fabricate evidence or help anyone else do so.

"What are you going to do?" I asked Lenny

"I was hoping you'd tell me that," he replied. "You know that this sort of thing's not my strong suit. Do I sack him, suspend him or what?"

"You can't sack him before he's even been charged with anything," I said, "but you've got to suspend him. You can't have him working for you at the same time as you're building a case that could implicate him."

Lenny seemed relieved at being told what he had to do.

"So I'll suspend him this afternoon. O.K."

I hated to be the bearer of bad news but there was something I had to point out to Lenny.

"I don't think suspending MJ is going to be enough, Lenny. There's the conflict of interest angle as well. At the very least you have to explain the position to Beppo and offer him the option of going to another solicitor. If you don't do that and the case doesn't go the way he wants he'll make all kinds of allegations against you."

Lenny's face brightened up.

"I've done that already," he said. "I spoke to him before Christmas and explained everything. He says he wouldn't dream of going to another firm. We were his dad's solicitors and it's only right that we should be his. That's what he said. He's happy for the firm to continue acting for him although there is a condition he has insisted on."

I suddenly felt uneasy as I asked the obvious question.

"What condition?"

Lenny proceeded to pick up his glass. My unease grew.

"He wants you to handle the case for him."

"Me? That's ridiculous, Lenny, I'm retired."

"Don't worry, I've thought of that. I'll employ you on a temporary basis. I'll make it worth your while, honest."

"But I live in Spain."

"That's O.K. Martin says you're here for another ten days. That's plenty of time to see everybody you need to. Then when you go back Pauline will look after this end and keep you posted."

At least I knew that if Pauline were to be involved the case would be in reliable hands. She had been my secretary for the last fifteen years of my career and, although not legally qualified or particularly well educated in a formal sense she made up for those deficiencies with generous quantities of common sense, attention to detail and an uncanny ability to grasp concepts that baffle many qualified lawyers. Once she learned the job she was an invaluable help to me and saved my professional skin on more occasions than I cared to remember. It was only the knowledge that Pauline would be more than capable of carrying on my role of watching Lenny's back that allowed me to retire in the confidence that it was safe to leave him in sole charge of the firm.

"How is Pauline?" I asked.

"As indispensable as ever," was Lenny's response.

"And Sam, what about him?"

Lenny shook his head at the mention of Pauline's husband.

"No better I'm afraid. He still sits there on that bench in all weathers staring into space and threatening Terry Driscoll. It's a tragedy isn't it? Pauline lost a daughter too but you don't see her act like that. She channelled her grief in positive directions like that charity she runs for the parents of kids killed in accidents. That's what Sam ought to be doing instead of all those threats. Pauline's never forgiven Terry either but she doesn't waste her energies on threats against him."

As a matter of pure logic Lenny was right of course. Perhaps, however, logic doesn't get much of a look in when your child is suddenly taken away from you. Perhaps hating Terry Driscoll was all that was left for Sam, the only way he could cope with the pain. There was good reason for Sam to feel bitter against Terry Driscoll even if, in the difficult driving conditions that night, his fatal error was a minor one. What made the case so much worse was that Terry had left the scene with Debbie dying in the van and had not even bothered to call an ambulance. On a dark winter's night the van would have remained unseen on the side of the mountain had it not been for the fact that Terry's parents had insisted on taking him to hospital with comparatively minor injuries after he turned up at home. Only then had Terry told the doctor of the accident and only then, when it was too late to save Debbie, had the police found the van. Maybe everyone is judging Sam too harshly. Maybe if it was their daughter that Terry Driscoll had abandoned dying they would do exactly as Sam was doing. Pauline had conducted herself with extraordinary courage and dignity and, compared to that, Sam had seemed weak and irrational. Perhaps, though, that's an unfair comparison. Perhaps Sam is just being human. Of course it was tragic and of course it was illogical for Sam to act as he did but I for one was in no hurry to judge him.

Lenny wasn't inclined to let me change the subject by talking any more of Pauline and Sam. Grasping his glass he asked me straight if I was prepared to take the case on.

"Why me?" was all I could think to say.

"Because you were Beppe's brief. He trusted you and his son trusts you. Beppo knows that you will fight to clear his father's name just like you always did in his lifetime."

It was all very flattering but I was still looking for an excuse to refuse.

"Be realistic, Lenny," I said. "It's far too late to investigate now. Nobody is going to be able to give any useful information. The only person who could is dead. Don't the police solicitors realise that they can't do any more than they've done? They know there was a stitch up. Tom Webster would have told them who was involved. They should turn that information over to the local force and then pay up on the claim and support the pardon."

"Unfortunately," Lenny said, "the solicitor who saw Tom Webster was unable to get names from him and Tom was dead before he could be asked any more questions."

"So he didn't name MJ?" I asked. I felt strangely relieved to hear that. Lenny shook his head in confirmation.

"Surely," I said, "there's a clear case of police malpractice here and the finger is pointing at MJ. He will know who was responsible even if he had nothing to do with it himself. If he's too stupid to name names he'll just have to take the blame on his own."

"And bring the firm down with him," Lenny added in a tone that made me feel uncomfortable. He was right, of course. If MJ was exposed as a bent copper we wouldn't be able to stop the mud sticking to the firm that employed him for the last ten years no matter how hard we protested that it all happened before he got involved with us. I understood why Lenny was asking me to be involved. It wasn't just that he resented passing a good case on to another firm. He wanted me to protect the reputation of the firm he and I had built up together. Maybe it was emotional blackmail but it was pretty effective blackmail. I tried another excuse.

"The case was twenty years ago," I said. "All the documents in it would have been destroyed. There's nothing for anyone to go on."

Lenny raised his index finger triumphantly.

"Actually," he said, "all the documents aren't destroyed. They should have been destroyed years ago but the clown who's supposed to look after our archives and destroy files after twelve years was so bloody inefficient that he'd overlooked a couple of boxes full of old files. I sent Pauline down to the storage facility to rummage through the mouse droppings and, sure enough, she's found a box of files that includes all the Beppe Contemponi papers. The box is at the office now, slightly smelly but otherwise intact."

Damn! That's another excuse I can't use. Despite a desperate mental effort I couldn't think of a further one. I decided to play for time and asked Lenny to ring me at Martin's house that night when I would give him my answer. I hoped that by then Sue would be able to suggest a form of words that would get me out of it without offending Lenny. I felt bad about letting him down but I kept telling myself that I was retired now and it wasn't my problem. In any case it was surely better to let him down by declining to help than to raise his hopes that I could work some kind of miracle when it seemed plain to me that the whole affair was going to end in tears.

"OK," said Lenny shrugging his shoulders, "I'll ring tonight and on the assumption that you say yes I'll ask Nigel to call round to see you at the office later in the week."

"Nigel? Who's Nigel?"

"He's the solicitor for the police authority, instructed by their insurance company to investigate the case. He says he knows you as a matter of fact. He said you met in Liverpool and you helped him out in a difficult case. He's down in London now working for one of those snooty outfits that write letters to firms like ours as if they were talking to their butlers. He says he's very much looking forward to meeting you again. Do you know him?"

Did I know him? I certainly did. We'd been thrown together when I had been unwise enough to help out a neighbour with a court case in Liverpool and found myself face to face with a psychopathic gangster threatening my family. I won't forget my meeting with Nigel in a hurry. I admitted to Lenny that Nigel was right, I did know him and would love to see him again.

"So you'll do it then," he said.

"Ring me after eight, Lenny, I'll tell you then."

I got back to Martin's just in time to see Sue proudly displaying the day's purchases. She had certainly hit the shops hard. I suspected that they were still vibrating from the impact. Certainly, if the shops weren't rocking our bank account would be. Sue has exquisite taste and there was no doubt in my mind that as a result of her efforts our modest retirement home in Spain would soon be adopting a more palatial appearance. The problem was that I wasn't convinced that my now depleted post retirement income could afford such sophistication. I felt the panic that grips the constitutionally tight fisted when in the presence of unrestrained expenditure but Sue was so pleased with herself that I didn't have the heart to say anything. It did, however, set me thinking of Lenny's offer of temporary employment. I persuaded myself that for no greater motive than the desire to replenish the family treasury coupled with the need for an excuse to meet up with Nigel, whom I rather liked despite his public school exterior, I should take up the offer.

In truth I had other, more powerful, motives. I could not have looked at myself in the shaving mirror each morning if I allowed my friends MJ and Lenny to be dragged through the mud without at least making some effort to help them. They had always been there for me when I needed them and, futile though my task seemed to be, I could not abandon them now. After a short debate with myself I decided that when Lenny rang I would tell him that I would do what I could to help.

"You'll need to speak to MJ straight away and suspend him," I said after formally accepting the offer.

Lenny paused before answering.

"There's a bit of a problem there, Gareth. I spoke to MJ just before I rang you. He's got a bit of a crisis on at home with Iris."

"Iris? What's the problem with Iris? She's not ill is she?"

"No, she's not ill. She's been arrested."

"Arrested? What for? She's not put the wrong bin out for recycling has she?"

Lenny paused again and took a deep breath.

"No, Gareth. It's more serious than that. She's just been charged with murder."

Seven

"There it is," said Nigel waving a tastefully expensive silver pen in the air. He was sitting at the desk that had been mine during my time as a partner in the firm of Stevenson and Parry. His immaculately tailored jacket was draped precisely on the back of the chair that had born the burden of my increasing weight over those years and the sleeves of his handmade shirt were rolled up to the elbows as if to signify the effort that he was going to put into the investigation. Before him on the desk were neatly piled papers fanned out so that his eyes could dart from one document to another with minimal movement of the head. He had extracted the Giuseppe Contemponi file from the rodent chewed box at his feet and systematically arranged its contents around himself. For half an hour he had studied the papers in silence before finally announcing that he had found something.

It had been a strange experience returning to work at the office after over a year of retirement. I had borrowed Martin's car and driven it along the same route as I had taken every morning since deciding that my status as a partner was not compatible with travelling to work by bus. The route was so familiar that by the time I arrived in Pentreglo I couldn't remember any details of the journey. I could not even remember seeing Sam on the bench as I passed it although he was almost certainly there.

My usual parking space was obligingly free. Surely it hasn't been kept empty all this time on the off chance that one day I would return. As I walked from the car into the main street I was able to see how little had changed since I left. I saw the real changes over the previous twenty odd years as I watched a once bustling town centre take on an air of dereliction and despair. The women who stood there sizing up and judging all who passed by as they completed their circuit of the shops were now gone. Not only that, the shops themselves were now almost all gone. The butcher, the grocer, the draper and the hardware shop had all withered away starved of the sustenance of the miners and their families whom they had served for generations. The new families of Pentreglo were the commuters who had gentrified the miners' cottages that had flanked the row of shops or moved into the mass produced boxes in the improbably idyllically named cul de sacs that had sprung up in the nineties. Those people have no need of and no time for the daily visit to the kind of shops where they can exchange not just money but their opinions. Instead they pile themselves into their cars once a week and head off to the out of town superstores that gleefully strangled the High Street of Pentreglo. It is of no concern to them that the High Street they have watched die had spawned a way of life that will never be seen there again.

The real shops have gone now. Those that are not boarded up serve the needs of the new population. There's the estate agent's where the commuters can exchange their overpriced homes and the charity shops where they can clear their cupboards and consciences while those from the old mining families can find a way to clothe themselves. I walk past my favourite Indian restaurant, housed in a building whose history might be that of Pentreglo itself. It had once been the local chapel but, following the change in priorities in the town it had become first a cinema and then a bingo hall before its rebirth as "The Athena" serving the best kebabs in the valley and proudly displaying on its wall a mural of the Acropolis. Improving living standards in Cyprus and increasing age took the owner, Mr Georgiades, back to the island of his birth and the old building became "The Rajah". The mural was not lost in the changeover. The wily new owner got a painter to fill in the spaces between the columns of the Acropolis and add a few minarets so that diners can now gaze at a rather questionable representation of the Taj Mahal as they enjoy their tikkas and chapatis.

A little way down the road, in a building that used to be the Miners' Institute there was now a furniture shop, the sort where there was always a sale on and the impression is given that you never have to pay for your purchases until some distant time when, with any luck, you will have won the lottery or, failing that, died. It was a sensible change of use. The people of Pentreglo will always need furniture but a miners' institute is of limited value in a town with no miners. At the side of the building there is a glass door leading to a narrow staircase that guides those seeking justice as well as those trying to evade it into the offices of Stevenson and Parry solicitors. This was where I had spent my working life and now, over a year after my retirement, I was back.

"Yes?" said a voice from behind a celebrity gossip magazine at the reception counter. There was a sign on the counter saying "welcome" in English and Welsh but the tone that greeted me was anything but welcoming. It was the sort of tone you might expect from a customs officer whose sniffer dog had suddenly developed a keen interest in your suitcase. The owner of the voice peered over the top of the magazine exposing an undoubtedly painful piercing and an unconvincing hair colour. I temporarily forgot that I was now retired and pointed out rather tetchily that this was not a way to address a visitor to the office. At first I was met by blank defiance followed by an ever so slightly sarcastic, "Yes, sir?" I abandoned my attempts to teach the art of good reception practice and told her who I was. In response she put down the magazine with sufficient force to let me know that I was interrupting her and screeched over her shoulder.

"Mrs Hopkins. There's a man called Parry here wants to see Mr Stevenson. Shall I tell him he's in a meeting?"

The door opened behind reception and out stepped Pauline, greeting me with a broad smile.

"Welcome back, Gareth," she said warmly. "I didn't think I'd see you back here again."

I was about to tell her that I was just as surprised when she turned to the receptionist who by now had returned to her magazine.

"Now, Cher," she said kindly, "remember what I said about shouting instead of using the telephone. It looks far more professional if you telephone me even if I am close enough to hear you shout and, also, don't automatically tell people Mr Stevenson is in a meeting until you find out from me if he's available."

Cher exhaled in frustration.

"But yesterday you told me to say Mr Stevenson was in a meeting when that bloke was looking for him."

Pauline smiled sweetly. Her explanation was patient.

"Yes, dear, that was because you'd told the caller that Mr Stevenson was on the toilet."

"But that's where he was. You told me."

"I know that's where he was but you don't say that to clients. They don't want to know about Mr Stevenson's morning routine. As far as they are concerned he is either available or in a meeting and I'll tell you which."

Cher was clearly not following Pauline who abandoned the lesson and invited me into her office. There she explained rather unnecessarily that Cher was new and still being trained.

"They don't make them like you any more, that's for sure," I commented and Pauline smiled modestly. I glanced at her desk. I felt the pang that I always feel when I look at the picture of a smiling Debbie on her sixteenth birthday. Pauline noticed my expression and gave me a look that told me she was thinking the same as I. Although subtle and well concealed there was an unmistakeable air of sadness in her eyes as she caught my glance.

That was how it always was with Pauline, friendly but efficient on the outside but always that inner grief just below the surface ready to emerge briefly and discreetly whenever her thoughts turned to Debbie. She had borne her loss with a courage and dignity that I had admired from the day when she first entered the office as a client. When she returned five years later looking for a job I did not hesitate. It was the best business decision of my life. She had some limited clerical experience from looking after the books for Sam's business, but when he removed himself from the world of work had become redundant not to mention facing the need to provide for the two of them. It wasn't her previous experience, however, that persuaded me to offer her the job as much as the strength of character that I recognised in her. I guessed that she was the kind of person who could pick up the necessary skills fairly easily and in that respect I was proved right as she rapidly transformed herself into the hub around which all that took place at the office revolved.

We were chatting about old times when a terrifying wail came from reception.

"Mrs Hopkins. There's a posh chap here looking for Mr Parry. Shall I tell him he's on the toilet?"

Cher had clearly misunderstood what Pauline had tried to teach her. I noticed Pauline wince as she went out to reception returning seconds later with a bemused looking Nigel. As I went to make the introductions I could see him staring at the surroundings in a state that I suspect resembled shell shock. I carried on regardless.

"Pauline this is Nigel Allerton, an old friend of mine. He's the one that will be working here for the next few days. Nigel, welcome to the world of small town solicitors. This is Pauline Hopkins who knows everything there is to know about the workings of the office so if you have any problems just ask her."

Pauline smiled warmly at Nigel who was still staring in astonishment at the décor.

"Don't worry, love," she said kindly. "I know it's not what you're used to but you'll find us a friendly lot and more efficient than you might think. Once you get used to things I know we'll get on like a house on fire."

Not what you're used to? That's an understatement if ever I heard one. This was a different world to what he had experienced to date. I had been to the offices of Nigel's last firm in Liverpool and he'd even progressed upwards from there. I knew just how big a culture shock this would be for him. His was a big city firm established centuries ago to serve the interests of the rich and powerful. The Liverpool that Nigel had cut his legal teeth serving was that of the merchants and the ship owners who had flourished in the city's long departed heyday. The clientele he now dealt with in London were the very pillars upon which the British Empire was built. I am sure there are just as many scruffy outfits like ours in Liverpool or in the more deprived areas of the capital, born out of the Legal Aid boom of the sixties and seventies and dedicated to steering the misfits of society through difficulties that are often as much social as legal. If there are such firms, however, I can guarantee that Nigel will know nothing of them. His firm would not dirty its hands with criminal law apart from the odd Jaguar driver with too many gin and tonics on board. When the marriages of Nigel's clients broke up the first question would be who gets the fortune held in a tax haven not who is best placed to keep the children out of care. The offices that Nigel is used to working from are all wood and leather and the receptionists (yes they have more than one) that he encounters look and sound like the products of an exclusive finishing school that they are. No wonder Nigel's exposure to the direct style and rough valleys accent of Cher had been so traumatic for him.

It was Pauline with her friendly and gentle manner who succeeded in putting Nigel at his ease. She has a knack of doing that with even the most difficult of people who come to the office. It is a skill that I exploited many times during our time working together. I am a grumpy bugger at times and I am not over endowed with patience or empathy. Left to my own devices I'd have probably alienated every client I ever had but Pauline always made sure that they developed an affection and loyalty for the firm that kept them coming back and sending their friends too.

Pauline saw Nigel eyeing the threadbare chair with suspicion as she waved him towards it.

"Come on, love," she said, "take a seat. You've no need to worry, we had them fumigated last week."

For a second Nigel looked uncertain but Pauline's giggle persuaded him that she was joking. Unable to resist directing a wiping motion at the chair Nigel sat down on it.

"That's better," said Pauline like a mother to a child. "Now how about some refreshment. Tea or coffee?"

"I don't suppose you have any Columbian do you?" asked Nigel. Pauline shook her head with a laugh as soon as he asked.

"It'll have to be Co-op instant," she said. "Is that O.K.?"

Nigel nodded and even smiled. Pauline was working her magic on him. A disgruntled Cher was sent off to pit her wits against the kettle and Pauline led us through to my old office. She had set it up for the two of us with a chair either side of the heavy and worm infested desk. On the floor was the box containing old files that she had rescued from storage and among these files was a pair of dog eared folders that contained the only surviving record of the case of Regina v Giuseppe Contemponi.

Cher entered and with a surly, "There you are," deposited mugs of coffee before us. Pauline took her leave with a friendly wink in Nigel's direction and he and I were now facing each other across the desk, ready to talk about what had brought Nigel so far out of his comfort zone.

"It's good to be working with you again," he said in a voice that suggested he meant it.

"I feel the same way," I said, "but are we really working together? Surely we are on opposite sides. I represent Beppe's family in trying to get as much compensation as I can and you represent the police who are going to pay as little as they can get away with."

Nigel nodded.

"Very true," he said, "but just because we are on opposite sides doesn't mean we don't have common interests. We were, strictly speaking, on opposite sides the last time we met but it did not stop us helping each other."

I acknowledged that this was the case but I still could not see what there was to investigate. Beppe Contemponi had been the victim of injustice and the police were responsible. It was as simple as that. All that was left was for Nigel and I to negotiate a suitable amount of compensation for the family and in those negotiations we would be on different sides with very different interests. Nigel would know that if we didn't agree then I would leave it for a court to decide. I wouldn't accept an inadequate settlement just to keep Nigel happy. I told Nigel bluntly that I didn't care who exactly was responsible for what had happened. Whoever it was the police would still have to pay out.

"Let us look at our positions," Nigel responded calmly and logically. "There has been a miscarriage of justice agreed, the police will ultimately have to pay for it agreed. However, they are going to have to pay for it with taxpayers' money and you know how tight the public purse strings are. The civil servants who look after the piggy bank will not authorise expenditure unless, at the very least, those responsible for what happened are prosecuted and the local police won't prosecute without evidence not merely that this took place but of who fiddled the identification. That way, like all bureaucrats, they can cover their backs against suggestions that they have spent money unnecessarily. So far as the police are concerned, they know that this man Jenkins must have played a part, if only turning a blind eye, but they're not going to be satisfied with that. Before they charge anybody they will want to know exactly who put him up to it so they can be seen to be clearing the rotten apples out of the barrel. They're not going to be satisfied with Jenkins because they know he had no reason to frame Mr Contemponi so he couldn't have been working alone. If they don't charge at least one other person everyone will be accusing them of a whitewash. Now do you see why we have to investigate this thing together?"

Frankly I didn't. It all made sense so far as Nigel's side was concerned but my concern was with getting Beppo's compensation without, if it could be avoided, giving him a name to exact Italian style revenge upon and without having MJ publically branded a corrupt cop.

"What's the advantage to me of taking part in all of this?" I asked. "Why shouldn't I just issue court proceedings tomorrow? The court will give my client damages even if there hasn't been a full investigation at your end and your pen pushers will just have to pay those damages."

Nigel had clearly thought of this. He was unruffled as he replied. "There are two things in it for your client. Firstly, he'll get his damages quicker and his father's name will be cleared quicker. You know how long cases like this take to come to court when they are fully contested and, believe me, Gareth, they will be fully contested if we can't agree a settlement. On the other hand, if we work together we could have the investigation sorted and hand the culprits over to the local police to charge by the time you return to Spain. Once we do that you have my word that you'll have a formal admission of liability and a generous offer of damages and a pardon within 24 hours."

That sounded like a threat to me and I said so. Nigel didn't seem to take it personally as he continued. "There's a second advantage, not so much to your client but to you and your pal, Lenny. If we simply dealt with the claim without naming the bent coppers then my people are still going to want prosecutions. At the moment all the suspicion falls on Mervyn Jenkins who, if I may remind you, is an employee of this firm. What's that going to do to the firm's reputation if he's the only one charged and what's it going to do to him if he's the only one punished? If someone else was involved isn't it better that we find that person? Isn't it in your interest to show that there was another mind at work and that the worst that can be said of Mervyn Jenkins is that he allowed a devious colleague to dupe him? If that's what we find then the odds are that the police may not even charge Jenkins with anything and they can't discipline him for neglect of duty because he's not in the force any more. Let's face it, Gareth, that's why Lenny Stevenson got you involved. If it was just a matter of issuing court proceedings he wouldn't have needed you. He wants you involved because he trusts you, he's got a high opinion of your ability and he's depending on you to keep him smelling sweet when the excrement starts hitting the fan. "

Damn Nigel and his logical thought processes. He may give the impression of being awkward and out of touch but beneath that elegantly coiffured skull was a very sharp mind. He had worked me out in seconds. I suppose the really powerful need bright boys like Nigel to ensure that even when justice is not on their side the law always is. Lesser creatures have to be content with dullards like me to look after their interests.

When put the way it was, Nigel's request that we work together seemed irresistible. I offered him my hand to signify my agreement and, with a friendly grin, he shook it. I then asked the obvious question.

"Has anyone asked MJ what happened?"

Nigel shook his head.

"They haven't been able to yet. Lenny Stevenson could have done when the whole thing came to light but he didn't feel able to until he had spoken to you. Since then the business with Jenkins' wife has come up and we've not been able to arrange a formal interview."

"So why don't we wait a day or two for him to get over the shock of his wife and then talk to him? He'll be only too ready to spill the beans when he realises that he can save his own skin by doing so."

Nigel smiled wryly.

"You don't know police officers like I do," he said. "They have a code of silence stronger than the Mafia. You'll never get a copper splitting on another copper whatever the consequences. You wait and see."

Actually I do know police officers like Nigel does. I may not have been on the same side as them but I have seen enough of them in the witness box to make me realise that he was probably right. MJ might well be hanging himself by doing so but I feared that his adherence to the "Coppers' Code" might override both his common sense and his instinct for self-preservation. If I was right then he would, in the process, reduce to rubble all that Lenny and I had built up over thirty years.

We agreed to speak to MJ within the next few days but not to delay the investigation while we waited to do so.

"In the meantime let's see what we can find in the papers." said Nigel bending down to reach the box at his feet. He gingerly extracted the file of Giuseppe Contemponi, pausing to wipe his hands after handling the folders, and arranged the papers methodically on the desk. It was after half an hour of silent contemplation that he spoke.

"There it is."

Eight

I walked round the desk to see what Nigel was looking at. He had before him the Custody Record, the chronological register of all that had happened to Giuseppe Contemponi from the time of his arrest until the time he was put before the magistrates charged with armed robbery. These days they are all kept on computers but in 1989 the Custody Record was a handwritten document prepared in triplicate by the custody officer. I could see the initials "MJ" beside most of the entries.

"Look at this," said Nigel stabbing the top of the page with his pen. "He was arrested in his car on the main Cardiff road at just before 5 a.m. on 16th December, 1989. The night duty sergeant booked him into the police station at 5.18 a.m. He then checked him every hour at exactly 18 minutes past the hour and made a note every time. There they are 6.18, 7.18 and 8.18."

Nigel moved the pen further down the page and pointed at the entry for 9.05 a.m.

"There we are," he said. "At 9 a.m. Sgt Jenkins came on duty and at 9.05 the night sergeant hands over the responsibility for the prisoner to him. It's all recorded."

Nigel then began tapping the page with his pen as he read the subsequent entries.

"9.18 – spoke to prisoner, all in order; 10.18 – spoke to prisoner, he requested a cigarette, supplied same from his property and lit it for him; 11.18 – spoke to inspector and tells him that they're still waiting for the CID to be ready to interview him and the inspector authorises further detention."

I knew that the Code of Practice for Custody Officers required there to be a review by an inspector within six hours of detention commencing to check that further detention is justified. MJ was doing the job by the book, carrying out the review at exactly the right time – not a minute early and not a minute late.

Nigel pointed the pen at the next entry and read it out.

"After Inspector Matthews authorised further detention I spoke to the detained person and explained that he was going to be interviewed about the offence this afternoon. He understood. Right to have legal representation explained; 12.18 – Given ham sandwich (2 rounds) and mug of tea (1 sugar)."

"It's all very meticulous," he said. "Every hour at exactly the same time, Inspector's review bang on time and he even records exactly what he gave him for luncheon."

I doubt whether anyone has ever partaken of "luncheon" in Pentreglo Police Station but I could see what Nigel was getting at.

"That's MJ for you," I said. "Very disciplined and organised. Good on detail."

"Exactly," said Nigel, "and it carries on. At 12.45 p.m. the duty CID man, Constable Powell, takes him to the interview room for interview and Sgt Jenkins notes this in the Custody Record but he doesn't leave him to the tender mercies of DC Powell. At 13.18 he insists on interrupting the interview to check on the welfare of Mr Contemponi. This is a man who is carrying out his job to the letter."

That was undoubtedly right but I had still not grasped what Nigel had found to be significant in what looked to me to be a shining, if somewhat pedantic, example of proper record keeping. I may, on reflection, have sounded a little impatient when I pointed this out to Nigel. In response he gave an enigmatic smile and turned the page.

"As it's getting a bit tedious for you I won't bore you with the entries between 14.18 and 18.18" he said, taking my show of restlessness in good spirit, "they are pretty uneventful, but what's interesting is what he did at 18.41."

"Which was?"

"He called the inspector again for another telephone review."

I failed to see the point.

"Isn't that what he's supposed to do?" I asked.

"Yes," agreed Nigel, "but not until 20.18, nine hours after the previous review. Why did he do it so early? Nothing had happened."

If this was Nigel's great discovery it was a distinctly disappointing one.

"All the Code says is that there has to be a second review within nine hours of the first," I pointed out with exaggerated patience, "there's nothing to say you can't do one early."

Nigel seemed a little frustrated as he explained. "Yes of course you can bring the review forward if there's a reason for doing so but the point is that there was no reason for doing so here. Mr Contemponi had been interviewed by DC Powell and DC Powell had gone off to carry out further enquiries before deciding whether to charge him. If there's no reason for a review why would he have one? All he's doing is bringing forward the time of the next review and potentially cutting down the time DC Powell has for his enquiries. I don't think DC Powell would thank him for that."

I acknowledged the point. Nigel continued his explanation, emphasising his words by waving his pen before my eyes.

"This is a man who has stuck rigidly to a timetable and then, for no reason, he suddenly abandons it. Not only that, there is no check made on the prisoner at 19.18 and the next check is not 20.18 but, for some reason, 20.11. He doesn't hand over to the night officer until 21.05 so he had plenty of time to call the inspector for review at the correct time instead of more than half an hour early. What has happened to throw out Sgt Jenkins' routine at exactly the time when, according to Tom Webster, he was being called to the police station and given a discreet and highly improper look at Giuseppe Contemponi?"

I didn't know whether Nigel was expecting an answer to that question but if he was he didn't allow me any time to give it.

"What we have here," he said in the manner of a professor lecturing on a subject in which he was a world leader, "is the background record of what Tom Webster told me about at the hospice. It tends to confirm the truth of what he said."

Nigel sat back and, when satisfied that the creaking noise his chair made was not a sign that it was about to collapse, clasped his hands together and began to reconstruct the night in question with all the drama and pomposity of a fictional detective who had gathered all the suspects together to show how his superhuman powers of deduction had drawn him to the conclusion that the butler had done it.

"Prior to about twenty to seven Sgt Jenkins acted in a perfectly unremarkable manner because, I suspect, he had no reason to do otherwise. The idea of framing Giuseppe Contemponi had not until then occurred to him or been suggested to him. At about twenty to seven that idea started to influence his actions. I don't know yet what happened at that time but something did. The most likely explanation is that it was at that time that he was approached by whoever hatched the plot, assuming of course that Jenkins wasn't acting on his own."

"Yes, let's assume that," I said a little too eagerly. Nigel gave a sharp nod of the head.

"Yes, I think we can assume from what we know so far that someone else was involved. We ought to give him a name, Gareth, even if it's only Mr X. What name would you give to a corrupt police officer who would interfere with evidence like that?"

I wondered for a moment whether Nigel was inviting me to swear but he seemed to be serious. In his tidy world everything needed a title so that it could be filed away in the right place.

"How about the Viper?" I suggested.

"Yes, the Viper. I like that name. He was contacted by the Viper and told to look the other way."

I suspected that Nigel had missed what had been intended as a bad pun.

"Good name for him eh, Nigel? The Viper seems appropriate doesn't it?"

Nigel nodded. He didn't seem to be laughing at the joke. If anything there seemed to be a crusading light in his eyes.

"It sums him up doesn't it?" he said. "Because he's poisonous. People like him don't just damage the one they target with their lies. They affect every decent copper, every decent lawyer and every decent person who tries to uphold a fair and honest legal system. People start mistrusting the law and that mistrust spreads like venom destroying all that it comes into contact with. That's what vipers do isn't it? They spread venom. I think the name sums up this creature we're looking for perfectly. His poison has affected Giuseppe Contemponi, Mervyn Jenkins and Tom Webster that we know about. How many others have there been?"

Now I was embarrassed. I pointed out sheepishly that "Viper" was the acronym for the modern practice of video identification parades that had replaced the face to face confrontations of Beppe's day. I acknowledged that it wasn't a particularly good pun but that I had not intended anything deeper by it.

Nigel looked disappointed for a moment before resuming the manner of the super sleuth who had worked out what was baffling mere mortals.

"Sgt Jenkins knew that there was a review due and he couldn't run the risk of the inspector barging into the police station while Tom Webster was still there with the Viper so he got the inspector out of the way by ringing him and having the review done early. That way he knew that the Viper would be left in peace to do the evil deed. Obviously, the Viper hadn't finished by the time the inspection of eighteen minutes past seven fell due so, rather than tell a blatant lie, Sgt Jenkins simply omitted that inspection. The Viper had finished by eleven minutes past eight so Sgt Jenkins carried out the inspection belatedly at that time and then handed over at nine. The night man would have seen the right number of hourly inspections and wouldn't have been bothered about the lateness of the last one. The irony is, of course, that Sgt Jenkins would not have known how long the Viper was going to be. Had he known he could still have got a review in by 20.18 and all we would have had would be one missed hourly inspection."

Nigel looked up at me still playing the part of the fictional detective. I wondered if I would hear "elementary, my dear Parry," but instead Nigel simply asked if I agreed with his interpretation of the facts.

"On that version of affairs," I said, running the implications through my mind, "MJ is guilty of no more than turning a blind eye to another officer's actions. The actual framing of Beppe was done by another, this Viper as we call him."

"I think that's so," said Nigel. "I'm a firm believer in looking for patterns in cases. People usually follow patterns. If a pattern is broken then there's a good reason for it. If Sgt Jenkins had intended to do this thing on his own he'd have fitted it around the pattern of hourly visits to the cell and reviews by the inspector at the prescribed times. The fact that he had to depart from that pattern means that something else, or rather someone else, intervened forcing him to do so."

"And that someone else is the Viper," I said rather unnecessarily. Nevertheless Nigel humoured me.

"Exactly right," he said. "Besides, what reason would Sgt Jenkins have to frame Mr Contemponi? He had no interest in him or the crime and he wasn't the investigating officer. What's more, if he was going to set Contemponi up like that he wouldn't do it in a way that would put suspicion right on him."

I agreed with all of that but felt obliged to point out that none of this led us any closer to the Viper.

Nigel had an answer waiting. He picked up a different pile of papers and extracted one of the documents which he passed to me.

"That's the transcript of DC Powell's first interview with Giuseppe Contemponi, the one at 12.45," he explained.

I read the first few pages before commenting. "I don't actually remember seeing this before."

"You must have seen it," replied Nigel patiently, "but you'll probably not have read it if you were representing Mr Contemponi on a charge of armed robbery. That transcript wasn't part of the prosecution evidence against him so you would have had no reason to read it. I found it among the unused papers that the police are obliged to send to the defence. What's significant is that the interview lasted three quarters of an hour yet at no time was any question asked about the robbery at Pentreglo Post Office. It's all about some boxes of stolen cigarettes that were in the car when Mr Contemponi was arrested."

"That's right, I remember that. Beppe was originally arrested for handling stolen goods. It was only later that the robbery charge arose." I turned the Custody Record back to the first page and pointed out the entry that showed the reason for arrest. Beppe had been taken to the police station on suspicion of handling stolen cigarettes.

Nigel had realised that already. He pulled out another document.

"That's a statement from the young bobby who stopped the car on the Cardiff road. He only stopped it because one of the brake lights was out but when he went to speak to the driver, Mr Contemponi, he saw the cigarettes and arrested him. Mr Contemponi gave some story in interview about buying them from a man in a pub. DC Powell asked him for details and then terminated the interview so he could try to trace the cigarettes before charging him. The case was so trivial Mr Contemponi didn't even bother to call on your expertise to represent him during the interview. He said he'd call at your office on the Monday after he got bail. Now you tell me this, Gareth, why did DC Powell waste his time investigating a few thousand cigarettes and never get round to asking any questions about an armed robbery? It's not as if you have an armed robbery every day down here but stolen fags would be hardly worth bothering about."

"That's obvious, Nigel, he didn't have any evidence linking Beppe to the armed robbery at that time."

Nigel beat the desk in frustration.

"But he did have evidence." Nigel emphasised his words by beating the desk again. "Look at the statement of Tom Webster made the day after the robbery and describing Giuseppe Contemponi perfectly. Are you telling me that an experienced detective sitting in an interview room for three quarters of an hour looking straight at a man who perfectly fits the description of the perpetrator of the biggest crime on his books doesn't put two and two together and, at the very least, ask him where he was on the night of the robbery?"

Now it was my turn to show frustration. I shook my head to illustrate my words. "Nigel you're forgetting an important point. Tom Webster told you that his original statement didn't give a description of the robber."

"Precisely," said Nigel, raising his index finger in triumph. "When DC Powell interviewed Mr Contemponi about the cigarettes he didn't have the damning description from Tom Webster. After that interview, however, he went off to make further enquiries including searching the Contemponi household and seizing the scarf that featured in the evidence. Then, I suspect, he came back to the police station, told Sgt Jenkins to look the other way and got Tom Webster in to make the new statement after he had seen Mr Contemponi in the cell."

I agreed with Nigel that this was a plausible theory. When I asked him who had taken the statement describing Beppe he did not even need to look down.

"Detective Constable Neville T Powell," he said with a smug smile. "The same Neville T Powell who had been assigned to the robbery case at the outset and the same Neville T Powell who, early on the Sunday morning, started to set up an identification parade fixed for the Monday."

Nigel went back to the Custody Record and explained.
"On the Sunday morning the night sergeant wanted DC Powell to charge Mr Contemponi with handling stolen cigarettes and intended to release him on bail before he handed back to Sgt Jenkins. There's a note here that he spoke to DC Powell at home on the telephone at 8.30 on the Sunday morning telling him that unless he arranged to charge Mr Contemponi without further delay he was going to release him without charge. DC Powell told him he'd come right down to the police station to charge him but as soon as he arrived at 9.15, by which time Sgt Jenkins was back on duty, he re-arrested him for armed robbery. In view of the seriousness of that charge Sgt Jenkins

decided to refuse bail and Mr Contemponi was kept in custody pending an identification parade on the Monday. It's all down here."

Nigel tapped the Custody Record.

"I suppose you know the rest," he said.

"Yes I do. I was called in at that stage sat in on an interview about the robbery which Beppe denied. We then had the identification parade and it was downhill from there."

As I was remembering that interview something struck me that I had not realised at the time.

"You know," I said, "that statement from Tom Webster, the one describing Beppe, was never referred to in the interview. I only saw it weeks later when the papers were served on me by the CPS. I remember thinking when I first saw it what a sly bugger Nev had been keeping that up his sleeve. Until then I thought we were in with a fighting chance of suggesting mistaken identity but that statement was what made me think Beppe had had it and Nev had just been playing cat and mouse with him."

Nigel thought for a moment. "More likely he didn't want to risk using the statement until he knew Tom Webster was going to go through with the identification. If he didn't he'd have to frame someone else and that statement with its precise description would have made it difficult."

"You suspect Nev Powell?"

Nigel answered my question with another one.

"What kind of person is DC Neville Powell?"

"A typical detective."

"Meaning what?"

I struggled to explain. I knew what I meant but I felt I had to pick my words carefully. Nigel was, after all, a man who spent a lot of his time defending the reputations of those I would call typical detectives. Finally I settled for, "Narrow minded, politically right wing but superficially pleasant enough."

"Do you think he could be the Viper?" Nigel asked.

I hesitated. I was not a great fan of Nev Powell but I had not regarded him as corrupt in any of the dealings we'd had.

Cunning perhaps and two faced when he needed to be but not downright corrupt. I decided to bat the question back to Nigel.

"Do you think he could be the Viper, Nigel?"

Nigel was not as hesitant as I had been.

"Yes I do," he said. "He's the most obvious one. He had the opportunity and a good motive for fitting someone up. News of the robbery would have shocked the community and people would have been feeling vulnerable. There would have been immense pressure for a quick arrest and most of that pressure would be on DC Powell's shoulders. More than two weeks had passed without a sniff of evidence and DC Powell would have been feeling pretty desperate when Giuseppe Contemponi came into his life. Unfortunately the late Mr Contemponi chose exactly the wrong time to handle stolen cigarettes. As soon as DC Powell saw him he must have realised he was perfect for a fit up."

Nigel paused before asking, "Did DC Powell get much credit for his part in the investigation?"

"He certainly did," I confirmed. "It was his first major success as a detective. He was promoted to detective sergeant on the back of it. From then on he developed quite a reputation. He's head of CID for the division now."

"And all on the back of a lie." Nigel seemed to direct that comment to himself rather than to me. He allowed a look of disgust to cross his face before resuming a brisk business-like tone.

"It's now clear what we have to do, Gareth. We have to speak to DC Powell but perhaps not until we have spoken to other witnesses. We need to be sure of our position before we confront Powell and, with any luck, we can pick up something useful from the others that'll strengthen the case. We'll tell Powell what we know and ask for his comments. Of course he'll decline to make any comment but at least he won't be able to complain that he wasn't given the chance to explain himself. Once we've done that we can hand everything over to the police and leave it to them to charge him with perverting the course of justice. My guess is that if they've got a strong enough case against Powell they won't bother with Jenkins.

They won't be too keen on charging two people with perverting the course of justice. It wouldn't be good for the image. One bent copper they can explain away as a freak but two of them begins to look as if the whole force could be rotten and they won't want to create that impression. One prosecution would be enough for my insurance clients and once it's under way I can report to them advising them to settle straight away."

It all sounded very simple to me and the outcome would give me everything I wanted, even the opportunity to finish off the investigation in sufficient time to enjoy a few days with the family before returning to Spain.

"Who else do we need to see, Nigel?" I asked wondering why all cases hadn't been this simple when I was working.

Nigel had already thought of that.

"You need to speak to Mr Contemponi junior but it's probably not a good idea for me to be involved in that as I'm representing the enemy. We'll obviously need to speak to Mervyn Jenkins though I don't expect much from him. Also, we'd better speak to this inspector who did the reviews and find out if he knows why he was asked to do one early."

Nigel looked back through the Custody Record. "What was the name of the inspector?" he asked before answering his own question. "Here it is, Inspector Matthews. Do you know him, Gareth?"

Yes I knew Stan Matthews alright. The mere mention of his name put me in mind of my Christmas humiliation. We had got on reasonably well after that on the frequent occasions when our paths crossed though he could never resist telling people the story of when we had first met. He was obviously good at making fools of defence lawyers and won rapid promotion to the rank of inspector. I haven't seen him for a few years, since he retired. He's apparently gone off to run a pub in West Wales near the sea. I understand that he got married late in life. The malicious gossip had it that he had got himself a Russian bride on the Internet. I told Nigel that Pauline would try to trace him for us if he thought it worthwhile paying him a visit.

"Right," said Nigel standing up and consulting the Rolex on his wrist. "Time for a break, it's one o'clock. This afternoon we can start sorting out the papers and arranging appointments. With any luck we'll have the Viper flushed out by the end of the week."

Nine

I accepted Lenny's invitation to have lunch with him in the pub. Despite having given up alcohol Lenny still felt himself drawn to familiar sounds and smells whenever one o'clock came. He justified it by his need to keep in touch with his clients and contacts, past, present or future, as they passed through the pub doors daily. Lunchtimes in the pub with Lenny were always truncated affairs as he repeatedly paused in mid-sentence to greet some passing wheeler, dealer or felon as if he were a long lost brother.

Nigel declined the invitation to join us, preferring to partake of the impressive looking hotel packed lunch in the office. He was clearly a man well insulated from the more downmarket aspects of lunch break cuisine and had not yet come to trust anything prepared by a chef with no stars to his name.

"Strange bloke that Nigel," said Lenny gazing forlornly at the tonic water in front of him. "He's pleasant enough but doesn't fit in too well here. He's too posh. The punters here would eat him for breakfast." Lenny looked pointedly at a pair of shaven headed hulks standing at the bar to emphasis the remark.

"Don't underestimate Nigel," I said. "He can't help his upbringing but never forget, he cut his teeth in a tough city and in a tough environment. We criminal lawyers may think we deal with some nasty characters but if you want to see clients who would stab their own mothers for a penny you need to spend some time in a commercial practice like Nigel's."

"He's not like a typical bloke from Liverpool though is he?" protested Lenny. "Scousers aren't like that. They all wear shell suits, fight in pubs and talk like Cilla Black."

I realised that Lenny was winding me up. As a proud valley boy he would do the same with the citizens of Cardiff where I was from, using the stereotype of urban softies and plastic Welshmen to provoke a reaction. He knew I'd been to university in Liverpool and was a dedicated fan of the city. I tried to ignore the provocation.

"I'm not sure whether Nigel's a typical scouser," I said, "but that's where he worked when I first met him. He was in a very respectable and long established firm with features that we don't have like video conferencing and matching furniture but, take it from me, Lenny, Nigel had to deal with far more dangerous people than this lot here. Believe me, I met one of them and I'm still having nightmares about him."

Lenny shrugged his shoulders. "If you say he's alright then that's fine by me," he said, "and he certainly seems to get on well with Pauline. She treats him like the son she never had."

"Perhaps that's to make up for the daughter she no longer has," I found myself saying.

"I'm glad Nigel and Pauline seem to get on," added Lenny. "She's been running the Contemponi case for me so far and hopefully she'll be a big help to Nigel after you go back to Spain."

"Aren't you involved in the case at all?" I asked.

Lenny shook his head. "Beppo wanted you and only you to handle it. Besides I've got enough to worry about without this case."

"Such as what?"

"The auditors. They're going through the books at the moment. Seems like there's quite a bit of money unaccounted for in the trust funds. I'm sure they'll find the mistake sooner or later but at the moment the books don't balance and they're trying to find out why."

Trust funds? The firm never handled trust funds when I was a partner. That wasn't for the likes of us. That was for the firms like Nigel's that represented people who had money they could put in trust. Our clients were lucky if they had enough to keep in the teapot at the end of the week. I asked Lenny about the trust funds.

"Remember the explosion at the old colliery site?" he said. "It's the money from that. We're looking after it for the children until they get to 18."

I remember the explosion only too well. In the name of free enterprise the site of the old defunct colliery had been sold for a pittance to a gang of cowboys who had seduced the gullible civil servants in charge of the sale with blueprints for an industrial park that would have kept every man, woman and child in Pentreglo in work for the next century if it wasn't for one small detail – they were completely non-viable as anyone with an ounce of foresight would have realised. I suspect that the cowboys themselves realised it since there was never any real effort to develop the site for sustainable industry. Instead it was let out to a succession of fly by night outfits who used it to store a collection of dangerous chemicals in conditions that didn't even pay lip service to health and safety. Spurred on by government entreaties to cut red tape, nobody made any serious effort to regulate what was going on until, after only a few months, the inevitable happened and the whole lot went up killing three local men who had been desperate enough to take jobs as security guards on the site. In a flash, literally, eight children became fatherless. Those responsible melted into the corporate shadows but, fortunately, the site owners were insured and I managed to extract substantial compensation from the insurers. That compensation, together with the proceeds of various collections and charitable events was being held on behalf of the widows and children of the men.

"Didn't we have some sort of financial adviser looking after the funds for us?" I asked Lenny.

"Financial adviser?" Lenny spat the words out scornfully "Oh yes we had a financial adviser. He called himself an Investment Manager but if you ask me he couldn't manage a fart in a baked bean factory. He was paid an obscene commission every year yet every year the investments were worth less than the year before."

Lenny gripped his glass as he warmed to the theme. I have never seen anyone's hackles rise and, if I am honest, I wouldn't know a hackle if I saw one but I am sure Lenny's hackles were rising as he spoke.

"I asked him why, if we were paying him to manage the money, he was losing it for us and do you know what the snooty bastard said? He told me I didn't understand the markets like he did. Well that was it. I told him I knew all about markets. My granddad had a stall in Pontypridd market all his life. I told him that if the markets have got the money I'd go there myself and get it back off them. Tell me which market it is I said and I'll have the market supervisor hanging by his ankles until the money fell out of his pockets."

"What did he say to that, Lenny?"

"He told me I was being facetious. I wasn't being facetious at all. I was being sarcastic but this high and mighty Investment Manager couldn't manage to tell the difference – the prick!"

I nodded in sympathy. In my experience contact with the so called financial services industry is about as beneficial as contact with a mosquito. They end up enriched by the experience but you end up sucked dry.

"So you decided to manage the funds yourself?" I asked.

Lenny nodded.

"I reckoned I could protect the funds better than that idiot even if I did no more than stick them under the mattress. The trouble is that I didn't realise how much bureaucracy it involved, it's all form filling, box ticking and auditors."

Talk of bureaucracy started us off on our favourite subject. The decline of the profession we had both dedicated our lives to in the face of the mindless box ticking that has replaced integrity and experience as the regulator of lawyers' activities. Lenny has a theory that every politician is at heart a frustrated lawyer. When you watch them trying to imitate advocacy with verbosity or getting excited about legislation that they don't understand you can see his point. Because politicians are jealous of us, Lenny's theory dictates, they are always trying to kill off the traditional solicitor or barrister. They starve the public justice system of funds not simply because they want to save money but because they wish to starve experienced and conscientious people out of that system. The result of all of this is that we are all being turned into the kind of spiv who harangues the viewers of daytime television until, in desperation they admit that they might have had an accident in the last three years or that they didn't really want the insurance that they asked for when they took out that loan.

When Lenny and I get onto that subject it's difficult to get us off it. We say the same things every time. We bemoan the fact that lawyers are now hustlers instead of servants of society. We look back to the golden (and probably non-existent) days when we were respected and valued. We express shock at the low standards now tolerated from the profession and then we shake our heads and acknowledge that politicians are really quite cunning. Nobody is going to feel outrage at attacks on lawyers in the same way as they do when nurses or teachers are involved. The public, when they think of lawyers imagine them all like Nigel, generating mind boggling fees in plush surroundings. They don't think of people like Lenny working at the other end of the social and income scale. We are a soft target.

Lenny was working himself up to his usual tirade about jealous politicians, box tickers and ambulance chasers when his attention was diverted by the appearance of an estate agent in the pub. Lenny saw the potential for boosting the meagre earnings he had been complaining about with a bit of conveyancing for the commuters so he took his leave of me to buy the estate agent a drink before anyone else could. I finished my sandwich, emptied my glass and returned to the office.

I walked through the door to a grunted acknowledgement from Cher whose social networking I had apparently interrupted and headed for my room. As I passed Pauline's door I heard carefree laughter from inside. There were two voices obviously sharing a joke. The door was slightly ajar so I looked in to see Pauline and Nigel chatting away like old friends. Nigel looked at his watch with an exaggerated gesture that provoked a giggle from Pauline.

"Is it time to go back to work already?" he said with what I could swear was a wink aimed at across the desk. "See you later, Pauline. Gareth is such a slave driver!"

"What a lovely lady your secretary is," said Nigel when we were back in my room. "Much more fun than some of the frosty faced specimens I have to deal with and, what's more, she's efficient too. While you were out imbibing with Lenny she's fixed up the next few meetings we need. We're off to the seaside tomorrow morning."

"The seaside?"

"Yes, the seaside. Pauline's traced ex Inspector Matthews to his retirement retreat. It's a pub in Pembrokeshire. Do you know Pembrokeshire, Gareth?"

"I certainly do. I went there for a holiday when I was a kid. I always remember that as the best holiday I ever had. Come to think of it, it was the only one I ever had as a kid so that's probably why I remember it so well. I can even remember the smell of the caravan we were in. It's a beautiful part of the world, beautiful beaches if I remember though I don't suppose we'll have time for building sandcastles will we Nigel?"

"Yes, Pauline was telling me about the beaches in Pembrokeshire," he replied, "and you're quite right, we just need to see the inspector to see if he can shed any light on the affair and then we need to get back. Pauline's arranged for your client to be here at 4 p.m. tomorrow so you can speak to him. I hope you don't mind but I thought we'd get everything organised at the same time."

I was about to tell Nigel that I had no objection to him taking the weight of scheduling meetings off my shoulders but he carried on laying his plans proudly before me.

"On Wednesday we'll see if we can get anything out of your Mr Jenkins in the morning and then we can review the position before the meeting that Pauline has set up with number one suspect Powell on Thursday morning. We'll then finalise our thoughts on Friday and I can then let you get on with your holiday. I'll return to London to touch base with my insurance clients and as soon as I am ready to talk figures I'll give you a ring."

Remarkable! Nigel and Pauline have planned the whole investigation in less than an hour and still had time to eat their sandwiches and have a laugh together.

"That's fine, Nigel," I said, "but what if I'm back in Spain before you have the go ahead to make an offer?"

Nigel clapped me on the shoulder.

"Then we will have to fly you back again for a couple of days. I'm sure the insurers will pay. They might even run to business class. You won't mind that will you?"

I couldn't help but notice that Nigel was suddenly in a more jovial mood than usual. He's not an unpleasant person to be with and has quite a sharp, if dry, sense of humour but outright joviality such as he was exhibiting this afternoon was not normally his style. Pauline certainly has a talent for putting people into an amicable frame of mind. Still smiling, Nigel leaned down to the box on the floor to retrieve the file. Suddenly his smile faded to be replaced by a puzzled frown.

"That's odd," he said. "I hadn't noticed that before."

"Hadn't noticed what?"

"There's a file missing. Look at this, Gareth. On the outside of the box it tells you the year and the numbers of the old files in the box. There it is, "1990 files 220 to 239." Presumably the files are each given a number when they are put into storage and then stored in numerical order. The individual numbers are written on the folders for each file and the range is on the outside of the box so that it's easy to retrieve papers."

I nodded in agreement. Nigel carried on.

"The Giuseppe Contemponi file is number 1990/226. There's the number written on the outside of the folder."

I nodded again. Nigel pulled out the file next to the Contemponi file and showed it to me.

"There you are; this is file 1990/228. The one before the Contemponi file is 1990/225 but there's no sign of 1990/227. Where is it, Gareth?"

There was no obvious answer to that question. The files had, as Nigel said, been numbered as they were put into storage and would not then have been touched again. There was no reason for one number to be missed out unless...

Nigel finished the sentence I had started in my head.

"Someone has removed a file since they were put in storage. Why would someone do that?"

"Obviously, if they wanted to check something like we're doing with the Contemponi file," I suggested "but then they would put the file back. That's the point of the numbering system. It allows you to put files back in the right place as well as finding them to get out."

Nigel took over. "Yet in this case someone has taken a file out permanently. Why would they do that?"

He answered his own question.

"Maybe it's because there's something in the file they don't want people to see. Any way of telling which file it was?"

"We used to have a book," I told him, "with the numbers down one side and the names of the files on the other but that'll be long gone. They use a computer now but nobody bothered to copy the book onto it."

"The file was next to the Contemponi file. Any chance it was another file for the same case?" Nigel asked. I agreed that it was a possibility.

"Or it could have been a different case but connected to the Contemponi case," he suggested and once again I agreed that this was possible.

Nigel carried on considering the implications of what he had found.

"The file must have been removed after the box was brought here from storage. It wouldn't have been removed before going into storage because it wouldn't have had a number at that point."

I had to agree with the logic and I knew what was coming next. Nigel continued. "Someone in this office has gone through the files after the box arrived and taken one out. It's the file next to the one we're interested in so it's surely too much of a coincidence that it's unconnected to it. What does that tell you, Gareth?"

I knew what it told me but Nigel answered his own question anyway. "It means that someone in this office is trying to keep us from getting at the truth. Who could that be, Gareth?"

We looked at each other. I knew what Nigel was thinking. Despite myself I was thinking the same thing. I couldn't bring myself to say it out loud so I left it to Nigel.

"It's Mervyn Jenkins," he said. "He shielded The Viper twenty years ago and after all this time he's still shielding him."

Ten

We sat in silence, turning this new discovery around in our minds. I felt my heart sink. I was reconciled to the fact that, under pressure from a brother officer, MJ had neglected his duty. I would have been prepared to forgive him for that. I am not naïve and I realise that a lapse of standards like that is all too easy in the close knit community of a police station. I am well aware that loyalty to colleagues and an exaggerated belief that they occupy the moral high ground sometimes affects the judgment of even the straightest coppers. However, this was something different. MJ, I had always thought, was not only a colleague but a friend too. Now I've caught him trying to deceive me and I take it personally.

I had, up until then, refused to accept that MJ was the sort of rotten copper who would deliberately set up an innocent man for his own personal benefit. That was my main reason for getting involved. I still refuse to believe it but I can feel my sympathy for him waning. I feel betrayed.

The silence was broken by the phone. It was Cher telling me in her blunt and inelegant way that there was someone who wanted to see me urgently. Of all the people I didn't want to see at that moment, this was the one above all others. Sitting in the waiting room refusing to take no for an answer was, I was told, none other than my former colleague and perhaps soon to be former friend, Mervyn Jenkins.

I asked Nigel whether he thought the time was right to put our suspicions to MJ without further ado and in particular to confront him about the missing file. He didn't think it a good idea.

"I don't know why he's here but I'd be astonished if his intention is to help the enquiry," he said. "It's more likely he's here to throw some more obstructions in our path. Why don't you let him do the talking and see what his game is. At worst you'll learn nothing but at best he might let slip something we can use against Powell in due course. I'll make myself scarce in the meantime."

I watched Nigel leave the room and then asked Cher to show MJ in. I thought of what my approach to MJ should be. Nigel was probably right that it could be a tactical blunder to weigh in with accusations against him or Nev Powell but, on the other hand, knowing what I did, I could hardly treat him like the old mate he was. It would have to be stern and formal, I decided. I was gearing myself up to adopt that unnatural stance when he entered. I saw his face and my plans were instantly abandoned. He looked distraught. MJ is a strong character with a forceful personality and a radiating self-confidence. The man I saw following Cher through the door seemed weak and vulnerable. He looked overwhelmed by fatigue and an air of hopelessness that I would never have associated with the Mervyn Jenkins that I knew. Instead of following my intention of coldly enquiring as to the nature of his business I found myself directing him to a seat and waiting for him to speak. When he did his voice was breaking.

"You have to help me, Gareth," he said. "This is all wrong and I know you can put it right."

Had MJ taken leave of his senses? Surely, whatever stresses he was under and whatever our past friendship, he couldn't expect me to tamper with the investigation for his benefit. He must surely realise that I would fight his corner as far as I legitimately could but how did he think he was helping by spelling it out like that? I knew that I needed to make my position clear from the outset but I found myself doing it in a far more sympathetic voice than I had planned.

"You know I can't do that. I'm on the other side. My job is to expose those who set up Beppe Contemponi not to protect them and, sorry, MJ, I can't leave you out of that. You're not even supposed to be here, you're suspended. What do you think Lenny would say if he saw you?"

MJ stared at me with uncomprehending eyes.

"What are you talking about, Gareth?"

"The Contemponi case of course. What do you think I'm talking about?"

MJ blinked and shook his head as my words finally sank in. "The Contemponi case? I'm not here about the Contemponi case. Load of rubbish anyway if you ask me. He was a villain and he came to a villain's end. That's what happens when you break the law. I don't know why everyone's getting so excited about it. I don't care about the Contemponi case. I'm here about Iris."

I felt instantly ashamed. I had become so preoccupied with the investigation that I had forgotten the news that must have had every man and woman in Pentreglo shaking their heads in disbelief. Give me a list of people likely to commit murder and Iris Jenkins' name would be at the bottom of it. When Lenny told me about it we both agreed that it was some kind of bizarre mistake and that we'd have an embarrassed correction from the police within hours. When Nigel and I had discussed speaking to MJ about the Contemponi case I had envisaged that it would take a day or so to get over the shock and then he would be back to normal and ready to answer some testing questions. Looking at his face now I realised that this wasn't going to be.

"What's it all about with Iris?" I asked.

"Political bloody correctness that's what it's all about," said MJ bitterly. "Iris gets home from shopping and there's this bastard in our bedroom. He attacked her. He would have killed her. She happened to have a knife in her hand and he gets accidentally killed. Instead of saying, 'well done, Mrs Jenkins' they go and charge her with murder."

"Someone attacked Iris? Why?"

MJ became more animated as he replied. "That's the thing these days. They don't just burgle houses, they've got to damage them and attack anyone they find inside. Some lowlife enters my home and goes upstairs to do who knows what to my wife and when she defends herself they charge her with murder. They should be giving her a bloody medal not treating her like a criminal but that's the trouble. They're so wrapped up with human rights and all that crap that the villains get the sympathy and decent people are locked up."

As he finished his diatribe MJ seemed to slump forward in his chair, his head in his hands. I tried to think of something helpful to say. I was not used to seeing this strong man so helpless.

"I assume that the police are investigating the question of self-defence," was all I could say.

"That's what Nev Powell said they'd do," said MJ. "He's been alright Nev has. If it was up to him Iris would be free now. He's a good lad. He'd do anything for you."

"And you'd do anything for him," was the response that came into my mind but I decided that this was neither the time nor the place. I let him continue.

"They won't let him near the case. They've got these boneheads from Cardiff investigating and they're so afraid of offending anybody that they can't see the wood for the trees. Apparently there's nothing offensive about attacking a middle-aged woman but if you don't properly investigate the death of those who would do it then that's a cardinal sin."

"Surely they can see that this was a case of a burglary and a house holder defending herself," I said. MJ shook his head.

"They're saying it wasn't a burglary," he said. "They put a lot of importance on the fact that nothing was taken. It doesn't occur to them that the only reason nothing was taken was that Iris disturbed him. That's the trouble with them; they know all about procedure and bugger all about common sense. It's the same with the knife. They say it was our knife that killed the man as if that proves some kind of premeditated murder. If Iris had gone out and bought a new knife specially for it I could understand what they were on about but if someone breaks into your home you've only got what's there to defend yourself with. What do they think? That Iris lured some passing bloke into the bedroom so she could stick our vegetable knife in him? Does that sound likely to you, Gareth?"

I had to confess that it didn't but, equally, I could see why the police, who wouldn't know of Iris' gentle nature, might be suspicious of someone they find with a blood stained corpse in their bedroom, a blood stained knife in their possession and no obvious signs of burglary. I didn't expect MJ to see it that way and I couldn't blame him. I tried a different approach.

"Surely they'll be checking on the identity of the man. Once they find out who he is I'd bet my pension he'll have a record long as your arm for burglary and probably violence too. Once they realise that even the worst box tickers will see what really happened."

"That's the other thing." said MJ, looking up with a puzzled expression. "It's another reason why they don't accept it was a burglary. Nev tells me they've checked the man's DNA against all known burglars and robbers and there's no match. Nev thought the same as you and, be fair to them, so did the woodentops from Cardiff but there's absolutely nothing. Nobody recognises the picture of him either."

"Perhaps he's not local," I suggested. "Ty Gwyn is pretty isolated. It's just the kind of place that would attract roving professional burglars from out of the area." As I knew from my time in practice there are gangs that operate out of London or even the North of England that target lonely houses in Wales just like Ty Gwyn. They are ruthless professionals who often work in daylight so they won't look suspicious driving home in the middle of the night.

MJ shook his head emphatically. "They've tried that already. They're even asking Interpol."

"That's a thought," I said, trying to sound encouraging, "maybe he was foreign."

My remark didn't have the desired effect. MJ could just about accept that his wife could be attacked and nearly killed by someone with Anglo Saxon or Celtic blood in his veins but the thought of a foreigner being responsible turned his face immediately purple.

"That's all I need!" he spat. "They take the side of an asylum seeking murderous bastard before they stick up for a decent British lady in her own country. I suppose they think they'll be hauled before the European Court of Human rights if they don't and for all I know they might be. That's how mad the world's gone."

Normally at that point I would have shared with MJ my recent discovery that my own great grandfather had been a tailor from Krakow who had come with his family to these shores in the nineteenth century fleeing poverty and persecution but I felt that the time was not right for my "we are all immigrants if we go back far enough," speech.

As MJ spoke his eyes were not focussed on me but on the space above my head as if there was an audience somewhere in the ceiling that would understand his frustration.

"Can't they see that Iris would never kill anyone deliberately? She wouldn't hurt a fly that woman. Doesn't it occur to them that it was that bastard who came to her? She didn't go to him. Isn't it as obvious a case of self-defence as you could find?"

He was right about Iris. I feel I know her pretty well and to say that she was not a violent person is simply to state the blindingly obvious. Iris is an inoffensive and largely ineffectual woman who has lived all her adult life in her husband's shadow. So far as I know she doesn't have an enemy on this earth. She doesn't really do enough to make enemies. She can be seen pottering around Pentreglo or standing dutifully at MJ's side, never expressing in public an opinion about anything that might provoke any strong emotions, always content to let MJ do the talking and thinking for her. She is the sort of wife who is fully prepared to live her life through her husband. When you get to talk to her about anything other than the trivial she comes across as an intelligent woman who makes sensible and perceptive comments but she seems to believe that nobody would be interested in what she has to say when they can listen to her husband instead.

Nobody would call Iris a natural beauty and under MJ's influence she does not even make the best of what she has. She is quite short and can only be described as dumpy in appearance. Her hair is rarely in place and the unfashionable clothes she wears stifle any feminine allure that she may have. It's curious that MJ should want it that way because he is a man who has an obvious eye for an attractive woman and a strong confident manner that women seem to find attractive. When he was younger he could surely have had the pick of the local girls and it's common knowledge that he is not averse to the odd extra marital dalliance. Why then does he stick with Iris?

The only answer must be that with Iris he has the opportunity to mould and dominate her in a way that a more obviously desirable woman would resist. Maybe the intelligence that occasionally displays itself during Iris' unguarded moments is something that MJ wants to keep hidden from the world for only him to enjoy like an ancient sultan keeping his concubines locked up in the harem.

There is a certain type of man who lives in perpetual fear of being upstaged by his wife. Such a man makes it his business to remove every ounce of self-confidence from her to prevent it from happening. They enjoy the dependence which comes with the belief that they instil that their wives cannot live their lives except through them. I don't know why men do it unless it is because deep down they feel inadequate themselves and I certainly don't understand why intelligent women fall for it. I would be bored to distraction with a wife like that. Whatever the psychology of it MJ is certainly that type of husband and Iris that kind of wife. I blame MJ for the way Iris is.

I have seen MJ with Iris. He tries to control every aspect of her life. He doesn't miss the opportunity to tell us, in front of her, how little she knows about the world or to invite a laugh at her expense. He makes it sound like a joke, even a show of affection, but I often suspect a more calculating motive. If you go to dinner at their house he'll apologise on Iris' behalf for the state of the place or the quality of the food. Try to have a serious conversation and he'll be interrupting her as if the subject were too much for her little head.

He's the same with driving. Whenever he is a passenger and Iris the driver MJ carries out a running commentary like a driving instructor telling her when to change gear and unnecessarily pointing out pedestrians, other vehicles or red lights. Very often he will insist on driving even when he has had a bit to drink because, according to him, the roads are a bit wet or the journey is further than to the local supermarket. He banned Iris from driving his own cars on the grounds that they were too powerful and bought her a succession of overlarge, underpowered and brightly coloured vehicles on the grounds that she needed a big car to protect her from the inevitable impacts and a brightly coloured one to warn other road users. The consequence, inevitably, is that Iris has lost all confidence on the roads and confines herself to short journeys at slow speeds turning into just the sort of driver that MJ had told her that she was.

In all aspects of life it is the same. To the casual observer he is an attentive and protective husband whose wife manifestly adores him but for those who have seen the intelligence behind the timid façade it seems like sickening manipulation.

Still there was no doubting MJ's concern for Iris on this occasion. Even if I suspected his motives in adopting the role of Iris' protector it was a role he was now performing with obvious sincerity.

"I'd like to help you, MJ," I said, "but you realise don't you that I can't. I'll tell you what I can do though. I can put you in touch with a mate of mine in Cardiff, a top notch solicitor. I'll ask him as a favour to me to take on Iris' case and give her special attention. He'll do the business for her; I'll make sure he does."

"O.K., Gareth," said MJ allowing himself a friendly smile. "I would appreciate that. I understand your position. I know you have to pursue this Contemponi case and I'm grateful to you for listening to me and offering to help as best you can."

As MJ had mentioned the Contemponi case and as he seemed to be well disposed towards me I decided the opportunity was too good to miss, despite what I had agreed with Nigel. I would ask him about it without, of course letting him know exactly what we were thinking. I hoped that his concern for Iris and apparent gratitude to me would lower his defences and allow him to speak frankly. Perhaps it was a bit underhand but ultimately if it shifted the responsibility from MJ to Nev it would be for MJ's own good. I was disappointed.

"Don't know anything about it," was the immediate reply to my question. His eyes challenged me to pursue the subject. I accepted the challenge.

"Come on, MJ, you know that won't wash. You were the custody officer for God's sake. You were either a major player in what went on or you know who was. Do you really want to end up taking it all on your own?" I realised I had said too much but it was too late. The words were out.

"Gareth," said MJ through pursed lips, "we've known each other a long time and I hope you accept that I wouldn't lie to you about this. What I am saying to you is that I was not the one, if there was a one, who took Tom Webster to the cell corridor and I was not the one who prepared the backdated statement. I want you to believe that, Gareth, I am telling you the truth."

I did believe him. He was right. He was an old friend and I could not see him lying to me. However, I was conscious of the care with which he picked his words and though I would not suspect him of telling me lies I was not sure if I could rely on him to tell me the whole truth.

"I believe that, MJ," I said, "but I think you know who it was that did these things. Tell me who it was. It can only help you."

The reply was equally cleverly crafted.

"I did not see anyone else take Tom to the cell corridor and nobody told me they had rewritten the statement. You can believe that too, Gareth."

I knew that further questions would be futile but I had one last try.

"Would you like to tell me anything else that you might know about what happened?"

The reply was as succinct as it was literally accurate.

"No," was all MJ said. After a short pause he went back to talking about Iris and the solicitor I had promised to contact. I made the call there and then. MJ left the office, grateful but unresponsive.

Nigel was still talking to Pauline when I passed her door. I told him about our conversation and MJ's reluctance to speak about the case. We agreed that Nigel would have another go at him at a later date though we did not expect any change in his attitude. We also agreed that Nigel would raise with MJ the question of the missing file when he spoke to him.

As we walked back to our cars I realised that I had been a bit rude to Nigel, who still seemed to be in a state of mild panic to be here in South Wales, so far out of his comfort zone. I decided to make amends.

"You don't want to be alone in your hotel tonight," I said. "I'll give Sue a ring and we can arrange to go out together. We can have a meal and then, if you're up to it we can sample the night life of Cardiff. Nothing too wild, I'm afraid. I'm too old for debauchery these days."

"That's very kind of you," said Nigel with a smile, "but I'm afraid you'll have to stick to gentle debauchery with your wife tonight. I'm already booked for dinner. Pauline was kind enough to invite me to join her and Sam at their home. I'm just going back to the hotel to change and then I'm coming back to Pauline's."

I was surprised at how quickly Nigel had got his feet under the table. Pauline is a naturally friendly person who has a knack of making everyone feel special but I had not really considered her and Nigel to be natural dinner companions.

"OK," I said. "We'll do it another night. Meanwhile what have you got lined up for the morning, a trip to the seaside?"

"That's it," said Nigel. "Tomorrow we intrude on the retirement of former Inspector Matthews, the man whom, with singular lack of originality, you call Stan."

Eleven

The Bentley purred westward along the motorway while I sat back in the thick leather seat and enjoyed the experience. I gazed idly out of the window as Port Talbot and Swansea were swiftly bypassed. I did not feel like making the effort of initiating a conversation and, fortunately, I did not have to. Nigel was particularly talkative and particularly enthusiastic about his subject, my former secretary.

"Do you know," he said lounging casually in the driver's seat, "she's a remarkable woman. Runs the office like clockwork. I gave her a list of people to meet and with no fuss she set it all up. That's not like our office. Ask someone to do something and they'll do it alright but then they'll send you a memo to tell you they've done it. The memo will tell you how difficult it all was and how clever they are for having done it. They're all obsessed with self-promotion and they're all ruthlessly competitive. They suck up to you like the class swot with the prep school master and it's not very enjoyable I can tell you."

Nigel paused to concentrate on an aggressively driven BMW beside us. Its driver seemed to be aggrieved that Nigel had a smarter car than he did as if his manhood was being challenged. Nigel saw him off easily and then returned to singing Pauline's praises.

"The thing about it is that she's such a pleasant person as well as being efficient. She's a real joy to work with. The personal assistants in our office are very efficient but you'll never get a genuine smile out of them. They're all so serious about what they do and if they do smile at you or say something friendly you can guarantee that they're after something. Pauline is just so genuine. It's such a refreshing change. I hope your friend Lenny appreciates her. If you don't mind me saying so I strongly suspect that if Pauline were to go the office would descend into chaos within days."

Nigel was right about that and Lenny knew it only too well. Both of us had good reason to remember with gratitude the day we offered Pauline a job in the office. It wasn't the first time I had met her. That had been about five years earlier and in far less happy circumstances. She was a grief stricken mother who had come into my office trailing in the wake of her husband as he burst in demanding vengeance for the death of their daughter. Pauline didn't say much at first. Nobody said much as Sam Hopkins, demented to the point of aggression by their loss, shouted and bawled insisting that I "do something" as if I were a doctor with some wonder drug to kill the pain. Try as I might I could not get it over to Sam that it was not within my power to drag Terry Driscoll off the street and march him off to the nearest lock up. It is always a hard job explaining to the recently bereaved parents of a teenager who did not work, that in such a case they were entitled only to a fixed and modest sum by way of compensation for the death, whatever the depth of their sense of loss or their loathing for the person responsible for it. Sam simply wouldn't have it. He seemed to feel that all he needed to do was to convince me of what a perfect daughter Debbie was for me to say that in that case I had some magical remedy that would make everything good again. Pauline simply sat in stunned silence.

When Sam's aggression started to be aimed at me and not simply Terry Driscoll I turned in desperation to Pauline. Gently but firmly she ordered Sam out of the room before listening patiently and tearfully to what I had to say. After I had explained how the law worked in these situations I waited in anxious silence for her reaction. Had she descended into a rant like Sam's I would have been at a loss to know what to do. Thank goodness she was different. When she spoke it was in a calm voice punctuated by intermittent but well controlled sobbing. She told me that she understood what I had told her even if she did not agree with it. She hated Terry Driscoll and would always hate him but hatred would not bring Debbie back. She knew that she had to be positive and focus on the future. She wanted to honour Debbie's memory in positive ways rather than allowing hatred to destroy her. I was so impressed by her dignity and maturity that I found myself, very unprofessionally, choked with emotion and I had to pretend to be looking down making notes while I composed myself. With the same quiet, sad dignity Pauline apologised for Sam's behaviour and thanked me for my understanding before going out to gently guide her still simmering husband away from the office.

Once Pauline grasped the reality of her situation the compensation claim proceeded swiftly and smoothly, the pittance was paid and the file was closed. I didn't forget Pauline though. There are some clients you never forget and Pauline's courage and clear thinking at a time of desperate distress ensured that she would be one of them. I often thought of her when I had to deal with the histrionics of clients who had suffered no more than the legal equivalent of a nosebleed but who carried on as if the ills of the world had all descended upon them in unison.

I was pleased but not surprised when I next came upon her as the energetic and vocal local organiser for a charity dedicated to helping parents of teenagers killed in road accidents. Our paths crossed a few times a year as Pauline came to the office to give support to other parents whom she had referred to me and her help was invaluable in cutting through the barriers of grief and anger that prevented their claims being progressed.

One day she stayed behind after the bereaved parent she was helping had left. She said she had something to ask me. At first she was reluctant to spell it out. She talked about everything except what she wanted to see me about. I realised that whatever it was would be difficult for her so I let her do it until eventually she got to the point. As she fiddled with her wedding ring and stared at the floor she told me quietly that she had finally come to accept that Sam would never work again. All their savings were spent and the debts were building up. The charity couldn't afford to pay her so she had to find a full time job. She had no qualifications and no recent experience but she had taught herself office administration looking after Sam's business, was hard working and eager to learn. She wondered if I knew anyone who could employ her.

The idea came to me immediately but I didn't let on to Pauline. I told her I would ask around. That evening I gatecrashed Lenny's nightly visit to the pub and, with the help of copious amounts of Brains Bitter, sold the idea to him. I am not sure that he actually remembered agreeing to it but he has never regretted it. The following morning I contacted Pauline and offered her a job, initially as a receptionist. From the first day she started to make her mark on the office and soon progressed to become my secretary as well as the office manager. Those titles, however, were inadequate to convey what Pauline really gave to our office. She was the human face that put at ease all who crossed our threshold, the ambassador who brought us new levels of trust and loyalty from the people of Pentreglo, the cool headed antidote to every crisis that life threw at us and the glue that held together what was otherwise a chaotic imitation of a legal practice. Lenny and I had no doubts as to Pauline's worth and I felt a proprietorial pride in the fact that Nigel had seen her qualities too.

"She's got a tattoo you know."

My reminiscences were interrupted by a seemingly disjointed remark from Nigel.

"Who's got a tattoo?" I found myself asking.

"Pauline," he said impatiently, "that's who we're talking about isn't it?"

If I'm honest I felt a trifle cheated. I've known Pauline on and off for about 20 years and I counted her as a close friend. In all that time she's never mentioned a tattoo to me. Now along comes Nigel and on the briefest of acquaintances she's showing it to him.

"You can't see it normally," he went on. I felt no better. Not only was she telling him secrets she had never confided in me but she was apparently giving him access to parts of her anatomy that I had neither seen nor ever felt it appropriate to seek to see. What had been going on at that dinner?

"It's on her shoulder right at the top," he explained. "It's a tribute to her daughter that she had done on holiday last year.

It's Greek and it shows that Debbie is still in her heart even if she is not there with her. It's very moving."

I felt strangely uncomfortable listening to Nigel talking about the shoulder of a woman old enough to be his mother so, in an effort to move on, I asked how dinner had gone the previous evening. After describing Pauline's cooking in the same glowing tones as her secretarial skills Nigel turned to the subject of Sam.

"I met her husband. He's an interesting character isn't he? Even after all these years he's still obsessed with that accident that killed their daughter. You can't get him off the subject. The hatred he feels is frightening. I'm amazed that Pauline puts up with it."

I'd often thought the same thing. "I suppose she thought at first that if she left him alone to mutter his threats he'd get over it with time," I suggested, adding, "She was wrong, though. He's still as bad as ever."

Nigel seemed to be thinking deeply about my words. "It's a defence mechanism," he said after a while. "The hatred's like a drug to him. Take it away and he'd have withdrawal symptoms. He would have to face the fact that his daughter is gone. As long as he has the hatred he can deceive himself that once he's extracted his revenge everything will come right again. There will have been no accident and he will be able to go back to life as it was."

I had not analysed Sam's motivation that closely. To me he was simply a tragic figure and Pauline was a saint to tolerate him. My concern had always been whether his threats really were as empty as everyone took them to be or whether Terry Driscoll had been wise to leave Pentreglo. I wondered whether Nigel agreed with me that Sam was a sad but ultimately harmless character.

"Of course he'll never do it," he agreed. "I suspect that beneath the obsession there's a piece of Sam's rational mind that tells him that if he ever carries out his threats he'll be left with nobody to hate and if he can't hate he would have to grieve which is what he can't do. If Sam Hopkins were to carry out his threats it would be like throwing his drugs away permanently. He doesn't feel strong enough for that."

That was something else I had not thought about but I felt that Nigel was probably right.

"Pauline suffered the same loss," continued Nigel, "and she feels the same grief but that tattoo is a symbol of how she deals with it. It shows how strongly she feels but she keeps it out of sight. Sam feels the need to parade his grief before the world at every opportunity. Pauline shouldn't let him get away with it. She should stop it."

"But you've said yourself that Sam's harmless," I said without necessarily believing what I was saying but feeling the need to put both sides of the argument. "Surely Pauline is right to let him carry on as he does. If the alternative is grief he can't handle then maybe it's the lesser of two evils to do nothing."

"No it's not!"

I was surprised by the vehemence of Nigel's response. He elaborated and there was an edge to his voice as he did so.

"This obsession is destroying him and it's destroying Pauline. She may think it's a kindness to leave him alone but it's not. He has to confront his situation. He has to experience grief. It will be a painful journey but it has to be undertaken and eventually he will come out on the other side. If he does not face his demons they will kill him. Surely Pauline sees that. If she loves him she has to make him see it. She can't let him die before her eyes."

I was taken aback by Nigel's obviously strong feelings about something which was really none of his concern. I decided that a period of silence might be called for. I stared out of the window as the signs for Carmarthen came and went pretending to be fascinated by the hard shoulder and the scenery beyond. It was Nigel who broke the silence.

"I'm meeting him tonight."

"Meeting who, Nigel?"

"Sam. I'm meeting him tonight. I've invited him out for a drink in that pub that Lenny seems to treat as his second home. He and Pauline weren't willing to listen to me last night. She made that quite clear even if she did so very gently. I was hoping that if it was just Sam and me I could talk to him some more and persuade him to snap out of it, for Pauline's sake if not for his own."

I winced. Nigel was getting too deeply involved in a complex problem after such a short acquaintance. I felt that he was needlessly meddling in something that could only end badly. The selfish side of me was also concerned that if Nigel upset Pauline, as he surely would, the repercussions for the firm that I still felt parental about would be disastrous.

"Do you think that's a good idea?" was what I wanted to ask but something in Nigel's expression told me that it was a comment best left unmade. Nigel's strong feelings on the subject of Sam Hopkins didn't make sense to me but I decided that diplomacy required me to let the matter drop.

The voice on the Bentley's satellite navigation system was as genteel and refined as one might expect in such a vehicle. With immaculate courtesy it guided us off the motorway and past the fields and hedges of rural West Wales. The countryside was not looking its best under the hostile January sky. Seeing the landscape of Pembrokeshire gave me the opportunity to talk about a less controversial subject than Sam Hopkins obviously was. I reminisced about my childhood and the magical holiday I spent in Pembrokeshire in a caravan. Nigel relaxed and the atmosphere in the car lightened. Reverting to his dry, laid back self, Nigel confessed that he had never experienced a caravan or camping holiday and had spent his adolescent summers in a villa near St Tropez.

"You haven't lived," I told him but, try as I might, I could not convince him of the virtues of communal shower blocks and sleeping on beds that converted into dining tables by day.

Like a well-trained domestic servant the satellite navigation system ushered us into the car park of the "Smugglers' Arms" a large country pub at the side of the road that led to the beach past fields that in season were campsites and caravan parks. It was the kind of pub that would have flourished in the days before the breathalyser and cheap foreign travel. I suspected that it still did a reasonable trade among the campers and caravan dwellers in the summer but now, in the middle of winter, it looked abandoned. The car park was empty apart from the Bentley and a battered old Mercedes tucked away in the corner. The right wing slogan on the sticker in the rear windscreen suggested to me that it was Stan's.

As we entered the pub I noticed the sign above the front door that announced that E. D. Matthews was licensed to sell intoxicating liquor for consumption on or off the premises. So Stan has put the pub in the name of his wife, the Internet bride. Was that an act of love, I wondered, or Stan using the guile that had made him such an effective detective to keep one step ahead of creditors? I would imagine that with a business like a beachside pub you'd always be in danger of going under when custom dried up in the winter. If the car park was anything to go by there'd be very little going through the tills of the Smugglers' Arms today.

As we entered the near deserted bar we were greeted enthusiastically and noisily.

"How's it going, butty?" called Stan as he strode across to us arm outstretched while the two old gents in the corner paused briefly in their game of dominoes to take in the rare sight of strangers in the bar in winter. Stan smiled broadly as he pumped my hand and told me with apparent sincerity how good it was to see me. I noticed that he had put on a considerable amount of weight since retirement and his hair had thinned. The Hawaiian shirt that fought a losing battle to contain a newly acquired paunch did him no favours in the dignity stakes and his complexion was several shades redder than that of the canny police officer I had known. I suspected that this change of hue owed more to sampling the stock than to the fresh air of Pembrokeshire.

"Alright, Nigel?" said Stan as I introduced my companion. "Gareth and I are old butties. We used to cross swords in the old days in the court at Pentreglo didn't we, butt? We had some run ins didn't we, but no hard feelings we're still good butties."

As if to emphasise our closeness Stan squeezed my arm till it hurt while Nigel looked obviously confused. Stan ventured to explain.

"He's my butty," he said with a laugh, "that's what we call our mates round here. I'm not talking about sandwiches. I know you scousers call sandwiches butties but not round here. They're our mates."

Stan paused for a second and looked Nigel up and down, beginning to doubt the intelligence he had received.

"You are a scouser aren't you?" he asked tentatively. "Pauline said you were when she rang. I must say you don't look like one. You've got a suit on. Round here they say the only time you see a scouser in a suit is in the dock in the Crown Court."

Stan was alone in laughing at his joke. Nigel simply explained patiently that although he came from Liverpool he had attended boarding school in Surrey and now worked in the City of London which might explain his noncompliance with the stereotype.

"That's ok then," said Stan giving Nigel an unwelcome slap on the back. "People don't have mates in Surrey. Come to think of it they probably don't eat sandwiches either."

Stan laughed heartily and alone at his failed attempt at social comment before ushering us towards the corner of the bar. He pointed to a door.

"Let's go up to the living quarters," he said. "It'll be easier to talk there."

I glanced around. The two old gents were engrossed in their game of dominoes and in the opposite corner was a customer with a newspaper over his face apparently sleeping. Apart from us and a bored looking barmaid they were the only occupants of the vast expanse that was the public bar. We could have discussed the most sensitive of state secrets in stage whispers without much risk of being overheard. Nevertheless, we accepted Stan's invitation and followed him through the door and past two more doors marked "Cocks" and "Hens". Stan jerked his head towards them as he explained.

"It's a bit inconvenient having the bogs right next to the door to the living quarters. Every year you get some drunk pissing on our stairs by mistake. We really ought to get a lock fitted."

With another loud and unreciprocated laugh he led us through a door marked "Private" and up a narrow staircase to a small but tidy lounge. We declined the offer of anything stronger so Stan disappeared into the kitchen to make coffee. Nigel stared at the walls, his brow furrowed, as we waited.

"I suppose Gareth has told you about the first time we met," said Stan to Nigel as he sat back in his armchair balancing his coffee cup on his stomach. I tried to change the subject but there was no stopping Stan. He regaled a bemused Nigel with the full story, Hooky Hughes, the pub, everything. He punctuated the account with frequent bursts of exaggerated laughter as he worked up to the climax. The buttons on his Hawaiian shirt were hanging on grimly as the shirt was buffeted by Stan's heaving chest. As he described my vomit drenched scarlet clad body being dragged into the patrol car he leaned forward and clapped me on the shoulder.

"Tell him what happened next, Gareth," he said. "Tell him what happened when you got home."

I declined the invitation with a modest wave of the hand like an Olympic triple gold winner insisting that it really was nothing. Stan filled in the detail.

"Thought he was bloody Santa Claus they did. That's right, bloody Santa Claus and there's him lying pissed on his front doorstep cuddling a chicken, that's right a bloody chicken."

Stan laughed heartily and alone, the shirt buttons continuing their desperate struggle. After a while, when he saw Nigel's impassive face, he stopped and shook his head.

"It's all a game isn't it? That's what I always said. Just a game."

He then looked over at Nigel expectantly signalling that the banter was over and it was time to get down to business.

Twelve

"I presume Pauline told you why we wanted to see you," began Nigel, calmly and politely.

"Beppe Contemponi?" asked Stan. Nigel nodded.

"A low life who got what he deserved and who should be left to rot in hell," was Stan's verdict. I don't know what I had expected his reaction to be but I suppose, thinking about it, there was nothing surprising in it. Coppers, even retired ones, don't take kindly to those who investigate other coppers. I had sensed the undercurrent of resentment in MJ and here it was again in Stan. This was not going to be easy. Nigel was at his dry understated best.

"You didn't like him then, Mr Matthews?"

"Well spotted."

"Any particular reason?"

Stan fixed Nigel with an expression usually reserved by patient but patronising teachers for the slowest of their pupils.

"Because he was a villain, butt, and my job was to lock villains up not to like them. I don't hate them, they're not worth wasting hate on, but I don't like them either. "

He winked at me as he continued. "Some of their lawyers I got to quite like. It was a game with them, but the way I look at it is that if a villain falls off a roof and croaks then that's one less villain in the world and in my book that's something to celebrate not investigate."

He knew he was winding Nigel up. There was a faint smile on his face as he awaited a reaction like a naughty schoolboy who'd said "bum" in front of the teacher. Nigel remained calm, injecting the barely discernible cold courtesy in his voice that I knew to be his signal to say that he was not going to rise to the bait.

"You know he's an innocent man," he said.

Stan smiled as he replied. "Depends what you call innocent doesn't it? He was a bad man from a bad family. You might call that innocent but I don't."

Patiently and with the cold courtesy now more evident Nigel explained what Tom Webster had told him on his deathbed. Stan was unmoved and unrepentant. He shrugged his shoulders.

"So Tom Webster was on the take was he? I hope that doesn't mean he's burning in hell because if I were St Peter I'd let him straight through those pearly gates just for putting that Italian mobster behind bars."

Now it was me he was winding up and he knew it. Unlike Nigel I reacted to the jibe.

"Italian mobster? What on earth are you talking about, Stan? Beppe was a petty criminal not a mafia don."

Stan smirked in satisfaction at having got to me. It was a game to him as he was always reminding me and he had got the better of me yet again. He was able to lay on the patronising tone even thicker than he had with Nigel.

"The trouble with you, Gareth," he said with a smile, "is that you're too naïve, always have been as long as I've known you. You're a nice bloke, I like you and I know your heart's in the right place but it happens to all of you that spend your time speaking up for villains. You end up believing your own bullshit about someone beating up an old granny because he wasn't potty trained as a child and all that crap. You refuse to believe in evil, you're all the same."

I had been at the receiving end of that speech from people like Stan for all of my professional life and I wasn't going to let it divert me from my point.

"You called him an Italian mobster," I repeated. "All I am saying is that just because he's originally from Italy doesn't mean you can use words like that about him. You make him sound like someone out of a George Raft or Jimmy Cagney film."

Stan gave me a pitying smile and explained himself.

"I'm not saying that Beppe used to go round in a striped suit with padded shoulders carrying a gun in a violin case.

What I am saying is that he was a member of an Italian criminal gang. These gangs exist you know, Gareth. They don't necessarily swear oaths of allegiance or leave horse's heads lying about but they exist and they are dangerous. I'm not having a go at all Welsh Italians. God knows they've done enough for the country. We wouldn't be able to get a decent cup of coffee or an ice cream without them. All I'm saying is that within the Italian communities, in Wales just like in New York or Chicago, there are gangs with links to their old country. They use the community as a cover for their nasty activities. The late Giuseppe Contemponi was a member of such a gang and I'd bet my pension that his son, your client, is one too. Let me tell you as a friend, Gareth, be careful who you're dealing with."

Nigel could see that I was getting nowhere with Stan and decided to take over again. He was polite and spoke without raising his voice but his tone was fast approaching freezing point.

"Let me make it clear, Mr Matthews, that I have long shared with you the belief that the world would be a safer place if we spent more time letting the police do their job and less time pandering to criminals but that rather misses the point in this particular case."

"And what is that point?"

Nigel remained polite. "It is that, whatever you may say about him, Beppe Contemponi was convicted of a crime he did not commit. What is more, he was convicted of that crime because at least one policeman deliberately broke the rules and at least one other let him get away with it. You may think me the worst kind of limp wristed liberal for saying this, Mr Matthews, but I happen to find that state of affairs offensive to my sense of justice."

"So in order to satisfy your sense of justice you want me to betray Nev Powell?"

Nigel looked up sharply at Stan. "Do you believe it was Nev Powell who interfered with the evidence?"

"Don't you?"

"I don't believe anything, Mr Matthews, until I have investigated thoroughly and that's all I'm doing here. All I want is for you to tell me what you know."

"What I know," responded Stan, "is that Nev Powell is a good copper, and more than that, he and MJ were my colleagues. We relied on one another, trusted one another to watch our backs and owed one another a hell of a lot more than we could ever repay. That's how it was in the days when coppers came from the community and understood the community instead of descending from ivory towers with their flow charts and mission statements. They've all got honours degrees these days but put them in a pub at closing time when the punters don't want to leave and there's nothing in the manual that tells them what to do. We used to be like a family and, like all families, we stick together. Good, bad or indifferent we supported each other because to us there were only two most important qualities a copper needed, loyalty and the common sense to tell right from wrong. As long as we remembered who were the good guys and who were the bad guys that's all that mattered. If one of our colleagues cut a few corners to help the good guys or beat the bad guys we weren't going to turn on him. That's where the loyalty came in. You knew that any one of your colleagues would put his life on the line for you and you weren't going to repay them by stabbing them in the back. I'm well aware that in the modern police force that you represent it's those that step on their colleagues who climb to the top but I'm afraid that I'm from a different age."

Nigel wasn't going to be diverted. "Tell me about DC Powell and Sgt Jenkins," he asked. "Do you include them when you talk about those who cut corners to get the right results?"

"They're ordinary decent blokes and, like I said, good coppers."

"No vices at all?"

Stan smirked at the question. "Well we know that MJ can't keep it in his trousers if that's what you mean but I've always forgiven him that. After all, with no disrespect to poor old Iris, if you were sleeping with her every night you'd want a bit of variety wouldn't you?"

Once again Stan had successfully avoided the question. Nigel pressed on. "What about DC Powell? Is he a ladies man?"

Stan laughed out loud. "Nev? Do me a favour. He's happily married to his childhood sweetheart that one. His only vice is singing. He never bloody stops. A big booming voice, baritone I think. It used to drive me nuts when we were on duty together but I forgave him."

He looked straight at Nigel as he finished the sentence.

"...and I wouldn't do him down, not for the sake of some low life I wouldn't."

Nigel tried a different approach. "Would they have any reason to frame Mr Contemponi?"

Stan shrugged.

"Who says they did?" he asked. "Who says anyone did? How do you know it's not just Tom Webster deflecting the blame from himself?"

Nigel shook his head firmly. "Because, Mr Matthews, I saw Tom Webster. He was dying before my very eyes. I knew he was dying and so did he. If he hadn't spoken, his secret would have died with him. What was the point of him saying it if it wasn't true? People don't set out to deflect blame from themselves unless they've been blamed in the first place. Tom Webster could have died quietly and nobody would have thought to blame him. If he knew he was going to die how do you explain his confession unless it was true?"

Stan had no answer to that question and he knew it. He shrugged his shoulders and sat looking at Nigel with a firm expression that made clear where his loyalties lay. Nigel was equally lost for words. I felt obliged to break the silence.

"Something like this wouldn't happen today would it, Stan?"

I meant by that remark that policing had changed out of all recognition since the days we were talking about. Prisoners aren't kept in cells in small, local police stations any more. They are taken to specialised "custody suites" a name that makes the grim reality of incarceration sound like a weekend hotel break. Records are kept on computers, CCTV cameras observe all that transpires. Identification parades are carried out on laptops rather than in police station corridors. Reliance on personal initiative has largely gone out of that aspect of policing and with it has gone the risk of misguided use of that initiative. Prisoners might still get fitted up by dishonest policemen these days but the fitting up is far more subtle and sophisticated than it was. Stan chose to misunderstand me.

"You're not wrong there, butt," he said nodding enthusiastically. "In those days if you caught a criminal you got a slap on the back for doing a good job. Now you get a slap on the wrist for infringing the poor darling's human rights."

I glanced at Nigel for his reaction but he seemed to be more interested in scanning the walls of the room as if looking for clues in the wallpaper. Warming to his theme Stan continued.

"Look at poor Iris Jenkins, MJ's wife. Some bugger breaks into her house ready to do God knows what to get away with burgling it and when she stops him they charge her with murder. Murder for Christ's sake! What do they think he'd have done if she'd left him alone? MJ must be going demented at what's going on. Nobody seems to want to help Iris but all they want to talk about is what he did twenty years ago."

As Stan paused for breath I saw my chance to get him on side. "You're right, Stan," I said. "MJ needs help with Iris' case and I've arranged it for him. I've got one of the top men in Cardiff to represent her."

I told Stan the name of the lawyer I'd arranged. It was one he recognised and he nodded in approval.

"Good choice. He's a tricky bugger that one. Totally up himself, of course. I can't stand him personally but he's smart and cunning, like a fox with O levels. Just the man Iris needs."

I hammered home the advantage I was gaining.

"That's what I'm interested in, Stan. MJ's a good mate and I don't want to see him blamed for something he didn't do. That's why I'm working with Nigel. We can only clear the suspicion from MJ by getting to the truth. We're not here to do anyone down. We're just trying to find out what happened."

I doubt that Stan was totally convinced of the purity of our motives but he seemed pleased with what he heard.

"What do you want to know, butt?" he asked, sitting back in his chair.

"What part did you play in the Contemponi case?" I asked the question we should have asked in the first place.

"None." The reply was swift and succinct.

"But your name is on the custody record as the reviewing officer."

Stan smiled smugly. "Exactly! I was the reviewing officer and you know the rules. The reviewing officer can't play any part in the investigation and the investigating officer can't conduct reviews. They must have taught you that at law school or wherever you go to learn to be smart arsed pricks. You know the system, Gareth, keep the investigation of the offences separate from the detention of the suspect and no clever dick lawyer can accuse you of a stitch up, not that it stops them anyway."

Stan was literally correct, of course, but he and I both knew that he was dodging the question. Even though we were both retired Stan couldn't resist the temptation to make life difficult for me.

"If you were the reviewing officer, Stan, you'd have to know what was going on with the investigation. That was your job; to make sure everyone stuck to the rules."

Stan nodded in agreement so I pressed on. "Was there anything unusual that came up on the review?"

Fair play to Stan, he seemed to be genuinely trying to recall. His brow furrowed as he cast his mind back through the years. Eventually he shook his head.

"To tell you the truth, Gareth, I can't really remember anything about it. There was nothing memorable about the case. At the time I was involved it was just some local baddy caught with some dodgy stuff in his vehicle, absolutely routine. I'm sure it would have been the talk of the town in Pentreglo when Beppe was charged with the post office job but, don't forget, by then I was no longer involved in day to day policing there. I was in uniform as an Inspector at Divisional Headquarters. I'd get phone calls from custody officers in all the little police stations they had in those days and I'd just ask a few standard questions. If they gave me the right answers I'd tick the boxes and that would be that. Within five minutes I'd have forgotten about it."

Nigel had finished staring at the walls and decided to join in. "How would it have gone with a typical case like Mr Contemponi's? Talk me through it."

"MJ would have rung me and told me he had someone there who needed reviewing and he'd give me his name and what he was in for and I'd ask MJ if he was satisfied that he's been lawfully arrested. MJ would obviously have said yes. Well, he's hardly going to say no is he?"

Stan laughed out loud at his own attempt at wit. When we failed to join in he carried on with his explanation.

"I'd then ask whether Nev was ready to charge him and he'd say no. I'd ask him why and he'd say that Nev was carrying out further enquiries. I'd ask what further enquiries and if MJ's answer sounded credible I'd authorise further detention and give a little talk about making sure that the enquiries were carried out promptly. That's the way it always was and I've no doubt that's the way it was in this case."

"But in this case," Nigel asked, "you would have recognised the name of Giuseppe Contemponi. You'd come across him before hadn't you?"

"Of course I had but there would be nothing strange about that. I recognised the names of most people who get locked up in Pentreglo. They're all regulars you know."

Nigel was still not satisfied. "What about the timing of the review? Didn't it strike you as odd that it was hours earlier than it needed to be?"

Stan seemed to be agreeing with Nigel. "You're right," he said. "You almost always get the reviews a few minutes early or late because of pressure of work but hours early that's odd. There's no obvious reason for it."

"So didn't you pick up on it at the time?"

"I would have done if I'd have known but MJ needn't have told me. I'm only concerned with doing the review I'm asked to do. I don't bother with the time of the last one unless something special happened that I had a note to look out for and in this case there was nothing special at all."

Stan looked across at Nigel with eyebrows raised inviting further questions. There were none. What a waste! We had travelled all the way out to Pembrokeshire to be told nothing. Stan seemed to have enjoyed it but Nigel and I had more important things to do than sharing Stan's bonhomie.

"If there's nothing else I'd better get down to relieve the barmaid," said Stan getting to his feet. "The wife's off shopping and there's only me and the barmaid looking after the place, not that we're exactly run off our feet but you need to give the barmaid a break every so often from listening to the regulars going on about milk quotas or livestock prices. The poor girl will die of boredom if I don't get down there."

Stan offered us each an overtly masonic handshake and we, without betraying any indication of irony, thanked him for his help.

"Any time, boys," he said jovially. "Come and see me any time you like. Maybe next time we can have a pint in the bar and chat about old times. It's good to see my old friends from Pentreglo once in a while."

As we took our leave of Stan he was installing himself behind the bar preparing, no doubt, to regale his clientele of inebriated farmers with a selection of tasteless anecdotes about life at the sharp end of old fashioned policing.

"So we can cross Stan off the list of useful witnesses," I said as I settled into the thickly upholstered passenger seat for the journey home. Nigel said nothing as he directed the smooth glide of the Bentley onto the road from the car park. His brow was furrowed. He seemed to be preoccupied with something. It was certainly nothing Stan had told us because Stan had told us nothing and I doubted if he would have told us anything even if he could. Our trip to Pembrokeshire had reminded me of something I had forgotten since retirement; how different old school coppers like Stan are from the modern breed. To Stan and his ilk loyalty to colleagues was all that counted and the world was divided in the most one dimensional of ways into the good guys and the bad. Human Rights, proportionality of response, ethnic awareness and all the other buzzwords of today's policing would be like a foreign language to Stan. I was idly wondering whether the changes actually made the life of the average law abiding citizen better or worse when Nigel broke the silence.

"It's a paradox isn't it?" he said as much to himself as to me. Nevertheless I felt obliged to respond and asked him what he meant.

"He was a successful detective in his day wasn't he, Gareth?"

"He certainly was. Not much got past Stan."

"So you'd say he had a good mind, an organised, logical one."

"Well, I wouldn't call Stan an intellectual, Nigel, but he was always very sharp. He tended to see things quicker than others. He was a complete nightmare to cross examine in court, always a step ahead. Beneath the vulgar exterior I suppose you would say there was a very efficient brain."

"Exactly." Nigel nodded and thought some more. I was beginning to feel stupid. Nigel had seen something that had passed me by. My worst fears were coming to pass. I was getting slow witted in my old age.

"It's the room," said Nigel finally. "It's not the room of someone with a well ordered mind."

"The room? What do you mean?"

"Didn't you see? It was disorganised, lopsided. I can't put my finger on what it was exactly but it just wasn't set out properly. Too much at one end and not enough at the other."

I was both disappointed that there was not some critical clue that Nigel had found and relieved that I had not after all missed it.

"Stan's a slob, Nigel, he's not that bothered about external appearance. If he were bothered about it he'd not wear revolting shirts like the one he had on today and wouldn't let his gut hang out of the top of his trousers like that."

"It's not a question of taste, Gareth, it's one of organisation. Whether you're a slob or a dandy if you've got a methodical organised mind you arrange things in a methodical, organised manner. That room was not the product of someone with an organised mind."

So that's something else I didn't know about Nigel. He's into feng shui. I might have known. I looked across at him with his perfectly fitting suit, carefully fastened tie and every hair in its allotted place. A mental picture of his office in Liverpool came into my mind. The papers were neatly stacked on the desk, all pens pointing the same way, no half eaten sandwiches or half read newspapers to clutter it up. Yes, Nigel was the sort of person who would notice an ornament out of place or an armchair at the wrong angle. He calls it an organised mind but I'd call it obsession. I saw no paradox. Stan was a sharp witted narrow minded ex small town copper who'd derived much satisfaction from locking up those he regarded as villains and didn't regard it as the end of the world if his curtains didn't match his carpets. As far as I was concerned Nigel's observations about Stan's living room told me far more about Nigel than about Stan.

We were just joining the motorway when my phone rang. It was Lenny.

"I'm afraid you're going to reschedule your meeting with Beppo," he said. "I've just had Nev Powell on the phone. He's got Beppo locked up for conspiracy to murder."

Thirteen

As Nev Powell sat back in his chair looking across at me he couldn't resist a smirk. I saw it clearly enough. He made no attempt to hide it. He was being perfectly polite, even friendly towards me but he didn't want me to be in any doubt that as far as he was concerned it was police one lawyers nil. I don't suppose I can blame him. He would have felt himself over the past few weeks being thrust into an unwelcome spotlight by the re-opening of the Beppe Contemponi case. Beppo had been treated as a victim, almost a hero, while he, Nev Powell, would have had a worse Christmas than a supermarket turkey as he felt the finger of suspicion cast its shadow over him. Now the smirk was telling me that he had turned the tables. Beppo was about to be exposed for the criminal Nev always suspected he was and it was he, Detective Inspector Neville Powell the self-proclaimed brightest detective in the South Wales force, to whom the honour had fallen of tearing away the veil of sympathy spun by interfering lawyers and journalists. In his eyes it was poetic justice. No wonder he was smirking.

For my part I was still in the dark. Lenny hadn't been able to tell me much. All he knew was that Beppo was sitting in a police cell refusing to ask any questions until his "brief" arrived and that "brief" he had insisted, would be me.

"He won't talk to me," Lenny had said. "He still doesn't trust me. He wants you down there and you'll need to be quick. Nev Powell is straining at the leash to interview him."

I had a quick word with Nigel before heading off to the police station. We agreed that Nigel would use the time talking to MJ to see if he could succeed where I had so miserably failed. He wasn't expecting to get anywhere but it was worth a try.

Before speaking to Beppo I went to see Nev to learn what the case was about. He was only too happy to oblige. Maybe it's my age but I'm still taken aback by the way that before interviewing a suspect the police these days disclose to his solicitor the outline of the case so that he knows what questions are likely to be asked. They've been doing it for years now but, throwback that I am to a different age, I still think of it as a new procedure like identification parades by DVD or electronic breathalysers. When I started in the job you would be told nothing before an interview. You'd be lucky if you knew what charges the police had in mind let alone what evidence was going to come up in interview. You needed to keep your wits about you to spot the bombshells hidden among the apparently innocuous questions. I suppose it's a sign of getting old when standard procedures still seem novel to you. It's like the first time you hear yourself saying "That's not music, that's just noise" or when you catch a whiff of "old man smell" and realise that you're the only one in the room. Maybe I retired at the right time.

After a brief exchange of pleasantries in which I told Nev of my new life in Spain and he pretended to be interested we got down to the business of the reason for Beppo's arrest. Nev's opening remarks were straight from the "How to be a detective" manual.

"Your client has been arrested on suspicion of conspiracy to murder and as part of my investigation into that alleged offence I intend to interview him. However, the decision as to whether he is to be charged with an offence and, if so, what offence, will be taken by the Crown Prosecution Service to whom all evidence including that arising from the interview will be submitted."

Nev couldn't keep the formality up any further and allowed himself a heartfelt aside.

"Knowing the bloody CPS the charge could be anything from obstructing the highway to high treason. Nothing would surprise me about that shower."

He rolled his eyes as he spoke. Like many police officers he had an uneasy relationship with the CPS or "Couldn't Prosecute Satan" as they were sometimes cruelly called in constabulary circles. Nev, like many of his colleagues, was too ingrained in the practice of deciding charges himself with the compliance of sympathetic custody officers to take easily to allowing outsiders to do it.

I decided to respond to Nev in the same formal terms as he had used to open the proceedings. Employing sufficient grammatical pedantry to remind Nev that I was still a lawyer I asked, "With whom is he supposed to have conspired and whom had he conspired to murder?"

Nev reverted to the manual. "Subject to what emerges in interview it will be my recommendation that your client be charged with conspiring with Milan Jankovic and others unknown…"

"Milan Jankovic? Who the hell is Milan Jankovic?"

I realised that I had spoken my thoughts out loud and interrupted Nev in full flow. He carried on regardless.

"…to murder Mervyn John Jenkins."

This time I had no need to ask. I knew who that was but I was still confused. Why did Nev think that Beppo was conspiring to murder MJ and why would he involve Milan Jankovic who I still knew nothing about? Nev started to explain patiently reading from his notes but failing to conceal his self-satisfied grin.

"On 4th January of this year a call was received at this police station at 15.51 and fourteen seconds…"

Once again I spoke my thoughts out loud. "That's a very precise time, Nev. You must have replaced the old station clock since I was last here."

"It's the computer," Nev explained. "It automatically records the time of calls into the station. It makes life a lot easier now that we don't have to enter them all in a big book."

"A big book? I didn't know you used to have a big book for telephone messages. Nobody ever told me about it."

Nev allowed himself to be distracted from his formal briefing to explain with a slightly triumphant air how every call had to be logged and timed in a book in the old days and then reconciled with the telephone records on a monthly basis so that no smart arsed solicitor could ever catch them out with technicalities based on timing discrepancies.

"You didn't know that did you, Gareth?" he asked with a smile. "You must have wondered how all the statements tallied exactly on timings so you could never get one over on us. Anyway we're even better now we have a computer. You'll never trip us up."

Satisfied at how he had demonstrated his superiority Nev went on.

"The call was from Ty Gwyn. The computer logged the number. It was Iris Jenkins reporting an intruder. She said she'd found a strange man in her bedroom and he attacked her. She thought he was going to kill her. Next thing he dies on top of her. She said she had a kitchen knife in her hand and he must have fallen on it. The Desk Sergeant reckoned it was a wind up at first. It all sounded so unlikely but apparently Iris really sounded distressed and with her house being so isolated we went along to investigate. We didn't expect to find anything but sure enough when we arrived, there was this body in the bedroom and a hysterical Iris covered in blood."

"So you arrested Iris."

Nev raised his palms in a self-justifying gesture.

"We had no option, mate. There was a body on her floor, a blood stained knife right by him that Iris said was hers and a blood splattered Iris telling us she'd killed him. You can't ignore that. Even the Chief Constable's wife would get collared for it."

I'd heard this story before from MJ's perspective although I still couldn't see why Nev was telling me about it. He continued trying to justify his actions.

"What I thought was that we'd bring Iris to the station and while we were waiting for MJ to pick her up we could identify the bloke on the floor. I didn't recognise him as one of the local villains but I was sure he'd be on the Police National Computer. The way I saw it was that we could release Iris on bail while we tied up the loose ends and then, once we had proof that the bloke was a burglar or a rapist or whatever he was, we would recommend no charge against Iris on the basis that it was an act of self-defence. Even the CPS would have to agree with that."

"But it didn't work out that way."

"No it bloody didn't." Nev's smug nonchalance was supplemented by a touch of anger as he continued.

"As soon as the yes men at headquarters heard about the case they ordered me off it. Conflict of interest or some such crap they said, just because I knew Iris and MJ. Within the hour they'd sent in a team from Cardiff complete with clipboards and university degrees but bugger all common sense. Before I knew it they'd charged Iris with murder. Iris of all people! Murder! What were they thinking of?"

The formality was now abandoned. Nev was speaking from the heart.

"Do you know," he said, "when I started in this job they used to say that the force was built on its PCs. They might still say that now but PC doesn't stand for Police Constable any more, it stands for political bloody correctness. That's what's driving today's police force."

Nev raised his hands to make quotation marks in the air as, with no attempt to hide his contempt, he continued. "Apparently it's not the done thing for a middle-aged woman to defend herself in her own home. Apparently it would have been a dereliction of duty to release Iris without charge. The press would have said it was a cover up because she's the wife of an ex copper and apparently we care about the crap the press write so in the name of political correctness and to keep the press happy Iris had to be charged with murder and kept in custody. Never mind the muggers and kiddy fiddlers roaming the streets. We've locked Iris up so the world is safe for decent folk."

He shook his head in frustration as I wondered why it was that every copper or ex copper I spoke to would rather talk about Iris Jenkins than the matter in hand. Nev then picked a piece of paper up from his desk and as he read it his mood changed instantly back to the self-satisfaction that had originally greeted me. He settled back in his chair again as he explained the contents of the paper to me.

"Today this came along and it changes everything. I've already been on to the CPS about it. Needless to say they're too bone headed to drop the charge against Iris but even they can see that things are different now and they can't keep her locked up any more. They've agreed not to oppose bail so Iris is going before the court in the morning and they'll release her on the condition she lives with her sister in Swansea until we complete the investigation. Once we've done that I reckon we can drop the charges and Iris can go home."

Nev sat back smiling as he waited for me to ask the obvious question. I wasn't going to give him the satisfaction so I stared back at him knowing he was bursting to tell me what the paper was. He didn't hold out for long.

"It's from Interpol," he said. "We drew a blank over here so we asked them if they could identify the body of the intruder from DNA records."

"And he is…?"

Nev read the name from the paper in front of him. "Milan Jankovic, he's a Croat last heard of living in Southern Italy."

Suddenly I knew where the conversation was going. Nev carried on reading from the paper.

"He first came to attention during the Yugoslav Civil War. His family was wiped out by the Serbs and he decided to avenge them, except that for him it wasn't so much an eye for an eye as whole villages of Serbs in return for each of his family members. He turned into quite an efficient killing machine, totally ruthless and with nerves of steel. When the war ended, the UN War Crimes Tribunal wanted to speak to him but he got out of the country and resurfaced as a contract killer. He'd go anywhere and kill anyone he was asked to. He didn't care. They reckoned he left his human emotions behind when he lost his family. There was nothing left but killing. According to Interpol there was one criminal gang for whom our friend Jankovic was the assassin of choice, a nasty bunch who liked everyone to know when a killing was their handiwork. They insisted that Jankovic left some sign whenever he killed. One of their favourites was to get him to cut off the victim's nose after death. He would leave it in the victim's hand as a warning to others to keep their noses out of the gang's business."

I shuddered at the thought as Nev continued. "Do you know what was found in the pocket of the body in Iris' bedroom?"

"A knife?"

Nev nodded in triumph. "Not just a knife, a bloody sharp one," he said.

This sounded ridiculous and I told Nev so. "Someone put a contract out on Iris? Come off it, Nev. Who'd want to do that?"

Nev shook his head vigorously. "Not Iris. I don't reckon there was a contract out on Iris. I reckon it was MJ they were after. Iris was just unlucky, or perhaps lucky in the circumstances, that as Jankovic waited for MJ to come home she must have found him and seen him off, the plucky old bird. Marvellous isn't it? The UN can't get him, Interpol can't get him but up against a valley girl he had no chance. It makes you proud to be Welsh doesn't it?"

Nev laughed out loud at the thought. I suspected I knew what was coming so I asked the question. "Why was a contract killer after MJ and where does Beppo feature in all this?"

"Didn't I tell you the name of the gang Jankovic did the killing for? It's all down here from Interpol."

Nev was playing with me now. He looked down and paused before reading further as if he was announcing an Oscar winner.

"It's an Italian gang based in Naples. According to this the head of it is a man called…"

Yet another pause. Nev was milking this for all it was worth.

"…Luciano Contemponi, the elder brother of the late Giuseppe Contemponi and, according to Interpol, a serious player in organised crime in Southern Italy and…"

I finished off the sentence for him.

"…the uncle of my client whom you've got locked up downstairs. I think I'd better go and see him."

The last time I had seen Giuseppe Contemponi junior he was a frightened seven-year-old clutching his mother's hand outside a court building. His mother had left the area soon after the trial and I'd heard no more of Beppo until Lenny had brought him back into my life.

Now I was looking at a grown man sitting opposite me in the cell. He was unmistakably his father's son complete with the broad shoulders and the dark wavy hair. When he looked up at me I saw the same dark eyes to which, all those years ago, I had delivered the news that the last appeal had failed. If anything, despite his mixed parentage, his complexion was even darker than his father's had been when I knew him, a result, no doubt, of two decades' exposure to the sun of Southern Italy.

I offered him my hand and he shook it warmly. When he spoke it was with the same valleys accent of the seven-year-old I had known but the voice was deeper and stronger now and with the unmistakeable intonation of Italy.

"I'm very pleased to see you, Mr Parry. My family always spoke well of you. I have wanted to meet you to thank you for all you did for my father but I didn't expect to meet you like this."

He looked around at the cell walls to emphasise the point.

"I'm afraid, Beppo," I said, "that when you make the sort of allegations against the police as you have you can't expect them to take it lying down. If they have a chance of getting back at you they will. They're like that."

"I didn't start this, Mr Parry. It was that man Webster. When I heard what he was saying what would you expect me to do? That man Jenkins killed my father as sure as if he'd shot him in the head. I couldn't let that pass."

"I appreciate you couldn't ignore it but I didn't expect you to put a contract out on him."

My reply had left my mouth before I had the chance to think of it. I was out of practice and I had forgotten the first rule of criminal lawyers. You never act as if your client is guilty until he tells you he is, no matter how strong the evidence. I started to apologise but Beppo waved the apology away.

"I was actually referring to the legal action I've started, nothing else," he explained patiently. "I can understand why you may think otherwise though, it's natural. I have grown up with hate in my heart for what they did to my father. There has not been a day since his death when the family hasn't spoken of avenging him. Now, after all these years, we know who was responsible for his death. What could be more natural than that I would want to have him killed?"

I was tempted by Beppo's candour to break another important rule. In my head the obvious question formed but, fortunately, I was able to supress it this time. Beppo picked up on my expression and saved me from having to ask.

"No I didn't put the contract out on Jenkins, Mr Parry, if that's what you're thinking. It's true Jenkins took my father's life and I know why they say that he should lose his own life in return but if I believed that Jenkins deserved to die then, believe me, I'd do it myself. I wouldn't need to hire anybody to do it for me."

"Does that mean you don't believe he should die, Beppo?"

Beppo shook his head. "I don't believe he should die. I believe he should be brought to justice, to face up to what he has done. I don't believe in blood feuds. I'm too British for that."

"But some people believe he should die, Beppo, you said it yourself. You said you knew why they say he should die. Who is 'they', Beppo? Do you mean your family in Italy, your Uncle Luciano?"

Beppo avoided a direct answer. "Uncle Luca is a very traditional Neapolitan," he said. "He believes in doing things the traditional way."

I felt that the time had come to spell out the predicament Beppo was in.

"You may say that you don't believe in a life for a life and you're only interested in justice but that's not how the police are going to put it. They will say that you, whether alone or with your uncle, engaged Milan Jankovic to kill Mervyn Jenkins. They know he was hiding in MJ's house waiting for him to come home, complete with a knife. They will ask themselves why an Eastern European contract killer should be hiding in the bedroom of a retired policeman in South Wales. They'll decide that he was there to do what contract killers do – to kill him. They would then ask themselves two questions, firstly who would have a motive for wanting MJ dead and, secondly, who usually uses Jankovic's services. They'd get the same answer to both questions, Beppo, whether right or wrong. Everything would be pointing at you."

Beppo seemed surprised by what I had said. I couldn't think why. It seemed, unfortunately, all too obvious to me.

"MJ?" asked Beppo. "You called Jenkins MJ. Is that how he's known?"

"Yes, it's his nickname. They were a sporty lot at Pentreglo Police Station. Mervyn Jenkins' initials are the same as the American basketball star Michael Jordan so they gave him the same nickname, MJ. They were always doing it. They had a senior fellow there called Matthews. I met up with him again today as it happens. Everyone called him "Stan" after the footballer. There was one poor bugger they had there who was PC King and he had to go through life called 'Billie Jean' so I suppose MJ wasn't so bad by comparison."

My attempt to lighten the mood didn't seem to work. Beppo's brow was furrowed and, for the first time, he looked worried.

"If Jenkins is known as MJ," he said eventually. "I could be in more trouble than I realised."

Fourteen

"I think you'd better tell me about it," I said, so he did.

"You probably know that after the trial my mam took me to me to Italy," he began. Actually, I only found that out recently from Lenny but I nodded. Beppo continued.

"We went to live with my father's family."

"Uncle Luca?"

He nodded.

"Yes, Uncle Luca. He was the acknowledged head of the family, the eldest son. My grandfather was dead by then and Uncle Luca was the one everyone looked up to."

The word "godfather" passed through my mind but I kept it to myself and allowed Beppo to carry on.

"We lived in Naples. The family was very protective towards me and I certainly didn't lack affection from them in my childhood. As I got older, though, I began to realise that Uncle Luca was involved in a lot of stuff that I didn't want to know about. He wasn't like my father. I know now that my dad was a bit dodgy at times but Uncle Luca was far worse. He was a serious player and the older I got the more I understood. He had a lot of enemies did Uncle Luca and I began to notice that when he made an enemy that person tended not to stay healthy for very long. To be fair, he didn't ever try to get me involved. He always kept business and family separate and I was able to get through life shutting my eyes to the nastier side of Uncle Luca. He was always kind and gentle with me. I don't remember him ever raising his voice to me let alone raising a hand. Believe it or not he was quite a quiet person in the house except where my mother was concerned."

"Your mother?"

Beppo looked nervous as he explained.

"Yes, the way he treated my mother was the only way I was able to see first-hand what he was capable of. It wasn't just that they didn't get on. He hated her."

"Hated her. Why?"

"Because he was convinced that she had cheated on my father."

"Had she?"

Beppo nodded gravely.

"I think she had but it was worse than that. Uncle Luca blamed my mother for my father's death. It all came out in a blazing row one night. Uncle Luca was in a terrifying rage, worse than I had ever seen. He was saying that my father had died because of my mother's infidelity. He said she'd betrayed him. He was going on and on, getting angrier and angrier and then he said it. He said that my mother's lover had been the one who set my father up over the post office robbery."

Beppo was getting upset. I allowed him a few moments to compose himself before asking, "Did your mother say anything when he said that?"

Beppo took a deep breath before replying. "She denied it, of course. She was screaming and crying and swearing on my life that it wasn't true but that just made my uncle worse. When she said that he had no proof he suddenly went very quiet and when he replied he sounded a hundred times more frightening than when he had been shouting. He just looked my mother in the eye and told her that if he ever found proof he would make it his business to kill her and her lover to avenge the family honour."

"But he didn't did he?" I don't know why but I was trying to look on the bright side.

"Not yet," was Beppo's discouraging reply. "He didn't know who the lover was by the sound of it. All he had was a name she had used to describe him and, ruthless though he was, he was still prepared to give her the benefit of the doubt while he didn't have proof. My mum wasn't taking any chances though. Soon afterwards she did a runner leaving me with Uncle Luca. He always used to tell me that she'd abandoned me because she didn't love me but, thinking back, I think he terrified her so much that she had to get away quickly and didn't want to risk my life by taking me."

"Did you ever see your mother again?"

Beppo shook his head.

"Do you know where she is?"

He shook it again.

"So how do you know he hasn't already carried the threat out?" It was a pretty clumsy question on my part but I could see where the conversation was leading and in my desperation was trying to send it in another direction.

Yet again Beppo shook his head. He struggled with his words as I suppose one would when talking about the potential murder of his mother.

"If he'd done the deed he wouldn't have kept going on about her," he said. "He would regularly talk about her to me and he always uses the present tense as if she were still alive. He would tell me that she was no good and use some crude, hurtful words to describe her. He said that if he ever found proof that she and her lover had betrayed my father they'd both be dead. He often used to say that. I love my Uncle Luca in spite of everything and I can never repay all that he did for me but the way he talked about my mother. I hated that."

"But your Uncle Luca never did find the proof he talked about." Once again I was trying to sound more positive than I felt.

"Not until now," was the inevitable response.

"What's more," continued Beppo, "I was the one that gave Uncle Luca the proof."

"What do you mean, Beppo?"

"Well, when I heard from that man Webster I asked Uncle Luca what I should do to get justice for my father. He was the one who recommended you as my solicitor and he was the one who got in touch with your office on my behalf. He developed quite a rapport with your secretary, what was her name?"

"You mean Pauline." I was well used to the fact that clients always looked on me with reserve bordering on outright suspicion yet developed an instant bond with Pauline. What is it that she has that I don't? A personality I suppose.

"Yes, Pauline," he confirmed "They got quite friendly chatting on the phone and it must have been her who told him about Jenkins, how he was involved in the case and how he was known as MJ."

I asked him why that was important.

"It was important," Beppo replied slowly, "because it was the proof he needed. When he was repeating his weekly threats against my mother through my time living with him he would name the man he blamed for my father's situation using the only name he had for him, the one my mother apparently knew him by. He called him 'M'. That was the man he swore to kill and until I got your law firm involved in the case he didn't know who he was. Now, thanks to me, he's found him."

It was all too clear to me now. Nevertheless, I spelt it out to Beppo persisting in the hopeless notion that perhaps I had got the wrong end of the stick.

"Your uncle had heard that someone called "M" had framed your father for a crime he didn't commit and he swears to kill him if he finds him. Pauline tells him that someone called 'MJ' is suspected of having a hand in falsifying the evidence. Your uncle puts two and two together and decides MJ was the man who he's been swearing vengeance against all these years so…"

Beppo finished the sentence for me.

"…he sends his pet assassin round to his house to kill him."

"Do you think that's likely, Beppo?" I was really clutching at straws now.

Beppo didn't need words to answer that question. His expression said it all. Nevertheless, he drove any doubt from my mind with his reply.

"Not just likely. It's exactly what Uncle Luca would do. He's spoken about it often enough."

I had to ask the next question. "Did you know anything about the plan to kill MJ before today?"

I looked him straight in the eye as I awaited his reply. He did not look away as I had seen so many guilty clients do in the past. Holding my gaze and in a clear voice he replied, "No, Mr Parry, you have my word on that."

Do you know what? I believed him. I had seen too many liars during my undistinguished career defending the indefensible that I was able to recognise all the giveaway signs, yet this young man looking apprehensively at me displayed none of them. I hadn't expected him to answer my question with a confession. Whenever I used to ask that question of a client I would always expect a denial. That denial would often be accompanied by a glance in the direction of heaven and sometimes even an anguished howl at the very suggestion of a departure from the paths of righteousness. My clients all knew the rules of the game. A lawyer cannot go into court to assert the innocence of someone who has told him he is guilty so the experienced clients know better than to do so. Most of them were wise enough not to expect me to believe their protestations of innocence, even if sworn on the lives of their dear mothers or unborn children, but they knew that it was necessary for them to go through the ritual of denial just as it was then necessary for me to pretend that I believed them. With Beppo it was different. He was either a superb actor or he was genuinely innocent and genuinely shocked by the realisation that had just come to him.

He wasn't the only one shocked as the implications of what he had said sunk in. I had conducted the whole investigation on the assumption that MJ was at worst a loyal and misguided dupe for a more sinister character. I had set out to demonstrate that this was so and thought I was succeeding. My faith had been rocked a little by the realisation that MJ was prepared to extend his assistance to tampering with evidence but my basic belief remained. I got involved because I wanted to protect MJ and the strongest weapon I had for doing so was the complete lack of any motive for wanting to frame Beppe. As a result of what Beppo had now told me I could no longer draw comfort from my ignorance. He had supplied the motive and a powerful motive at that. Not only was it a powerful motive but it was a credible one too. MJ was a good friend and colleague but his penchant for a bit on the side was legendary. Rumours had circulated for years of a secret mistress while MJ played the public role of a devoted husband blind to Iris' unattractiveness and tolerant of her foibles. I had never doubted the truth of those rumours but, to be honest, had preferred not to know the details. I was content to swallow the illusion of a happily married man that MJ would foster when in the company of anyone who might be less tolerant than I of his philandering. I couldn't ignore it any more though. That very philandering had cost a man his life and nearly caused MJ to lose his life in return. I would have to tell Nigel as soon as possible.

So preoccupied was I at the effect of Beppo's revelations on my relationship with MJ that I temporarily forgot the more immediate effect on his situation. I might accept his denial of involvement but I wondered whether Nev Powell would be so trusting. Worse than that, how bad would it all look before a jury? Beppo comes to Britain from Italy precisely because he believes MJ to have been responsible for his father's death and no sooner does he do so than MJ's home receives a visit from an armed killer employed by his uncle with whom he lives. Would there be any juror trusting enough to believe, as I believed, that Beppo knew nothing of what his uncle had planned?

I decided that I had no alternative but to give to Beppo the advice that every solicitor gives to a client before a police interview when he believes that client's position to be hopeless – to say nothing in the interview.

It had been a while since I had needed to give that advice but the mantra came back to me without effort.

"At the start of the interview confirm all your personal details and take the first opportunity to deny the allegation against you. After that, tell Inspector Powell that you've been advised to make no further comment about the case. He'll carry on asking questions though but you carry on saying 'no comment'. He'll ask you why you're not answering questions. He'll suggest that it's because you know you're guilty and ask you whether he's right. Don't fall for it just keep saying 'no comment'. He'll warn you of the consequences and no doubt try to drive a wedge between us by telling you I'm giving you bad advice. At times he'll be 'good cop' and at times he'll be 'bad cop' but it's all a ploy. Whatever he says and however he says it you just say 'no comment' every time."

I've given that advice hundreds of times and I've seen it ignored almost as often. Clients will always nod wisely, tell me they understand why I have given them the advice and assure me they will heed it. Then, ten minutes into the interview, arrogance will take over and they will persuade themselves of the entertainment value of a few smart answers to make the slow witted interviewing officer look particularly stupid. Only then will they realise that he wasn't so slow witted after all and they will turn to me with an expression resembling that of an animal caught in a trap but it will be too late. They will talk themselves into a conviction (deserved or otherwise) and I will be left wondering, yet again, why the average suspect seems congenitally incapable of simply saying two simple words and no more in answer to questions. The irony is that those who pull it off and are able to face everything thrown at them with a contemptuous "no comment" are the most cold blooded and unemotional and therefore tend to be the nastiest of criminals. Relatively normal human beings who find themselves in trouble are simply not ruthless enough to supress the natural tendency to unburden themselves.

In Beppo's case, however, he understood the position he was in and was intelligent enough to realise where his interests lay. He followed my advice to the letter. We sat for over an hour in a cramped and overheated interview room while Nev Powell fluctuated, with the skill of a true professional, between expressions of sympathy and thinly veiled threats. Nev went through his full repertoire of roles during that interview. At times he was Beppo's best friend offering help in presenting his case to the jury in the best light possible. At other times he was a cynical bully, dismissing Beppo's refusal to answer questions as "pathetic". Sometimes he was shouting, banging his fist on the desk and leaning forward menacingly towards Beppo. Sometimes his tone was kindly or even light hearted. He tried every trick he knew to coax something more substantial than "no comment" out of Beppo. Throughout it all Beppo stood firm and stuck to the script. He refused to be intimidated or flattered and maintained a calm and courteous demeanour. It was a master class in how to handle police interviews and I suspected that, innocent though I believed him to be, he had the genes of a professional criminal firmly embedded in his DNA.

Eventually a frustrated Nev Powell gave up. The interview was terminated. Beppo had won the first round. The "no comment" tactic had worked in the short term. Nev only had a circumstantial case and he knew it. He would have to release Beppo on bail while he made further enquiries. I suppose I should have felt elated at the effectiveness of my advice but what I was feeling was far from that. As I reflected on what would now follow my heart sank. It was my duty to tell Nigel of MJ's connection with Rita Contemponi and it was a duty I could not ignore. Nevertheless it was a duty that was going to send my old friend to prison and, more than likely, destroy the reputation of the firm that Lenny and I had built over so many years.

That wasn't the worst of it though. Although I had won a breathing space for Beppo I knew that it was no more than that. Nev Powell's investigation would soon uncover the identity of MJ's "bit on the side" and, once it did, the case against Beppo would become as close to watertight as you could get. Nobody would believe that he had played no part in his Uncle Luca's plans for vengeance; nobody that is apart from poor trusting me. Beppo would be charged and would find himself before a jury in a trial where, far from being his saviour, the refusal to answer questions in the interview would be the final factor that the jury would need to be certain of his guilt. With an increasing sensation of nausea I realised that, for the second time in my life, I would watch a member of the Contemponi family being sent to prison for a crime he did not commit.

Fifteen

They were just getting ready to close the office when I returned. Cher was preparing the mail for posting while a lank-haired acne scarred adolescent stood on the other side of the counter staring vacantly in her general direction. I must have given him a suspicious look because Cher quickly introduced him to me as Wayne, her boyfriend. As Wayne grunted in apparent recognition of my presence Cher explained that he gallantly accompanied her to the post office each evening to ensure her safety. I wondered who it was that might wish to relieve Cher of the confirmations of appointments, notification of court dates and the other standard letters that formed the bulk of the firm's postal output and I wondered further how such a person might react to a confrontation with a taciturn teenager clad in heavy metal T shirt, a coat several sizes too big and sagging jeans that exposed the waistband of his underpants.

"Wayne love, can you back up the computer for me?" called Cher from behind the counter. Wayne grunted again and shuffled over to her like an obedient mongrel. Cher paused to point out to me, with more than a little pride, that Wayne was a self-taught computer "genius" to whom the firm turned whenever there was an IT problem. That struck a chord with me. My son, Martin, is a computer whizzkid and I knew only too well from the succession of eccentric looking but technically gifted friends that he had that appearances can be deceptive in the cyber world. Perhaps I had misjudged him.

When I entered my room I found Nigel there sitting at my desk reading over the notes of his meeting with MJ. He looked exasperated. He had got nowhere with him.

"He's in total denial," he said. "He must know who the Viper is and he must know that we know yet he won't help himself. He just clams up and refuses to talk about it. I'm sorry about this, Gareth, because I know that you want to help him but, frankly, short of a confession from Inspector Powell, which I'm not holding my breath about, I'm going to have to advise my insurance clients that Mervyn Jenkins is the one that's going to cost them all this money. They're going to want him prosecuted unfortunately and you know what the result of that will be."

Nigel shrugged his shoulders in a gesture of helplessness. I knew I'd have to tell him what I had learned.

"Perhaps MJ has a good reason for not wanting to talk about it," I began hesitantly.

"I know his reason well enough," was Nigel's immediate response. "It's this bloody loyalty coppers have for one another. It's all very touching and a welcome contrast to the backstabbing that goes on among lawyers but it doesn't help in investigations like this."

"It's not that, Nigel."

He looked up waiting for me to explain and so I did. I told Nigel as succinctly as I could about what Beppo had told me in the cell, emphasising the relationship between MJ and Rita Contemponi but omitting, on the grounds of client confidentiality, mention of the threats Luciano had made against MJ. Nigel pondered for a moment.

"So it's looking a lot clearer and simpler now," he said. "MJ was carrying on with the man's wife so when he had him in custody he took the opportunity of arranging things so that he'd be out of the way for a long time. Only MJ wouldn't have known he'd be getting rid of the competition permanently. It sounds credible enough to me. Sex is a pretty good motive for perverting the course of justice, wouldn't you agree, Gareth?"

I didn't want to agree but I knew I'd have to. Like Nigel said, it was all now clear and simple. Nigel didn't dwell on the point. Instead he moved on to something that hadn't crossed my mind with all the other concerns I had.

"This puts the claim for damages against the police in a different light of course," he said, avoiding my eye as he spoke. "Just as sex can be a credible motive for perverting the course of justice so vengeance can be a credible motive for attempted murder."

"You mean Beppo."

Nigel nodded in confirmation. "We know now that Sgt Jenkins did for your client's father but your client himself would have known that for even longer. He's tried to have him bumped off in revenge hasn't he?"

Even though I had not given him all the details of what Nev had told me Nigel was rapidly working it out for himself. I knew that his suspicions would grow stronger once he spoke to Nev but in the meantime I resorted, unconvincingly, to bluster.

"What makes you think Beppo had anything to do with the attack on Iris?" I asked trying to inject just the right amount of outrage into my voice that Nigel would back down. Unsurprisingly he didn't.

"Look, Gareth, you're going to speak up for your client, of course you are, but my insurance clients are going to jump on this to try to get out of paying young Contemponi any damages for what Sgt Jenkins did. You may say he's innocent but that's obviously not what Inspector Powell thinks otherwise he wouldn't have arrested him. My understanding is that he's being accused of sending a hired assassin after Sgt Jenkins. Apparently the police have evidence linking the man found at Jenkins' house with the Contemponi family."

Nigel looked straight at me waiting for the expression that would confirm his suspicions. I tried staring straight ahead betraying nothing. He wasn't impressed.

"In case you're wondering, Gareth, Sgt Jenkins told me that when I spoke to him today. He'd just been told by Inspector Powell who, as we speak, is arranging bail for Mrs Jenkins. Needless to say Sgt Jenkins missed out the bit about carrying on with Mrs Contemponi but now you've filled in that detail the picture's complete wouldn't you agree?"

Of course I agreed but I wasn't going to admit it.

"Of course, Nigel, the fact that Beppo may have wanted to get revenge, which hasn't been proved, doesn't alter the fact that his father was unlawfully framed and wrongly convicted.

If anything, the discovery of MJ's fling with Rita makes the claim stronger because it shows that the framing of Beppe Contemponi wasn't just a case of over zealousness, it was downright malicious."

Nigel's expression didn't change. He'd obviously considered that point. He replied in measured tones.

"The reality, Gareth, is that no court is going to fall over itself to award damages to someone who doesn't simply take the law into his own hands but hires war criminals to help him do it. What's more they're not going to be too happy to order a pay out to a man who's serving a long prison sentence for conspiracy to murder, and a foreign resident to boot. Imagine the headlines in the 'Daily Mail' if that happened."

I could smell defeat on all fronts as I asked Nigel what he intended to do next. His reply was friendlier than it needed to be in the circumstances.

"Gareth," he said, "whatever the position that my insurance clients require me to adopt I want to tell you that I regard you as a friend and I'm not in the habit of letting down my friends. You've helped me in the past and you've helped me with this case. I know that you only wanted two things, damages for Mr Contemponi and clearing the name of Sgt Jenkins so far as that was possible. I promised you I'd help with both those wishes and, though it may be impossible to deliver everything you want I'm going to do the best I can to help you. We'll stick to our plan to speak to Inspector Powell. I doubt it will get us anywhere but you're welcome to try to get something from him that will at least allow responsibility for what happened to be shared rather than resting totally on Sgt Jenkins' shoulders. I'll do everything I can to help you in that. After we've done that I'll let you enjoy the rest of your holiday and then get back to Spain while I make my report in which I intend to recommend that we offer compensation to Mr Contemponi rather than forcing him to take us to court. I can't make any promises about the size of the compensation they'll offer. It'll have to reflect what we now know and I can't even promise that they'll take my advice and make an offer at all. Either way, I'll get in touch with you in Spain and let you know. If you need to come back to discuss matters formally with me I'll make sure my clients pay your expenses. I'm afraid, Gareth, that's the best I can do."

He smiled and made a raised palm gesture as he finished. I thanked him. I knew my position had been weakened and I trusted Nigel to keep his word.

"I take it that you still want to see Inspector Powell about this?" he asked. I told him I certainly did if only so that I could try to puncture the smugness that Nev had exhibited when he knew he had Beppo in the frame for conspiracy. It would be nice to reverse our positions and for me to throw accusations at him for a change. In any event it was my last chance to do something to salvage MJ's reputation and, with it, that of the firm. Nigel got up to see Pauline to make arrangements. As he walked past me he smiled reassuringly and squeezed my shoulder. It was a welcome if uncharacteristic gesture from him.

I followed Nigel out of the room and was just passing Lenny's room when I heard my name being called from inside.

"Can I have a quick word before you go?" said Lenny in a voice that sounded strangely subdued. Surely the doctor hadn't followed up the ban on alcohol by banning Lenny from going to pubs at all; that would be a sure way of killing him.

Lenny looked up as I entered. "Shut the door," he said curtly but his voice betrayed anxiety rather than rudeness. He motioned me to sit down and proceeded to focus his attention on the empty coffee cup that sat in the middle of his desk. This was not like Lenny at all, even the new sober Lenny. He seemed to be avoiding my eyes. When eventually he spoke there was a flatness about him that I did not recognise.

"You know about that missing money I mentioned in the pub?" he asked without looking at me. I said that I did.

"Well," he continued, "the auditors have got back to me. It's not just a clerical error, the money's actually missing, someone's made off with it."

"Where has it gone, Lenny?"

At any other time Lenny would have burst into sarcastic laughter at such a stupid question and proceeded to tell me, in characteristically colourful language, that if he knew where the money had gone it wouldn't be missing. Instead he just shook his head slowly. He was in no mood for sarcasm. He pointed at the laptop on his desk.

"I tried to be a smart arse, to do things the modern way." he said. "I used this thing to manage the funds. It seemed like a good idea but then I didn't bargain for some bugger hacking into the system. Over the last few months investments have been sold and the proceeds, instead of going back into the fund, have been shipped off to an offshore bank account that I've never even heard of."

He sank deeper into his chair as he went on. "I can't even blame that useless prick of an investment manager for this one. It's all my fault. He'll be laughing his socks off when he hears what a cock up I've made of things. Serves me right, that's what he'll say and he'll be speaking the truth."

I tried to be constructive. "Who could have hacked into the system, Lenny? Did the auditors have any idea?"

Lenny looked pained as he answered. "There are two possibilities apparently. One is that a gang of professional hackers got into the system via the bank account. They tell me there're plenty of gangs in Eastern Europe and Asia who specialise in that sort of thing according to the bloke I spoke to."

"That sounds serious, Lenny."

"Maybe it does," he agreed, "but I hope to hell that's the answer. The alternative is too horrible to contemplate."

"What is the alternative?" I asked rather unnecessarily.

Lenny didn't answer. It was as if he didn't want mention of the other possibility to pass his lips lest that might make it true. Instead, he looked pointedly over my shoulder towards his door.

"An inside job?" I spared him the ordeal by saying the words for him.

As Lenny nodded in agreement I could see the tears forming in his eyes.

"I just can't believe it," he said in a voice breaking with emotion. "I simply can't believe that any of them would do this to me, none of them. They're more like family than staff. They just wouldn't, would they?"

Lenny was waiting for me to give him a comfortable answer but I saw no point in ignoring an obvious possibility.

"Could anyone here have got access to the funds, Lenny?" I asked. Lenny responded by pulling out his key ring and unlocking a drawer in his desk.

"All of the codes and passwords are in there taped to the bottom of that drawer. If you ask me whether anyone here could find them then I've got to say yes but if you tell me someone would want to do it I'd say no or, at least, that's what I would have said yesterday."

I remembered the conversation I had had in reception earlier. "How well do you know Cher?" I asked. "Has she been here long?"

"Cher?" Lenny shook his head. "I don't think so. I know she's not the world's most polished receptionist but I'm sure she's honest and, let's face it, she's not really bright enough to find her way around an offshore bank account."

I told Lenny what I had heard about Wayne. I suggested that maybe he'd put her up to it or even that she had used him to steal the money. Lenny didn't reply. He was still unprepared to countenance the possibility of one of his employees, his family, wanting to steal from him. Eventually I broke the silence.

"Have you contacted the police?"

"Not yet," said Lenny. "I know I need to but I was hoping you might do something for me first." I noticed that he had picked up his coffee cup, the closest thing he had to the glass he always seemed to have in his hand when trying to persuade someone to do something they might not want to do. Oh dear, another favour for Lenny! Haven't I done enough for him already? I looked across at him ready to cut him short but he looked so pathetic that I held my tongue.

"Your place is near Gibraltar isn't it?"

I nodded to confirm, I didn't like the way the conversation was going.

"Well, by coincidence Gibraltar is apparently where the money is now, in a bank account at one of those dodgy banks they have there for people who don't like paying tax."

"Do we know whose bank account it is?"

For the first time Lenny almost smiled as he picked up a piece of paper from his desk.

"The auditors were able to get details of the transfer from our bank. The account it went into is in the name of a woman."

"Have you got her name there?"

"Oh yes, I've got her name." Lenny held up the paper and read slowly from it. "Miss Monica Bent."

I have a talent for stating the obvious. It's an important attribute in any lawyer, the ability to state the obvious as if it were profound wisdom. My talent did not desert me at that moment.

"I think that's a false name, Lenny. No one has a name like that. She chose it as a laugh."

At least it made Lenny smile again.

"Well spotted, Sherlock," he said. "According to the auditors it's quite common to give Mickey Mouse names when opening that sort of account. The banks don't care. All they want is the money."

"Did the auditors tell you how to get the money back from Gibraltar?"

"That sort of bank is pretty difficult to deal with," Lenny replied. "They'll only pay money out on the express instructions of the account holders. They say they do not want to get involved in disputes between third parties, the miserable hypocrites. In practice, of course, the account holders will only authorise repayment of the money if they are getting their collars felt by the police as they're doing it."

"So you need to identify Monica Bent and put the law onto her."

"Exactly," said Lenny.

"Isn't that all the more reason to get the police involved sooner rather than later, Lenny?"

He looked pained at that comment.

"You're right, Gareth, but I thought before I did that..." he couldn't finish the sentence so I did it for him.

"You want to find out for yourself first."

"Just in case it is someone here," he explained before adding, "Not that I think it is but if it is then I would want the chance to ask them why before getting the police involved. Maybe I'm being soft but perhaps if I could talk to them and persuade them to return the money voluntarily..." His voice trailed off as if he was ashamed to admit that his loyalty to his staff was so great that he would even contemplate forgiving such a betrayal.

"Worry about that if it happens," I said before remembering that Lenny was about to ask a favour of me. I braced myself as Lenny grasped his coffee cup tightly and uttered words that I had often heard from him before and which inevitably lead to disaster.

"I was talking to a bloke in the pub a while ago," he began. "He's a retired investigator for the Inland Revenue. He spent his life chasing tax evaders. Didn't win him many friends but in my book he's a hero. I can't stand those arrogant pricks who make a bob or two and then decide they don't owe the country anything. They conveniently forget the free education they received to give them the skills to grow rich or the NHS that kept them healthy while they were doing it."

I gently steered Lenny back to the subject in hand and he continued. "Anyway, this bloke was telling me that they keep a lot of moles to use in their work."

A lot of moles? I had visions of "Wind in the Willows" or of little nocturnal animals burrowing under the lawns of the mansions built by the tax evaders with their ill gotten gains before I realised what Lenny was talking about.

"You mean informers," I said.

"Yes, informers in the banks. People who get pissed off at working for a pittance bowing and scraping to those who'd rather hide their money than let it help some poor kid get the same chances in life they had. Not the senior people of course, they're as bent as the customers most of the time, and as rich, but this bloke was saying there's enough minor clerks in these places with no love for the banks and only too willing to pass on information to those who grease their palms. I thought of the bloke when this came to light and gave him a ring. He rang me back a few minutes ago. He says he knows someone in the bank where the account is who'll tell you what you need to know. Only problem is he'll only do it face to face. He'll show you the file for the account but he won't let you make copies and won't put anything in writing in case things get traced back to him. He's good and reliable according to my source."

"And expensive no doubt."

Lenny looked hurt.

"A hundred Euros, apparently but don't worry I'll give you the money to pay him, of course. All I want is for you to meet him, find out who runs the account and tell me."

"And if I find out that those running the account are not strangers? What then, Lenny? You can't just slap them on the wrist."

Lenny stared hard at the desk for a few seconds before taking a deep breath.

"I know, Gareth, I'll have to involve the police but, before I do I want to talk to them, try to understand why they did it. I reckon that's worth a hundred Euros don't you, Gareth?"

I'm not sure that I do but it was perhaps to Lenny's credit that he was still contemplating forgiveness despite talk of going to the police. I wasn't going to upset him any more than he was so I didn't press him further.

"OK, I'll do it," I heard myself saying. "Tell your mate to set up a meeting."

Lenny passed a folded sheet of paper to me.

"It's already set up," he said. "Next Wednesday at 7.30 in La Linea. The details are all here. I won't ask you to eat it after you've read it." Lenny allowed himself another smile.

"What if I'd said no?" I asked.

Lenny walked around the desk and clapped me on the shoulder.

"If you'd have said no then you wouldn't have been the Gareth Parry who's been a good and loyal friend of mine for over thirty years."

There was nothing more to be said. Lenny was right of course. There's no way I would have refused to help him any more than he would have refused to help me had the shoe been on the other foot.

Sixteen

Cher had already left by the time I walked out of Lenny's room. Reception was in darkness. The light was still on in Pauline's room though and I went towards her door to turn it off. I may not be a partner in the firm any more but the penny pinching habits die hard. I realised before I got there that the room wasn't empty. There were raised voices coming from it. One of them was Pauline's. She sounded upset. I didn't recognise the other one at first and then it struck me. It was Nigel. I'd never heard him raise his voice before and the sound was therefore new to me. What on earth was going on? Nigel never raised his voice. Even when he was angry he resorted to cold sarcasm, never shouting. And what was upsetting Pauline? I couldn't ignore it. I went over to the door and gingerly poked my head round. I needed to investigate but I didn't want to seem as if I was prying so I coughed loudly as I looked round.

Nigel and Pauline were standing either side of the desk. They seemed to be glaring at each other as if they had just been arguing. They stopped when they saw me and looked embarrassed. I waited for an explanation but when none came I asked what was going on. They stared at each other, each defying the other to explain. Eventually Nigel spoke first.

"Pauline and I were just having a discussion. It got a bit out of hand. I'm sorry."

"A discussion? What about?"

Pauline and Nigel exchanged glances. She nodded and Nigel took that as his cue to tell me.

"We were talking about Sam."

"What about Sam?"

"I've been talking to Sam," explained Nigel. "Giving him some advice that I thought might be helpful. He doesn't seem too keen to take it so I've repeated it to Pauline. She doesn't like it either."

I was now confused. Why did Nigel think it to be his place to give advice to a man who clearly hadn't asked for it and what had he said that had visibly upset the usually resilient Pauline?

"What was that advice, Nigel?" I asked when it became obvious that neither of them was going to tell me unprompted.

Nigel didn't reply. Instead he looked at Pauline and she in turn looked at the photograph on her desk. I realised, with some surprise what they had been arguing about.

"Is this about Debbie?" I asked.

They nodded together and I saw tears form in Pauline's eyes.

"He told Sam to snap out of it, that's what he did. Snap out of it as if he was talking about a teenage crush or something." Pauline looked accusingly at Nigel as she spoke.

Nigel had recovered his composure and when he spoke it was with his usual calm but firm tone.

"What I said was that it was time for him to move on. I offered to help him do it. I suggested that instead of spending so much time on that bench he could start working again, do a few jobs, get involved in charity work, anything to give him something to think about or talk about other than hatred and revenge. When I went to dinner at Pauline's he hardly spoke and when he did everything he said was about his daughter and that boy. I took him for a drink willing to talk to him about every subject under the sun; football, politics, the weather anything that two men might talk about over a drink, anything but self-pity and getting even but it was hopeless. In the end I dropped the pretence and told him straight that unless he got a grip on himself he was going to destroy Pauline's life just as he was destroying his own."

I was taken aback by Nigel's bluntness. He was probably right in what he said but to say that he was being tactless didn't do justice to my reaction. I didn't need to say anything. Pauline said it for me, anger and hurt battling for supremacy in her voice.

"Just what do you think gives you the right to come down here and tell my husband, who you've only known five minutes how he should behave?"

Nigel was sheepish as he tried to explain. "I'm not trying to upset you or him, Pauline. It's just that perhaps as an outsider and as a fresh pair of eyes I can see what maybe you can't and what I can see is a man destroying himself over something that can never be put right. Don't you see, Pauline, it's desperately sad but it can't be put right by hatred."

Perhaps Nigel was trying to be conciliatory but I could see that he was having the opposite effect. Pauline's face was showing an aggressive expression that I can't recall ever seeing before.

As she replied her voice was approaching a scream. "Don't you think I bloody well know that? You come here with your posh voice and your fancy manners treating me as if I'm *twp*, telling me the bloody obvious as if you're the only one clever enough to see it. Of course I know he's destroying himself. Of course I know hatred won't bring Debbie back. We've lost Debbie and instead of her all Sam has is hate. He's lost everything else. I'm not going to take that from him. You may have a fine education, Nigel, but it didn't teach you about me and it didn't teach you about my husband."

She paused and seemed to be calming herself but instead she wiped the tears from her eyes and resumed the attack.

"I can't believe that a man who's supposed to be clever can be stupid enough to think I like having my husband turned into a rambling bitter man, old before his time. I can't believe that you're arrogant enough to believe that I haven't tried everything to help Sam 'snap out of it' as you so elegantly put it. I have lived for twenty years watching the man I love suffer pain, terrible pain. I would give anything to take that pain away from him but there's nothing I can do. Year after hopeless year has taught me that. I won't give up on him and maybe one day I'll find a way to heal the pain. Until then I'm not going to take away the hate because that hate is the only medicine that can make the pain bearable. Above all I don't need some posh boy who doesn't understand what we're feeling making the pain worse by sticking his middle class nose into our business."

Nigel looked stunned at the ferocity of the reply. Things were now seriously out of hand. Nigel had been stunningly insensitive towards Pauline and she was being unnecessarily offensive to him. I had to intervene to defuse the situation or I could see the working relationship on the Contemponi case breaking down irretrievably. Adopting the tone of voice that I imagine U.N. peace envoys adopt with megalomaniac presidents I began. "Look, Nigel, mate, I know you think you're helping but maybe this is something Pauline's better off dealing with by herself. She's obviously upset and I'm sure she doesn't mean what she's been saying. She'll be fine in the morning. Shall we get off now and forget about it?"

"I can't," was Nigel's blunt and frankly surprising reply. He didn't seem offended by Pauline's tone. Instead, to my astonishment, he seemed determined to carry on the argument. What on earth was he thinking? I stayed conciliatory and tried another approach. If I could just get Nigel to leave the visibly upset Pauline alone I was sure I could persuade her to withdraw her hurtful and uncharacteristic remarks.

"Perhaps, Nigel, the problem is that you don't understand what Pauline and Sam have been through. How could you? How could anyone who hasn't experienced it?"

Nigel looked up sharply but didn't reply. For what seemed an uncomfortably long time he seemed to be staring not so much at me as through me. His expression seemed to change as I watched him. It was disconcerting. I knew Nigel as a clever, meticulous man with a dry sense of humour and a calm, sometimes cold exterior. Emotion was something I simply did not associate with him yet, before my very eyes, super capable controlled Nigel was disappearing and in his place was somebody altogether more human, even vulnerable. I saw his lip quiver and his eyes blink. He took a deep breath. His voice was breaking as he finally spoke.

"You're wrong there, Gareth. It's because I know only too well what Pauline and Sam have been through that I won't let this go. I can't let it go. I know what will happen if I do and I wouldn't be able to forgive myself."

Both Pauline and I looked at Nigel inviting him to go on. Three times he tried and three times he failed. Nigel, the man who had an answer for everything simply couldn't form the words he was struggling to find. I tried to sound as sympathetic as I could. I knew that at that moment I was looking at a troubled, tormented soul.

"Don't say anything you don't want to, Nigel, but if it helps to talk we'll listen."

Nigel did talk. There were tears in his eyes as he did so. He talked at length but in a hollow voice that did not seem to acknowledge our presence. He spoke of his childhood, living in a big house by a park in a wealthy suburb of Liverpool. I knew the area he was speaking of, where the comfort and apparent wealth of the inhabitants must appear even more desirable than usual because it is perched on the end of a notoriously poor and depressed city whose run down terraces and sprawling, vandalised estates seem to be in such a contrast to the leafy avenues and solid airy dwellings that they might as well be part of a different civilisation. Nigel's parents, he told us rather unnecessarily, were well off and gave him almost everything parents could give to a child except for the two things he wanted most, their attention and a family life. They were too busy, he told us wistfully, being successful in their careers to spare any time for him and too conscious of their standard of living to give him a brother or a sister that he could share his time with. As soon as he was old enough they packed him off to school and every school holiday they entrusted him to the care of a child minder.

"She wasn't the conventional kind of nanny like many of my friends had. They all tended to be looked after by girls from similar backgrounds to them, filling in time between leaving boarding school and ensnaring a husband of sufficient means to keep them in idle luxury. It was either that or foreign au pairs. My friends used to tell some horror stories about the au pairs and the things they'd get up to with the local boys or sometimes the man of the house. Fortunately, I was spared that experience. My mother farmed me out to a woman her parents used to employ in their factory. She had left to have children and needed the extra money so my mother came to an arrangement with her that she would look after me at the same time as her own children while I was home for the holidays. I think that my mother wanted me to see how the other half lived. It wasn't creeping egalitarianism or anything like that. It was more a case of teaching me how to communicate with those whom she fondly expected I would be exploiting in later life.

I would be taken to the child minder's house. It was so different from what I was used to, like breathing fresh air after being in a stuffy room. She lived in a little terraced house in a street full of them. I'd never seen a street like that, apart from on television. From our house, just a few miles away, we could hardly see our neighbours' houses let alone get to know the people who lived in them. In Auntie's street everyone knew all the neighbours and all the neighbourhood stuck together whatever was thrown at it. In happy times you never celebrated alone there and in sad times you always had someone to cry with. Yes they would interfere and yes there'd be terrible fights sometimes but compared to where I lived it felt alive and real. They may be swearing at you or chasing you down the street for some reason or other but you knew that they cared about you and you knew that if you were in trouble they wouldn't turn away."

A faint smile had formed on Nigel's lips as he remembered those times. He seemed to be reliving them, oblivious to the two of us listening to him.

"I got to know the family better than my own, that's why I called her Auntie and him Uncle. Apart from Auntie and Uncle there were three children and although they didn't have much money they were close, happy and to my mind the kind of family I wished I'd belonged to. I loved my parents of course and they were very good to me but to be honest Auntie and Uncle were more like my family. They treated me like their youngest son. They only had one son and he was a few years older. The other two were girls so I think it was a relief for

Auntie and Uncle to have a boy again to play football with in the park or make model boats. He was really into model boats was Uncle. He used to sail them on the boating lake in the park near the house, but the real obsession he and his son had was football. They were fanatical about it and they'd take a delight, even though they had so little money, in buying things for me like football boots and annuals. They could only afford to buy them second hand but to me the love that went into those presents made them so much better than those my real parents spent lots of money but no thought on. Then when I was old enough they started taking me to matches with them and I grew to love the game as much as they did. It was a new experience. We didn't play football in school, it was all rugger."

Pauline and I looked at each other and both winced at the use of that English public school name for the sport that we who grew up in South Wales treated as a religion. We didn't interrupt Nigel though. We could see from his face that he was about to come to the point of what up to then had been a gentle reminiscence of childhood.

"One day," he began, with his voice now sounding flatter and more distant and the smile fading from his lips, "when I was back at school the son went to Sheffield for a cup match. Uncle had a ticket but he couldn't go. Work was hard to find and he'd just started a job which involved Saturday working. He couldn't afford to pass the work up so his son went alone."

I felt my chest tighten. I realised now what he was leading up to. I felt myself mentally willing him not to go on but at the same time I knew that there was a horrific inevitability about what was coming next.

"He never came back alive from that match. Along with 95 others he was crushed to death and in a few short minutes I'd lost a friend, a big brother and a hero because that's how I always regarded him, as a hero that I wanted to be like when I was older."

I heard Pauline catch her breath involuntarily and, out of the corner of my eye, I saw her reaching for a tissue. Nigel wiped his hand across his eyes and continued.

"What was tragic, really tragic wasn't just his death but what it did to my Auntie and Uncle. They were never the same again but though the events of that afternoon changed them both the changes were very different. Auntie was nothing short of heroic. She drew energy and determination from her loss and came out fighting. She got involved with those who committed themselves to honouring their dead and battling for justice for them. She was typical of the best kind of mother, sacrificing herself for her children when they were alive and, in the case of her son, fighting his corner after his death. She didn't wallow in self-pity, she didn't bemoan the hand that fate had dealt her. She campaigned for truth and justice not just for her son but for all who had so cruelly been cheated of life along side of him and so scandalously vilified in death. She was an inspiration to me, the reason I resolved to be a lawyer. I was determined like her to dedicate myself to the pursuit of justice for all those who could not stand up for themselves. Unlike her, sadly, I've gone astray over the years and I doubt if what I do now can really be called fighting for justice but I have her to thank for any good that I occasionally do and it's because of her that when I started to practise law there was only one city where I wanted to do it. I had the chance to go to big City of London firms after I left Oxford but I stayed in Liverpool right up until Auntie's death last year. Only then did I succumb and leave the city and, to be honest, I have a bit of a conscience even now about it. Even if the realities of legal practice have taken the self-righteous shine off my principles I can at least say that I stayed loyal to the city of my birth and the city of my heart until my last link with it went. It was my way of saying thank you for the lessons that a remarkable family taught me."

Nigel turned to Pauline, now listening intently, as he continued. "Do you know, Pauline, when I met you and spoke to you about Debbie and Sam I saw Auntie in you. You are so like her in so many ways. Sadly though, when I saw Sam it brought back darker memories of Uncle. He reacted so differently. Auntie was galvanised by what had happened. She was forced out into the world because she had a cause to fight for and that meant she never became self-obsessed or felt sorry for herself. The whole experience gave her strength. With Uncle it was the exact opposite. It was as if you'd taken a balloon and let all the air out. He'd been a strong man, a funny man and an active man but all that changed when he lost his son. He never worked again and hardly went out unless it was to sit for hour after hour at the grave. He was even found sleeping there some nights. He lost interest in doing anything except hating, hating the police for their part in his son's death and then hating the whole world because as he saw it no one else had suffered as he had so he hated them all for not suffering. Auntie tried to get him involved in her meetings and campaigns but he didn't want to know. If meetings and campaigns couldn't give him his son back then he wasn't interested in them. He became more and more reclusive. The world couldn't bring his son to life so what was the point engaging with it? All he did was hate because only by hating could he find a stronger emotion to block out the grief. What happened that day killed my big brother but just as surely it killed his dad who so far as I was concerned had been a father to me too. When he had run out of people to hate he turned on the only one left and started to hate himself. He hated himself because, just like all those he'd hated before, he couldn't stop the pain of losing his son in that way. I saw him change before my eyes into a bitter, pathetic shadow of the man he once was until…"

Nigel's voice trailed off and I felt the tightness in my chest again. There was more to come. Nigel took a deep and laboured breath before finishing the sentence.

"…until one day Auntie came home from a meeting and found him hanging from a beam in the attic. The hatred had finally finished him off."

Nigel looked again at Pauline. Suddenly the sadness in his voice was being overlaid with anger.

"The point is, Pauline, that I stood by and let it happen. I saw what was going on and I didn't try to stop it. I thought I was being kind to Uncle. I didn't want to upset him any more by telling him to get a grip. I thought time would be the healer but instead time just let the grief and the hatred fester and eat away at him. Auntie was the same. She may have been a hero with her campaigning but did it help her family letting him surrender and not forcing him to fight as she had fought? She was so busy dealing with the loss of her son that she failed to see that she was losing her husband as well. Do you think that did her and the girls and me any good, Pauline? Wasn't one loss enough without us standing by and letting another one go? You think I'm just some interfering smart Alec sticking his nose into your business don't you? You think I got involved just to show you how clever I am. You're wrong, Pauline. I got involved because I had to get involved. I've seen this story before and I know how it ends if you don't stop it. I've seen it in Uncle and I see it again in Sam. I let it happen to Uncle because I didn't know how it would end. Now that I do know I can't let it happen to Sam. I'd rather be struck down where I stand than to live to watch it happen again knowing that it was my fault because I was too polite to get involved. You have to tell him, Pauline. You have to say that he must face his grief and fight it, however painful that must be because if he doesn't fight it he'll be finished off by it. Do you think that's what Debbie would want? I may be interfering in things I've no right to be involved with but you know why I do it and if that upsets you then I am most terribly sorry."

Nigel's head dropped and his shoulders started shaking. The ice cold unflappable lawyer that I'd known had been shown to be, beneath the expensive suit and the superior airs, a human being as haunted by demons as the rest of us who have never sought to portray perfection. I had learned a lesson in not judging books by their covers.

Pauline said nothing but moved across to Nigel, taking hold of him in a tight maternal hug.

"Don't you worry about it, love," she said softly. "We can help each other. As long as we stick together we'll all get through this, even Sam. If I need to I'll do the fighting for the three of us."

I let myself quietly out of the office. As I left, Nigel abandoned any remaining self-consciousness and I heard

Pauline's soothing words intermingle with his uncontrolled weeping.

Seventeen

I deliberately delayed my arrival at the office the next day. If anything more was going to be said between Nigel and Pauline I reckoned it would be said first thing so that by arriving late I would avoid being stuck in the middle again. In fact, when I saw Pauline she seemed her normal self again, smiling and efficient.

"Is Nigel in yet?" I asked as casually as I could but Pauline knows me too well not to understand the question I was really asking.

"Don't worry," she said with a grin, "we haven't killed each other. In fact it did us both good to have it out. We went back to ours last night and the three of us, Sam included, had a long chat way into the early hours. Nigel even ended up sleeping in the spare room we went on so long. Nigel's a nice lad you know but he's not as insensitive as he likes to make out. He seems to feel the need to put a hard shell around himself as if he's afraid of people finding out he's got feelings. I asked him about it. He said it's something to do with boarding school."

Nigel's probably right about that. I've heard it from many colleagues over the years who were sent away to school. It dehumanises them. I suppose in days gone by it was a necessary process for training future leaders of men. It wouldn't do for aspiring members of the Establishment to be held back by human emotions. Greed and single mindedness are the qualities you need to develop to be one of the elite. You don't want to be clogging up the corridors of power with empathy or compassion.

Pauline wasn't so sure. "I think there's more to it. I think he was deprived of affection as a child and he missed it. That's why he latched on to that family in Liverpool even though it doesn't sound like he had anything in common with them. He relied on them for all the love that he should have had from his parents. It's no wonder it affected him so badly when that substitute family collapsed in front of his eyes. Now he's afraid that if he shows affection like that again he'll be hurt again so he builds this barrier around himself and everyone thinks he's not got feelings like the rest of us."

"Quite the psychologist aren't you, Pauline? You're wasted working for an unfeeling brute like Lenny."

Pauline laughed at my deliberate attempt to steer her away from deep contemplation. It was still too early in the morning for it.

"It's nothing to do with psychology," she said. "It's simpler than that. What that boy needs is a hug now and again."

"Good grief, Pauline, you're not planning to hug Nigel in the office are you? It'd ruin his image not to mention traumatising Cher."

Pauline gave me a playful dig. The atmosphere was now nice and light as I wanted it.

"Don't worry, Gareth, I won't embarrass you with open displays of affection. Sue told me how distressing you find them. It's just that Nigel needs a proper mother figure in his life and I'm about the right age so if he needs someone to talk to he knows where to come. It'll do all of us good. We had a very useful session last night where all three of us were able to gain something. I've got someone to mother, Nigel's got someone to talk to him about his feelings which you'll never do and as for Sam…"

"What about Sam?"

"It was good for him too. When he heard me and Nigel talking it encouraged him to join in. He even started to talk about his own feelings. That's something new for him."

"Perhaps the first step on the road back do you think?"

Pauline shook her head but accompanied the gesture with a kind smile. "I think that's putting it a bit highly, Gareth, but there's one encouraging sign."

As she spoke she pointed down to the floor where there was a large metal case.

"Sam's toolbox," she explained. "He's lending it to MJ but, more importantly, he's also agreed to give him a hand with some jobs in the house. MJ wants to give Iris a surprise when she comes home. Apparently he's taking out that old coal fire that they used to have in the living room and having one of those modern gas fires put in that looks like a log fire but that Iris won't have to get on her knees to build every morning. I suppose it's long enough now that people round here can take out coal fires without feeling they are betraying the miners and gas is so much cleaner."

"It would be if Ty Gwyn only had mains gas," I pointed out.

"Yes, I asked Sam about that," she said. "MJ has a tank in the garden that he runs the cooker off and Sam reckons that it can be used for the fire without it costing too much. Obviously they need a special fire to use the bottled gas but MJ's looked into it and put an order in."

To tell the truth I wasn't particularly interested in MJ's house heating arrangements other than to reflect in passing that, in freeing Iris from the burden of looking after a coal fire, MJ was showing rare sensitivity to her needs. What interested me was that Sam was taking an interest in something that didn't involve Debbie, Terry, car accidents or revenge. I said as much to Pauline who told me excitedly what was planned.

"I've persuaded Sam to help him take out the fire and run a pipe to the fireplace to the gas. Apparently he's not qualified to actually fit the fire so they are going to board up the fireplace while they wait for delivery of it. He's also putting in built in bedside lighting to replace the old lamps they used to have. That at least will save MJ from having to find a match for the lamp that the burglar broke. They were ancient those lamps. He may have had other things on his mind but he did them a favour breaking that old lamp. Sam's going to build a fixed headboard with reading lights in it. He's quite enthusiastic about it. You don't know how happy it makes me to see it. Iris is going to love it too. MJ was saying how fond she is of reading in bed even though he's not too impressed by her taste in books. She reads historical romances apparently."

Hearing mention of Iris coming home reminded me of the events of the previous day.

"You've obviously heard the news," I said. "Iris is getting bail and it's only a matter of time before they drop the charges and she's back home again."

"Yes," said Pauline. "MJ was so pleased when I saw him this morning. It's a great weight off his mind."

"Where did you see him this morning?"

"When he called in to arrange to borrow Sam's toolbox. He told me all about it then."

I tried to approach the subject delicately.

"You know, Pauline, MJ shouldn't really be coming to the office. He's suspended."

"Oh that nonsense," she said dismissively. "I thought you and Nigel were sorting that one out."

I should have told Pauline then that all our investigations had achieved was to shine the light of suspicion even more brightly on MJ but I didn't have the heart to do so. I felt sick enough thinking about it without having to come out and say it. I restricted myself to saying how pleased Iris would be when she saw what had been done to the house in her absence.

"Oh yes," agreed Pauline, "she'll get the welcome home she deserves. I'll make sure of that."

Nigel seemed subdued when I looked in on him. He was obviously still embarrassed at the previous night's show of emotion. I therefore kept the conversation focussed on our investigation, a subject he felt more at home with. His tone was brisk and business like as usual. Watching him running through the results of our efforts so far slowly and methodically you wouldn't believe that he was capable of caring about another human being let alone being reduced to tears by memories of someone he wasn't even related to.

"Our next port of call is Inspector Powell," he said after running through what we had learned to date. "Once we have spoken to him I should be in a position to make my report to the insurers."

"Is there any point?" I asked. "As you've just said MJ had the best opportunity of anyone to get at Tom Webster and now we know he had the perfect motive to stitch Beppe up. Like they say in all the cheap detective novels, show me the motive and opportunity and I'll show you the culprit."

"The trouble is," replied Nigel, "we are neither cheap nor detectives. Sgt Jenkins undoubtedly has a lot of explaining to do and he hasn't helped himself by not doing it but I've spoken to him and I can't see him being that sophisticated. He strikes me as one of life's followers not a leader. Someone else pulled the strings here and I still think that Inspector Powell's the obvious candidate. He's a bright chap or he wouldn't have made the rank of Inspector. He's bright enough to have organised the whole thing to give himself a leg up the career ladder."

"Come off it, Nigel," I said. "It doesn't take much sophistication to nobble a witness. The lowest forms of petty criminals do it all the time." I realised as soon as I said it that far from defending MJ, as I had started off with the intention of doing, I was arguing the case against him. The trouble was that, try as I might, I couldn't see an answer to that case that would stand up to scrutiny. Nigel, logical as ever, provided that answer.

"What about the statement?" he asked. "If all that had been done was to fix the Identity Parade by showing Mr Contemponi to Mr Webster then I'd agree with you but how does a custody officer with no role in the investigation prepare a false statement for a witness, get him to sign it, backdate it and switch it for the original one. That took someone smarter and closer to the investigation than Sgt Jenkins."

Nigel had a point and I was only too pleased to latch onto it. Although my head was telling me that MJ was not going to emerge well from the investigation my heart was still hoping for a breakthrough, some lucky chance that would prove that, despite all the signs, he really was guilty of nothing more than being the randy old goat we had always known him to be. I asked Nigel how he intended to approach the interview with Nev Powell.

He furrowed his brow and thought before replying. "I don't think we have any choice but to work on the hypothesis that he is the one behind all this, the Viper as you called him. We need to challenge him to show us that the hypothesis is wrong. After all he's the one who suddenly came up with the allegation of robbery where there had been no evidence before of Mr Contemponi's involvement and he's the one who is on the record as the witness to Mr Webster's signature on his false statement. He needs to explain those matters doesn't he?"

"So what are you going to do, Nigel? Walk in and accuse him of perverting the course of justice before he's even got the coffee and biscuits out? That should be fun to watch."

Nigel permitted himself a smile.

"Not quite," he said. "I'm not Perry Mason and I don't expect him to break down and confess all at the first hint of a difficult question. I won't pussyfoot around, there's no point. I'll ask for his explanation and he'll give us some bullshit answer that I will dutifully record before thanking him and taking our leave. I will then report to the insurers the questions, the answers and my opinion that Inspector Powell is lying. That's all we have to do, just marshal the facts. We're not here to force confessions out of anyone, someone else can do that."

As he was driving us to the police station in the Bentley Nigel suddenly and without prompting spoke. "I had a long talk with Pauline and with Sam after you left. You've no need to worry, everything will be fine. I'm sorry you had to witness my inappropriate behaviour last night."

I was going to tell Nigel that he had no need to apologise and to wish him and Pauline well in their efforts to help one another but as I looked across I could see from his face that, as far as he was concerned, he had had the last word and further discussion of the subject would not be welcome.

There is a standard response which, in my experience, every serving police officer gives to allegations of malpractice in the force. They are always hostile and always aggressive. It is a well known and perhaps unsurprising phenomenon that police officers can deal with the most unpleasant of criminals without seeming to care whether their efforts result in conviction or acquittal. "It's a game", "We'll get him next time" or "our job is to put them before the court not to be judge and jury" are the sort of good natured clichés you will hear from them, often accompanied by a shrug of the shoulders, when a charitable jury allows an obvious felon to escape from the clutches of the penal system. The vast majority I have dealt with are far too professional to make their daily battle with crime personal. Make an allegation against a police officer, however, and it becomes very personal and very nasty. A police officer accused of misconduct makes a cornered rat seem resigned to his fate by comparison.

Nev Powell did not disappoint. He was unpleasant and defensive from the outset. He began with a ploy straight out of the Police Training Manual, trying to take charge of the interview and put us on the back foot.

"I can't believe you are still pursuing this," he said with an outrage that I found almost convincing. "Young Contemponi's decided who he's going after and he doesn't need any help from you two in doing it. Are you seriously going to ask a court to give compensation to someone who thinks he can bump people off like that? Is this what the taxpayers are going to have to pay for?"

Nev had picked the wrong person to try that on. Nigel, showing no signs of the vulnerability he had displayed the night before, was at his cold, firm best.

"Actually, Inspector Powell," he began, "I'm not asking the court to give anything to Mr Contemponi, Mr Parry here is and if the court decides he should be compensated then they will order that he is. They won't care what you think and frankly Inspector neither do I."

There was an unmistakable note of challenge in Nev's voice as he responded. "Aren't you supposed to be on our side?"

Nigel was unfazed. "Indeed I am," he said, "and if I feel that there is any risk of Mr Contemponi receiving compensation to which he is not entitled then I will ensure that it does not happen. In performing that function I would be greatly assisted if you would help me with the facts of the case but I am considerably less assisted by your ill thought out opinions."

Nigel, a past master at the art, injected exactly the right degree of sarcasm and calculated rudeness into that final sentence to silence Nev. Taking advantage of that silence he launched straight into his questions.

"On Saturday 16th December, 1989 Giuseppe Contemponi was in custody on suspicion of handling stolen goods."

"Correct."

"There was no suggestion that he might be guilty of robbery at the time."

"Correct."

"Yet by Monday 18th December he was being put before an identification parade in relation to that very charge."

"Correct."

Nev was clearly in no mood to fill in the gaps. He simply sat staring at Nigel with unblinking eyes as he barked out his single word answers. He accompanied them with the faintest of smiles to make it quite clear that, although Nigel was asking the questions, he was in charge. The expression was telling Nigel that he wasn't going to get anything that he didn't want to give him.

Eighteen

Nigel wasn't intimidated. Retaining his air of exaggerated formality he pressed on.

"What changed between the 16th and the 18th?"

"Information received."

Nev was still not making it easy. Nigel pulled some sheets of paper from his file.

"What about this statement?" he asked matching the intensity of Nev's stare. Nev was unimpressed.

"What about it?"

"This is the statement put before the court as the first statement made by Tom Webster after the robbery. It was put forward as having been taken in the immediate aftermath of the robbery."

"I believe it was."

"According to the note on the bottom you took this statement, Inspector Powell."

"I believe I did."

Nigel looked down. Nev's smile became ever so slightly broader. He had outstared Nigel. In fact Nigel was looking down at the statement. He adjusted the position of his glasses, more for effect than out of necessity, and read out the detailed description from the statement. Having done so, he looked up again. This time it was his turn to engage Nev with a piercing stare. Nev's face seemed to betray the first signs of uncertainty as Nigel asked the inevitable question.

"Any detective worth his salt would have recognised that as an excellent description of Giuseppe Contemponi, so good that he would immediately make the connection as soon as he came into custody. Why didn't you?"

"I don't know," Nev looked flustered. Nigel moved in for the kill.

"It's because you know that this statement didn't exist when you first took Mr Contemponi into custody. You created it after the event and substituted it for the original in order to frame him."

"No I didn't." The defiance had disappeared from Nev's demeanour. He sounded confused and the vehemence of his denial seemed convincing. Nigel didn't let up.

"Yes you did. It says here that you took the statement. It has your signature on it."

Nev's confusion was increasing. He abandoned any attempt to outsmart Nigel.

"I know I took a statement from Tom Webster," he said, "and I know that it's been a few years since then but I genuinely don't remember Tom Webster giving a detailed description of the robber at the time. If he had I'd have nailed Beppe straight away. I don't understand why I didn't."

He furrowed his brow, straining at the effort of trying to recall the events of 20 years earlier. Eventually he spoke in a voice that was quiet, respectful and in complete contrast to his earlier hostile self-confidence.

"May I see the statement please?"

Nigel handed it over without relaxing his stare. He had the fish on the hook and it was as if he feared that if he blinked he would lose it.

Nev studied the document shaking his head as he did so. When he spoke he did so slowly, weighing every word as he uttered it.

"I don't think I've ever seen this statement before. It isn't the one I took. The first bit is, where he describes the robber entering the living quarters, but then when he goes on to talk about the scarf falling and seeing the bloke's face I've no memory of that and I'm sure that if he said that I'd remember it."

He continued to stare in disbelief at the statement and then stabbed the page with his finger.

"Look at this," he said, his voice growing in confidence. "It says here *'The view that I had of the man's face was more than a fleeting glance. It was sufficient to allow me to absorb and retain the image of his features. I feel confident of recalling those features should I be called upon to do so.'*

There's no way Tom Webster would have expressed himself like that and, what's more, no way I would. I'm a simple valley boy. I wouldn't have put it that way."

"That's what you say." Nigel was unimpressed.

"Look at it," said Nev, pushing the statement in Nigel's direction. "Look at the language where he describes the man and compare it to the rest. It's not the same."

It was Nigel's turn now to study the statement and as he did so I could see a look of doubt on his face. He changed the subject.

"You signed to say you had taken the statement," he said. Nev was quick to respond.

"How do you know?" he asked. "What you have there isn't the original handwritten statement it's a typed copy. My name's been typed on but it's not my signature."

He had a point there. The original handwritten version of the statement would have been on the Crown Court file which would have been destroyed long ago. What Nigel had produced was a typed transcript produced as a working copy and served on me by the prosecution in the course of the case.

"If you could show me the original I'd be able to tell you if it's my genuine signature," said Nev with the renewed confidence of one who knew perfectly well that Nigel couldn't comply. Nigel wasn't going to be diverted.

"The whole point of this working copy is that it's an exact copy of the original and the whole point of having the original on the Crown Court file was in case anyone suggested that it wasn't an exact copy. If your name is typed on there then it means that your signature was on the original which was there to be checked."

"All it means," said Nev, his initial self-assurance now fully restored, "is that the original bore a signature that was supposed to be mine. Without examining it we wouldn't even know if it looks anything like my genuine signature."

He looked at me as he continued. "If you ever checked the handwritten copy against the original, Gareth, you wouldn't even consider making sure it was a genuine signature would you? You'd just take it at face value."

I was forced to agree with him. Nigel was still not beaten but I could see that he was beginning to wonder whether the fish was about to swim free.

"How did this statement get on the file?" he asked. Nev shrugged.

"I've no real idea," he said. "I'd just put all the statements together in a file and send them to Divisional HQ who'd produce the typewritten working copies and keep the originals safe. It was up to HQ to then send everything to the CPS who'd send the originals to the court and a working copy to Gareth. I wouldn't have seen the original again after sending it off and I don't think I'd ever see the working copy."

Nigel mounted one last attack. "What was there to stop you altering the statement before you sent it off? How do I know you didn't nobble the identification parade by showing Mr Webster Mr Contemponi through the observation hatch in the cell and then persuading him to alter his statement?"

The smile returned to Nev's face. He was back to being arrogant and confident of defeating Nigel. He opened a drawer in his desk and took out what looked like an old style photograph album. Placing it on the desk he explained.

"I thought that as you were going to persist in this ridiculous investigation I'd better check up on my alibi. All my notebooks and diaries have long gone but, thankfully, I still have my scrapbook."

He thumbed through the pages deliberately slowly until he found the one he wanted to show us. Adopting heavy sarcasm he said, "I'm afraid you've caught me out. I have a guilty secret and now I'm going to confess to you."

We looked at the page. It contained a cutting from the "South Wales Echo" for Monday, 18th December, 1989. It was a report of an event in Cardiff the previous Saturday, a Christmas Concert and dinner in aid of a local children's charity. Giving the concert were, it said, the Pentreglo Male Voice Choir among others. There was a picture of the choir to accompany the article and there, in the middle of the back row resplendent in a dinner jacket and bow tie, was a youth bearing the unmistakeable features of the young Neville Powell.

Nev was now laughing openly as he held his hands up in a mock gesture of defeat.

"There you are gents," he said, "the shameful truth is out. I'm a secret baritone."

"Why didn't you mention this before?" asked Nigel impatiently.

"You didn't ask," was the smiling reply.

Nigel accepted defeat and moved on to other things.

"If it wasn't the description in the statement that made you suspect Mr Contemponi what was it?"

"I told you, information received." Nev was back to the smiling non co-operation with which he'd started the meeting.

"What information?" Nigel was becoming frustrated and it was starting to show. Nev thought for a moment weighing up whether to give proper answer or whether to continue to obstruct the enquiry.

"A phone call," he said choosing the latter course.

"When?"

"On the Sunday morning."

"Saying what?"

"Saying I might like to investigate Beppe Contemponi for the Pentreglo Post Office job."

"Who was it from?"

Nigel had realised that Nev wasn't going to do any more than literally answer the question he was asked so he kept the questions short and specific. Nev shrugged to make it clear that he didn't regard the questions as anything approaching important but was prepared to humour Nigel.

"Don't know," he said. "It was an anonymous call. I don't know who she was."

"She?" Nigel pounced on the word. Nev winced. He had said more than he needed and broken the rules of his own game.

"Yes she," he agreed.

"So it was a woman."

Nev mimed applause.

"Well done," he said. "Your university education wasn't wasted then. Yes it was a woman, I remember that particularly. I had my own theory about it at the time."

Nigel paused to allow Nev to finish his sentence but when it became clear he was going to say no more he asked the obvious question.

"What was your theory?"

Nev smirked.

"I thought you weren't interested in my opinion," he said.

Nigel paused again but Nev had nothing more to say. With a stiff handshake and an openly sarcastic expression of thanks for his assistance he took his leave of Detective Inspector Neville Powell, amateur baritone and professional protector of bent police officers.

"I'm sorry about that, Gareth," said Nigel when we reached the office. "Believe me I genuinely hoped that I could help you clear the name of Sgt Jenkins but this seems to be the final nail in his coffin. The charming Inspector Powell is in the clear and we now not only have motive and opportunity pointing to Sgt Jenkins we have the means too. He got his girlfriend to tip off the police after he's done the dirty deed. I'm afraid that this is what I'm going to have to report to the insurers. Tell Lenny I'm sorry."

With sinking heart I agreed with him. The whole point of working with Nigel on the investigation had been to deflect blame from MJ and, in so doing, preserve the reputation of the firm. Now it was clear that the whole exercise had backfired in spectacular fashion. If I had simply declined the offer to work with Nigel and insisted that his clients paid up without wasting time investigating the fine detail then we would have been left, it's true, with a cloud of suspicion over MJ. As a result of my efforts suspicion was no longer the problem. There was now positive proof that the senior criminal clerk of Stevenson and Parry, solicitors of Pentreglo, was the Viper, a bent policeman who, in order to satisfy his own lust, sent an innocent man to jail and ultimately to his death.

Nigel tapped his file of papers briskly on the desk and placed them back in his expensive briefcase. "That seems to be it for now," he said briskly. "I can go back to London and you can fly off to Spain. I'll make my report and then we can set up a meeting when the insurers have decided how much to offer your client."

We shook hands and told each other how much we'd enjoyed working together. I suggested a farewell drink.

"I can't, I'm afraid," said Nigel. "I'm addressing a meeting tonight and I need to work on what I'm going to say."

"A meeting? What meeting?"

He looked slightly sheepish as he told me.

"Pauline asked me to speak," he explained. "It's a meeting organised by the charity she works for. I'm talking about how to deal with grief to people who have lost loved ones in tragic circumstances. Sam's coming along as well."

"Sam? That's a breakthrough. It should do him a lot of good."

Nigel smiled at the comment. "I don't think it was Sam she was thinking about," he said. "I rather think she's doing this for my benefit. I've said it before, she's a remarkable woman."

III

DEJA VU

Nineteen

When you are a lawyer there are days when everything goes right for you in court. As you stand up and start speaking you find the right words presenting themselves obligingly to your tongue at exactly the right time. Everything you say strikes home. You can see the impact you are having on the faces of the magistrates, their clerk and all the witnesses. You feel that anything you say will bring forth enthusiastic nods of agreement. There is nothing that the power of your advocacy can not achieve.

I was having one of those days. What had started in my brain as a mundane statement of the obvious was somehow miraculously transformed en route to my mouth into pure wisdom delivered with the elegance of a poet. Those receiving such prose looked on transfixed by the erudition and sheer beauty in what I had to say. So well was it going that I was drifting into autopilot. I was simply standing there allowing my words to float across the courtroom to be received with unqualified acclaim while my conscious mind detached itself and floated to a point near the ceiling there to gaze down in awe at the beauty of it all. The magistrates nodded with increasing enthusiasm at each point I made while my previously hyper anxious client Reg Cummings was able to relax his diminutive five-foot frame and sit back to enjoy the spectacle of an advocate at the top of his game fighting his corner.

Every advocate has days like that and every advocate knows, or should know, that it is during such purple patches that they are most prone to making the sort of calamitous errors that can change the complexion of a case in an instant.

"And so," I heard myself say in an almost Shakespearian voice as I approached the long awaited climax to my oration, "I ask you to look upon my client's shortcomings…"

I got no further. The atmosphere in the courtroom changed in an instant as the spell was broken. The hitherto sour faced clerk started to crack his features into a smile. The magistrates, who seconds earlier had been listening intently to my every word, began to struggle manfully but unsuccessfully to supress giggles.

"Who are you calling short Cummings, fatso?" asked an indignant voice behind me as my client, his mood having changed from admiration to outrage, retaliated against the supposed insult to his body shape by flinging one back at me.

The Chairman of the Bench had by now abandoned attempts to stifle his giggling and decided to join in the fun.

"Do you think it appropriate, Mr Parry, to use this courtroom to make observations about your client's stature?" he asked winking theatrically at the harridan with the extravagant hat who sat beside him on the bench.

I tried to explain but it was no good. The court was descending into uncontrolled ridicule directed at me. I looked to the back of the court and there he was, Stan Matthews, surrounded by his police cronies conducting the laughter as if he had an audience before him. Things just couldn't get any worse – or could they?

"Gareth!" cried a familiar voice from the back of the court "Why haven't you written home? You know I worry about you."

I had no need to look. There was no mistaking the voice of my mother. I'd been promising to write or telephone but I just hadn't got round to it. Despite the fact that I was a qualified solicitor and had long since flown the nest she still thought of me as a six-year-old who would be bound to come to grief without her firm and close guidance. If I didn't contact her regularly to assure her that all was well she assumed that it wasn't and started to worry. That was why she insisted on a weekly debrief and she often threatened desperate measures to ensure compliance. Now the threat was being carried out.

"He never writes," she was complaining to the Chairman of the Bench who nodded in sympathy before sending a venomous look in my direction. My mother then directed her attention back to me.

"Gareth, Gareth," she called, the volume of her voice rising to ensure my full attention. "Gareth, can you hear me?" she repeated in an accent that suddenly didn't sound like my mother's any more. In an instant I realised the horrible truth. My mother's voice and that of my wife, Sue, were the same. Somehow, the spirit of my long dead mother had entered the body of her replacement as the voice of female authority in my life in order to ensure that I would be treated like a six-year-old for the rest of my days. It was a prospect too frightening to contemplate.

I opened my eyes wide in terror. I wasn't in court at all. Instead I was sitting in my favourite armchair in my home in Spain while Sue tried to rouse me from the deep sleep into which I had fallen as soon as my head had made contact with the thickly padded back of the chair.

"Been dreaming again?" Sue asked with a smile. I nodded in confirmation.

"How did you know?" I asked.

"Maybe because you were shouting '*may it please your worships*' over and over," she said with a laugh.

What an irony. I had only been back in Spain for less than 24 hours yet the nightmares had returned. In the time I had been back working at the office I had slept like a baby every night without a sign of a bad dream but as soon as I return to the tranquillity of life as a retiree in Spain I am plagued with the stresses and anxieties of legal practice every time I close my eyes. It's as if my sub conscious is telling me that when I signed up for life as a small town lawyer I committed myself to a permanent state of apprehension over what disaster will strike next and I can't use the excuse of retirement to break that commitment. Meanwhile my conscious mind battles to persuade me that I am retired and there is no rational reason why I have to concern myself with the calamities that lie in wait every time a lawyer stands up to speak. Sadly, my sub conscious tends to win those particular contests and the price I pay for no longer experiencing the emotional roller coaster of a small town solicitor's life in my waking hours is to do so with enhanced intensity when I sleep.

Sue knew the answer to the dilemma, of course.

"Let's go to Rafa's for lunch," she suggested. Nothing can be more effective at driving away all memories of life among the vices, weaknesses, temporary triumphs and enduring tragedies that those working in the sub-basement of that grand edifice they call the legal system have to confront than to spend time among the relaxed and friendly inhabitants of the Spanish village that has been our home since I retired. Despite the best efforts of my sub conscious I find it impossible, during my waking hours at least, to feel anything but relaxed and at piece with the world when I am in this tiny piece of Iberian heaven among people who know what's important in life. Despite the best efforts of the international financiers and those politicians who are subservient to them the people of the village, my village, are never foolish enough to be seduced into believing that material wealth can ever be a substitute for friendship, family and simple but good food and wine. Several times during the day I find myself silently giving thanks for the good fortune that brought me here and if nightmares based on my former life are the price I have to pay for such fortune then pay it I will.

Perhaps it's true to say that the person I have to thank more than anyone for the chance to indulge in this love affair is Rafa, whose bar and restaurant in the main square we were now heading for. He was the first of the locals I got to know and has been the key to my meeting all the others. We had stumbled into his bar one August afternoon after we had escaped in a hire car from our uninspiring hotel in a tacky tourist trap and driven off in search of the "real Spain". Rafa had been there just as he was on every subsequent visit of ours, behind the bar dispensing the drinks and the tapas as he bantered with customers who looked as if they had been welded into their seats at some point in the distant past and never moved since. When he heard me talking to Sue, Rafa had asked me if I was Welsh. That endeared him to me instantly. When I am abroad the majority of people, whether locals or British, label me as English and when I point out that I was born and bred in Cardiff look at me as if I were the worst kind of pedant. It was refreshing to find someone, particularly a foreigner, who actually respected the fact that there are four nations in the UK and not just England. He surprised me even more by talking knowledgeably about the Welsh rugby team a subject that is close to the hearts of very few Spaniards.

We spent the rest of the afternoon in a wide ranging conversation in English while the locals around us looked on in friendly curiosity. Our conversation was punctuated by Rafa laying before us a variety of small dishes from plump green olives to crunchy fried squid via salty cheese and exquisitely thin ham that he carved before our eyes. He also ensured, after Sue had done the decent thing and volunteered to drive back to the hotel, that the chilled local wine kept flowing into my glass. At regular intervals he would switch from cockney tinged English to flamboyant Spanish as he sought to bring his other patrons into the conversation and then obligingly translate their contributions for our benefit as they smiled and raised their glasses as if to acknowledge authorship of what was being said.

We left the bar with multilingual farewells ringing in our ears resolving to return before the end of our holiday. That night, as we played with the bland fare on our plates and listened to the sanitised flamenco of the hotel entertainment team we made a decision. The next day we returned to Rafa's and asked him if he knew of any properties for sale in or near the village that might be suitable for us after my impending retirement. He assured us that we were in luck and within thirty minutes had summoned his cousin, an estate agent, to the bar. Within three months of my retirement and with the help of Rafa's seemingly inexhaustible supply of relatives in influential positions we had bought and furnished a beautiful house overlooking the sea and cleared the numerous bureaucratic hurdles that face anyone seeking to relocate abroad. Rafa became a firm friend as we adjusted to our new lives and, whenever a job needed doing, he would produce a relative who could sort it out for us.

I have to admit that what first drew me to Rafa's company, apart from the fact that he sold alcohol, was that he spoke perfect English. Although all of the villagers were happy to chat to us in the street or in the shops I found listening for more than a few minutes to Spanish spoken with an accent and at a pace that bore no resemblance to the "Teach yourself Spanish" CD's to be an exhausting process.

Unlike the majority of the villagers, who have never seen the attraction of venturing far from the village, Rafa had spent a number of years in London as a young man. The experience had not only taught him English but guaranteed him the status of village entrepreneur. His fellow villagers bowed to his superior insight into the seemingly inscrutable workings of the Northern European mind and allowed him to adopt the role of chief provider for the needs of the "*Guiris*", the relatively small band of foreigners who, like me, had either retired to the village or holidayed there. Whilst there was a minority that was alarmed by Rafa's cosmopolitan ways, most of the villagers recognised that he performed an important social function. As long as Rafa kept the Guiris happy they wouldn't need to change their ways to accommodate them. The more pragmatic amongst them even acknowledged that it was only the money that the expat residents and tourists brought into the village that allowed them to carry on very much as before despite the demise of the traditional fishing industry.

What makes Rafa acceptable to native and newcomer alike is the ease with which he bridges the two cultures. Although he can speak English with the ease and accent of a native born Londoner and understands British cultural references he is, underneath it all, a true son of Andalucia. He is popular among the other villagers not least because he seems to be related to most of them. To look at him you would be in no doubt as to his origins despite middle age taking the edge off the Latin good looks that, according to his stories, were the passport to his success in London. He is as much at ease gossiping with the old men in flat caps as he is sharing memories with me of a wild night in 1960's Soho. In a village where religion is still woven into the fabric of the community his strong support for the local church allows him to escape resentment of what might otherwise be regarded as his dangerously modern ways.

A good deal of the credit for Rafa's reintegration into Spanish village life must go to Maria-Carmen his wife of some twenty-five years. She is as we all imagine Spanish women to be, smart and elegant, a faithful wife and a dedicated mother whose maturing features still retain much of the eye catching beauty of her youth. Over the years she has been the constant at Rafa's side and, he tells me, the reason why he is able to look back on his time in London with affection but without any sense of loss.

Rafa was in his usual place as we entered the bar. Maria-Carmen was there too. However, there was definitely something different. Rafa was wearing a suit. To my knowledge he only wears suits for weddings and funerals; they are neither appropriate wear for the Andalucian weather, even in winter, nor expected by village etiquette. I walked across to ask him about it. Before I could speak an inadequately covered and sun dried expanse of bosom thrust itself into my line of vision. Attached to that bosom and dressed, as always, at great expense but with little taste was Brenda, the female half of the ex pat couple who have the doubtful privilege of being my next door neighbours.

"Doesn't he look smart?" she said talking over Rafa's warm greeting. "He's got an important meeting today in Cadiz. Haven't you, Rafa?"

Brenda is one of those people who has a compulsion to tell you things before anyone else can. I have often imagined her as a Greek maiden waiting with all the other, more modestly dressed maidens, for the messenger to complete his epic run from Marathon before elbowing him out of the way at the vital moment so that she could announce the victory first.

"I have followed your example," explained Rafa, "and decided to investigate my family tree just like you did last year. I thought it would be easy with so many of us living nearby but none of my cousins seemed to be interested. They couldn't understand why I was doing it. So far as they were concerned we were here and that was all that was important.

Typical peasant stock! They don't have the feeling for history and heritage that the British have!"

Rafa adopted the slightly haughty expression that he tended to display whenever making the point that, unlike the rest of the native inhabitants of the village, he had been infused with the sophistication of the urban Anglo Saxon. He carried on his explanation. "I spoke to a professor at the University at Cadiz and told him what I was doing then last week the professor got in touch with me and said he had something very important to tell me about my family. It must be important because he would not tell me on the telephone or even in a letter. He said he had to see me in person so this afternoon I am off to meet him. What do you think it is, Gareth? Do you think that I am related to Juan Carlos himself?"

Rafa laughed at his own joke while Maria-Carmen humoured him with an exaggerated curtsey. Brenda, frustrated at not having contributed to the conversation for the last thirty seconds, chipped in.

"He's got you to thank for that, Gareth. It was the talk of the village when you found out your family secrets. What a surprise that was! Who would have thought you were a Jew?"

From the way she said the word she might as well have added that I looked so normal, no beard, no disproportionately long nose, not even a penchant for demanding pounds of flesh as security when her husband, Trevor, borrows my ladders. Brenda's view on life is particularly one dimensional and I don't think that the news that they lived next door to a person with Jewish immigrant ancestors went down particularly well when I broke it to her and Trevor following an eventful trawl into my family history last year.

Brenda, at least, was circumspect enough to hide her inbuilt anti-Semitism, at least in my company. To my amusement I would find her apologising every time she ate a ham sandwich or pointedly insisting that Trevor paid half whenever we had a drink or a meal together. On the other hand, the less socially gifted Trevor didn't seem able to prevent himself from the tedious routine of making outrageously anti-Jewish comments rapidly followed by insincere apologies and assurances that he didn't mean me.

Actually I don't feel in the slightest bit Jewish so I don't let their ignorance worry me. It was certainly an educational experience learning of the Jewish heritage that had, in a spirit of overprotection by relatives traumatised by wartime experiences, been hidden from me, but it was not life changing. Nevertheless, I felt flattered that my experience had inspired Rafa to follow a similar path and I told him that I hoped that his search would yield similarly fulfilling results.

After Rafa left for his meeting I chatted to Maria-Carmen for a few more minutes before joining Sue who had been steered by Brenda to the table she was sharing with Trevor.

Trevor seemed preoccupied as I sat down opposite him. Sue and Brenda were deep in the sort of conversation that wives have and that husbands are not welcome to join. I tried to strike up a rival one with Trevor by asking him how things had been in the village during my absence. He didn't answer. He was muttering something to himself but I couldn't catch what it was. I asked him if anything was the matter. That, at least, caught his attention. Eventually he let me into the secret.

"Ghosts," he said in a loud enough voice to wake the old fisherman who had been having a siesta over a glass of wine at the next table. I assumed that I had misheard him. Perhaps he's talking about goats. There are a few farmers around who keep them and occasionally a stray one can be seen wandering through the village. Surely this was what Trevor was talking about. It wasn't.

"Ghosts," he repeated just as loudly. "I can't get rid of the bloody ghosts. What do you think I should do, Gareth?"

I found myself lost for words. What on earth was Trevor talking about? Has he gone mad? Our houses had been built in 2002 by an ex pat builder from Doncaster who had teamed up with one of Rafa's relatives to develop a strip of decommissioned military land between the main road and the beach at the edge of the village. The houses simply weren't old enough to be haunted.

I began to wonder if I had taken too idealistic a view of retirement to Spain when I decided to give it a try. Perhaps after a few years the idleness and the steady intake of alcohol get to the brain and make you delirious. Trevor had lived in the village longer than I had. Perhaps these ravings were a foretaste of what was to come for me. Trevor had a habit of frequently talking nonsense. I had put it down to the fact that he was an avid "Daily Mail" reader but, surely, even that can't be blamed for Trevor's latest outburst. It must be the sun or maybe the sherry. I decided to humour him.

"When do you see these ghosts?" I asked, commending myself on my straight face.

Trevor considered the question carefully before replying in a voice that sounded surprisingly rational. "Every night when it gets dark. It's really annoying me, Gareth."

Every night? The man's clearly lost his marbles since I've been away. What have we let ourselves in for moving next door?

Twenty

"Did you hear that, Sue?" I butted into the women's conversation so that I could have an ally in dealing with Trevor's delusions. "Trevor's complaining about ghosts."

"I know," said Sue, irritated at the interruption. "Brenda was telling me."

The two of them resumed their conversation seemingly unconcerned that they were sitting with a deranged man. I had to tackle this one alone.

"Trevor," I began gently. "How can your house be haunted? It's not even ten years old. There hasn't been enough time for anyone to die there let alone return to haunt the place."

Had Trevor possessed a sense of humour he'd have laughed out loud at that point. Instead he gave me one of those condescending looks you give to a child when he tells you in all seriousness that babies are born under gooseberry bushes. Brenda, who had heard what I had said, was not so restrained. Throwing her head back she let out a noise intended to represent extreme amusement but actually more reminiscent of a horse being strangled. Sue at least had the decency to look uncomfortable at what was apparently my stupidity and refrained from joining in with the laughter.

"Not that type of ghost," said Trevor in the manner of a teacher addressing a particularly slow pupil, "ghosts on the television. You know, outlines on the picture that shouldn't be there."

Whilst relieved that my next door neighbour, for all his other faults, wasn't paranoid I was also a little angry at the reaction to my perfectly understandable mistake.

"How the hell was I to know?" I said just a trifle too defensively.

"Because that's what we were talking about before," said Trevor. "Weren't you listening?"

"No I wasn't," I was quick to point out. "I was over there talking to Maria-Carmen. I've only just joined you."

"Oh have you?" said Trevor without a hint of an apology. "That explains it then."

The trouble with Trevor is that he's so self-obsessed that he simply doesn't notice who he's talking to. I suppose that everyone else is so unimportant compared to him that he has never found it necessary to register their presence. I suspect that if you left Trevor overnight in a mortuary he would happily spend his time telling the corpses there how important he was and never wonder why nobody was responding to him.

I was anxious to demonstrate that I was in full command of my senses so I applied myself to solving Trevor's problem for him.

"It'll be the dish," I suggested in a reference to the oversized metal monstrosity that protrudes from next door's roof. "It's probably moved."

Trevor thought about it and eventually nodded. "You're probably right," he said. "Come to think of it we had some pretty bad winds on New Year's Eve and it was on New Year's Day that we started getting the ghosts. The wind will have moved the dish."

"That's a relief," cackled Brenda. "I thought Trevor had forgotten to pay the subscription again."

As she laughed at her own wit Trevor threw a withering glance in her direction before applying his mind to a solution to the problem.

"I'll have to get up there and sort it out," he said. "Do you mind if I borrow your ladders, Gareth?"

"You'll do no such thing," said Brenda sharply. "You know you're afraid of heights. I'm not having you falling off a ladder."

Trevor took that to be a public rebuke to his masculinity and was in the process of lifting himself to his full insignificant height for a response when I decided to come to Brenda's aid.

"She's right you know, Trevor. It's not as easy as it looks. You have to get the adjustment just right or you could make it worse."

"It can't be that difficult," retorted Trevor. "Can't I just fiddle with it until I get it right?"

"Sounds like our wedding night," chipped in Brenda digging Sue in the ribs for emphasis as she let out a laugh like a donkey watching a "Carry On" film.

Trevor didn't see the joke and, to spare him further embarrassment, I continued as if I had missed Brenda's remark. "Why don't you ask Rafa when he gets back? He's bound to know someone who fixes satellite dishes. He's probably related to him. He seems to be related to everyone else in this part of Spain."

Trevor was not impressed by the suggestion.

"That won't be any good," he said scornfully. "Anyone Rafa puts me in touch with will be Spanish and it's British programmes that I want."

I was about to point out that when it came to tuning televisions it didn't actually matter whether the engineer understood the subtleties of an "Eastenders" plot provided he knew the name of the desired channel but instead I suggested that if Trevor wanted an English speaking engineer he could find one advertising in one of the ex pat magazines that drift our way from the Northern European ghettos further along the coast. Trevor continued to insist that he could do it himself so I allowed Brenda to change the subject.

"How is that beautiful grandson of yours?" she asked. "I bet it was even worth going back to Cardiff to see him."

So keen am I to talk about the magical things that my grandson Jake does every hour of his waking life that I allowed the slur on my home city to pass and, as Brenda nodded enthusiastically, I meticulously listed everything that I had found cute and clever since the last time she had mentioned Jake in conversation. A proud grandparent is a fearsome beast, unrelenting in the elevation of trivia into wonder until physically prevented from speaking. Most people, I notice, visibly shrink away when I am holding forth on the subject of Jake but Brenda is a welcome exception. A woman more transparently eager to join the ranks of grandparenthood is hard to find. To date the single minded pursuit of material wealth has distracted her son and daughter-in-law from breeding but I can sense that Brenda's patience is wearing thin with them. I fear that unless they present her with news of an impending happy event soon she will take it upon herself to enter their bedroom in order to direct operations personally! Brenda is a competitive creature who is never slow to trump every possession or every experience of yours with one of her own. So far the existence of a grandchild is one area in which Sue and I have an unassailable advantage.

Trevor, as usual, glazed over at talk of Jake. It's nothing personal that he holds against the little chap but Trevor feels profound disinterest in any conversation that does not have him as its focus. While Brenda lapped up every detail he stared pointedly at his gin and tonic and, when it was empty, loudly informed his wife that it was time to go home.

The next morning the storm struck. Sue declared in a voice that invited no dissent that the house needed cleaning. I knew better than to disagree despite the fact that Sue had spent the three days before we left for Cardiff in a frenzy of scrubbing, mopping and polishing. She's the same whenever we go away. If during our absence a burglar were to enter our home and, whilst rooting through our possessions, found dust on the furniture Sue would not be able to live with the shame. We had not in fact been burgled over Christmas but Sue had detected something far more sinister. The house had become dirty again, so dirty as to be unfit for human habitation without another concentrated bout of cleaning. My presence, I realised, would simply add to the air of untidiness so I went off into the village in search of some fresh bread for breakfast. At the same time I was hoping that the local shop, which received sporadic supplies of English language newspapers, would have something I could read while waiting on a bench in the square for the detergent fuelled orgy to abate.

As I drove into the square I noticed that a crowd had gathered at the side of the church. They all seemed to be looking at the same thing, pointing and shaking their heads. They were clearly not happy. I parked the car and walked over to investigate and then I saw it. Daubed in red paint over the hitherto pristine white wall of the church was the cause of the crowd's concern.

"What does it say?" asked a familiar voice and I turned to see Trevor and Brenda behind me. I translated the words literally for them.

"It says all priests are sons of bitches."

"That's an odd thing to say," commented Brenda dismissively. I felt that she had missed the point. While "son of a bitch" comes across as a fairly innocuous, even good humoured expression to Anglo-American ears it is far more offensive to Spanish ones not least because it is aimed at that most sacred of Spanish institutions, motherhood. To attack motherhood and the Church in one splash of graffiti was, in a village like this, something very serious indeed, as the shocked expressions on the faces of the crowd confirmed.

I too felt shocked and disgusted. It's not that I have any great affection for religion, far from it, but you would need to be blind to fail to recognise the respect and even affection with which the Roman Catholic religion is regarded in the village and others like it in Spain. The Church and the family are the two ingredients in the glue that holds the community together. It's one of life's ironies that the waning influence of the Church in countries like Britain may have created a more tolerant and progressive society but, in doing so, it has removed all unifying force from that society turning us into a collection of individuals with no purpose in being on this earth beyond self-indulgence. I like to regard myself as part of the community of the village rather than some foreign interloper so although I consider the Roman Catholic Church to be as hypocritical and corrupt as any other religion I still feel the pain of an attack like this upon it.

Amongst the assembled villagers speculation was rising as to the identity of the culprit. I realised with a degree of discomfort that the consensus seemed to be that it was the work of a foreigner since none of the locals would commit such blasphemy. Somebody, it was decided, was seeking to wage war in the name of Protestantism or perhaps Islam. There was always a steady stream of Moroccans passing through the area since we were so close to the ferry ports and the idea was mooted that one of those might have paused en route to strike a blow for Allah. To my relief I heard the idea that any of the British population of the village could have been involved being quickly dismissed. It was pointed out that no Anglo-Saxon would have thought to insult the Church in Spanish; they would have insisted in doing so in English. The notion raised a laugh which lightened the atmosphere a little. Fortunately, Trevor couldn't understand what was being said as fingers were pointed at us to the accompaniment of laughter or he would have mortally offended. Nevertheless, among the generally good humoured reaction to our presence I could hear some voices saying that this only proved the truth of what they had always said about the folly of letting "*guiris*" live amongst them.

I felt that I needed to get close to Rafa in case the crowd turned nasty. He, I was sure, would look after us. I couldn't see him in the crowd and when I turned to look at the restaurant and the living quarters above I saw that they were still shuttered. Brenda saw me looking and couldn't resist telling me that she had spoken to Maria-Carmen earlier in the day. Rafa had apparently got home late from Cadiz with some important news to share but first he was catching up on his sleep and would be holding court in the bar of the restaurant later in the day. That was a shame. I was going to miss it. I was due to go that afternoon to meet the rogue bank employee who, in return for cash, was going to enlighten me and, through me, Lenny on the identity of those who had been siphoning money from the children's trust fund. I was not looking forward to the meeting and a sickening feeling inside was telling me that I didn't want to know who had betrayed Lenny. Nevertheless I had made a promise and I intended to keep it. The price I would pay was that when Rafa announced to the world that he now had nobility to stand alongside the wheelers, dealers and fixers in his family group I would have to rely on a maddeningly smug Brenda to tell me all about it.

In the absence of Rafa to act as a buffer between us and the outraged citizens of the village I suggested to Trevor and

Brenda that we would be better removing ourselves from the area. In order to keep myself away from the hygienic hyperactivity at home I spent nearly an hour at Trevor's house as he told me in a variety of contexts what a wonderful person he was. I knew better than to attempt to get a word in, even as he announced his blinkered and xenophobic solutions to the ills of the world in his usual dogmatic terms that neither required nor deserved intelligent debate. Trevor, like most people on the right of the political spectrum had the habit of elevating misinformation and petty bigotry to the level of universal truth that only the feeble minded would seek to question. When Trevor paused for breath Brenda started and I had to look interested as she proceeded to list all that she had that was superior to anything Sue and I could aspire to, dropping names as frequently as a butter fingered slip fielder might drop catches.

Eventually the prospect of dodging my wild eyed spouse as she fanatically wielded a vacuum cleaner became more attractive and I went home. Trevor and Brenda probably didn't notice and would have carried on talking at me for some time after my exit.

Every time I tried to place my foot on the ground in order to walk from the front door to a chair I was told in a panic stricken voice to watch out for a wet floor here or a pile of dust there until I resembled a child playing hopscotch as I crossed the room. I had learned not to attempt to engage Sue in conversation mid-clean but, at last, as the intensity of her brush movements abated, I felt able to suggest that she accompanied me on my journey that afternoon. I agreed to drop her off at a shopping centre while I went on to my meeting and to take her out to dinner at one of the superb roadside restaurants on the way home. It was a small price to pay in return for being allowed to sit quietly in the corner with a crossword as Sue finally restored our house to the status of somewhere you would be proud to have burgled.

Twenty-one

There's only one good thing that can be said about the Spanish city of La Linea de la Concepion or La Linea as it is generally called by those who bother to talk about it at all; it is not Gibraltar. Apart from that undoubted advantage it has little going for it. It is a charmless, seedy place separated from its even less charming neighbour by the road that gives the lie to the oft repeated myth that Gibraltar is an island. That myth is itself part of the collective delusion that supports the preposterous notion that, in the twenty-first century when the concept of empire lives on only in the memories of an ageing minority, a rocky outcrop of the Spanish mainland is as legitimately part of Britain as Scunthorpe or Eastbourne. That particular notion never ceases to outrage the Spanish who, with a sense of irony that is largely lost on the majority of British visitors, periodically clog up the border crossing with lines of vehicles that they insist on stopping and inspecting as if they really were crossing an international border.

As shirty as the Spanish get about the status of Gibraltar it doesn't seem to occur to them to smarten up La Linea, the first bit of Spain that those crossing from Gibraltar see. The opportunity to show those people just what they are missing is therefore spectacularly lost. In the days of the Cold War no effort was spared to create in West Berlin an image of wealth and comfort that evoked such envy in their East German neighbours that their country was undermined far more effectively than with bombs or bullets. You would think the Spanish would do the same in La Linea but they haven't bothered. Instead the border crossing sees a steady stream of shifty looking characters with carrier bags mingling ineffectively with the British tourists heading from the airport to the Car Hire offices across the road and the Spanish workers returning home from keeping the economy of Gibraltar ticking over. As the tourists disperse in their hire cars heading for the

Costas the carrier bags are emptied with little attempt at subtlety and the cargo of smuggled cigarettes is revealed. Shoving a handful of crumpled banknotes into their socks or the waistbands of their shabby trousers the smugglers then return across the road with the regularity of a metronome to replenish the now empty carriers.

I had dropped Sue off at a smart retail centre near Algeciras and I was now parking my car just opposite the border before proceeding on foot to the address I had been given for Paco, the contact who was going to reveal the current holders of the funds that should have been in Lenny's bank account. The address was in a rundown apartment block not far away. As I walked through the communal entrance I felt uneasy. My instincts told me that this was not somewhere I should be on my own and the hairs on the back of my neck felt as if they were standing to attention. I watched and listened intently for the first shadow or the first sound that would tell me that someone was behind me. I was ready to turn and run at the first hint of a hostile presence.

Paco lived on the third floor but I decided that using the lift would make me too vulnerable so I walked up the worn and dirty staircase. When I reached the third floor I found myself on a landing from which led six identical doors. None of them had a number. Apartment D, where Paco lived, would either be the third or fourth away from me depending on whether the door nearest to me was to apartment A or apartment F. I went to look at the third door. Beside it was a small nameplate announcing the occupant of the apartment to be "Snr. P Torres" I didn't know Paco's surname but this looked promising. In order to double check I looked at the nameplate outside the next door. It bore the name "Snr. F Hernandez". Paco Torres it was then. After a quick look round to ensure that I was not about to be mugged I knocked on the door.

As it opened, an overwhelming smell of cooking fish flooded out of the apartment followed by a squat, swarthy man with a pencil moustache and greasy dark hair. He was dressed in a discoloured vest and worn trousers. A cigarette hung from his lips wafting smoke into my face. The man looked at me curiously and not particularly warmly making no attempt to speak.

"Paco?" I asked tentatively and the man grunted something that sounded hostile while jerking a nicotine stained thumb in the direction of Snr. Hernandez' apartment. Without further explanation he slammed the door in my face. I was ready to give up my mission there and then. Only my long friendship with Lenny prevented me from walking back down those dirty steps while I was still physically able to do so. I gathered all my courage and knocked on Snr. Hernandez' door with a firmness that suggested confidence I did not possess. At least, I reasoned, Snr. Hernandez might be able to direct me to Paco's apartment before relieving me of my wallet.

The man who opened the door was young and smartly dressed. Before I could say anything he greeted me in English and ushered me inside. The apartment was small but clean and tastefully furnished so that it seemed out of place in such a grubby building. Calling me by name the man directed me to a chair beside a table near the small window. He took his place opposite me and, extending his hand he announced himself in clear and confident English to be Paco Hernandez.

"Paco?" I said, confused. "It doesn't say that outside. You're down as F Hernandez."

Paco laughed at my error and explained. "I am Francisco Hernandez," he said, "and when you are called Francisco in Spain everybody calls you Paco. It's like the English calling William Bill or Anthony Tony."

Of course, how stupid of me I should have realised. It's funny how you can be misled by someone's initial when you see it written down. The thought sparked a memory, a sort of déjà vu. Something had happened to me recently where I was misled by a name. When was it? I thought hard but I couldn't recall. Something inside me told me that it was important but I couldn't think what it was that I should be remembering. That's the trouble with getting to my age. You keep thinking you should be remembering things and when you can't it ends up annoying you far more than it should. My trouble, I have decided, is that I simply can't get used to the idea that I'm over sixty. I keep thinking I'm twenty-five. I'm one of those poor deluded men who are flattered when an attractive young female smiles at them in the street without realising that she's not doing it because she fancies them but because they remind her of her dad.

As I was mentally lamenting my lost youth Paco was pulling a file out of a briefcase that was beside the table. He placed it on the table and put his hand over it as if to bar my access to it. He looked up at me expectantly like a head waiter when he brings over the card machine and enquires whether the meal was to my liking. I took the hint and slid over two crisp 50 Euro notes that I had drawn from the bank that very day. Paco nodded curtly in acknowledgement as he stuffed the notes into his shirt pocket. He then pulled some sheets of paper from the file.

"These are the statements of the account," he explained in a level voice. "It was started in the early 1990s by a Miss Monica Bent and over the years the balance was reduced to a fairly nominal one until a few months ago when there was suddenly a large injection of funds from the UK."

Paco stabbed one of the pages with his forefinger to point out the deposit. I could see details of the bank from whence it had come. I recognised the code number of the branch which was no surprise considering that it was the branch where Stevenson and Parry, the firm I had so recently been a partner in, had always had all of its accounts. I reached for the piece of paper on which Lenny had written the account number for the trust fund and compared it to the details on the statement. There was no longer any doubt. I had found where the missing money had gone. Unfortunately, I had found something else as well. It was no longer there. The balance was back down to a nominal amount. I asked Paco to explain.

He responded by pulling out another sheet of paper. "Not long after the money went in Miss Bent called at the branch with a gentleman friend and they asked us to arrange the onward transfer of the funds to Switzerland."

Switzerland? I don't remember Lenny mentioning Switzerland. This was getting too confusing. Paco stabbed another entry with his finger.

"Here is the entry here. The money that had come from the UK was shipped to this account in Zurich on the client's instructions. It's all gone from here. The note on the file says it was the gentleman who asked for the transfer but the account was in Miss Bent's name and she had to agree to it which, according to this, she did."

I had mixed feelings as I considered the implications of this latest piece of information. On the one hand it was now going to be even more difficult to get the money back but on the other Lenny would have the satisfaction of knowing that this had not been an inside job. These movements of funds were clearly the work of international criminals not, as Lenny had feared, a bent employee. I took down details of the Swiss account to pass to Lenny with what I guessed he would find to be the good news that he could go back to trusting his staff.

"I don't suppose you have details of the account holder do you?" I asked without any real expectation of a helpful answer.

"I told you, Monica Bent," was Paco's deadpan reply.

"Actually, I think they're false names," I said, giving him the benefit of the doubt.

"It's a British joke, I think," said Paco eager to demonstrate that he was not the ignorant Spanish peasant he obviously thought I had taken him for. "Monica is a slang term for a name and Bent means that it is dishonest, isn't that right?"

I agreed, feeling a little embarrassed at having doubted his perception.

"We know it's a false name," he explained patiently. "Most of the accounts we hold are in false names. We use passwords to do business with the customers so their identity is protected."

"So you don't have any idea of her true identity?" I asked, thinking that the prospects of bringing the criminals to justice were becoming remote.

"Only the photographs," replied Paco with the faintest hint of a smile disturbing his deadpan features.

"You have photographs?"

Paco responded by extracting another sheet from the file and placing it face down on the table. He covered them with the same protective gesture that it had taken 100 Euros to counteract.

"We took this one on Miss Bent's last visit. It shows her and her friend," he said. "We always take photographs for our own protection. "The customers don't know we're doing it but it prevents fraud."

Prevents fraud? That's rich! Most of the money in these accounts was probably the product of fraud so it seemed to me that it was a bit late to be preventing it.

"May I see the photograph?" I asked.

Paco's hand did not move. "The agreement was that I show you the statements," he said. "There was nothing about the photograph."

He smiled at me for a few seconds until the penny or, to be precise, the 100 Euros dropped. I slid two more notes over the table making a mental note to ensure that Sue and I ate our dinner that night in a restaurant that took credit cards. I would need to get the money back from Lenny in due course but I thought that he would appreciate photographs of two of the hackers, or at least two of those who laundered money for them, to hand over to the police.

Paco slid the photograph over. I turned it face up, curious to see the faces of international criminals. I had not seen that many in my time. In Pentreglo they think you are an international criminal if you burgle a house in the next valley. As I focused my first reaction was disappointment. The woman in the picture may not have realised that she was about to be photographed but she had turned up well prepared for that eventuality. A thick pair of sunglasses and large straw hat made it impossible to be sure who she was. Nevertheless, there was something familiar about the face shape and the posture that awakened memories of seeing that same person in the witness box at the trial of Giuseppe Contemponi. Even without seeing her features clearly I had a good idea who it was.

I turned my attention to the man standing behind her and I realised that I didn't need to see the woman's face or hair to confirm my suspicions. I could work out her identity simply by who she was with. My heart sank as all my assumptions about anonymous hackers faded away. Lenny wasn't going to like this. I certainly didn't. I could feel the nausea building up as I surveyed a face I had seen many times before. He was red faced from the sun and wearing a casual shirt with shorts that made him look faintly ridiculous like the stereotypical Brit abroad. Red face or not there was no mistaking the features of former police sergeant and erstwhile solicitor's clerk Mervyn Jenkins.

Twenty-two

The phone call to Lenny was not an easy one. In fact it is probably the hardest thing I have done in my life to tell my old friend that he had been betrayed by the man he had not only entrusted with a responsible position in the firm but also defended when the accusations had started to fly around. Lenny was devastated and his low mood dragged me down with it. I had just spent two weeks of what should have been a holiday trying desperately to find some way to clear MJ's name against a mounting wall of evidence. I had finally persuaded myself before returning to Spain that my task was hopeless but at least I had the satisfaction of believing that I had done my best for a friend who would have done the same for me. What particularly sickened me was the realisation that MJ had not been worth the effort. All the time I had been feeling the frustration of not being able to help him MJ must have been laughing at me behind my back as he cynically picked Lenny's pockets.

Lenny declared, overdramatically but perhaps understandably, that he wasn't going to trust anyone ever again and then, rather touchingly, assured me that I would be the exception. I gave Lenny the details of the Swiss bank account and he promised me that he would pass all that I had discovered to Nev Powell the next day. He assured me that sentiment would not hold him back from supporting a full police investigation. As far as he was concerned MJ had finally forfeited any last right to be treated as anything more than the thief and the perjurer that he had been shown to be.

I stayed on the phone for longer than I needed with Lenny. I sensed that he needed a friend to talk to and the least I could do was to be that friend. We talked about MJ and our shared memories of him, pausing at intervals to collectively declare that we could never have believed him capable of such treachery. We moved on from that to talking about our own relationship and the times we'd spent together building and maintaining a relatively successful if grossly unfashionable legal practice out of the almost fossilised remains of his uncle's old family firm. At least that got us laughing as we reminded each other of the eccentrics we had met, the calamities that we had always managed somehow to avoid and the outrage we always seemed to invoke in the more straight laced figures in the legal community. It was like being at a funeral when you want desperately to succumb to the misery of the loss of a loved one but you find yourself participating in a mass conspiracy to think only of the good times and to recall them with an intensity of positive emotion that you hope will somehow force the grief out of your consciousness. All along I knew that when the jollity subsided Lenny, like a widow after the last guest had left the funeral, would be plunged even more deeply into despair. I owed it to him to delay that moment for as long as I could.

Finally we ended our conversation with Lenny descending into a level of sentiment that I was uncomfortable with as he told me what a good and loyal friend I had been. I had been talking to him for so long that I was late picking Sue up. She was thankfully unconcerned having been adequately distracted by her single minded assault on the stocks of the various units at the shopping centre.

I called Nigel from the Shopping Centre and told him we had been right in the conclusions we had finally reached about MJ. He had stolen another man's wife and, in the process, stolen his life. Not content with that he had stolen money intended for grieving widows and fatherless kids and in so doing he had ensured that Lenny, who had done more for him than he would ever be entitled to expect, would never be the same affable trusting man again.

We speculated as to MJ's motives for stealing from Lenny. It didn't take too long. It was sickeningly obvious. MJ had realised that the net was closing on him when Tom Webster made his confession and was planning to make himself scarce. The money was to set him and his lover up somewhere where justice could not reach them. They had used the classic ploy of two money transfers in quick succession to throw anyone chasing them, or the money, off the scent. It seemed that not only was Lenny going to be left high and dry by MJ's scheme but so too was Iris. I wondered how she would react when her illusions about the man she worshipped were shattered and I felt a deep compassion for her. To Iris, that experience would be far more soul destroying than an attack by an intruder or even a murder charge. As Nigel and I talked it all through my instinctive feeling of intellectual satisfaction at having tied up all the loose ends was heavily outweighed by the revulsion I felt for the man whom we had unmasked in the process.

Nigel, to his credit, was sympathetic and sensitive to my feelings. He resisted the temptation of displaying any suggestion of smugness at the comprehensive case we had built against MJ. He knew that a feeling of achievement was the last emotion I would be experiencing. What I felt was something very different. I was disgusted, not simply with MJ for what he had done but with myself for ever having called him my friend. My only consolation was the thought that Beppe's untimely death had at least spared him the anguish of realising that he had been betrayed not simply by corruption in the police force but by the cold blooded scheming of the woman who at some earlier, happier time had promised to love and honour him.

By the time Sue and I got to the restaurant it was nearly ten o'clock. In Britain a request for a table at that time would have provoked expressions of incredulity and the news that, as the microwave was unplugged at 9.30, chef would not be able to work his magic for us on this occasion. Fortunately in Andalucia that's not a problem. The locals are only just starting to get peckish at that time and anyone seeking his dinner before about nine is generally regarded as a hopeless glutton or alternatively a foreigner.

I was not particularly good company during dinner. I was still angry at MJ for his betrayal and at myself for my naivety. Sue seemed to understand what was going through my mind and tactfully refrained from giving me the opportunity to transfer my anger to her or to the young waiter who tried repeatedly to engage me in friendly conversation. The food was as good as ever; fresh local ingredients prepared and served without pretension. My usual and wholly predictable reaction to a meal like that is to wonder aloud like the grumpy old git I have become why it is that British restaurants can either give you the best fine dining in the world at obscene prices or largely indigestible fare at bargain prices but seem incapable of reproducing what we found everywhere we went in Spain, simple food that was actually pleasant to eat served in surroundings that were neither intimidating nor debilitating on the wallet. Tonight, however, I was in no mood for such pontification and largely ate in silence.

Across from us there was a long table with three or more generations of the same extended family crowded around it and large plates of food in the centre for all to take from. The family members shared their food naturally, amicably and loudly just as they shared their everyday lives. As they ate they were alternatively laughing, arguing, reconciling and then laughing again, living their joint lives in public without any Anglo Saxon notions of image, status or propriety to restrain them. Nobody else was complaining about the noise, shaking their heads at the behaviour of the children or whispering disapproval through pursed lips. Normally, such a sight would set me off on another grumpy monologue about the decline of family life in Britain and the way that once we pass forty we forget that we were once children or even parents. Tonight I had more relevant things to regret than the British attitude to children. Instead I could reflect on the loyalty you can show to a colleague only to have it all thrown back cynically in your face.

Sue tried a few times to engage me in conversation so that I could snap out of the black mood I could feel engulfing me. I knew what she was doing and appreciated it. I knew that I owed it to her to respond but it was like climbing out of the sea onto slippery rocks. Every time I tried to escape my mood it just pulled me back again. As we drove back home in silence I willed myself to talk about something other than MJ and what he had done to Lenny and to me. With a degree of effort I told her about the graffiti on the church wall leading her to speculate as to the identity of the culprit.

"By the time we get home Brenda will know the full story," she said with a laugh. "She'll probably wake us up in the middle of the night to tell us just in case anyone else gets to us first."

That laughter helped lift my mood enough to allow me to have a normal conversation with Sue during the rest of the journey. We talked, as we often did, about how different the values and the priorities were in the tight knit community of the village compared to those in the city suburbs where we had both spent our lives. I told her, as I often did, that I had sensed that same community spirit in Pentreglo when I had first worked there but that I had seen it die slowly as the life blood was squeezed out of the community when the pit closed. This led us on to a familiar topic; how the British had, with honourable exceptions, stood back passively and watched the destruction of communities built around traditional industries while the Spanish seemed to want to preserve the values of those communities even after they had ceased to be viable by the standards of today's unforgiving economic forces. Was this something ingrained in the Spanish people, we wondered, or is it simply that we had a head start in sacrificing human values for the fickle mistress of material wealth and the Spanish will simply catch us up in time?

Those thoughts diverted me sufficiently that I had been able to put thoughts of MJ and Lenny to the back of my mind by the time we drove into the now deserted village square. Sue wanted to see the church wall for herself so I pulled up just outside the cemetery that is at the side of the church, fished a torch out of the glove compartment and led her over to where the wall had been defiled.

As we approached I heard a noise. It was a banging as if somebody was knocking down a wall. The noise reverberated around the square and I thought I heard a sound like stones falling. Surely nobody was trying to knock the church down in the middle of the night! Vandalising the place was one thing but demolition seemed to be a rather extreme way of making a point about the Catholic Church. I wondered whether the graffiti artist had returned to hide the evidence by knocking down the wall he had defaced but then swiftly dismissed that idea as too ridiculous for further consideration.

The noise was not abating and it was beginning to wake the neighbours. I saw a light go on in the living quarters above Rafa's and felt relief that my friend would soon be out to investigate. It was pitch dark apart from the torchlight and Sue and I were alone in the company of somebody who, by the sound of it, had a sledgehammer and was not afraid to use it. To put it bluntly I was scared. I didn't want to be the one to disturb this person and risk the transfer of his malice from the wall to my head. On the other hand, I owed it to the people of the village not to simply turn my back and pretend I had heard nothing. At least Rafa would know what to do. Whoever was out there, Rafa had probably known him all his life and, by the law of averages in this part of Spain, he might even be related to him. In any event all the villagers tended to treat Rafa with inordinate respect so it would be unthinkable for anyone to smash my skull with a hammer if they thought Rafa might not approve.

As I listened to the rhythmic pounding and crashing I was able to pinpoint it better. It wasn't coming from the church itself but from inside the cemetery. It was a typical Spanish cemetery with ornate memorials cramped together surrounded by walls containing remains and plaques to identify them. This realisation didn't help. Someone was attacking the graves. This was a situation I could not stand by and allow to happen. I had to go and at least try to stop him. I told Sue to get Rafa while, on legs that were decidedly shaky, I followed the thin beam of the torch towards the noise.

As I got closer to the banging I heard another noise. It was a man's voice shouting angrily. I could neither hear nor understand what was being said but the aggression in the voice matched that of the bangs. I could now hear that the source of the noise was an area of family memorials erected and thereafter diligently tended by the relatives left behind. I had been to that part of the cemetery before. Rafa's parents were buried there and he had proudly shown me the statue of two angels bearing ornately framed photographs of the couple that he had placed there in their memory. That decided it. Frightened though I was I could not look Rafa in the eye and tell him that I had done nothing as his tribute to his beloved parents was desecrated by some madman.

I raised the torch beam and scanned the area around. I froze as the light picked up a figure ahead of me. He was frantically swinging a hammer at a memorial and I could hear him screaming at it as each blow landed. I had to do something but my muscles were refusing to cooperate by carrying me any closer to the deranged character who was going about his destructive business seemingly oblivious to my presence. I decided to shout but then, in an almost surreal moment, found myself debating what the appropriate form of Spanish words is when you are trying to attract the attention of a maniac. What's the verb for stop and how do you put it in the imperative form? Where's the Spanish dictionary when you need it?

I was spared the ignominy of having to shout at the man in ungrammatical terms. I heard a voice, a woman's voice, behind me doing it for me. She sounded as if she was crying. I turned and shone the torch on a distraught Maria-Carmen accompanied by a horrified Sue. I turned back again. Maria-Carmen's shout had stopped the vandal in his tracks and he had turned to face her. I shone the torch into his face and realised why Sue was so horrified. I abandoned any thought of properly formulating a Spanish sentence. I spoke in English. I knew I would be understood. I found myself shouting

"Rafa, for God's sake, man! What the hell do you think you are doing?"

Rafa stared blankly at me and at Maria-Carmen who was now beside me. He allowed the hammer to drop at his feet. Maria-Carmen, in a tearful voice called on Rafa to come to her.

"Ven, Rafa, ven acqui."

He looked at her as if she were a stranger. When he replied it was in a loud and angry voice that was unfamiliar to me.

"Rafa?" he said. *"No soy Rafa, soy Carlos."*

He looked at me and even in his aggression he had the instinctive courtesy to translate.

"I am not Rafa, I am Carlos."

Maria-Carmen ran over to him and flung her arms around him. They were both crying now. I was able to see the memorial to Rafa's parents lying shattered at his feet. All that I could hear as Rafa buried his head in Maria-Carmen's shoulder was a repetition like a ritual chant of those same words. *"Soy Carlos, Soy Carlos. No soy Rafa, soy Carlos."*

Maria-Carmen walked Rafa past me and as she did so she gestured with her eyes for me to say nothing to him. "Come to see me in the morning and I will explain," she whispered. She then steered her sobbing husband out of the cemetery towards the restaurant. As we left the cemetery Rafa and Maria-Carmen were by their door. Rafa broke free from her grip and turned to us. As his wife tried to usher him through the door he called pathetically across to me in English.

"Remember, I am not Rafa. I am Carlos!"

Twenty-three

I awoke the next day to one of those mornings that reassures you that spring will surely come. A blue sky in January is always a bonus and although this one was marred by clouds they carried not the threat of storms but the seductive promise that, although there might still be miserable days to endure before summer, they would obediently disappear in the months to come leaving only the sun to break up unremitting blueness of the sky. It was the sort of morning that would normally make me feel glad to be alive but I still had the memories of the previous day to squeeze any such feelings from my body. I felt a sense of loss, loss of MJ as someone worth caring about, loss of Rafa as the imperturbable rock to whom I could turn for wise counsel interlaced with amusing banter as I adjusted to life in a new country. I stared morosely at the sea as I sat with a coffee on the balcony. It was beginning to show the first signs of losing the greyness and ferocity of winter. On any other day I could have spent a good hour eking out my breakfast as I studied the movement of the waves but my thoughts were far away. They were with Lenny as he painfully confessed his naivety to Nev Powell and with Maria-Carmen as she struggled to come to terms with her husband's mental breakdown.

I felt myself drifting off to sleep, not the gentle, refreshing sleep that is born of freedom from care but the troubled sleep that we turn to in a vain search for a refuge from pressures our waking body cannot take. In my dreams I saw Rafa on all fours howling pitifully like a wounded animal while a smiling MJ rifled through his pockets.

"Help me somebody, help me!" Rafa's cries were pathetic but somehow my muscles were frozen and I was powerless to stop MJ.

"Gareth, quickly, help me." Now Rafa was calling me by name but still I could do nothing.

"Gareth, I'm up here. Help me please."

That's strange. Why is Rafa saying he is up somewhere when he is clearly down on the ground? Come to think of it that doesn't sound like Rafa at all. I forced my eyes open and I was back alone on the balcony with my half-drunk coffee. The voice hadn't gone away with the dream though. I heard it again.

"Gareth, Gareth, quickly, Gareth up here."

I looked around but could see nothing to account for the sound. It seemed to be coming from the direction of Trevor's house. I looked across but still saw nothing. Perhaps Trevor had been right without realising it. Perhaps there was a ghost in his house. It would have to be a British ghost as it was calling me in English and, anyway, Trevor would not tolerate being haunted by a foreigner. Perhaps it was the spirit of an Irish plasterer or a Geordie bricklayer who had met a ghastly end while working, cash in hand and outside the reach of Health and Safety rules, on the site.

I stood up and looked over the balcony towards Trevor's garden. That, I realised immediately, was a particularly stupid thing to do. The voice wasn't telling me much but the one piece of information it had imparted was that it was up rather than down. I went down to my garden and looked up at Trevor's house. It was then that I saw where the voice, now descending into a frightened whine, was coming from. It was Trevor. He seemed to be on the roof and from the panic I was able to detect on his usually smug features I deduced that he was stuck there.

"What are you doing up there?" I asked a stupid question but, fortunately, Trevor was insufficiently quick witted to give me the sarcastic reply I deserved.

"I'm stuck up here," he said rather needlessly before explaining in tones rising towards hysteria that he had been trying to adjust the satellite dish when his stepladder had fallen over. He had been left hanging onto the chimney that had been included on the house not because it had an open fire but because the architect, to save money, had borrowed the plans of a bungalow development in Leeds.

"Where's Brenda?" I shouted up.

"Having her hair done," was the exasperated reply. That came as no surprise. In her quest to have the most outlandish of shapes and colours adorning her head Brenda had done much to transform Conchita from the next village from a modest ladies hairdresser to one of the wealthiest business women in the region.

"Is the door unlocked?" I asked. Trevor told me it wasn't.

"You'll have to throw me your keys then," I said, "so I can get up to the roof terrace and pick up the stepladder."

It took a terrified Trevor a full five minutes to summon the courage to take one hand away from the chimney and fish his keys out of his pocket. He shaped as if to throw them across to me. I could see that if he did that he was likely to follow the keys off the roof so while Trevor waited impatiently I had to climb over his wall into his garden, a task which my advancing years and expanding waist rendered far more difficult than it should have been. I stood below the roof to catch the dropped keys.

"The trouble is that I'm not good with heights," Trevor told me in a rare admission of non-perfection once I had helped him onto the restored stepladder and to the safety of the roof terrace.

"Why then did you go up there?" I asked. "And with a set of household steps instead of a proper ladder. You could have borrowed mine."

"I thought that if I borrowed your ladder you'd try to persuade me not to try it," was the sheepish reply. He was right, of course, but too stubborn to admit that I would have been fully justified as events had proved.

"I don't know how I'm going to fix that dish," he said ruefully. "It's really a two man job and needs somebody who's good with heights." He was looking at me as he said it but I had no desire to interfere in something I did not understand and which, particularly with Trevor holding the ladder, could quite possibly kill me. I took my leave of Trevor and went back home, returning shortly afterwards with a magazine in my hand. It was an ex pat magazine, one of those designed to extol the virtues of life in the sun while maintaining the illusion that its readers were really living in an outer suburb of a British city. A well-meaning friend had bought us a subscription to it when we first moved over to Spain and even when that subscription ran out they kept sending it to me in an effort to tempt me into renewal. At least half of the pages were given over to advertising and the selling point for every advertiser was that there were no Spaniards involved in their operation. Almost every advertisement had a Union Jack logo and assured the reader that English was spoken. Those using trading names tended to adopt ones that left no doubt about their origins like "Bulldog" or "Britannia". There was even a building maintenance company called "Thatchers". I wonder what that does – demolish workplaces and pinch the children's milk from the doorstep presumably.

I scanned the section headed "TV and Satellite Services" looking for the least jingoistic to recommend to Trevor. My eyes alighted on "Telstar Electrical and Aerial Services" which boasted a British trained electrician with over ten years' experience of satellite TV installation and maintenance. I liked the way he said "British" instead of "English". That's always a plus in my book. I circled the number and suggested to Trevor that he ring it before setting off to what I expected to be an awkward visit to Rafa's.

To my surprise Rafa was back to his affable self when I called on him. He answered the door himself and greeted me with an enthusiastic handshake before sitting me down and, with an instinct developed during his years in London, offering me a cup of tea. As I looked around the room there was something different about it but I couldn't put my finger on what it was.

"Thank you for stopping me doing anything too stupid yesterday," said Rafa as if smashing your parents' grave with a hammer wasn't a pretty stupid thing to do, "and sorry if you caught me at a bad moment. I'm alright now though. I've thought about things and I can now get on with my life."

I suppose what Rafa was doing when I last saw him might just about qualify as a bad moment though I'm more used to the expression when someone has put on odd socks or missed a bus. Rafa really was calm about what had struck me as a highly traumatic incident. He laughed but without the warmth that normally goes with such a gesture. "I suppose you want me to explain," he said and, when I nodded pointedly he agreed that it was the least he could do. His smile faded and he replaced it with an expression that told me that his was not a happy tale. He started with a question.

"When did you first come to the village?" he asked.

"About two or two and a half years ago," was my reply.

Rafa greeted it with a knowing nod. "Two and a half years ago," he repeated, "so you know the village as it is now and I couldn't expect you to have any idea what it was like before."

"Before when, Rafa?"

"When I was a child. It was all very different when I was growing up," he said before telling me of the Spain of his childhood.

The Spain that Rafa spoke of was not a Spain I recognised. The Spain I know is populated by friendly generous people who understood the value of family and community. They are a people with an endearing streak of anarchy about them. I remember the time when the powers that be painted blue lines along the sides of the roads and installed parking meters in an effort to derive some revenue from the summer visitors in their hire cars. As the Town Hall employees moved along the roads with their blue paint the locals followed them with a can of black paint which they used to cover over the blue lines as quickly as they were produced. Within days of their erection the meters were blocked up by heavy tape attached to which were graphic cartoons showing, with a clarity that did not require knowledge of Spanish, exactly what the Town Hall could do with their parking meters. Within a month the Town Hall caved in and on street parking is still free in the village. Some of the older locals are the same with the one way system that operates in the centre of the village. So far as they are concerned a few no entry signs aren't going to stop them from travelling in the same direction that they had always done since before motor cars came to the village. What Rafa described was very different.

To the casual observer, perhaps, the village was just a quiet sleepy backwater in those days. To those whose memories are distorted by nostalgia, perhaps, it was a place where there was more respect for authority, more obedience to the Church and more discipline than today. Those same people will tell you that things were better then, that everyone was safe and knew what to expect of life but, Rafa said, they are wrong. It wasn't respect they had then but fear. People did not respect their neighbours, they were afraid of them, afraid of what might happen if they were seen to step out of line. Because of this nobody did step out of line or question anything or try to lead a different life. That's why the casual visitor might not have noticed it. The village would have looked like somewhere where everyone was content with what they had and the life they led but they weren't content. They were just too afraid to say so. All in the village thought with one mind in those days. Nobody rocked the boat. Rafa was quick to dispel the impression that this represented an idyllic existence by asking me to think about the other side of the coin, how anybody that didn't share the collective beliefs of the village would find himself alone against them all.

I know of course that Spain has had a dark past but I also know that it isn't generally mentioned in company. The Spanish seem to treat those events in much the same way that a family might treat the time when Uncle George had too much to drink at cousin Katie's wedding and started touching up the bridesmaids; everyone in the family knows it happened but nobody wants to spoil things by mentioning it.

"I know what Spain was like under Franco, I've read about it," I said, trying to make Rafa's task easier, but he shook his head.

"You may have read about the power of the State, the mistreatment of people, the injustices and all the rest of it, Gareth, but what you must understand is how it affected people every day in villages like this. There was no need for any obvious signs of state power in this village. They didn't need the Guardia Civil dragging people off the streets. It was more insidious than that. Where you have open shows of force against the people all it does is turn people against the status quo and bring down the very system they are trying to preserve. Look at Northern Ireland where the more soldiers they put on the streets the more kids joined the IRA. In Spain it was different. People knew what the State could do; they had seen it during the Civil War. It had destroyed without pity all who openly opposed it so that those who were left did not need open force to keep them in line. It was far more effective to instil conformity into people so that if anyone questioned authority they could not expect their neighbours to help them avoid the often brutal consequences. In that way very few people did question authority. Freedom of expression was stifled by fear, by the collective obedience of the community and, of course, by the errand boys of the dictatorship, the Church."

I was taken aback by that remark. Although the questionable role of the Church during Spain's darkest days was something I was aware of I had always known Rafa to be a strong supporter of that institution. Something had changed his mind about it and the idea that Rafa might have been behind the painting of obscenities on the church wall suddenly didn't seem as ridiculous as it had.

"Even in a village like this," Rafa was continuing, "if you had Civil Guards in big boots telling people what to think they would soon rebel but it wasn't the Civil Guard doing it, it was the Church and, even today, if the Church says it, most people will accept it. The Church did the work of the dictatorship. It encouraged the people to turn a blind eye to what was bad in our country and to turn on those who wanted to change it."

"Is this why you left Spain and came to Britain?" I asked.

Rafa nodded. "I suppose I could say that I was a principled and courageous man who saw what was wrong and walked away in protest but it would not be true," he said. "I didn't think of politics in those days and I accepted the teachings of the priests like everyone else. I left Spain because of what it had become but when I did so I didn't understand that this was my reason. For me it was so dull, so lacking in variety or opportunity. When I was a teenager I used to like British pop music, the Beatles and the Rolling Stones and people like that. I used to listen to their music and wanted to know what they were singing about. I started learning English from a book so that I could understand them. I had to do so secretly because I knew that those who called themselves my parents wouldn't approve. That led me to start reading British newspapers that they used to sell in the holiday towns and listening to the BBC. It taught me about a new world that seemed so much more exciting than this dull old village so I left home. I suppose you could say I ran away. I didn't think that I was running away from a dictatorship because I don't think it occurred to me that this was what Spain was. What drove me away was the narrowness of life here and the attitude of the family I grew up with. When I settled in England I soon understood why life was freer there but it is only now that I understand why I wanted to leave that family."

"What was it about the family?" I asked. It was not lost on me that Rafa had referred to *"those who called themselves"* his parents and the family he *"grew up with"*. These were strange expressions to use and they did not seem accidental. I was curious to know more.

"I never felt that I belonged to the family I grew up with. I was the youngest child and I always had the feeling that my brothers and sisters rejected me. They did not seem to treat me as they treated each other. Their parents were the same, very cold and formal with me. They were strict parents, always insisting I went to church and worked hard in school and showed respect to my betters. They were the same with my brothers and sisters but somehow there was affection behind it where they were concerned which seemed to be missing with me. Other relatives, uncles, aunts and so on, were the same. They were very warm towards everyone else but with me there was a distance as if I was different. I didn't understand it at the time and couldn't put it into words. It was just something I felt. When I was in London and thought about it as an adult I decided that I was imagining it and that what I was feeling was just the awkwardness of adolescence. Eventually when things started changing in Spain I decided that it was time to go home. Life was better by then. I made an effort to develop a relationship with the family that I had not had before. I am not sure if I ever have but it's easier when you are an adult because you can have a friendly relationship without looking for affection. I think that the fact that I lived in London for all those years makes me a bit of a novelty to them so we get on well enough. For my part I made a conscious effort to blend into village life and to get involved in the Church, if only to keep those whom I knew as my parents happy. When they died I had that memorial made for them to show everyone that, whatever had gone before, I was a good and loyal son."

"You don't call them *your* parents or *your* family, Rafa. Why is that?" I had to ask the question.

His answer was disarmingly simple.

"Because they are not. I am not Rafa. I am Carlos."

Twenty-four

I couldn't help but notice the paradox. Rafa was totally absorbed in telling me a peculiarly and tragically Spanish story but as he did so he was instinctively adopting that most British of practices and dipping a biscuit in his tea.

"By the time I came back to Spain, got married and started my business I had put my childhood uncertainties to the back of my mind," he told me. "Which is where they remained until you brought them out."

"Me?" I was suddenly concerned that I might be responsible for all that had gone on. Rafa reassured me as he explained.

"It was the way you went back and tried to find an explanation for all those half retained memories of your childhood and the way you made such surprising discoveries, that got me thinking about my childhood and made me want answers as you had."

It was true that reflections on my past had led me to trace my family history to fill in the gaps and force any remaining skeletons out of their cupboards. It was equally true that this endeavour had revealed a fascinating history of which I had been previously unaware not least the fact that I was descended from Jewish immigrants, something Trevor had never really forgiven me for. I recalled with embarrassment how I had spent most nights after discovering the truth boring all who would listen, or could not avoid hearing, with tales of my grandfather's adventures as the East London-born son of Polish/Jewish parents determined to discover the wider world. Rafa, by virtue of his position as proprietor of the establishment where most of my tedious monologues were delivered, had been a captive audience. I didn't realise at the time that I was having any deeper effect than encouraging him to find someone else to talk to.

"I asked around the family but they seemed reluctant to tell me anything," he said. "They would change the subject or fob me off with clichés about living for the future instead of the past. I didn't think I would get anywhere until a few months ago when I got talking to a professor from the university in Cadiz who was spending a holiday in the village. He told me that he was researching the history of the region in the mid-20th century and it was when he said, as a way of illustrating it, that he was concerned with the time when I was born that I found myself telling him about my childhood. He was a good listener and we talked for quite a long time. I thought no more about it until he contacted me last week and invited me to visit him at the university. He said he had something important to tell me about myself. I wondered what it was but I never imagined that he would tell me that I was not Rafa, the son of the village storekeeper here but Carlos whose father worked at the docks in Cadiz."

"I don't understand, Rafa, what do you mean?"

"I mean what I said. My father worked at the docks in Cadiz. He was very active in politics and when my mother became pregnant with me he made it very clear that if I was a boy I would be called Carlos."

"Why, Rafa? Was that his name?"

I was being extremely slow on the uptake. Rafa showed the slightest hint of frustration as he made things clearer.

"No, Carlos was not his name but it was the name of the man whose teachings he followed to the end. He was a brave man and wanted to make a point that nobody was going to take his beliefs away whatever else they took."

The penny finally dropped. It was the Spanish version of the name, Carlos, that had thrown me. Had Rafa used the original German version I would have seen it earlier. He was talking about the name of Karl, Karl Marx, that most misunderstood, misquoted and generally misused figure of the last few centuries. It was a surprise to hear Rafa mention his name; so few people did these days. It's not like the heady days of the sixties, my teenage and student years, when the name of Karl Marx took its place with that of Che Guevara, Ho

Che Minh and all those that we long haired idealists were going to change the world on behalf of. Today it seems that few young people know who he was and those that do have no real idea what his message was. Some, even of my age, might tell you he was an American comic film star or the founder of a chain of food and clothing stores.

For my part, like most children of the sixties, I left my Marxist tendencies behind when I left university. It was one of those things like living in flea ridden digs cultivating a pseudo bohemian look and pretending to understand abstract art that people tend to abandon as soon as they emerge with a degree into the real world.

Despite this I never cease to be amazed at how little influence Marx has on modern politics at a time when everything that he predicted is coming to pass all around us. We all adopt the role of impotent bystanders as rampant capitalism marches through every aspect of our lives. We fail to see the message when even the old fashioned justifications for free market economics, like freedom of choice, competition driving up standards or customer focussed service become illusory with the rise of faceless monopolies. Nobody seems to stop and think whether there may a different way. We seem to accept it as ordained by some wiser power that our "betters" should treat the nation's wealth in the same way as old Mr Prosser, a neighbour from my childhood who seemed to reside permanently either in the pub or the bookies, used to treat his pay packets. We even accept that when things go wrong we should bear the loss in the same way as Mrs Prosser and the twins would be reduced to bread and jam whenever the head of the household's chosen horse decided to enjoy the scenery on his way round the track. We are told we are unrealistic if we expect the same level of job security or public service that our parents enjoyed in the years following a debilitating war. Nobody asks why that should be so in an age when technology has advanced to a level that our parents could not have dreamed about. Nobody bothers to ask the obvious questions but if they did they might find that old Uncle Karl has many of the answers.

Perhaps Marxism has suffered the fate of all religion since, to its followers, that's what it is, a religion. Those who believe in it look to it in vain for a comprehensive blueprint for all aspects of life. Those who don't believe in it convince themselves that it is so evil that it must be supressed at all costs. Just as with any religion Marxism has inspired some to dedicate their lives to the wellbeing of others, has encouraged others to such slavish adherence to its teachings that they lose all grip on reality and has attracted a host of non-believers who use it as a justification for their own lust for power. The fact that, whether it's Marxism or religion, the implacable fundamentalists and corrupt self-seekers tend to outnumber the idealists is perhaps the reason why neither plays much of a part in the lives of most normal people today. It's a pity that this is so. Just as we can seek guidance from the wisdom of the Bible or the Koran without being full blown Christians or Moslems we can appreciate the perception of Marx's analysis of history and the nature of power without wishing to replicate North Korea in South Kensington.

Rafa's father clearly belonged to a different generation, one that believed in absolutes in a way that our generation, knowing, as their parents were to learn, where totalitarianism can lead, never will. Rafa held a fading photograph of an earnest looking bearded man as he told me what he had been told about him.

"He had been a supporter of the Republic during the war," he said, "because he believed that it represented the opportunity to cast off centuries of exploitation and to build a new society where all could be equal. It sounds so simplistic now doesn't it, Gareth, but the professor was telling me that this was how people thought at that time. They were prepared to lay down their lives to build something worthwhile for those like me who would come after them. The professor told me that as a young man my father went to fight for the Republic convinced that he could save it and convinced that it was worth saving. He risked his life for the Republic but it was all in vain, the war was lost. My father returned to Cadiz defeated and angry because, like many who thought like him, he felt that in the end the Republic had betrayed its ideals and its forces had fought with each other rather than saving their energy for the enemy. He was convinced that if his side had maintained the same unity of purpose and the same faith in its principles that the Nationalists had then victory would have been theirs. He was a bitter man according to the letters I have been shown but, compared to those who had fought alongside him, he was also a lucky man. He escaped injury and he escaped capture by the Nationalists. He was able to resume his life in Cadiz where he met and married my mother."

Rafa looked lovingly at the fading photograph as he continued.

"For a few years he kept his head down and got on with life, keeping himself away from the attention of the authorities but he didn't lose his ideals and as he began to learn which of his workmates he could trust he started talking politics with them. He formed a branch of the Spanish Communist Party, in secret of course because such activities were illegal in Spain then. He also formed a secret union for the workers at the port. At first these were just talking shops but, as more people joined with them, they became more active. They began to circulate leaflets attacking the government and calling for workers' rights and, although they could not actively organise strikes, they would ensure for example that all workers in a particular part of the port fell sick at the same time and missed work just when it would have maximum effect. It was inevitable that the authorities would notice him and he knew that. He was prepared to make that sacrifice until…"

Rafa paused, overcome with emotion.

"Until when, Rafa?" I prompted him as gently as I could.

"Until my mother became pregnant with me. She begged him not to have anything more to do with the union. She told him that he had responsibilities that had to come first. He couldn't do it. He became convinced that he was of more use to his unborn child fighting, even dying, for a better Spain than if he simply lived as a family man. Two weeks before I was born they came and took my father away. My mother never saw him again and he never saw me."

Rafa was forced to pause again. I was torn between my respect for his feelings and my eagerness to hear his story. He drained his teacup of its now cold contents, looked again at the photograph and continued.

"I was born in the bedroom of the tiny house near the port in Cadiz where my parents lived. My mother was attended at the birth by a nun from a nearby convent who acted as a midwife in that quarter. As soon as I was born, according to one of the neighbours who was in the room, my mother declared that, in accordance with the wishes of her missing husband, I was to be called Carlos. The nun took me away to wash me and that was the last time my mother ever saw me."

"Did anything happen to her?"

Rafa shook his head and as he answered his voice was breaking. "No, nothing happened to her, she lived for another twenty years and for all of that time she believed that her only child, her son Carlos, had died within an hour of birth. Do you understand, Gareth? My mother lived and died believing that I was dead."

"Why, Rafa? Why did she believe that?" As soon as I asked the question I knew that the answer was obvious. Rafa told me anyway.

"Because the nun told her I was dead and then took me away and gave me to the people who I grew up believing to be my parents. They registered me as their child and called me Rafael and not Carlos. They brought me up as a good Catholic and until they died they never told me the truth."

"Why did the nun do this?" Once again I was asking a question to which the answer was obvious.

"It was planned as soon as my father was arrested. They couldn't have me growing up as the son of a godless father, a communist and an agitator. That's why they gave me to a good, loyal, religious family who, with the help of the Church would drive out the evil that I had inherited from my father. In that way there would be one less enemy of the state and one more loyal servant of it."

I was stunned. I told Rafa that I couldn't believe that anyone professing to be a Christian could act in such an unfeeling way.

"You do not understand, Gareth," he said. "In those days the priests and the nuns worked together with the army and the Civil Guard. They all thought that they were doing God's work and that communists were the messengers of the Devil. For those in power, even if they didn't believe such nonsense, it was a good excuse for supressing all opposition."

There was an obvious question for me to ask.

"What happened to your father, Rafa?"

Rafa squeezed the photograph harder and shook his head.

"Nobody knows exactly," he said. "The professor says that at some time after his arrest he was killed, murdered, but he does not know exactly when. They didn't bother to keep records then. They just disposed of their enemies with about as much ceremony as you throwing out your garbage at night. The professor was able to put the story together by talking to families that knew my parents in Cadiz and from the records of the convent. They believed they were doing nothing wrong taking babies from what they considered to be undeserving families so they had no reason not to keep a record. According to the professor my father will have been buried in a mass grave somewhere without any record being kept. They are digging up graves like that all over the country. I have given him a sample of DNA so if he finds a match in the future he can tell me where my father is."

Maria-Carmen had joined us by now. She stood behind Rafa leaning forward with her arms around his shoulders in a protective gesture as he sadly contemplated his empty cup.

"It all must have come as a terrible shock," I said with what I realised was a masterful understatement.

Rafa nodded. "Enough of a shock to make me do what I did. I'm sorry if that upset anybody but I felt I had to do it. I had to make some gesture against those liars who called themselves my parents and those hypocrites who preach about love and family yet helped to destroy my family. I had to do something and I feel better for having done it. I will of course pay for painting of the church wall and make good the damage to the cemetery. I will then be able to get on with my life without people pointing at me as the man who vandalised their church."

"Get on with your life? Surely you can't just forgive and forget, can you, Rafa?"

He looked serious.

"I will never forgive and I will never forget," he said. "I will not set foot in that church again and, as far as I am concerned, I never knew those who masqueraded as my parents for all those years. See, Gareth, they are gone already."

He gestured towards an empty area of wall to the left of the ornamental and rarely used fireplace. It bore the marks of pictures that had once hung there but were now removed. I realised now what had been different about the room when I first entered. Rafa had removed the large black and white framed photographs of an elderly couple whom he had in the past referred to as his parents.

"I intend to have copies made of photographs of my real parents to hang there," he said. "It would be good, also, if I could put a memorial to them somewhere in the village but not in the cemetery. It would be a final insult to put them anywhere belonging to the Church. Apart from that what else can I do? I cannot punish those who did this. They are long gone and if what they say about Heaven and Hell is true then they will, I am sure, be suffering eternal torment for what they did. I cannot bring my parents back to life. Spain today is very different from the country in which those terrible things happened so why should I live my life with a hatred for something that doesn't exist?"

He was absolutely right, of course, but I was nevertheless surprised and impressed by his sensible, logical approach. Others would be eaten up with hatred and a desire for revenge even as they saw the futility of such emotions. I told Rafa how much I admired his attitude. He shook his head with a smile.

"I do not take this attitude for anyone else's benefit so you have no need to admire it, Gareth. I can assure you that my actions are purely selfish. If there is one thing that I have learned in life it is that when somebody harbours hatred for another it is not that other who is destroyed by that hatred; it is the one who feels it. If you feel hatred about something you can't change then you will never find peace. You will live your life suffering but that suffering will not be because of the actions of whoever wronged you but because of the growing cancer of hate inside you. You cannot cure it because you cannot change what has happened and when you have a cancer that you cannot cure what does it do? Eventually it kills you. I don't want to die, Gareth, so I don't want to hate."

"So you do nothing?"

"Not nothing, Gareth. You do what you can but no more. I cannot right the wrongs done to my parents but that doesn't mean I accept them with a stiff upper lip like the Englishman they all say I have become. I showed my emotions, Gareth. I showed them how they had hurt me and what I thought of them for it. I am glad that I did it but now that I have there is nothing more I can do so what is the point of spending the rest of my life destroying myself with hate? I needed to paint on the church wall. I needed to destroy that meaningless memorial. Now I have done those things I can find peace and lead the kind of productive life I am sure my parents would have wished Carlos to lead."

Twenty-five

As I returned home I reflected on the good sense of Rafa and how his way of dealing with those who had injured him compared to Sam Hopkins who, after twenty years, still harboured thoughts of revenge that prevented him from ever finding relief from his pain. I thought of Pauline and how she had faced the same loss by concentrating, like Rafa, on what she could do, assisting others suffering bereavement, rather than focussing like her husband on a target she could never strike. I also thought of Nigel, more affected than his Anglo Saxon emotion free exterior allowed him to show by the tragedy that had befallen his substitute family. My visit to Rafa had stirred up many obvious comparisons with what I had seen and heard in Pentreglo these last few weeks. There was the same theme of tragedy and how the innocent victims deal with it. There was something more as well. I couldn't for the life of me drag what it was to the front of my mind but there was something else I had seen or heard at Rafa's that had put me in mind of recent events. It was that damned déjà vu again. I struggled to force it out from where, tantalisingly out of reach, it stood taunting me from the limits of my conscious mind. Try as I might to maintain the illusion of being in my prime, moments like these were a rapid reminder of my incipient senility.

I had left my phone in the car and when I checked it I noticed a missed call from Lenny. I was about to return it when the phone rang. It was not Lenny. It was Nigel instead.

"Have you spoken to Lenny today?" he asked with what sounded like a note of caution in his voice. I told him about the missed call.

"I suppose I had better give you the news then," he said in a tone that suggested that he would rather have left it to someone else.

"Do you want the good news or the bad news?" he asked cryptically. I elected for the good news. I had had enough of the bad.

"Your client, Beppo is off the hook," he said. "We can meet up as soon as you can get back to this country and sort out a settlement of his claim. The police have dropped the charge of conspiracy to murder against him. They are quite satisfied he had nothing to do with it."

"That's good," I said. "How did they come to that conclusion?"

Nigel coughed. It was a forced cough designed to buy time rather than to clear his throat.

"That's the bad news," he said.

"What do you mean?"

"The reason the police dropped the charge was that they realised that Mervyn Jenkins was not the intended victim of the attack. If he wasn't the intended victim then the fact that the Contemponi family have been after his blood for years is irrelevant."

There was an obvious question to ask and I asked it. Had I thought for a moment the answer would have been just as obvious.

"If MJ wasn't the target who was?"

"The victim," said Nigel carefully, "was the person who was actually attacked. Simple isn't it? We were all complicating matters unnecessarily by assuming there had been a mistake."

"You mean Iris? The man was trying to kill Iris. Why would a hired killer want to kill Iris for goodness' sake?"

"Doesn't that depend on who hired him?" was the cryptic reply. I was about to complain about not having time for riddles when realisation dawned on me. Nigel had said that there was bad news and this was what he was so uncomfortable about telling me. Suddenly I knew what Nigel was saying but my tongue wouldn't let me say it as if not saying it would somehow mean that it wouldn't be so. There was silence between us. I heard Nigel's deep breath as he prepared to break it.

"The police followed up the information you gave them about the transfer of the money in the Gibraltar bank account to Switzerland, the transfer your friend Jenkins set up. They traced the holder of the account from intelligence they had about international criminals. Do you know who the money went to?"

I already knew the answer but I left it to Nigel to say it.

"Milan Jankovic," he said, even taking care to adopt an authentic Slav pronunciation. "Your man Jenkins used the money he had stolen from your colleague Lenny Stevenson in order to pay someone to bump off his wife."

"Why?"

As soon as I asked the question I realised what a stupid one it was. I knew perfectly well why. MJ knew he had to disappear before our investigation was complete and start a new life far away from Pentreglo. He clearly wanted that new life to be with Rita Contemponi. There would be only one obstacle to that new life and MJ was prepared to pay someone to remove that obstacle. Not for him a messy divorce with the risk of his relationship with Rita coming under scrutiny or the prospect of having to share the value of Ty Gwyn with Iris. It was cheaper and easier for MJ to snuff Iris out like a candle at a dinner table once the seduction is complete. Twenty years ago the evil couple had conspired together to remove one barrier to their liaison and now they were conspiring again to remove another. Did MJ really think that Rita Contemponi was worth it?

I had already concluded that I did not know Mervyn Jenkins. The man I thought he was had never existed. I knew he was a philanderer and now regretted the blind eye I had turned to that knowledge. I now knew that his philandering had led him not just to theft from the man who had taken him in and given him a job after retirement. To MJ, Iris, with the almost childlike affection she had given him and the misguided awe in which she had held him, was no more than an inconvenience. The man I thought I knew was my friend, but the man I had now learned about was a cynical selfish coward whom I was ashamed ever to have associated with.

I realised that I didn't know MJ just like I didn't know Rafa, the tormented son of a martyr whom I had mistaken for a small town rural businessman warmly nestled in the bosom of a large and loving family, and just like I didn't know Nigel, a man living with the guilt of a suicide he didn't prevent yet giving the world the impression of being an immaculately mannered robot. Come to think of it do I really know anyone or am I too disinterested in others to ever be able to penetrate the masks that they all seem to wear?

I wasn't really concentrating during the rest of the conversation but I recall telling Nigel that I would book a flight back to Britain in a few days so that we could meet in the company of a newly vindicated Beppo and an insurance company representative with a chequebook in order to resolve a claim in which, if truth be told, I had all but lost interest.

It took me three days until I was able to raise the enthusiasm to contact Pauline and instruct her to set the meeting up. Having done so I was checking flight times when I heard a noise from next door.

"Brenda, for God's sake come in will you. It's unseemly standing there with your tongue hanging out. Leave the man alone." Trevor's irritated tones were instantly recognisable. I was drawn to look out to see what was going on.

Brenda was standing in the middle of her garden dressed, despite the modest temperatures and her own well established middle age, like one of those teenagers who, in the minds of the more archaic members of the judiciary, invite sexual assaults upon themselves every Saturday night. The vest top had abandoned any pretence of containment and the shorts, as tight as they were brief, allowed every ounce of excess flesh on Brenda's ample backside to be mapped out in fine detail.

"I was only offering him a cup of tea," she protested while maintaining a firm stare in the direction of the roof. All I could see of the object of her attention was that he was male but that was something I could have deduced from Brenda's conduct in any event.

"Good morning, Brenda," I shouted down. "I see you're getting the television sorted. It's a lot safer than Trevor doing it."

Brenda's instinctive response as she looked across in my direction was to allow a look of disappointment to cross her features. She clearly resented having to divert her attention from the apparition on the roof towards the vastly inferior example of manhood who was now addressing her. She greeted me politely enough and then returned to her ogling.

"Is that you, Gareth?"

Trevor must have heard my voice and came out to join Brenda in the garden. She was not pleased but Trevor clearly saw the opportunity to curtail his wife's shameless attempts at seducing the TV repair man.

"Come round," he said with more genuine warmth than I could ever recall him displaying before. "We're just about to have some tea. Why don't you and Sue join us? The workman's nearly finished up there haven't you, young man?"

He directed the last remark to the figure on the roof adopting a sufficiently patronising tone to make it clear to his embarrassingly lustful spouse that she was flaunting her ageing body at someone who was manifestly below her in status as well as years. His emphasis on the word "young" was not accidental.

Sue and I presented ourselves next door just as the proprietor of Telstar Electrical and Aerial Services was putting his tools away pretending to be oblivious to the wrinkled eyes that were trained on his muscled frame. Looking at his face I realised that, although well behind Brenda in the longevity stakes, he was older than I had imagined. He seemed to be in his late thirties or early forties but he had clearly looked after himself as evidenced by the torso that was now causing Brenda to drool ever so slightly. His jacket was open and I could see a medallion resting against his tight T-shirt. It was an unusual one, not the normal gold coin or cross. It was shaped like the outline of a heart but inside that outline was what looked like a triangle. Somehow it looked out of place on his unmistakeably masculine torso.

As he looked at us his eyes narrowed a little as if he recognised something. It was strange; I had the same feeling. I had seen him before but I couldn't immediately think where.

"I know you don't I?" he said in a voice that had the unmistakeable sound of the valleys. As I began to reply he stared intently, trawling his memory until the look of puzzlement was replaced by one of realisation and, or so I sensed, a look of sadness as if I had brought back a bad memory for him.

"It's Mr Parry the solicitor isn't it?" he said rather hesitatingly. "You used to work in Pentreglo. That's where I'm from though I've been here twenty years now."

Yes he was certainly familiar and it wasn't only the face. There was something else that was sparking a memory but giving no clues as to what that memory was. It was Sue who realised first who we were talking to.

"It's Terry, isn't it?" she said. "Terry Driscoll."

Terry nodded as I realised where I had seen him before. It was outside the Coroner's Court on the day of the inquest into the death of Debbie Hopkins. He had turned up in his best suit looking pale and puffy eyed to describe how the van he had been driving had left the road and rolled down the mountainside with him and Debbie in it and how he had escaped with comparatively minor injuries while she had been left dying from hers. He never got the chance to give that evidence. He was approaching the door when Sam Hopkins spotted him. Pauline and I needed all our strength to pull Sam, whose impotent rage seemed to impart to him the strength of a bull, away from a visibly shaking Terry. A policeman kept Terry out of the way while Pauline and I tried in vain to reason with Sam. There was nothing we could say to calm him. Eventually another policeman had come into the room to tell us he had spoken to the coroner and persuaded him, in view of the open and shut nature of the case and in order to defuse a nasty situation, to excuse Terry from giving live evidence and to rely instead on the statement he had made to the police. I was grateful for his help and common sense and once we got it through to Sam that Terry Driscoll was no longer in the vicinity his aggression started to wane.

With a shudder I remembered who that policeman had been. Little could I have realised at the time that the tactful and good humoured sergeant who had helped us avoid trouble that day would go on to become first a colleague then a friend and then the man who made me wonder whether I could ever trust anybody again. I had become so focussed on MJ the thief and would be murderer that I had forgotten that he had once been, to all external appearances, a normal and likeable human being.

Brenda served us tea and biscuits from an overpriced and hopelessly impractical set of crockery and then circulated clucking like a preening peahen while the conversation inevitably turned to Pentreglo.

"Have you ever been back?" I asked as I tried desperately to hold on to my teacup by its infuriatingly small handle. Terry shook his head.

"Not to Pentreglo," he said. "Old man Hopkins would have me shot if I went within a mile of the place. I'm not prepared to risk it. I'll come home when he sees sense. I don't suppose there's any sign of that yet is there, Mr Parry?"

I saw the look of expectation in his eyes as he asked the question. I wondered whether to tell him that Nigel, spurred on by his own experiences, had made it his business to direct Sam Hopkins' energy into more constructive channels but I didn't want to give him false hope. Nigel undoubtedly meant well but I was not convinced that he would succeed where others had failed. I shook my head and gave him what was intended to be an understanding smile.

"I don't want to sound callous," he said fingering his medallion nervously as he spoke, "but Sam Hopkins wasn't the only one who lost Debbie. I loved her, Mr Parry, we were going to get married. The way Sam Hopkins carries on you'd think he was the only one with the right to grieve."

I tried to make excuses for Sam pointing out how his life had been damaged far more by his irrational obsession with revenge than Terry's had. This angered Terry.

"Do you really think so?" he said slapping his hand on the table to make his point. That caused Brenda to put her hands protectively over the tea set as Terry answered me with an unmistakable note of bitterness in his voice.

"What about my mum?" he said "She died last year. All through her illness I couldn't visit her because she was afraid of what Sam Hopkins might do if he found out where I was. My dad had to move the funeral to Cardiff so that I could attend safely. How do you think that made my mum and dad feel? More importantly, how do you think I feel not being to see my mum for the last time? As if losing the love of my life wasn't enough."

He gripped the medallion tightly as he continued. "It's been twenty years now but there's never been anyone else. Even after all this time there's not a day when I don't think about Debbie. That's proper grief, Mr Parry, not the self-righteous, self-indulgent posturing of Sam Hopkins. Why does he think that losing his daughter gives him the right to persecute me and my family like this?"

Brenda, taken aback by the show of emotion in one she had so recently regarded as an object of desire, moved diplomatically away as I felt duty bound to defend Sam's position.

"I don't think it's the fact you were driving, Terry, I think he'd have forgiven you that. Everyone makes errors of judgment and I'm sure Sam recognises it."

Actually I wasn't sure at all about that but there was a point I felt I had to make. Terry was playing the victim and making Sam out to be the villain. I didn't think from what I knew that this was entirely fair. I approached the subject as gently as I could.

"I think that what Sam can't forgive is the fact that you left Debbie there. It may not have made a difference but he feels entitled to expect that you would have stayed with her or called for help instead of running away. Sam can't understand why you did that, Terry, and, to be honest with you, nor can I."

"Run away?" Terry looked puzzled.

"Yes, Terry, you ran away didn't you? The police were only called to the scene by the ambulance people and they only knew something had happened when you turned up at A and E with your parents. Don't you think you should have done something for Debbie instead of just thinking of yourself?"

Terry's expression as he looked up at me was a mixture of bewilderment and barely restrained outrage.

"Who the hell told you I ran away?" he demanded. "I only left the scene when the police told me to."

Twenty-six

Terry's expression was a mixture of frustration as he struggled to recall the events of that terrible night and pain as he began to do so.

"To be honest I still don't remember everything and what I do remember isn't too clear," he said. "I got a bump on the head and of course there was the shock of..." His voice trailed away before he could finish the sentence. He took a deep breath and seemed to be mentally counting to ten before continuing.

"We were on our way to Cardiff," he began. "A mate of mine used to sing in the choir and they were giving a Christmas concert there for charity. Debbie wasn't that keen on going but I persuaded her and she got her dad to lend us the van. I can remember Sam making me promise not to have anything to drink after the concert. He was very protective of her was Sam. He always made me promise not to drink when I was driving her and not to speed when she was in the van with me. I used to think he fussed too much but then..." It was obvious what he was thinking and I nodded so that he didn't need to torture himself by saying it.

"Do you remember the accident itself?" I asked as gently as I could.

"Not really," he said with a sigh. "It's all jumbled up like a bad dream, little bits of memory, impressions of things but nothing to hold it all together. I can remember we were laughing about something. I can't for the life of me remember what it was but I just remember Debbie laughing with me. She had a beautiful laugh, nothing self-conscious about it. If she thought something was funny she just let rip. She was like that with everything, no side to her. She displayed her emotions openly where everyone could see them. I loved that about her and, do you know, Mr Parry, I can hear her laugh still when I am alone sometimes and when I do she's with me again. It's only ever for a moment but for that moment we are together and then she's gone again and I am alone."

He smiled wistfully for a few seconds as he recalled those precious moments and then made a visible effort to pull himself together before continuing.

"She was still laughing as it happened. I was laughing with her and then, suddenly, there was something made me swerve. I still remember swerving and thinking I had to brake. I remember that but for the life of me I cannot remember what it was that made me do it. I've searched through my mind, I've relived it but I simply can't remember. I wish I could remember. I wish I could explain it. I wish I could tell myself that it was a stray animal or a fallen rock and that it wasn't my fault. I wish I could be sure that it wasn't just me laughing too much so that I wasn't paying attention to the road and overcorrected when I saw the bend ahead. I wish I could say that but I can't because I can't remember and the fact that I can't remember means I must live the rest of my life with the possibility that I may have killed the person I loved most in the world. I sometimes wish I could believe in an afterlife so that I can look forward to being reunited with Debbie and being told by her that it wasn't my fault but then I think what if it was my fault and what if Debbie won't forgive me? I'd really learn about eternal damnation then wouldn't I, Mr Parry?"

Terry had been waving his hands to express the strength of his feelings but now he let them drop, speaking with a quiet voice from a bowed head.

"I remember having to brake and swerve but that's it. The next thing the van's down the mountain on its side. Debbie's underneath me and she's not moving. I was talking to her trying to get her to answer me telling her she mustn't die and then, when I heard the woman's voice I thought for a moment it was Debbie. For a second I thought she was alright but then I realised. The voice was coming from outside the car and was asking if we were OK."

"A woman's voice?" I was puzzled. There had been no mention of any woman at the inquest.

Terry looked equally puzzled.

"Yes, I am sure about it," he said furrowing his brow as he grasped at what memories he had. "I'm certain I didn't dream it. There was a woman came on the scene after the van left the road. She shouted down to see if we were alright."

"Are you absolutely sure about that and you're not just remembering someone at the hospital, a nurse perhaps, asking you if you were OK?"

Terry at least had the decency to consider that possibility before firmly dismissing it.

"I am absolutely sure, Mr Parry. There must have been a woman there because she must have been the one who called the police. How else would they have known to come out to me?"

I could see what Terry was doing. He was trying to cope with the burden of guilt by rewriting events in his own favour. The police had not been called to the scene by a passer-by or even by Terry himself. They had only found out about the accident when Terry had come to the hospital for treatment for his own injuries later that night. That's why Sam could never forgive Terry. In Sam's book Terry had run out on his daughter in her hour of need and left her to die at the roadside. I can understand perfectly why Terry would want to blot that particular memory out.

Maybe the kindest thing would have been to leave Terry in his state of self-delusion. Nothing would be gained by putting him right and if it made the guilt easier to bear who was I to interfere? Nevertheless, I am one of those infuriating people who cannot bring myself to leave the errors of others uncorrected and the same obsessive pedantry that has me correcting the grammar of strangers before I can stop myself kicked in again.

"You were probably shocked and confused and you'd had a bang on the head," I heard myself saying. "I can understand why you felt you just had to run away but try to see it from Sam's perspective. As he sees it you left his daughter to die. It probably didn't make any difference. You probably couldn't have done anything to save her even if you had called the police or ambulance straight away but you can understand why

Sam thinks she might have lived if they'd have got to her earlier. That's what grief does to people. They don't think straight."

Terry stared at me in disbelief. As he started to answer me the disbelief began to turn to anger and the volume of his voice rose to a shout that caused a sudden jerking movement in Trevor and Brenda who had been listening quietly from the other side of the room.

"That can't be right. It can't be right. There was a copper there. I know there was a copper there. He was the one who told me to go. I wouldn't have left Debbie if he hadn't told me."

My pedantry wouldn't let me leave things alone. I knew it might make Terry more angry and achieve nothing positive but I pressed on. My only concession to him was to make an effort to sound conciliatory and non-judgmental.

"Are you sure about that, Terry?" I asked. "Are you sure it's not the bang on the head messing with your memory? Maybe it's your subconscious trying to stop you beating yourself up with guilt. If you are feeling guilty you don't need to you know. They were all very understanding at the inquest. The Coroner thought you probably took your eyes off the road for a second only and then overcorrected when the car drifted a bit. It's easy enough done. He said that. He also said he understood that in the state you were in you could have wandered away without actually consciously intending to abandon Debbie. He put it down to shock. Nobody blamed you, Terry."

That was a lie. Sam blamed Terry but I didn't see how stating that obvious fact would help. Terry was clutching at the most insubstantial of straws in an effort to fight enemies that, apart from Sam, did not exist. Maybe there's nothing wrong with that. Maybe only an irritating hair splitter like me would try to wave the unwelcome truth in the face of this troubled man but wave it I had. I had heard the evidence at the inquest and I knew the truth. There had been no policeman at the scene and no passer-by, female or otherwise. They were at best the products of post-concussion hallucinations of the type often experienced alongside traumatic events. At worst they were a lie that Terry had told himself so many times over the years that he now believed it and derived comfort from it. The truth was not so easy to face. Terry had, for good reason or bad, wandered away from the scene. He had left Debbie Hopkins dead or dying in the car where she was found, an hour later, by the ambulance crew. They had only been alerted by Terry's minor injuries when he presented himself at hospital for treatment. Sam would never forgive that act but, perhaps, with Nigel's help, he could learn to live with it. At the same time perhaps I could help Terry live with it instead of seeking refuge in fantasy.

In fairness to Terry he thought about my words instead of simply snapping back at me. There was a period of silence broken only by the sound of Brenda clearing up the tea set around us as if the conversation wasn't taking place. Eventually, carefully and emphatically, Terry shook his head. When he spoke it was slowly and clearly with each word stressed as if it had been the result of a long process of planning.

"If there was no copper there how did I get out of the van and if there was no woman there who called the copper?" He looked up at me. There was no aggression in his eyes. He was genuinely puzzled.

"Do you actually remember getting out of the van?" I asked. Terry started to shake his head and I was about to seize on that when he explained.

"I don't actually remember getting out of the van but I do remember being trapped and I do remember seeing a man at the window of the van asking if I could move. He had a uniform on, I am sure it was a police uniform."

Terry continued in the same careful monotone. "The van rolled over as it went down the mountainside. It got buckled on the way. It ended up passenger side down. I was lying on Debbie. The roof had buckled over her so I couldn't move her. I reached up to open my door but I couldn't push it hard enough without pushing down on Debbie and hurting her more. I remember shouting to the copper to pull the door from the outside. I don't know what happened next but the next thing I do remember is being outside the van. I remember my legs were shaking so I couldn't stand. The copper was holding me up."

He jumped slightly as he realised the significance of that memory.

"He was holding me up, Mr Parry. How could he hold me up if he wasn't there?"

Terry wasn't asking a rhetorical question. He was troubled and he genuinely wanted an answer. As I looked at him I found no reason to doubt his sincerity. Plenty of people have lied to me in the past, even those who swear by everything they treasure that they are telling the truth. It was part of my job as a solicitor to be lied to and to be lied to in the most superficially convincing ways. I believe I have learned how to see through the assurances and the shows of emotion with which most liars accompany their deceptions. I think I know it when I am listening to a liar but as I listened to Terry Driscoll, confusion in his eyes, his hands grasping his medallion for comfort I felt that I was in the company of one who was trying to be as frank with me as his traumatised memory permitted. I didn't know whether there had been a policeman or anyone else at the scene while Terry was still in the van but what I was now convinced of was that this was what he genuinely believed. The trouble was that his memory didn't accord with the facts as I knew them. After a lifetime plying my trade in the courts it's difficult to break the habit and I found myself switching into cross examination mode.

"Why was there no mention of this at the inquest? There was no mention of any copper at the scene and no eye witnesses. The first copper only got there because he followed the ambulance. That's what was said at the inquest."

"I wasn't at the inquest," was the curt reply. Terry was quite right but that wasn't the point I was making.

"There was nothing about it in your statement either. No mention of a copper, no mention of any woman. How do you explain that, Terry?"

"My statement?" Terry looked puzzled again "What statement? I didn't make any statement did I?" Once again the tone was questioning rather than argumentative.

"I mean the statement you gave to the police. From what I remember you gave it about a week or so after the accident."

I couldn't remember much about the inquest but an impression that stayed with me was that Terry's statement had been particularly brief and nonspecific. Had he mentioned anyone else on the scene I am sure I would have remembered it. I even remember Sam Hopkins commenting in the bitterest of terms on the fact that Terry had run away from the inquest just as he had run away from the scene and couldn't even be bothered to make a proper statement. I remember that at the time I had to concede that he had a point. I wouldn't have done so if there had been any suggestion in any of the evidence that Terry had spoken to the police before leaving the scene. I looked at Terry focussing on his eyes. I've noticed how, when they are trying to mislead me, my clients would always avoid looking into my eyes. There was no such reaction from Terry. He held my gaze and nodded slowly.

"I think I know what you're talking about now," he said. "When you mentioned a statement I thought you were talking about one on the night. They didn't take a statement from me then. With Sam Hopkins having a go at me like he was at the hospital they told me to get home as soon as the doctor finished with me. I didn't need telling twice. They said they'd call round later for a statement. I was beginning to think they had forgotten about it when the copper turned up at the door just before Christmas. It was the…"

He paused, considering the implications of what he had been about to say, and then continued in a more confident voice.

"It was the same copper who I'd seen on the night by the van, the one who helped me out. It was the same one who came to my house just before Christmas for a statement. I remembered him. Doesn't that prove it, Mr Parry? If I hadn't seen him by the van how did I recognise him when he came to the house?"

Twenty-seven

I felt that I was losing the argument but, like the thick skinned lawyer I had been, I pressed on.

"Maybe you didn't recognise him. Maybe you saw him for the first time when he came for the statement or maybe you'd seen him at the hospital and you imagined that he had been by the van when you were trying to reconstruct things in your mind. People often do that after accidents. Concussion does funny things to you."

Terry wasn't convinced and, to be truthful, nor was I. He shrugged his shoulders, once again demonstrating puzzlement rather than aggression.

"You may be right, Mr Parry, but I don't think so. It was so real."

He shrugged his shoulders again and continued to explain. "The copper didn't stay long. He was a decent bloke, very sympathetic. He advised me to steer clear of Sam Hopkins and then said he needed a statement just for the record. He said they weren't going to prosecute me so a short statement just saying that I remembered swerving but nothing else was all that was needed. That was a relief to me obviously. He reckoned there must have been a stray sheep on the road and he didn't seem to be blaming me. Thinking about it he's probably right about the sheep. You know what a problem they used to be on that road."

"Still are a problem," I found myself saying before returning to my cross examination.

"Why didn't your statement mention him being at the scene?" I asked, searching out his eyes again. He didn't blink.

"Why should I mention it? He was there. If he thought it important he'd have put it in."

A fair answer. I tried another question.

"What about the woman? Didn't you mention her? She could have been a vital witness."

The answer came straight back at me. "He must have known about her. She must have been the one who called him. If he thought she was a vital witness he didn't need me to tell him about her."

Another fair answer. I gave up the cross examination. I was now convinced that Terry was telling me the truth as he saw it. This wasn't the exercise in self-justification that I had originally imagined. I was satisfied with Terry's explanation for the absence of relevant detail in the statement. I have seen it countless times before – lazy police officers who can't be bothered to take proper statements from witnesses. They hate paperwork and just want to get it completed with the minimum of effort. The less detail they included in the statement the less investigation they would have to carry out. They were looking for simple cases and wouldn't let anything creep into the witness statements that might complicate matters. They would decide what they wanted the statements to say and wouldn't then let the poor witness get a word in edgeways. With a large measure of bonhomie and an occasional touch of irritability they would slap down any attempt by the supposed maker of the statement to say what he wanted to say in the words he wanted to use.

I have lost count of the number of times I have had presented to me statements bearing no resemblance whatsoever to the speaking style of the person whose name they bore. I've seen statements from university professors littered with the kind of grammatical errors that a probationary constable might make. I have seen statements written in standard vernacular English bearing the names of witnesses who, when they turn up in court, are seen to be non-native English speakers who struggle with the most basic of sentences.

The consequences of this sloppy attitude can be far reaching. If some of those retired army officers or Home Counties residents who flood the letters pages of the right wing press with hysterical rants about criminals walking free from courts actually knew how many seemingly perverse acquittals resulted from careless statement taking they'd be justified in calling themselves "Disgusted" or "Outraged". More worryingly for me is the thought that there will be innocent people languishing in jail because a witness wasn't allowed to tell the full story in his own words when he made his statement to the police.

Although lawyers like to cultivate the image of themselves as super sharp inquisitors breaking down obstinate and dishonest witnesses with a few perceptive questions the truth is more mundane. As any lawyer would tell you in one of those rare moments of frankness, the most potent weapon in any advocate's armoury is the ability to spot the inevitable products of lazy police work.

"Why didn't you say that in your statement to the police?" is a question that every lawyer knows is likely to reap dividends when put to a vital but inexperienced (and probably terrified) witness. The standard reply of "Nobody asked me" or "I'm sure I did but he mustn't have written it down," is then greeted with a world weary and sceptical smile directed by the questioner to the bench or the jury box where it is greeted by an almost imperceptible shake of the head or roll of the eyes that says that the unfortunate individual in the witness box might as well be reciting nursery rhymes for all the attention that will be paid to his evidence. This signals the steady descent of the witness from a usually firm and confident character to a self-doubting, quivering jelly who, in his blind panic will readily agree with anything suggested to him.

The path followed in such a cross examination is a well-trodden one. As soon as the slightest discrepancy between the evidence of the witness and his carelessly taken statement is exposed the questioner indignantly accuses the poor witness of misleading the court. The witness is so shocked as to forget everything except surviving the cross examination without being hauled off in chains for contempt of court. In a panicked voice that convinces the jury that he has something to hide he firmly denies the suggestion. This only succeeds in racking up the indignation in the voice of the questioner.

"So you are saying that the police officer is lying are you?" he will say as if it were the first time that he had ever heard such a monstrous suggestion in a court. The witness, if still able to speak, will then assure the questioner that he is making no such allegation.

"So if he's not lying you must be," will be the triumphant conclusion put by the questioner. Faced with that false choice and in a complete state of panic it is surprising how many witnesses cave in and in a frantic effort to make it all end, agree with that proposition. Whether the witness does so or not doesn't actually matter. The next stage of the cross examination is always the same. In a kindly voice, contrasting sharply to his previous hectoring tone the questioner will invite the witness to consider whether maybe he is mistaken in what he said with no intention to deliberately mislead the court. That invitation will be seen by the witness in much the same way as a lifebelt is seen by a drowning man and accepted just as readily. The remainder of the cross examination will then proceed far more amicably as every important part of the witness' evidence is repeated to him and he agrees that he might be mistaken about it. I have no doubt that, in the case of some of the more traumatised witnesses, they would agree, if it were put to them at this stage, that they may possibly have been mistaken when, at the start of their evidence, they told the court their full name.

So it is that every day in courts up and down the country perfectly honest and observant witnesses are taken down that route to being treated, if they are lucky, as idiots and, if they are not, as unprincipled liars. All of this is because police officers, looking for an easy life, can't be bothered to take proper witness statements.

Throughout my conversation with Terry I was developing the nagging feeling that perhaps this was what had happened to him. That feeling was now hardening into a firm belief. A lazy policeman determined to produce an oversimplified statement that accounted for Debbie Hopkins' death without the need for tedious investigation had given birth to the understandable but quite possibly incorrect belief of Sam Hopkins that Terry Driscoll had abandoned his dying daughter. From that belief it was only a short step to Sam's stubborn conviction that it was Terry rather than, for example, a stray sheep who was responsible for the loss that had destroyed him so completely. That conviction had in turn fuelled the twenty year search for vengeance that had taken over the being of Sam Hopkins and the twenty year exile of the man who now plied his trade among the expats of southern Spain as Telstar Electrical and Aerial Services.

I knew I couldn't leave it there. Nigel had made it his mission to bring Sam back to the land of reality. I had seen how important it was to him. Anything that brought out a display of human emotion in a calculating iceberg like Nigel had to be important to him. Now I knew something that could help him and I knew I had to use it. Nigel is a decent bloke for all his boarding school airs. When I needed his help in Liverpool, at a time when I had known him for only a day, he had given me that help. I could now do something to repay him. First I had to make sure the whole thing wasn't going to backfire on me. There was still a question I had to ask so that I could be sure. I adopted a sufficiently grave tone to leave Terry in no doubt about the importance of that question.

"Can you look me in the eye, Terry, and swear to me you didn't just walk away from Debbie, for whatever reason good or bad, after the accident? If you did I'm not going to blame you but I need to know."

Terry looked me straight in the eye and, before replying, lifted the medallion to his lips and kissed it. Then he gave me the assurance I needed.

"Mr Parry," he said, "I promise you on Debbie's grave that I did not just walk away from her. I would never walk away from her. I can't even walk away from her now after twenty years. She's still with me every second of my life and she will still be with me until the day it ends and we are together for ever."

He gazed lovingly at the medallion as he lowered it. I could see tears flowing down his sun tanned cheeks as he started to explain.

"When I got out of the car we tried to move Debbie but she was trapped. The copper said we'd need the Fire Service and an ambulance. He said he'd call them on his car radio. I said

I'd wait with him for them to arrive but he told me not to. He said I should walk to the phone box at the edge of the village and get a taxi from there to the hospital. He told me I needed treatment but it would slow things down if the ambulance had to break off from treating Debbie so as to take me to hospital. I know that sounds stupid now but at the time it made sense. I didn't want to do anything to slow down Debbie being saved. I said to the copper that I was OK and would wait for treatment but he insisted I left. He said I'd get in the way but I still said I wanted to stay. Then he changed his tack. He said that if I was still there when more police arrived they would have to arrest me on suspicion of dangerous driving and lock me up until I could be put before the court on the Monday. That scared me. I wasn't worried about myself but I wanted to be there at Debbie's bedside and I couldn't do that if I was locked up. It was a risk I couldn't take so I said I'd go. He said he'd square it with the other coppers to make sure I wasn't arrested and I should say nothing to them about the accident. It seemed sensible at the time so I left. I never should have done that but I wasn't thinking straight. I didn't call a taxi, I just wanted to walk. I didn't want to talk to anyone else, I just wanted to get home to my mum and dad and tell them all about it. I wanted them with me at the hospital. When I got home they took me straight there. It was weird. Nobody seemed to know where Debbie was when I asked to see her. When I told the doctor what had happened they put me in a cubicle and I was still there when Sam Hopkins arrived. I heard his voice and went out to see him and that's when he took off on me. A couple of coppers rescued me. They gave me a breath test and when that was negative they told me to get off home straight after treatment. They also told me Debbie was dead so there was nothing to wait around for. I thought when they didn't arrest me that the first copper must have spoken to them like he said he would. That's what happened, Mr Parry. I swear it was."

I gave Terry a moment to compose himself. His voice had been breaking as he revived the memory and had been punctuated by sobs particularly as he recalled being told that Debbie had been killed. I then asked him, trying not to appear too pushy, whether he wanted to me to tell that to Sam Hopkins. I explained how Sam's anger had been caused by a misunderstanding of what actually had happened and that it might do both of them good if that misunderstanding were cleared up. Terry started to reply.

"But I've…" He then seemed to think better of it and stopped himself. Eventually, he spoke, asking me how I thought Sam would react. I told him I didn't know, which was no more than the truth.

"I'm going to Pentreglo for a few days and I can test the water for you if you like. That's, of course, if you do want to make your peace with Sam Hopkins. Do you want that, Terry?"

"Of course I do," he said quickly. "Sam Hopkins and I have too much in common even after all this time. Both of us lost the dearest thing in our lives that night and neither of us has been able to move on properly. We should be able to share our memories and help each other to make sense of it all. Besides, I want to see Pentreglo again. It's where I grew up and where all my happy memories of Debbie are. That's why…"

His voice tailed off again as, once again, he thought better of saying what he was thinking.

I heard Trevor coughing rudely behind me. He had clearly decided that Terry had outstayed his welcome while Brenda, having decided that there was no prospect of drawing out Terry's flirtatious side, seemed to have lost interest and had even covered some of the vast expanse of flesh that she had previously exhibited for his benefit.

"TV working alright now?" asked Trevor pointedly.

Terry's expression changed as his mind moved from a twenty-year-old tragedy to a current malfunctioning TV set.

"Should be fine now," said Terry as he jumped up to demonstrate. Trevor's ghosts seemed to have been exorcised and I wondered whether the more tangible ghosts haunting Terry and Sam could be disposed of as easily. Meanwhile, Trevor allowed himself a brief grunt which was as close as Terry was going to get to an expression of gratitude.

Terry wrote out his bill and handed it to Trevor who spent a full minute staring at it in the hope that it might miraculously shrivel if subjected to sufficient scrutiny. When that failed he pulled out his wallet and counted the notes out on the table accompanying each one with a pained sigh as if they were his children whom he was giving up into slavery.

Before Terry left I took his contact details and promised to get in touch once I had spoken to Sam. At least if I could right this twenty-year-old wrong I would have achieved something positive from the trip to Pentreglo. I wasn't looking forward to it particularly. Any satisfaction I would derive from securing proper compensation for Beppo on behalf of his dead father would be more than outweighed by having to accept the reality that could not be ignored at such close quarters – that Mervyn Jenkins, whom I once called my friend was a corrupt copper who had gone on to be a thief and a would be murderer.

IV

THE CORONATION COACH

Twenty-eight

"Well!" I demanded. "Which are we?"

The poor girl behind the check in desk looked confused as I pressed the question. Sue had more sense than to attempt to explain. She studiously rummaged in her hand luggage, unconvincingly pretending that she hadn't heard me. She knew me too well to encourage me. As years of experience had taught her I was in one of my awkward moods and when in such moods I am best ignored. If only the girl at the check in desk had known me as well she would never have made the remark that she had. Surveying the passengers sauntering up to the check in desk at the airport and, wanting nothing more than to be friendly, she had commented that they were arriving in dribs and drabs. That was enough to set me off and, pedantic as ever, I had demanded to know whether we were a drib or a drab. Of course it was a matter of complete unimportance to me. I have no idea of the difference between a drib and a drab. I don't know whether one aspires to be a drib or is ostracised if labelled a drab. Nobody save for the saddest of woolly jumper wearing, bushy beard sporting, pub quiz winning bores knows where the expression comes from and in all probability nobody cares. It's just that when I am feeling frustrated with life it's my natural defence mechanism to pounce on a harmless grammatical error, ambiguity or cliché and persist tediously in exposing it long after such exposure has, if it ever was funny or clever, ceased to be so.

There was the time when Sue and I were about to drive onto a car ferry. I was feeling distinctly at odds with mankind after a stressful drive to the port so that when I saw the sign that said "Please use all lanes" that gave me my chance. Before Sue could stop me I was asking the bemused young man directing the traffic whether I should go up and down each lane in turn or cross them diagonally on my way to the boat. Even after an embarrassed Sue apologised for my "little joke" I was still unrepentantly muttering that if they meant "any lane" they should say so. Another favourite target of mine is that mistranslation one often sees next to lifts in Spanish hotels. As we approach the lift I can hear a sharp intake of breath from Sue who is wearily aware of what comes next. I come to a halt, point at the sign and loudly demand that we use the stairs. If anyone is ill advised enough to ask me why I triumphantly point to the sign that, underneath the perfectly correct Spanish, reads in English "Do not use the lift in case of fire".

"I'm not going to be responsible for the hotel going up in smoke," I declare self-righteously to pitying looks from strangers and a low groan from my long suffering wife. I sometimes annoy people sufficiently for them to call me names. "You're the kind of person who worries about misplaced apostrophes" they might say and, of course, they are absolutely right. I worry incessantly about misplaced apostrophes and never let one go without comment. I'm the same with people who misuse the word "literally".

I think of my habit as a pretty harmless if somewhat irritating way of coping with all those challenges that life throws at me. Surely it's a better way of reacting to the vicissitudes of human existence than beating my wife or voting UKIP. By behaving occasionally in a childish manner I can pretend for a few moments that I am still a young man with life's multitude of experiences still to unfold before me. I can forget that in reality I am closer to being an ageing, greying and declining being who is acutely aware in his more serious moments that the only new experiences I am likely to be visited by in the future are dementia, dependency and ultimately death.

I have lived since completion of my thirtieth year in fear of the inevitable arrival of that day when my marbles gently roll away from me never to return.

The most frightening aspect of that process to my mind is the fact that when it happens I will be the last one to realise it. For all I know it happened years ago but I like to practise on myself the deception that while I can still occasionally adopt the persona of an intolerant but sharp witted grammar Nazi I still have the mental acuity of a twenty-year-old. Those who associate increasingly curmudgeonly behaviour in others with the ageing process are only half right. It is true enough that it tends to appear in and after middle age but far from being a sign of deteriorating mental abilities it is more often than not a desperate reversion to the ready wit of youth in a Canute-like stand against onrushing senility.

It is, I am sure, that fear of ageing that causes me, for example, to overreact rudely to that standard greeting of the modern shop assistant who spots a customer who isn't actually buying anything. They all say "are you alright there?" It's not intended to be a profound comment but merely a substitute for a greeting. Nevertheless, it makes me all defensive as I demand to know why she assumes that because I am standing still in the middle of her shop I am about to croak at any moment. Do I look so frail that she equates my lack of movement with my imminent demise?

I was feeling particularly old today. We all forget names or numbers from time to time or remember that there was something important that we had to do without being able to recall what it was. To those of us who are the wrong side of sixty, however, such routine lapses become the cause of blind panic lest they are the heralds of that final descent into mental deterioration. Of course, the more distressed I become at a forgotten name or the fact that I have just climbed the stairs with not the faintest idea why I did so the less likely I am to think calmly and the greater the distress becomes. It's at moments like that when I am at my most annoyingly pedantic and today was one of those moments.

I had spent a lot of time reflecting on what I had observed during my relatively brief return to Spain. I had thought of Paco who had provided the means whereby the true character of my former friend, Mervyn Jenkins had been revealed. I thought of Rafa who had found all the smug certainties of his life being torn away from him yet was able to reconcile himself to it all with a few acts of frenzied vandalism. I thought of Sam Hopkins and Terry Driscoll separated by a misunderstanding that had grown into bitterness and fear. Yet through all those musings I was aware of something else. The feeling returned to me every time I thought of my recent experiences. They had taught me something important but for the life of me I could not bring to my conscious mind what it was. There was a pattern to all I had seen, a pattern that would provide the answers to the questions that were troubling me. The problem was that I could not see that pattern and worse still I could not even identify the questions it would answer. I had that feeling that often accompanies the most subtle of nightmares – something was worrying me but I could not recognise what it was.

I felt as I used to feel as a child surveying the pieces of a new jigsaw. Everything was there and, if put together properly, it would reveal the full picture but at this precise moment all I had was a collection of jumbled pieces the importance of which was yet to become clear. I had loved jigsaws as a child. I remember one in particular. Like all children born on the cusp of the 1940s and 1950s I had been given a jigsaw of the 1953 Coronation in what in my case was an ultimately doomed attempt by my doting and ultra-patriotic Uncle Stanley to instil in me a love of tradition and monarchy. The centrepiece was the coronation coach with all its intricate detail. That was the part you did first. Once the coach was in position it became an easier task to position the Horse Guards with their plumed helmets who rode beside the coach and the bearskin clad guardsmen who lined the route. If only I could now understand how the nagging thoughts that were lurking in my mind fitted together to show me the big picture, the coronation coach, I would surely be able to work out rest. The trouble was that, unlike a jigsaw, there was no box with a picture on it to guide me.

I could feel myself frowning as I took my seat on the plane and watched my fellow passengers seemingly incapable of reading the row numbers and then shoehorning their oversize hand luggage into the overhead lockers. I allowed myself a mental tut of disapproval as I noticed that one of the TV screens failed to drop with the others giving the cabin, to my jaundiced eye, a lopsided appearance like a mouth with a missing tooth. I watched a bored looking stewardess mechanistically donning a demonstration lifejacket for the benefit of an audience as unreceptive as in one of those long gone northern music halls of whom old style comedians still speak. I was simply itching for something to complain about, so frustrated was I by my failing powers of recall and their unsubtle message to me that my dotage was nigh.

"Good evening, ladies and gentlemen. On behalf of Captain Billy Rawlings and his crew I would like to welcome you..." I heard no more of the patronisingly delivered message that was issuing forth from the public address system. Billy Rawlings? What sort of a name was that for a man into whose care I and over a hundred others had delivered ourselves for the duration of the flight? I was quite happy to be flown by a William. Such a name conveyed sufficient gravitas to inspire confidence that our pilot wouldn't attempt the aeronautical equivalent of a handbrake turn whilst conveying us to our destination. Billy, however, was a different proposition altogether. It evoked the image of a mischievous little boy, the type who would ride his bike over your flower beds while his mother smiled indulgently or a teenage joyrider looking for someone to race. In my depths of grumpiness I concluded that any captain who would permit his crew to adopt the degree of familiarity that allows them to refer to him as "Billy" clearly cared nothing for his dignity and, I inferred by an inescapable process of logic, cared nothing for the safety and comfort of those he was flying.

It struck me that Billy was one of those names like Beppe or Paco that started with a different letter from their real initial. How many ignoramuses, I pondered intemperately, would refer to him as Captain B. Rawlings rather than Captain W. Rawlings? I was asking myself this question and staring at the undescended TV screen when the pattern presented itself to me. I saw the coronation coach even if I hadn't yet found the Horse Guards. In a flash I remembered the questions that had been nagging at me and I suspected I had the answers. I was like Archimedes as the principle of displacement appeared before him, except of course for being fully clothed and considerably dryer. I had the firm sensation that matters were not as straightforward as I had believed and I knew that Nigel and I had some further enquiries to make.

Suddenly I felt liberated. I was not senile after all. I was still capable of reason and deduction. Smiling to myself at my cleverness I did what I always did when aboard an aeroplane. I fell into a deep sleep before we had even reached the end of the runway. I remained deeply asleep with a self-satisfied smile on my face until awoken by the wheels hitting the rain sodden runway as we landed. Contrary to my fears Billy Rawlings had brought us home safely. As I awoke I knew I should be pleased with myself for solving the mystery but then horror struck – I had forgotten what it was that I had remembered!

It was late on Saturday night when we arrived at my son Martin's house. Jake, my grandson, was already asleep in bed so I would have to delay seeing him until the next morning. Despite the fact that Cardiff, as always in early February, was looking cold and unwelcoming it would feel worth leaving the milder climes of Spain to see Jake's smiling face when he realised that Grandma and Grandad were back. That's the beauty of children. Whatever adults do to you or think of you, however false their smiles, compliments or declarations of loyalty you can always depend on a child to tell you in his face the truth of what he thinks of you. To be the recipient of the type of simple, non-judgmental love that only children are capable of makes all of life's other achievements fade into obscurity in comparison.

I was feeling particularly frustrated at my latest display of mental ineptitude but I resolved to put it out of my mind until Monday. I was due to meet Nigel then and I hoped that if I relaxed I would by then have remembered what I had forgotten remembering. In the meantime I would confine myself to being a father and grandfather. I would do the normal things that normal people did when visiting their family. I would play with Jake, find out how Martin was doing at work, nodding sagely as he descended into technical jargon, compliment Charmaine, my daughter-in-law, on her cooking and drift reflectively over our shared memories in front of the fire. I would cast from my mind thoughts of corrupt coppers, thieving employees and all the other glimpses into the nastier side of life that I had experienced since Christmas. I told myself that, after all, none of it was my creation and none of it was my problem. I didn't fix an identification parade to frame an innocent man any more than I stole money from a trust fund, drove a car off a mountain or snatched a new born child from his mother's side in the name of political purity. Nothing I could have done would have changed any of that so why was I letting other people's misdeeds and other people's traumas monopolise my thoughts? I suppose it's because that's the way I am. I simply can't avoid making other people's problems my own. Some may call that a virtue but I call it a curse. I have great empathy with the Good Samaritan. People praise him and hold him up as an example of a saintly character motivated only by love of his fellow man. I know better. He was in truth a miserable wretch who would have liked nothing better than to have the ability to pass by on the other side but was blighted by this uncontrollable impulse to get involved. Like the alcoholic who cannot walk past a pub without feeling drawn through its doors he, like me, could not see anyone else's business without sticking his nose in it.

I long to be the kind of person that Thatcher would have wanted me to be, ruthless and uncaring, seeing only where my personal advantage lay. My life would undoubtedly have been less complicated and materially richer if I had achieved that lofty state but I cannot change who I am. At the drop of a hat I assume the burdens of the world. When I was working I would become far more nervous at the outcome of trials than my clients whose liberty or livelihood depended on them. Whenever I lost a case I would subject myself to a ruthless examination to ensure that there was nothing more I could have done and not simply settle for "you win some you lose some" or Stan's irritating "It's only a game". That is how I am, it is how I have always been and I know it is how I will always be. That's why whatever the temptation to turn up on Monday, accept the offer of compensation on behalf of Beppo and cast the whole business out of my mind, I knew that I would not rest until I had reached the truth.

Bearing in mind my inability to switch off I made a pretty fair attempt to do so on the Sunday. Jake helped enormously. As soon as he saw me he started to jump around like a mad thing and demanded that, despite the near Arctic temperature, I take him to the park. I spent a fulfilling hour freezing to the spot as I watched him, oblivious to the weather, launching himself onto the play equipment. I complied with his entreaties to push him higher and higher on the swing and faster and faster on the roundabout. When I dragged him away from those I found myself chasing a football as Jake, and I, entered a fantasy world where Cardiff City, with our help, were humiliating the top teams of Europe as they progressed through the Champions League.

By the time we had finished I was breathless but exhilarated. So completely had Jake monopolised my attention that thoughts of Beppo, MJ and all the others whose affairs I had become entangled with had moved to the back of my mind. When Martin suggested a pub lunch I felt I had deserved it and readily agreed. Jake was deposited with his doting grandmother, who found his company infinitely more intoxicating than anything the Red Lion had to offer, and Martin and I set off to enjoy that experience which every father of sons looks forward to, being bought a pint by one of them.

Martin and I were sitting in the corner feeling at peace with the world. The beer was going down easily and satisfyingly, the food was surprisingly tasty and the roaring fire was keeping the bite of a British winter at bay. I allowed Martin to lead the conversation. I feared that if I initiated talk on any subject it would end up with me telling him of the ordeal of Rafa, the bitterness of Sam Hopkins or, even worse the treachery of Mervyn Jenkins. He spoke of his work, of Jake's progress at school and other such easy subjects. Before we knew it the clock was showing four o'clock and we had promised to be home by three. We decided, in the way you do when in the welcoming embrace of a good pub, that the only thing for it was one last pint. Martin insisted on paying; I have obviously brought him up well. He went off to the bar and I was idly contemplating the beer mat when I heard my name being called. The voice was familiar to me but it was not one I wanted to hear. I ignored it but it didn't go away. The voice continued to call my name and I was conscious of its owner walking towards me.

"Gareth," he said as he drew near, "I have to talk to you. I'm in a desperate position."

I had no reason to doubt that the man now standing over me was in a desperate position. However, so far as I was concerned it was a position entirely of his own making and I felt insulted that he should even contemplate that I would provide him with a sympathetic ear. I made a point of turning my head away in an exaggerated manner to signify that his approach was unwelcome. I felt an idiot as soon as I did it. I am not one for theatrical gestures and realised how ridiculous I must have looked.

"Gareth," he persisted. "You've helped me in the past. I know you won't turn your back on me now. You're too good a friend for that. I need your help and I know you won't let me down when you hear what I have to say."

The trouble was that he was right. I should have walked out on him but a voice inside me was telling me that I wasn't going to do so. My Good Samaritan complex was about to take over me again. I tried to rationalise what I was about to do by telling myself that maybe I could gain some advantage from the situation by having him confirm my suspicions or even jog my memory as to the great insight I had experienced on the plane. I was lying to myself. I had been asked for help and it is my lot in life to help those who ask me to whether I want to or not. I needed time to think, though, and I didn't want to involve Martin who I could see returning to the table. Against my better judgment I heard myself saying.

"OK, MJ, I'll listen to what you want to say but not now. I'll call round at seven o'clock and we can talk then in private."

Twenty-nine

As I approached the front door of Ty Gwyn I asked myself why I was there. What was the point of listening to the pathetic self-justification and transparent lies that I was going to hear? Why did I need to pretend that I cared about what was to become of the man I was going to meet? Whatever it was would be richly deserved and I had neither the ability nor the inclination to change any of it. The answer to my rhetorical questions was all too obvious. It was that old vice of mine that had brought me here, the inability to keep out of other people's affairs, the morbid desire to help everyone I come across, no matter how unworthy of such help they might be. Who knows, someone might put my name forward for a sainthood at this rate – either that or have me committed for being so naively trusting of everyone as to be dangerous to be let out unaccompanied!

I justified my actions to myself by thinking back to my meeting with Terry Driscoll. I had been ready for the last twenty years to write him off as a coward who deserved to be shunned even if not to be subjected to the irrational obsessions of Sam Hopkins. I had listened to what he had to say and my opinion had changed. Perhaps I could end up the same way with MJ. Maybe I would start to understand what drove him to steal money from innocent children and use it to try to have his wife bumped off. I only had to say it to myself to realise how stupid it sounded. Try as I might to rationalise it there was no hiding from the fact that what I was doing was at best a waste of time and at worst positively dangerous. I was leaving myself open to being compromised over the missing money, the murder plot and maybe even the very case that had got me involved in the first place, the framing of Giuseppe Contemponi. What a fool I am! What a gullible, naïve, soft hearted fool!

MJ opened the door before I could even ring the bell, thus saving me from agonising further over whether to do so. It was too late to turn away now. The house smelt like I imagine buildings smell before a royal visit, fresh paint and detergent. MJ explained as he ushered me through the hall.

"We have been getting the house ready for Iris' return. I've had Sam Hopkins helping me. I thought I'd surprise her by doing all the jobs she's been on about for years. Everything's had a fresh coat of paint and Pauline volunteered to do the cleaning. Meanwhile I've got rid of the old coal fire and Sam's rewired everywhere and added built in reading lights over the bed. She loves reading in bed does Iris but those old bedside lamps were such a nuisance even though one of them probably saved her life."

I couldn't believe my ears. MJ had hired a hit man to kill his wife, let her be accused of murder and now here he was talking as if it all had nothing to do with him. As he continued it got worse.

"She's not been back to the house since she was arrested," he said. "After all she's been through I wanted her return home to be something special but no sooner does she have her bail conditions removed to allow her to come home but I have bail conditions put on me so I can't stay here with her. As soon as we finish here I'm off to my nephew's house in Cardiff where I've got to sleep every night until this ridiculous business is over. I'm not even allowed to communicate with Iris. Imagine that, Gareth, I can't even speak to my own wife!"

There was genuine outrage in his voice. I was overwhelmed by the arrogance of the man. He was complaining because he was being kept apart from someone he had tried to have killed. What the hell did he expect? Undaunted, he carried on.

"Nev Powell actually arrested me the other day. Do you believe that? He actually arrested me and told me I was suspected of conspiring to kill Iris. Fair dos to him, though, he was pretty decent about it and seemed almost apologetic. I'm sure he didn't want to do it but he obviously had orders from above. Anyway he didn't charge me then and there because, as he said, he'd have had to keep me in custody if he charged me. Instead he said he had further enquiries to make and that allowed him to release me on bail for the time being. The trouble is that he had to make it a condition of the bail that I kept away from Iris. It's bloody crazy isn't it?"

It crossed my mind that Nev Powell had indeed been particularly generous to MJ to an extent that wouldn't have been the case had he not been an ex copper. Anyone else would have been charged straight away and remanded in custody. Nevertheless, MJ didn't seem to appreciate the favour Nev had done him and was actually angry at bail conditions designed to ensure that he didn't finish off the job which Milan Jankovic had so ineffectively started. It was time, I thought, to bring the conversation back into the realms of reality.

"What do you want me to do, MJ?" I asked. I suspected I knew the answer and I was not disappointed.

"I need your help," he said. "They say I was behind the bloke who tried to kill Iris. They say I hired him so I could run off with another woman. They seriously think I'm so keen to be with her that I'd hire someone to kill Iris."

He had injected a sufficient degree of incredulity into his voice for me to reflect that if, as I had been sure, he wasn't telling the truth, he had missed his vocation as an actor or in some profession that requires the telling of lies convincingly, like politician or tabloid journalist for instance.

"Did Nev tell you of the evidence against you?" I asked as I watched him closely ready to pounce on the slightest sign of insincerity as he answered. He shook his head.

"Not much," he said. "Nev just said they had reason to believe I and this woman had made a payment to the bloke who attacked Iris. He didn't tell me anymore. He said they'd formally interview me when I answered bail in three weeks' time and they'd disclose the evidence then."

MJ winked conspiratorially as he went on.

"I reckon that was Nev trying to do me a favour, letting me get my story straight before the interview. It was nice of him but…"

Just as I thought MJ was going to confess something he finished the sentence.

"...there was no need for him to have done that. I've nothing to hide. I've been stupid of course. I let my dick rule my head – not for the first time – but murder? That's something different again – and Iris of all people. She's the last person I'd want to harm. She's my wife, the only woman I've ever loved. I've made love to enough of them, I'll hold my hand up to that but I've never loved any of them, never cared for any woman the way I care for Iris. I could as soon tear my own guts out as hurt the most insignificant hair on her head. It's just crazy what they are saying."

I had to admit he was very convincing and if I didn't know better I'd be persuaded by his over-elaborate protestations of undying affection for the person who, I had to remind myself, had come close to a terrifying death that he had cold bloodedly planned and commissioned. Instead I was sickened at his hypocrisy and the superficial conviction with which he spoke simply made me feel worse.

"What was your relationship with this woman?" I asked, unconsciously following his lead of not naming her. He responded with a short bitter laugh.

"Purely sexual," he said, "very active, always exciting and at the end bloody frightening."

He knew I was seeking more than that flippant response so he sat forward, dropping his eyes in what I took to be shame and expanded on it.

"She was one of those women who I got involved with when I was with the police. On and off I suppose I'd been knocking her off for the best part of twenty years. She wasn't the only one and she wasn't particularly special. The fact is that a lot of women go for a man in uniform. I was self-indulgent enough to take advantage of it. I'm not the first bobby to feel more than collars when on the beat and I can tell you I'm not the last either. It was just a bit of fun as far as I was concerned. All the women I went with were married to other people so there was no question of any commitment. I wasn't interested in commitment because I had Iris. She was the only one I felt any commitment to. Maybe our relationship didn't have the excitement of forbidden fruit or the intensity that comes with snatched meetings when the husband's back is turned but my love for Iris was something so much deeper. You could put together all of those women I had over the years, line them up naked against a wall and every time I'd choose Iris above all of them. The trouble was that while it was all going on it wasn't a question of having to choose. I could have them all so I persuaded myself what was the harm in it? I was having fun, the women were having fun and Iris was happy in her ignorance. She knew I would always come home to her so she didn't need to know what else I was doing."

I must have betrayed my thoughts in my face because MJ paused to tell me.

"Don't look so bloody disgusted, Gareth. These things go on. Maybe being a solicitor makes it easy to cope with routine. Maybe you didn't have to look for some way of using up the excess adrenalin. Perhaps solicitors don't have attractive women throwing themselves at them but it's different for bobbies. We were going to work every day not knowing what the shift had in store for us, constantly on edge looking at danger. We couldn't just go home to the little woman at the end of the day, eating our ready meals in front of the telly before putting the cat out and doing the crossword in bed. When you do a job like mine you need stimulation and you get it. I'm not asking you to approve, Gareth, and with hindsight I'm not proud of what I did but for Christ's sake try to understand."

Not only was I offended by the suggestion that I was too sad and boring an individual to understand the heat of passion but I was sufficiently experienced in life to spot bullshit when I hear it. Life as a small town copper is not that dramatic with probably no more challenges per day than the average school crossing warden. I would readily accept that there existed thrill seeking housewives in this world (though none had ever sought their thrills in my company) and I was aware that to many such women the lure of a uniform rather trumps that of a briefcase but what I refused to accept was MJ's pathetic assertion that somehow it was his unavoidable destiny to cheat on his wife and other people's husbands. If he genuinely believed that he was hurting nobody by his actions then this could only be because he never bothered to spare a thought for anyone's feelings but his own.

I mentally took a grip on myself. I wasn't here to talk about the morality of MJ's philandering, an open secret to all but Iris for a good many years, but about the circumstances in which he had the nerve to deny that it had led him to a far deeper betrayal.

"Is that as far as it went? A bit on the side now and again?" I knew in asking that question that the relationship had involved more than just casual sex. I'd seen the bank statements and the photograph. I was interested to see if MJ would admit it. If he denied any further relationship with Rita Contemponi I would know he was lying and, in a strange way, that would make me feel better. I could satisfy myself that MJ had tried once again to pull the wool over my eyes and had failed, thus relieving me of the obligation to give a toss over what fate awaited him. Far more disconcerting would be the conclusion that MJ was being honest with me because if he was then I would once again find myself involved in somebody else's problems. MJ did not give me the easy way out.

"That was how I planned it but she proved to be a determined woman," he said before explaining further.

"When I left the police I didn't have the same opportunities for outside entertainment as before. Working for Stevenson and Parry wasn't as sexy and one by one all the women dropped off, apart from her. She wanted us to carry on and I was naïve enough to feel flattered that she fancied me for myself and not just the uniform. I used to call and see her on a regular basis when the hormones needed damping down. I'd wait till I was doing a job away from the office where nobody was timing me and then call round on her. I'm sorry about that, Gareth, most of it was happening in your time."

He looked at me as if he expected an expression of forgiveness or an assurance that I had no problem with my employee pursuing an adulterous affair while I was paying him to work. I gave him no such encouragement so he continued.

"Everything was fine until her husband died. When I heard about it I tried to look sympathetic but it turns out it wasn't sympathy she was after. She couldn't stand the bloke. She said I was the one she wanted to spend the rest of her life with. Christ, Gareth, I nearly crapped myself. She'd fallen in love with me or at least she said she had. Very flattering at my age but it wasn't part of the plan. I was panic stricken. I had to end the relationship but I had to be careful how I did it particularly after she told me her secret."

"Her secret?"

"Yes, she told me that she was the one responsible for all that missing money from the post office. She said she'd salted it all away in Gibraltar. She said that it was all gone but we could get some more. She had a big insurance policy on her husband's life and she reckoned she knew enough about the way banks worked to be able to steal some more to set us up together."

I was now confused. Tom Webster had made it clear that Beppe Contemponi had not robbed the Pentreglo Post Office. Was MJ telling me that Rita had actually done it? There was another thing as well.

"Beppe Contemponi didn't have any insurance policies, "I said. "He was hardly the sort of bloke who'd bother with such things."

"Beppe? What's he got to do with it?" MJ was equally confused. Suddenly I realised the mistake I'd made.

"The woman you were involved with, it wasn't Rita Contemponi was it?" I asked. MJ looked appalled at the thought.

"Of course not," he said. "It was Angela Webster."

Thirty

MJ looked genuinely scared by the enormity of what he was telling me.

"She told me there'd never been a robbery at the post office. She said that Tom had taken the money and she had the idea of a fake robbery to cover it up. As soon as she told me that I realised how deep in the nasty stuff I was. If there was no robbery Beppe was innocent after all. He'd been framed and I was the custody sergeant in charge of the identity parade. If it got out what Tom had done and if I got linked to his wife, who was going to believe that I wasn't the one who framed him?"

There was an obvious answer to his rhetorical question. Nobody would believe him, just as I didn't. What I had just learned confirmed in my mind that Nigel and I had correctly identified the Viper even if it was a begrudged identification on my part. Not only did we have the right person but we had the right motive, a woman. The only mistake we had made was that we'd assumed it to be the wrong woman. So convinced had I been of Rita Contemponi's involvement that when I vaguely recognised someone who had been a witness at Beppe's trial I thought no further than her.

Angela Webster had also been a witness at the same trial, tearfully describing a robbery that had never taken place. With those crocodile tears she had deceived the jury just as she had deceived her unfortunate husband. Poor Tom Webster must have gone through agonies of conscience doing what he did but had done so comforted by the illusion, shattered only in his last pain-racked months, that what he had done had been for the benefit of someone who loved him and would be at his side until the end. Poor Tom Webster facing his end as a lonely, used, cuckolded shadow of the man who had invested so much in his relationship with the woman who repaid him with betrayal. The only consolation he would have had was his ignorance of what seemed so plain to me now; that his wife and the man with whom she had betrayed him had also been the ones who set him up to compound his wrongdoing by involving another in their deception, the ill-fated Giuseppe Contemponi whose death had weighed so heavily on him in his last miserable days.

No, I had no doubt about MJ's guilt. The only thing that puzzled me was why he was bothering to tell me what he had. He surely didn't expect me to believe that the whole thing was a terrible coincidence! I would normally have been inclined to believe MJ when he said that he was desperate to extricate himself from the relationship. MJ would normally have no interest in converting his affairs into anything more than the intermittent illicit copulation that was their trademark. I could also accept that if he really had wanted to extricate himself from his relationship with Angela Webster then he would have to be very careful about how to go about it. However, all of that was irrelevant in the light of what I knew and MJ didn't realise I knew – that he and Angela Webster, far from ending their relationship, had worked together to steal money which they then used to try to kill off the only remaining obstacle to that relationship.

I decided to put MJ on the spot. I asked him exactly how he intended to end his affair with Angela Webster. He was quick to reply.

"I knew I was in trouble as soon as her husband was diagnosed. She started talking about it being our chance to be together for ever. That's when I started laying the groundwork for an amicable exit, you know all this, 'it's not you it's me,' stuff and 'you deserve better' but then she dropped the real bombshell."

"You mean there was something worse?" I didn't immediately realise what MJ was leading up to and I allowed myself a small joke "Surely she wasn't pregnant. She must be too old for that!"

MJ allowed himself a brief grin at the suggestion before replying.

"No, Gareth, pregnancy I could have coped with. I had the snip years ago. I would have welcomed it if she'd been pregnant. It would have given me the perfect excuse. It was more serious than that. Once I found out what she had done I knew I had to stay with her until I could put it right."

I asked MJ what he meant. He refused to look at me as he whispered the reply.

"She stole money from the firm."

My reaction probably surprised him. I was relieved because he wasn't trying to fool me. He wouldn't know what I knew about the missing money so he had no need to mention it. Perhaps I could listen to him with a slightly more open mind. With that hope I waited for MJ to tell me more. After a pause he duly obliged.

"It was not long after Tom received his diagnosis and she was full of talk about us going off together. As you can imagine I was less than enthusiastic at the idea and I must have shown it. She was self-centred enough to believe that my reluctance was caused by money worries. It never occurred to her that I loved my wife and had no desire to leave her particularly for anyone as shallow as she was. Anyway, it was then that she told me about the money she had taken from Lenny. She was boasting about how clever she had been, taking it with nobody realising she was doing it. She thought that made her more desirable but all it did was to show me what a devious bitch she really was. I'd underestimated her. I always thought she kept her brains in her tits but I had to admit, she was a smart one. I knew I'd have to be doubly smart in dealing with her."

"How could she steal money from your employer without your help?"

I didn't expect an answer to the question. I had only asked it because I didn't want MJ to think I was gullible enough to acquit him of any responsibility for what he claimed Angela had done. Surprisingly, he answered me.

"It was simple, brilliant and took plenty of nerve. Apparently Lenny had set things up so that everything could be done online. He got Wayne, that rather strange bloke that hangs round Cher's neck, to set the system up for him. All he needed was a password to gain access to the account and move money around. It made it easy for him to change investments and things like that. Angela and I bumped into Cher and Wayne one night in a bar in Cardiff. On the odd occasions I went out for a drink or a meal with her it had to be far away from Pentreglo and we always chose places that people who knew us wouldn't be seen dead in. That bar in Cardiff was perfect, hardly any lighting and constant tuneless drivel passing for music. The only problem was that the beer was crap, watery foreign stuff that tastes so bad they have to serve it at below freezing point, but at least we were pretty sure we couldn't be recognised there. I should have realised it was exactly the sort of place Cher and Wayne would spend their Saturday nights at. I nearly died when I saw them and they saw me. I had to introduce Angela as my sister; she thought it was a great laugh but I was on pins and needles all the time.

It seems that while I was talking to Cher, Angela was pumping Wayne for information. He was bragging about how he ran the computer network at Stevenson and Parry and, like a typical computer nerd, he couldn't resist showing how clever he was and how technologically backward Lenny was. With the combination of Wayne's ego and his inability to hold his drink it wasn't long, so Angela told me, before he was boasting about how easy the password was to crack and demonstrating by telling her what it was. Angela, as I found out, knows all about transferring money to foreign bank accounts. She'd done it with the post office money. He'd paid the cash into a bank and she'd transferred it to an account she'd set up in Gibraltar. Apparently all you need is a pair of codes for the accounts you are transferring to. You don't need the account name or the postal address of the bank or anything like that. You just type in the codes and the money goes into the account."

I nodded. I had experience of transferring money abroad from when I bought my home in Spain. The two codes are called the BIC and the IBAN and, with them, you can send money almost anywhere.

"So she used the password she'd got from Wayne and the BIC and IBAN from her Gibraltar account to steal the money from Lenny?" I finished the story for MJ who nodded sadly in agreement.

"How's that for opportunism?" was his only comment.

"And you knew nothing of it at the time?" I was sceptical as I asked the question but the emphatic shake of the head from MJ was clear enough.

"She only told me about it a few days later," he said. "She thought it was a great laugh. I couldn't believe she could do such a thing."

"What did you do when she told you?"

"I know what I wanted to do. I wanted to ring her scrawny neck. It's bad enough she stole from a friend who trusted me and had given me a job when I needed it but what really made me sick was that she thought I'd be pleased with her for doing it. I knew I wasn't dealing with anyone normal so I decided to tread carefully. I decided I had to get the money back into the right account without anyone realising it had gone or, at least, not realising who had taken it. I suppose I should have just gone straight to Lenny and told him the truth but I didn't. I thought I could sort it all out without anyone having to find out about me and Angela."

"So how did you do that, MJ?" I asked, wondering if he'd realised that I knew what the money had been used for and wasn't therefore going to believe whatever he was about to tell me. Whether he realised it or not he started to explain.

"The first thing I did was to play along with her. I pretended to be impressed and to be keen for us to go away together after Tom finally went. I told her we had to transfer the money out of Gibraltar. I gave her some bull about there being too many bent bank clerks there who would give her away. Fortunately, she believed me. I then had to tell a few white lies to Pauline to get her to tell me the codes for the trust account. I told her Lenny had asked me to pass them on to the organiser of one of the fundraising events and I'd lost them so I wanted to get them again without him knowing. I was afraid she'd see through me but I used my charm and she suspected nothing. She gave me a piece of paper with the codes on and I gave it to the bank in Gibraltar right in front of Angela who was stupid enough to think I was setting up our life together instead of setting up my escape route from her. The money should be safely back in the trust account by now. Lenny will realise something dodgy has happened but he'll never find out what. Now I can dump Angela with no fear. She can hardly complain about me stealing money that she stole in the first place and, having told me her shameful secrets, wouldn't be too keen on making a fuss when I leave her. Pretty clever work from an ex PC Plod if I say it myself."

MJ looked so pleased with himself that I could have sworn he genuinely believed he had paid the stolen money back. He obviously thought I'd been thoroughly taken in so, without ceremony I told him I had not been.

"The money's not in the trust fund, MJ, you know that. It was transferred to an account in Zurich to pay the man who tried to kill Iris."

His first reaction was to ask me to repeat what I had just said. A nice touch, I thought, that might have fooled someone more gullible than I. After I said it again he fell silent for a few seconds, seemingly weighing up the implications. It was almost as if I could see realisation slowly penetrating his mind. Whatever else I could say of him it was an impressive act he was putting on. He spoke slowly and with a tremor in his voice as if afraid of the very words he was speaking.

"You are telling me that Angela wasn't fooled by what I did?"

I nodded.

"She changed the codes."

Another nod. "It seems so," I said.

He swallowed hard and continued at the same slow apprehensive pace. "She planned to have Iris killed."

I nodded again. It seemed clear at least that somebody had planned Iris' murder but I was keeping an open mind on the identity of that person or persons.

MJ's response was immediate and impressive. He leapt out of his chair sending a coffee cup flying into the air. He seemed oblivious of my presence as he started to pace the floor muttering obscenities as he did so. Eventually he stopped but instead of turning back to me he faced the wall and directed more obscenities, louder this time in its direction pounding it with his fists to emphasise each syllable. He turned from general obscenity to berating himself, still ignoring my presence.

"How could I be so stupid? How could I be so fucking stupid? I thought I was so smart but she was too good for me. I thought I'd done it to her but she's done it to me."

Finally he turned, hyperventilating, towards me and finally seemed to register my presence. He took some time to focus on me and control his breathing. At last he spoke directly to me in a voice that was no longer angry. In place of the anger was despair and self-pity.

"She conned me didn't she, Gareth? She conned me like she conned Tom and Lenny before me. I rejected her so she was prepared to kill the woman I love in revenge. What kind of a twisted evil character is that, Gareth?"

I always feel inadequate at times of great emotion and now was no exception. I could think of nothing helpful to say so I said nothing.

MJ seemed to be staring beyond me as he thought further. Having done so, he spoke quietly.

"She is so evil that she didn't just try to have Iris killed. I realise it now, she arranged it in such a way that I'd get the blame." He seemed to shudder before completing what he had to say.

"Do you know what, Gareth? She's going to succeed."

I looked at the fear in his face as he realised the full horror of the position he had been put in. I couldn't believe that the outpouring of emotion I had just witnessed and the look of anguish I was now looking at had been calmly manufactured for my benefit. MJ was telling me the truth. His weakness for a pretty face and a shapely body had led to him being prime suspect in a theft and a murder and there was no obvious way out. He may be telling the truth but he would have a hard job convincing a jury of that. It was only Nev Powell's alarming propensity to apply double standards to ex colleagues who got into trouble that was keeping MJ out of prison and that state of affairs couldn't last for ever.

I told him, rather unconvincingly that I would do what I could to help him but in truth I had no idea what I could possibly do.

I realised as I was about to leave that there was one subject we had yet to cover adequately. One part of me was saying that MJ was in enough trouble already without me rubbing salt in his wounds but another, more pragmatic part, reasoned that if I was going to help MJ in his current dilemma the least he could do was to come clean with me about everything. The pragmatic side won and I asked the question.

"What happened on the night Beppe was arrested, MJ? You must know and if I am to help you then you might as well come clean about it."

There seemed to be disappointment in MJ's eyes at the fact I had raised the subject again, as if I had somehow broken the rules of a game we were playing.

"I've told you already," he said. "I played no part in what happened to Beppe. I've told you that before and I'm telling you that now. I'm not saying anything more."

So that was that. MJ was following the example of every copper, saying nothing and trusting in that disturbingly frequent phenomenon – the reluctance of British juries to accept that police officers can be guilty of wrongdoing however compelling the evidence against them. It was an irony that MJ the copper might well get away with what he had done in his career but that would be little consolation if, as seemed frighteningly likely, MJ the adulterous ex solicitor's clerk ended up being convicted of far more serious charges that he was entirely innocent of.

I turned that thought over in my mind as I stood to leave. I could see MJ's suitcase, packed for his unwelcome journey, beside the fireplace or, to be more accurate, beside what used to be the fireplace. Where there had once been an impressive space that dominated the room there was now just a sheet of painted hardboard covering the recess completely. The absence of the fireplace seemed to alter the whole character of the room; it's funny how taking away something familiar can do that. Suddenly, as I reflected on that observation I remembered what it was I had forgotten in my sleep on the plane. The outline of the coronation coach was back in my view. I realised that I needed to get into the office early the next day. There was something I needed to check on the Giuseppe Contemponi file. If it said what I expected it to say I would have pieced together every last component and embellishment of that coach.

Thirty-one

I was at the office at 8.30 the next morning. My meeting with Nigel was fixed for 9.30 but I wanted the chance to look at the file in peace. I lifted the old box onto the desk and flicked through the collection of files until I came to the one I wanted, the case of Regina v Giuseppe Contemponi. I had become sufficiently familiar with the important statements that I could have quoted all of them verbatim. That's a power lawyers develop, the ability to digest and store a staggering volume of information for the purposes of presenting a case. It's a frightening process. If you stop and think about how much you must remember in the course of a case you panic as if you fear that your head will explode. It's like breathing. If you simply get on with it the whole process is reliable and painless but if you are conscious that you are doing it you start to doubt that you can keep it up.

The secret behind absorbing such a daunting volume of material for each case lies in concentrating on the important aspects of it and ignoring those secondary details that do not need to be remembered because they can easily be looked up if needed. That is why so many lawyers know everything about their cases except their clients' names. They can always look on the outside of the file if they want to know what to call the person they are representing but do not have the same luxury when they have to think on their feet about how an unexpected answer to a question might affect what they ask the witness next. Those pretentious halfwits who make it their mission to criticise or ridicule the legal profession often cite the inability of lawyers to recall their clients' names as proof positive that they care little for those clients and are focussed only on their fees. If only they realised!

As I flicked through the pages of the Contemponi file I was looking for the kind of statement that I would normally not waste my time on. Criminal files are full of the kind of formal statements that do not actually affect the important issues in the case but are nevertheless vital in ensuring that the case is a watertight one. There might, for instance, be a highly significant statement about a blood stained knife being found at the scene of the murder and an equally significant one about the blood being found to match that of the victim but in between those two would be a thick pile of statements describing each pair of hands through which firstly the knife and then the blood sample passed between those two points. If any stage in the process is missed out the whole case could collapse but, once he has satisfied himself that there is no break in continuity, no lawyer is going to waste his time memorising the detail of who exactly handled the evidence.

Today I was looking for just such a statement, one of a type that I would have looked at in a cursory fashion when first familiarising myself with the case but would never have looked at again. Certainly, since my recent reintroduction to the file I had concerned myself only with the evidence surrounding the identification and nothing else. Now I was interested in a statement that covered a point of detail having nothing to do with the meat of the case against Giuseppe Contemponi.

It didn't take me long to find it and when I found it I only needed to read the first line. It told me what I wanted to know. My suspicions had been confirmed. I must confess that I allowed myself a moment of self-congratulation at seeing what Nigel had missed. I was still smiling smugly as I went to return the file, minus the statement, to the box making sure that I put it in the right place. It bore the number 1990/226 so counting the files from the end I parted them to read their numbers. The first number I read was 1990/227. I had found the right place first time. This was clearly going to be a successful day for me. As I slipped the file in next to 1990/227 I caught a glimpse of the file in front of it. By rights it should have been 1990/225 but it wasn't. I paused for a second. The number on the file was 1990/235. Someone had obviously put it in the wrong place. It was strange that I hadn't noticed it before as I must have removed and replaced the Contemponi file scores of times over the past month. Then I realised that the mistake was mine. In front of 1990/235 was 1990/236 and behind 1990/227 was 1990/234. I was replacing the file at the wrong end of the box. I gave myself a mental slap on the wrists and started to count from the right end. It was only as I was going to replace the file that I realised. Someone else had made the same mistake. File number 1990/227 was the one I'd thought had been removed by MJ but, although it had clearly been out of the box since its delivery to the office it was not missing at all. It had simply been misfiled because somebody, when replacing it, had done so at the wrong end.

I pulled out the misplaced file in order to put it in the correct place. I also wanted to sneak a quick look at it before doing so. Now that I realised that it had never been deliberately hidden away I reasoned that it was unlikely to have any relevance to Beppe's case. Nevertheless, somebody had thought it important enough to have taken it out of the box and I was curious to see why.

That file never did go back in the box. It had nothing to do with the Contemponi case but as soon as I saw it I realised who had looked at it and why. I began to feel that it wasn't only the coronation coach that was becoming clearer. The file I was looking at might just allow me to add the Horse Guards and the bearskins.

Before any of that, however, I needed to postpone the morning's meeting. There was a further enquiry Nigel and I would have to make before we could tell Beppo and the insurance company's lackey that the investigation was complete. I went to find Pauline but she was not at her desk. I called Cher in. She told me Pauline was at Ty Gwyn having taken a couple of hours off to finish the cleaning and get things ready for Iris. As I turned away from the desk my leg clattered into something hard and I started to fall before recovering my balance with an athleticism that I thought had deserted me years ago. I looked down in the direction of my feet. There was a large metal case by the side of the desk. I seemed to remember seeing it before but I opened the lid to see exactly what it was that would be responsible for the bruise I anticipated on my shin. It was a tool box, one of those with different sections for different tools. Clearly it was the property of a professional or at least a very keen amateur. I remembered when I'd seen it before. It was Sam's toolbox. I looked over at Cher.

"It's not mine," she said defensively. "Mrs Hopkins must have left it there at the weekend. It wasn't there on Friday. I think it belongs to her old man, I mean her husband. He was doing some jobs for…"

Her voice trailed off as she wondered whether she should reveal the identity of the beneficiary of Sam's efforts. Even Cher was sufficiently in touch to realise that the name Jenkins was not one to be freely uttered within the premises of Stevenson and Parry.

I was standing there massaging a throbbing leg when Nigel came in. He was accompanied by a representative of the company that insured the Police Authority. He had no need to introduce him. I can recognise easily enough the mixture of anguish and disbelief that inhabits the features of an insurance company representative who knows that he is to be asked to put his hand into the corporate pocket of his employers. They are a strange breed insurance company people. They sell their policies on jovial assurances of how delighted they would be to help out in times of trouble but when they sense that they might have to deliver on those assurances it all changes. They have a unique way of making even the most modest of claimants feel as if they had just proposed the commission of an unnatural act with their grandmother. The stout, unsmiling character at Nigel's side was no exception. His eyes shone with "how dare you" indignation as I greeted him and his finely trimmed moustache quivered at the prospect that I might be so impertinent as to expect him to part with any of the funds that had been solemnly entrusted to him.

I lost no time in taking Nigel aside and explaining to him that we would need to make one more visit before we could truly say that we knew where responsibility lay for the conviction and ultimate demise of Giuseppe Contemponi. When I explained he readily agreed.

A look of palpable relief crossed the face of the insurance representative as Nigel told him the meeting would have to be postponed. It was the sort of look you used to see in those corny old films where a condemned man learns of a last minute pardon as he is being prepared for execution. The fact that the day of reckoning was merely being postponed rather than going away didn't concern him. The philosophy of those in his position is that if you can't avoid paying out to someone the next best thing is to delay payment as long as possible.

As we were preparing to leave, Beppo arrived. As the insurance man glowered at him I explained that if he was prepared to wait a day or so I could not only secure him the right amount of compensation but I could tell him the whole truth of what happened to his father. I heard what sounded like a low moan from the direction of the insurance man when I mentioned compensation. Beppo was only too ready to agree, telling me that he was more interested in seeing those responsible brought to justice than in receiving compensation. That brought a smile to the insurance man's lips. There was however, one thing I had to ask Beppo to do for me.

"Do you have a phone on you?" I asked.

Beppe said that he did and I noted down the number. I asked him to await a text message from me and to make sure that he replied to it as soon as it arrived. Pausing only to receive an insincere and perspiration laden handshake from the temporarily reprieved custodian of the insurance company's funds I walked with Nigel in the direction of the Bentley.

I could have sworn that the old gents in the bar were engaged in the same game of dominoes as when we were last there. They were certainly sitting in the same seats with the same type of drinks in front of them as engrossed as they had been before in the combinations of spots before them. There was even the same old man dozing in the corner. At least, I assume it was the same man; you can't be sure when his features are concealed by a newspaper over his face. I satisfied myself from the headline that it was today's paper so he must have moved since I last saw him. That was reassuring, I could quite believe that in a pub as quiet as this one in winter someone could lie dead in the corner for weeks and nobody would notice until he started to smell.

I saw Stan behind the bar apparently swapping anecdotes with a scruffily dressed man who was nursing what looked like a large whisky. Stan looked up as we approached the bar and for an instant I saw concern in his face before he broke into a welcoming smile.

"Hello, butties," he said, opening his arms in a gesture of welcome. "I didn't expect to see you two so soon."

I could sense the insincerity but I ignored it and explained. "You said we should drop in for a pint one day so now that we've finished our work we thought we'd take you at your word."

"You've finished your work have you?" he asked just a little too anxiously. "So this is a social call."

"What else?" I avoided a straight answer. Stan seemed to relax and walked round the bar to join us. I accepted his offer of a pint while Nigel's wish to maintain the Bentley in pristine condition led to him settling for mineral water.

"Before I do, though…" I gestured in the direction of the door marked "cocks". Stan gave an understanding nod.

"I know, long journey," he said. "When you get to our age you can't hold it in so easy eh, Gareth?"

I walked away and when I reached the door in the corner I looked round. Stan was already deep in conversation with Nigel who had positioned himself so Stan had his back to me. I ignored the "cocks" and instead opened the door to the living quarters as quickly and as quietly as I could. Speed was of the essence and although I anticipated an imminent collision between excrement and ventilating device I preferred, ideally, to remain undiscovered until I had done what I set out to do.

I poked my head gingerly into the living room at the top of the stairs. There was nobody there. I was in luck. I wasn't exactly sure what I would do if confronted by Mrs Stan as I snooped about. I looked to the wall opposite me. I had mocked Nigel when he spoke of the lack of balance in the room but when I looked at Rafa's room that day after the incident in the cemetery I saw the same thing only I hadn't realised it. I saw how the bare wall that once held pictures of his erstwhile parents made the room look strangely asymmetrical when the other wall was crammed with pictures of Rafa, Maria-Carmen and their children. I thought then that it reminded me of something but I couldn't think what. I had the same feeling at MJ's house when I looked at the blank space where the fireplace had been. That was what started the process of recall. My memory had been jogged, albeit temporarily by the missing screen on the plane and re-jogged by MJ's missing fireplace. Until I looked at Stan's living room I wasn't sure if it was a false memory but now I knew that my instinct was spot on. The room was no longer out of balance. The wall that had been blank for our last visit now had photographs on it to match those on the opposite wall. They were photographs that I suspected were a permanent fixture and which had been removed for our benefit. I got out my phone, selected a suitable photograph and took a picture of it. I then turned, closed the door gently and tiptoed back down the stairs. Before emerging into the bar I sent the picture I had taken to the number Beppo had given me, accompanying it with a simple question.

Thirty-two

"Bigger job than you thought?" called out Stan with a vulgar laugh as he turned to see me return to the table. I smiled in acknowledgement of his wit and listened for a few moments as he told me how he had been keeping Nigel amused with tales of the clangers I would regularly drop as I cut my advocate's teeth in the courtroom at Pentreglo. Within a few moments I felt the vibration in my pocket. I removed my phone keeping it under the table so Stan couldn't see it. Beppo had replied to my message. I read his reply and looked towards Nigel. He was watching me whilst pretending to listen to Stan who was sufficiently taken by his own wit and eloquence to be oblivious to what we were doing. I tilted the phone so that Nigel could read the message. He nodded almost imperceptibly. The time had come to change the subject.

"Do you know one funny thing about all the time I've known you, Stan?" I asked cutting casually across his anecdote.

"What's that, butty?"

"You never told me your real name. You've always been Detective Constable Matthews and then Sergeant Matthews and Inspector Matthews. Even when we got to know each other well enough for first names, it was always Stan. That wasn't what you were christened was it?"

Stan laughed. "No, it was a nickname, butt, after the footballer. I don't suppose you remember the footballer Stan Matthews do you, Nigel? It would have been before your time. Well, he was one of the most famous footballers in Britain at the time I was starting in the force and you know the lads, always up for a joke. Every new bobby had a nickname and mine was Stan because my name was Matthews. The name's stuck and it's only my family use my proper name these days. I don't mind it really; they could have called me a lot worse."

Stan chuckled at the thought and was about to launch into another bout of embarrassing nostalgia when I pressed the question that I noted he had avoided.

"So what did your mother call you, Stan? It couldn't have been that bad could it? It wasn't Adolf or Beelzebub or anything like that?"

"No but I never use it, I'm happy with Stan after all these years."

He still wasn't answering the question so I decided to do it for him.

"The funny thing is, Stan, that I would see your name at least once a week probably during the time I was working, on the top of statements you'd made but I never took it in. I'd just go straight to what you had to say. It's a bad habit all we lawyers have. We never bother with names only facts."

"I didn't used to make that many interesting statements anyway after I was made an inspector. Just routine stuff that I don't suppose you even bothered to read. You know the amount of paperwork..."

Stan was about to commence his oft repeated speech about the tedium and bureaucracy that surrounded the post of a Police Inspector tasked with administrative duties. I wasn't going to let him change the subject. He was right about me not reading with particular care the mundane offerings that he had put his name to in the latter years of his career. It was no wonder that I had never been particularly conscious of the name at the top. The statement he had made in the Giuseppe Contemponi case was typical of those that passed my eyes with minimal attention being paid to them. It merely described the fact that he had reviewed his detention and found nothing untoward. I don't recall even reading it at the time of the original trial. I only went back to it today because of something nagging in my mind, something that had finally re-entered my consciousness on the plane as I thought about captain Billy Rawlings and how he reminded me of Paco who was really Francisco and how that in turn reminded me that I had missed something important. Only on the plane was I able to complete that aspect of the coronation coach in my mental jigsaw. My subsequent sleep had hidden it from me but now it was back. The irony was that even though I was telling nothing less than the truth when I said I had never consciously known Stan's real name, I had seen it so many times that I had remembered it after all. The sub conscious mind is a wondrous thing. You absorb a piece of information and store it for years without even knowing that you absorbed it in the first place and then, at the right cue, it comes back to you and you can't for the life of you remember where it came from. It was a phenomenon that had brought me modest success in pub quizzes and now it had served me well again. Stan's name had come back to me, at least until I fell asleep, on the plane. That had started me thinking but it wasn't until the empty space where MJ's fireplace used to be jogged my memory of Rafa's half empty wall and then of Stan's empty wall that I realised where the horses fitted on the coronation jigsaw. This morning at the office I had confirmed my recollection, as I was about to tell Stan.

"Let's see if I can guess your name," I said, trying to disarm him with a jocular approach. "It's not Rumpelstiltskin I suppose."

Stan shook his head indulgently.

"...so how about Emrys? That's your name isn't it? Emrys David Matthews. It says it on the sign above the door, 'E D Matthews'. I didn't realise at first it was you."

Stan attempted to share the joke. "Not very sexy is it? That's why I prefer Stan."

"I don't suppose your wife calls you Emrys does she?" I teased. "What does she call you? Em?"

Stan grinned sheepishly to acknowledge my discovery of his secret. "Funny name Em isn't it?" I continued. "Hear it spoken rather than written and it sounds like the letter M."

Stan was obviously wondering what I was talking about. He didn't seem able to decide if these were just ramblings inspired by the few sips of the local beer or whether I was leading somewhere. A small twitch of the neck suggested that he feared the latter.

"I have a confession to make to you," I said, placing my phone on the table. "I've just sneaked into your living room and taken a photograph of one of the pictures you have hung on the wall, one you took down when we were here before. You know the one; it's your wedding photograph. I sent it to Beppo and asked him if he recognised the woman on it. Do you want to know what he said?"

Stan didn't want to know but I showed him Beppo's message anyway. It simply said "THAT'S MY MOTHER".

Stan smiled weakly. He knew the game was up. He knew what I knew, that he was the Viper. Stan can't resist telling a story and when he knew he could supress it no longer he told us everything. He started with his affair with Rita Contemponi taking care to assure us, as if it mattered, that it was based on real love and not just illicit sex. He described the phone call he had received from MJ asking if he minded carrying out the review of Beppe Contemponi's detention early. He had asked him why and MJ had told him that something had come up that needed his attention for the next hour.

"I saw my chance then," he said in a voice that sounded as if he was doing nothing more than recounting one of those anecdotes of police life with which he would keep his customers' interest on quiet evenings in the bar. "I saw how I could remove Beppe from the scene then once he was sentenced Rita could divorce him and nobody would expect anything different. We could then marry and go off somewhere like, well, somewhere like here. All I needed was to get Beppe and Tom Webster together. I asked MJ if it would help if I took over from him for a bit. He sounded very grateful and more than a little flustered so I went straight over to the station. As soon as MJ's back was turned I called Tom Webster and set him up for the identification parade. I didn't tell him why I was doing it of course. I just told him we had evidence against Beppe that we couldn't use so I was helping the wheels of justice to turn. He seemed unusually surprised, even relieved when I suggested it. I didn't know why then but I do now. I hadn't factored in that Tom Webster was as bent as I was."

He allowed himself a little laugh at that remark and then continued in the same anecdotal tone without a trace of shame.

"I then sorted out a new statement for Tom. I knew the jury would probably throw out the identification evidence unless we could show that Tom had already described Beppe so I needed that statement. I had to wait till Nev sent the file up to divisional HQ and then I made the switch."

"And the tip off to Nev Powell?" I knew the answer to that question before asking it.

"Rita," confirmed Stan. "I got her to ring Nev at home on the Sunday."

"What part did MJ play in all of this?" I asked.

Stan was quick to answer. "None," he said. "He left Beppe in my care and left the station. When he came back I just handed back over and told him nothing. He never knew what went on. He's probably twigged now with Tom Webster spilling the beans but he wouldn't have known before then."

"Why did he leave the station?"

Stan shrugged his shoulders. "To this day I have no idea. He didn't tell me and I didn't ask. I assumed at the time it was something to do with one of his girlfriends, you know what he was like."

"Was Rita one of his girlfriends?"

Stan seemed offended at the question.

"Of course not," he replied quickly. "I told you. Ours was a proper relationship. Rita wasn't interested in other men. We're still married and still happy after all these years."

Looking at Stan's face you would be forgiven for thinking that he'd just been telling us a heart-warming love story instead of confessing to a crime that had cost a man his life.

"Don't you feel any conscience at all about this, Stan?" I asked him. "Beppe killed himself because of what you did."

For the first time a note of anger could be detected in Stan's voice.

"Grow up, Gareth," he said. "I know I did wrong and no doubt I'll have to pay for it but if you expect me to feel bad about anything other than getting caught you'll be disappointed. Consciences are for people like you with your fancy degrees and your sweet talk in court. I was the poor bugger that had to deal with the consequences when you waved law books at gullible softies so that some psychopath could go free to harm decent people. I did the world a favour by taking Beppe Contemponi out of circulation and at the same time I gave the woman I love the chance of real happiness."

He fixed me with a stare defying me to reply. I knew that talk of the rule of law would fall on deaf ears so I kept silent and tried to stare him out. He cracked first. His face broke into a smile and he put his hand surprisingly gently on my shoulder as he said, "You never did learn it, did you? It's all a game. That's what it is, all a game."

Thirty-three

MJ sounded defensive when I rang him from the car. I could hardly blame him. I hurried to give him reassurance.

"I'm calling to apologise," I said. "I'm on my way back from Stan's pub. I know what happened to Beppe. Stan assured me you were not involved. I may not believe much of what Stan tells me but I believe that. Did you know he was married to Beppe's widow?"

MJ's air of surprise as he told me he didn't convinced me he was telling the truth.

"I was wrong to ever believe that you'd been involved with her," I said sheepishly.

"Yes you were," was the stern and not completely friendly response. Despite my willingness to eat humble pie I was taken aback by the tone of apparent indignation from MJ. After all, it's hardly an outrageous thing to believe him to have been led astray by the scent of perfume. Only the previous night he had confessed his infidelity. All I'd done was to pick the wrong woman to suspect him of sleeping with. His disapproval of my error was about as worthy as Genghis Khan pointing out that some of those his hoards had slaughtered were in pretty bad health beforehand.

"Are you about this afternoon?" I asked him, eager not to let our conversation drift into acrimony. "I'd like to apologise in person." That wasn't the complete truth. Although I wanted to mend my fences with MJ I wanted to talk to him for another reason. Questions were still unanswered. There were still gaps in the jigsaw and I felt that one of the missing pieces was in the file I discovered that morning. MJ, I believed, would be the one to tell me where it fitted.

"I'm going to Ty Gwyn in about an hour," he said. "Iris is due back there at about four. Her sister finishes work at three and she's bringing her home. I need to be away by then so I'm calling in first to make sure everything's right for her. Even though nobody seems to believe this, I care about Iris you know."

We agreed to meet at Ty Gwyn. Nigel dropped me off at my car and went into the office to explain the latest revelations to his insurance client. I suspected that he, in common with all insurance company men, wouldn't be in the slightest bit interested in the justice or morality of what Stan had done but would demand to be told what his "exposure" would be, a euphemistic way of asking how much it would cost. What a simple life those in the rarefied atmosphere of high finance live. They need not trouble themselves with love or hate, grief or anguish. Everything in their world can be measured in money and nothing that cannot be so measured exists in that world.

I passed Sam Hopkins on my way to see MJ. He was sitting in the usual place staring in the usual way across the valley and, no doubt, thinking the usual thoughts of why she had been taken away from him and what he would do to avenge her. I had time to spare before my meeting with MJ and it occurred to me that now might be the time to set in motion the reconciliation I had determined to effect between Sam and Terry. If I could take the first step today it might do something to sweeten the bad taste that had been left in my mouth by the visit to Stan.

Sam hardly acknowledged me as I sat down beside him on the bench. His eyes remained focussed on the edge of the road as I began to speak. I wasn't even sure that he was listening as I told him of my meeting with Terry and how maybe we had all misjudged him. I paused after telling Sam what Terry had told me but there was no reaction. Sam continued to stare silently ahead. I took that as encouragement. Maybe he wanted to hear more.

"I know Terry wants to meet you," I said. "He's been afraid of how you might react, that's why he's not been in contact before."

I realised that I had put it rather tactlessly so I quickly corrected myself.

"He didn't want to upset you, that's what he was saying but I told him that now you know the truth, now you know that he didn't abandon Debbie as we all believed you'd want to meet him."

I paused again inviting Sam by my silence to tell me whether I had been right in what I told Terry. Still there was no response. I had no alternative but to ask outright. I stood up blocking Sam's view over the valley. There seemed to be irritation in his face as he was forced to look at me.

"Well, Sam, do you want to meet Terry? Do you want to hear his side and see whether you can help each other?"

Sam stared at me for what seemed like a long time before replying. When he did it was with a soft voice bearing no discernible trace of anger but with a firmness that left me in no doubt that the conversation was over.

"You can tell Terry Driscoll that I would be happy to meet him, wherever and whenever he likes and tell him to be in no doubt that when I do I will kill him just like I've always said I would."

Sam's expression was blank, his features fixed. He stepped to his side so that he could look past me at the valley, ostensibly oblivious to my presence. Failing to take the hint I started to address him but he cut me off.

"I have nothing against you, Gareth but you have betrayed me talking to that man. I don't have anything to do with those who talk to him. Please remember that in future."

As if to emphasise the point he half turned so as to present his shoulder to me. I realised the futility of continuing the conversation and returned to my car.

MJ was already at Ty Gwyn when I arrived. Everything in the house looked immaculate. There was a strong, almost overpowering odour of air fresheners yet underneath it I could smell something else. It wasn't so much a smell as a memory. A carefree summer of long ago drifted into my mind. It was the year my mother came up to a modest extent on the Premium Bonds making just enough money available to hire a caravan for a week in Pembrokeshire. It was my first real holiday and I thought it was magical. For what seemed like years afterwards I could still taste the chips we bought by the harbour, hear the sea breaking against the stones on the beach and, if I closed my eyes see the sweep of the bay in the distance. Those memories had become buried beneath layers of the practical and the mundane as life's experiences lined up to be sampled by me. Now, one of those memories, the smell, had returned and I couldn't for the life of me think why. I tried to ignore it as gave my apologies to MJ and then turned my mind to the true purpose of my visit. I derived some satisfaction from resolving the question of the missing money and I looked forward to telling Lenny that he had not been betrayed as he had feared. However, there was an unanswered question and now was the time to ask it.

"Where did you go that night when you left the police station?"

"Out," was the unhelpful reply.

"Was it to see Angela?"

"Maybe."

"It wasn't, was it? You weren't with Angela that night, were you, MJ."

"You're talking as if you know." MJ tried to sound sarcastic but he couldn't hide the uncertainty in his voice. Did he realise that I had worked it out? I showed MJ the file I had found that morning misplaced in the box. It was a particularly slim file. Tragically, there wasn't much we could do at the time for the clients whose names appeared on the cover so there was no need to generate any great quantity of paper. As far as the legal system was concerned it was an open and shut case with only one outcome. It mattered not to the system that it dealt with an event that had changed the lives of my clients. I remembered those clients and the first time they came into the office, one restrained and dignified the other screaming revenge. MJ studied the names on the cover and I could see the colour drain from his face as he read "Samuel and Pauline Hopkins v Terence Driscoll re Deborah Hopkins deceased". He knew then what I knew and nodded with resignation as I pulled out one of the documents from the file. It was the official police accident report that reduced into figures, measurements and matter of fact statements the death of a bright teenager whose love for the life that was to be snatched from her was matched only by the love felt for her by those who had shared that life.

A little while ago Nev Powell had told me something I didn't know. He had glibly told me how everything used to get timed at the police station and how all times had to tally. When I had looked at the police report in the office this morning I had understood how the system worked. Near the top of the first page of the report was recorded the time of the first telephone report of the accident. It was noted to be 6.15 p.m. and I knew it had to be right even though, as I now noticed but had failed to spot at the time, there was a massive discrepancy between that time and the time shown for the arrival of the ambulance. That ambulance had been dispatched nearly an hour later, and then only because of the appearance of an injured Terry Driscoll at the hospital. The accident had been reported to the police yet nothing had apparently been done about the report. It had simply been ignored and it had been left to chance for the alert to be raised. How could that have been? Why was nothing done? Why was Debbie Hopkins left dying while those charged with her protection turned their backs on her? There was only one person to whom those questions could be asked, the person whose initials appeared alongside the note of the initial report.

"What did you do when you got that phone call?" I asked MJ.

"You know what I did," was the curt reply.

"You went out there didn't you?"

MJ nodded.

"You knew the person who made the phone call didn't you?"

He nodded again.

"It was Iris wasn't it?"

Another nod. MJ looked at me. He could read my thoughts. He was quick to answer my unspoken question.

"It wouldn't have made any difference. I could see Debbie was beyond help when I arrived. She was dead and she wouldn't have been any more dead by being left for a bit. I let young Driscoll go. I knew he'd have to tell someone so they'd find her sooner or later. There was no rush."

"Why didn't you call for help there and then? The delay may not have made things any worse but it hardly made them better."

"You know the answer to that one don't you, Gareth?"

He was right. I did.

"It was Iris. She caused the accident didn't she? You needed to get her out of the way and you needed to keep Terry Driscoll from talking to your colleagues. When Terry was told to leave the hospital quickly that was your suggestion wasn't it and the officer who turned up and took a statement from him that said nothing, that was you too."

MJ acknowledged that I had it right. He began to explain slowly and in an unsteady voice.

"Iris told me she took the corner too wide and forced the other car off the road. She was hysterical. She guessed she'd killed someone or at least seriously injured them. She was afraid of what would happen to her. So was I. She could have been charged with a serious offence and could have gone to prison. She's not a strong woman. She could not have taken prison. I had to help her. I phoned Stan early for the review and then I asked for a favour. He's an old mate is Stan. He agreed to take over at the station while I went out. I told him it was something personal. He didn't ask what it was. That's the kind of mate he is. It was so quiet at the station that I knew nobody would notice if I went missing for a while. That's how local police stations used to be in those days, nothing used to happen most nights. I didn't know what Stan got up to while I was out. I had no reason to think anything untoward had happened until all this started to come out about the rigged identification parade. As soon as I heard that I knew it was Stan but what could I do? He stuck up for me so I had to stick up for him. We were both bobbies and that's what bobbies do, they stick up for each other. They don't tell tales."

It had only been 24 hours since MJ had assured me that, for all his reputation as a womaniser, he had only ever loved Iris. I had been sceptical. Now I see I was wrong. I was now looking at a man willing to risk everything to protect the woman he married, the woman whom he loved far more deeply than anyone outside the marriage had realised. He had put his job on the line by covering up her role in the accident. He had left himself open to being convicted of perverting the course of justice not only by keeping quiet about what he had done for Iris but also by refusing to tell anyone why he could not have been the man who framed Beppe Contemponi. He had done this for one reason only, love and loyalty directed at one woman and all this from a man whose name had become synonymous among all who knew him in Pentreglo and the surrounding valleys with infidelity and contempt for his marriage vows. Mervyn Jenkins was no saint but I had to admit that we had all misjudged him.

As I reflected on how to deal with the new information that had come to my notice I realised that the holiday smell was not going away. If anything it was getting stronger and I tried to remember what it was about the smell that was so evocative. My memory wandered to the caravan my mother had hired for the week. It had been small and cramped, lacking in the luxurious fittings that the current more pampered generation of children associate with static caravans. In my memory I was squeezed into the corner, fighting with my brother Owen for space on the bench seat that opened out at night into a bed while my mother cooked favourites like beans on toast on the inadequate hob. Lurking below the smell of the beans was that same odour that was now beginning to win its battle with the air freshener.

I looked across at the board where the fireplace had been. I had looked at it the previous night and wondered what its significance was. Now I was doing the same thing again. MJ was deep in thought when I interrupted him with my question.

"When you fitted that board over the fireplace did you paint it before or after fitting it?"

"After," said MJ. "We fitted everything first then redecorated the whole room."

"Then the screws would have been painted over?"

MJ looked at what I was looking at and his brow furrowed. We could see the screws that fastened the board in position. The heads were bright and shining. The paint had been scratched off them. MJ muttered something to himself as he walked into the kitchen returning with a screwdriver. I watched him as he methodically removed the top screws until he could pull the top of the board away. I leaned in over his shoulder to have a look. Slowly it dawned on me what I was seeing. At the same instant MJ turned. I felt him pushing me backwards with such force that I had to move with the pushes to avoid falling over.

"OK, MJ, I'm going," I said as he started to drag me with him towards the patio doors. What I had seen caused me to panic but that panic had been matched by MJ's swift reaction as his police instincts kicked in. I caught a glimpse of his face. The subdued expression that had accompanied the knowledge that his secret was out was now gone. In his place was a look of firm determination. Beneath it I could see fear. It was controlled fear but fear nonetheless. His eyes had widened and a pulse throbbed visibly in his temple. His voice when he spoke was clear and authoritative.

"Get out!" he shouted flinging open the patio doors as he threw me into the garden. "Get out and get as far away as you can!"

Thirty-four

As he followed me out of the doors MJ made no effort to close them. There was a fixed stare in his eyes as he ran to the top end of the garden dragging me with him.

Next to the shed was a small compound. MJ rummaged in his pocket and pulled out a key with which he unlocked the gate to the compound and the door to the brick structure that was inside it. I could see gas cylinders inside. MJ picked up a large spanner from beside the cylinders and turned something with it.

"Panic over, it's off now," he said calmly turning to me. "Just don't light a match until the gas clears."

His face became serious as we compared notes on what we had seen. The gas pipe which had been fitted in the fireplace ready for connection to the new gas fire had an open end. Gas had been freely flowing out of it. That's what had caused that familiar caravan smell.

"Surely it should have been capped?" I said. MJ agreed.

"I could have sworn it was," he said. "I checked it myself before fitting the cover over the fireplace. That could have killed us," he added with a shudder.

"Only if we'd been incredibly unlucky," I replied. "The smell would have tipped us off before any significant amount could have built up as indeed it did. Anyway, most of the gas would have just escaped up the chimney."

"Not if it had been closed off at the top," said MJ.

"Was it?"

He nodded.

"It was part of the removal of the coal fire," he explained. "The chimney was blocked temporarily until a proper gas fitter could come in and fit a flue."

"In that case," I conceded, "we have had a lucky escape and you have learned a valuable lesson about not getting involved in DIY projects you don't understand."

I was always happy to advise householders against undertaking jobs around the house that they weren't totally confident of completing properly. It was advice that I always followed in my own life. I have no confidence in ever being able to do anything around the house properly so I never try.

MJ didn't share my readiness to pass the whole thing off as a botched job.

"What about the cable?" he asked pointedly.

I'd noticed the cable myself but in the split second before being bundled out of the house I hadn't really thought of its significance.

"Presumably that's a wire that's going to be connected to the new gas fire in due course," I suggested. "It'll work the ignition or the light that makes the fake coal glow or something like that."

In truth I know nothing about household maintenance let alone the intricacies of electrical wiring. MJ must have realised that as he gave me a pitying look.

"Why would you run a wire like that from upstairs downwards?" he asked. "You'd run it from a junction box or the main fuse box, somewhere downstairs."

I couldn't see what he was getting at. The last thing I wanted from MJ was a lecture on how to wire a house. I told him, with a slight sulk in my voice, that if that wasn't the explanation I had no idea what it was and frankly couldn't care either. He persisted with commendable patience.

"If there's an electrical cable hanging down the chimney with a loose end we can assume it's connected to something upstairs," he began. I gave petulant jerk of my head to acknowledge the point.

"In this house, like in many of its age, the chimney forms the central structure of the house," he continued. "If that goes, the whole house collapses."

I said nothing, still waiting for him to come to the point.

"The cable was left just above where the gas was escaping from. The ends of the two wires were exposed and they'd been twisted so that they were almost touching but not quite."

At last I realised what MJ was getting at. What he was describing wasn't just a gas leak. It was a bomb. As soon as current was applied to the wires it would try to jump across the gap causing a spark that would ignite the accumulated gas. The explosion that caused would be enough to send Ty Gwyn into the next valley.

"What were the wires connected to? Could you see?" I asked.

MJ shook his head. "All I could see is that they had been dropped from above but I've got a pretty good idea where they came from. Directly above the lounge is our bedroom and directly against the chimney flue is the headboard of our bed. We fitted a new built in headboard with drawers and a wardrobe and..."

"Built in reading lights," I finished the sentence.

MJ nodded grimly. "Good God, Gareth," he said. "Iris always reads in bed before she goes to sleep. She would have got into bed tonight and turned on the reading light and..."

He put his hand to his mouth. He didn't need to continue. By the time anyone got to the house there would be little left of it, or Iris for that matter and the devastation would be so widespread that the chances of working out what had caused it would be nil. MJ read my thoughts.

"People would just think it was a gas leak caused by me messing about with the supply when I don't know how to do it properly." His face darkened as he considered further how people would react.

"Or they'd think I did it deliberately. After all it's a gas leak. I'm the one who interfered with the gas supply, I'm the one with a bit on the side who's desperate to marry me and, to cap it all, in their book I'm the one who paid for some heavy to finish Iris off. I've been completely stitched up."

MJ looked sick as he considered what we had just prevented. We were not even supposed to be at Ty Gwyn that morning and had we not decided to meet there Iris would have come home, thought nothing of the smell in her excitement at the renovations that had been carried out and retired to bed with an over sentimental historical novel and a feeling of contentment. Before the first sentence of that novel had been read Iris would have ceased to be.

"It was deliberate wasn't it?" As he asked, MJ must have known my reply but nevertheless he looked at me pathetically in the vain hope that I could offer him reassurance. I could not.

MJ looked again at the keys that were still in his hand.

"She's still got one, Gareth," he said with a note of panic in his voice.

"Who has?"

"Her, Angela, the mad woman. I gave her a key a long time ago for when Iris was away and she's still got it. She's still after Iris. I've got to warn her."

As he was saying this, I must confess that I wasn't really listening. My attention had been caught by the tree just behind where he was standing. There was something familiar about it. As MJ debated his next step I looked at the carving on the tree trunk above his shoulder.

"Has that always been there?" I asked. He looked at me blankly and then followed my gaze to the tree.

"No it hasn't," he said vaguely, "I hadn't noticed it before but then I don't go into the garden that much in the winter. I'm pretty sure it wasn't there in the autumn."

He paused for a moment to consider who would want to carve anything on his tree and then shook his head dismissively, deciding that it was just one of those mysteries of life that can't be solved. He returned to the subject in hand.

"What do you think, Gareth? Should I call Nev Powell now?"

I didn't answer. I was too deeply into my own thoughts. I was thinking back more than fifty years. I was thinking of a jigsaw, a jigsaw of a coronation coach and I was thinking that I could now see every detail. The coach in its gilded magnificence, the elegantly dressed footmen, the Horse Guards with their plumed helmets, the bearskins and even the flags being waved by the crowd, I could see it all. MJ had become so obsessed with Angela Webster as to miss the obvious but there was nothing to gain by putting him right.

As soon as I got out of Ty Gwyn I rang Nigel. I told him what I had seen and what I suspected. I told him that he needed to locate Sam Hopkins urgently. He would need careful handling and Nigel seemed like the best person for the job. I headed back to the office. While Nigel dealt with Sam I had some unwelcome news to pass to his wife.

Pauline was at her desk when I returned to the office. I almost tripped over the toolbox for the second time as I entered her room. She gave a laugh.

"Sorry about that," she said, "but, to be honest, I'm rather glad people are tripping over Sam's toolbox again. It used to be a standing joke when he was working. He'd always be leaving it in people's way. I'd almost forgotten about it this last twenty years. The toolbox hasn't left the house in all that time."

"Yet he's kept them all this time," I added.

Pauline smiled proudly. "I made sure they weren't thrown out," she explained. "I always hoped he would take an interest again and, although it's slow progress, with Nigel's help he's starting to do just that. He really enjoyed working at Ty Gwyn."

"What are the tools doing in the office?"

Pauline looked sheepish again. "I hope you don't mind. He left them at Ty Gwyn when he finished on Sunday morning. He rang me up in a bit of a state. He'd been thinking of Debbie while he was finishing the job off and he just left and went to his bench leaving everything behind. I'm afraid that for all the progress he's been making he still has relapses like that."

Pauline's expression became serious at the thought of the considerable distance her husband still had to travel. Only I knew that the journey was going to be a particularly difficult one from this point on. Pauline's expression lightened as she continued. "I picked them up this morning. I did a bit of cleaning while I was there. I'll take them home tonight."

"Iris will appreciate your help," I said.

Pauline smiled dismissively. "It's the least I could do after all she's been through recently. She doesn't want to start cleaning as soon as she gets home."

Pauline paused and her brow furrowed. "I've left it as best I can," she said, "but there was a funny smell I couldn't quite get rid of. I've flooded the place with air fresheners so hopefully it'll go away."

"What sort of smell?" I couldn't resist asking.

"A sort of gassy smell," she said. "I wondered whether MJ let any escape when he was setting up the piping for the gas fire but he'll know what he's doing won't he, Gareth?"

I agreed with her and then changed the subject. I flicked open the lid of the tool box.

"An impressive array," I said, surveying a selection of implements the function of which I could only guess at.

Pauline smiled and nodded in agreement.

I could not delay the inevitable for ever with small talk. The time had come to talk to Pauline about what I knew. I called out to Cher that we were not to be disturbed. I then closed the door and sat down opposite Pauline, preparing myself for the difficult message I had to deliver. She picked up on my expression immediately.

"What is it?" she asked, suddenly concerned. By way of reply I reached into my briefcase and produced the file I had found. There was a sharp intake of breath from Pauline as she saw what it was.

"You know what that is don't you, Pauline?" I asked. She nodded, her hand over her mouth as she did so.

"You've seen it before, haven't you?"

She nodded again.

"I mean recently."

This time she was more reticent. She looked down to the floor avoiding both my eyes and an answer. I didn't waste time asking the question again. I knew the answer.

"Did you show it to Sam, or tell him about it?"

She was quick to look up again and deny it.

"You know how Debbie died don't you, Pauline? You know it was Iris Jenkins who drove Terry off the road."

Pauline looked to the floor again.

I carried on. "It's in this file. MJ received a call at 6.15 but he didn't pass it on. Instead he went to the scene himself and even then didn't report it. Why would he do that unless someone close to him had something to hide?"

Pauline's voice was barely discernible as she spoke. "Has MJ told you that, Gareth?"

"He has but I'd already guessed from this file just like you did when you looked at it."

Still no acknowledgement so I continued.

"Mind you, I doubt if it would have meant very much to me if I didn't already know that MJ had been seen near the car by Terry Driscoll."

Now I had Pauline's full attention. I pressed home the point I wanted to make.

"How come you worked it out just from the file without speaking to Terry first?"

Pauline smiled, raising her palms in a gesture of incomprehension. "I'm sorry, Gareth, but I don't understand. What are you saying?"

I didn't answer that question directly. Instead, I started to tell Pauline of my encounter with Terry in Spain.

"What I noticed," I said, "was the medallion he wore on a chain around his neck. Every time he mentioned Debbie I would see him gripping it as if it symbolised her. I couldn't work out how it symbolised her at first but then I realised. It's a triangle inside a heart. The triangle is the Greek letter delta or "D" as in D for Debbie. It's a very subtle way of saying that Debbie is always in his heart. That use of a Greek symbol reminded me of something Nigel told me a while ago. Can you show me your tattoo, Pauline?"

She didn't even try to feign ignorance. With a blank expression she revealed the tattoo. I saw it again then, the heart with a triangle inside it, the same heart containing the same triangle as hung from the chain around Terry Driscoll's neck.

"It's not coincidence is it, Pauline. You've met Terry haven't you?"

"Is there any point in me denying it?" she asked with the faintest hint of a smile. I smiled back and slowly but firmly shook my head.

"Then I won't," she said. "I met him when he was over for his mother's funeral. I knew he'd come for it so I found out where it was and waited for him. I've always wanted to talk to him, to ask him how the accident happened and why he ran away. I never got the chance when Sam was around."

"And he told you about the woman and the policeman being there?"

"Yes but I didn't know whether to believe him at first. Then when the box of files arrived for this case of yours I wondered whether the file was there so I had a look, and it was then that I had a pretty good idea what had happened."

"And you told Sam."

She shook her head vigorously but I wasn't deterred.

"You told Sam and he decided to take his revenge, just like he always said he would."

She shook her head again. "I've told you I didn't tell Sam."

"But if you didn't tell Sam how come he rigged up a booby trap to blow Iris and Ty Gwyn off the face of the earth?"

Pauline ceased shaking her head. Suddenly she was giving me her full attention.

"I don't believe it," she said. "Sam wouldn't do that."

"No, Pauline, you're absolutely right. Sam wouldn't do that and he didn't do it did he? I saw him earlier today and he was still swearing vengeance against Terry. He wouldn't be doing that if you'd told him the truth. He didn't rig that device up at all."

I had played around for long enough. The final piece had been fitted into the jigsaw just minutes earlier. Now I had the full picture I had to tell Pauline the truth.

"Sam wouldn't do it and Sam didn't do it. You know he didn't do it because you did it, didn't you, Pauline?"

She said nothing. She didn't even react with the slightest body movement. I waited for her to speak but then broke the silence myself.

"It was all for nothing, Pauline. Iris hadn't even arrived at the house when MJ found the device you'd rigged up. He turned off the gas and by now he'd have disconnected the wire from the back of the light switch. You failed, Pauline, Iris is in no danger."

Still there was silence and I began to develop the sickening feeling that I had got it all wrong. I started to think desperately of how to talk myself out of it, how to repair my relationship with Pauline after my misplaced hammer blow. Suddenly, Pauline looked up. There was a burning rage in her eyes, her nostrils distended and she screamed.

"That damned Jankovic! If only he'd done what I paid him to do!"

Thirty-five

"You lied to me about the tool box. That was the final bit of evidence that told me it was you. That was what confirmed to me that you had set up a death trap for Iris. You even tried to shift suspicion from yourself by mentioning the smell but you knew Iris would be so pleased to be home she'd ignore it. That didn't fool me. Once you lied to me about the toolbox I knew I was right."

Rather pathetically having exposed the person behind a plot to cold bloodedly and spectacularly murder another human being I found myself justifying myself to that very person by suggesting that the pointers towards her were so obvious that I couldn't avoid following them. Surely Sherlock Holmes, Hercule Poirot or any of the other great detectives of fiction don't end up apologising to the villains they cunningly unmask. They like to revel in their brilliance, to rub the villains' felonious noses in it. If truth be told I was feeling anything but triumphant. Within twenty-four hours of rehabilitating one of my closest colleagues I was condemning another.

Pauline and I had been a team. We had stood together to face the ups, downs, triumphs and disasters of that circus that we called a solicitors' office. We had laughed at the absurd and railed against the outrageous as each crossed our threshold in what seemed like equal measure. Our relationship had never been based on romance or even lust but in its own way it had been closer than marriage. Now I couldn't resist being the interfering show off who ruined her life with my smart arsed detective work. That was nothing to be proud of but I retained enough objectivity to tell myself that I was doing a duty that I couldn't shirk.

"I was in earlier," I explained. "I saw the tool box then so I knew you hadn't just brought it back when you finished cleaning this morning. You must have brought it back on

Friday. I asked myself why you'd leave the tools here instead of taking them home over the weekend. There was only one answer. You'd taken some of the tools with you this morning and couldn't take the rest home until you replaced the missing ones in case Sam noticed."

Pauline avoided my gaze as I continued.

"That's why when I realised you'd lied to me I had a look inside to see if I could see what tools had only just been put in. I saw a screwdriver and it had paint on the blade. It's the one you used to unscrew the cover and get at the gas pipe isn't it? There was a hacksaw too. You made the cuts in the gas pipe with it didn't you?"

"Very clever."

Pauline didn't sound bitter or sarcastic as she said it. She almost seemed to be complimenting me as she used to do in our working days whenever I managed to sort out a difficult case.

"There was another thing," I continued, "I saw something in MJ's garden just now. Someone had carved something on a tree. I recognised it. I'd seen that design before at the end of the medallion round Terry Driscoll's neck and I've just seen it again. It's your tattoo isn't it? What was that all about, Pauline?"

Pauline was matter of fact and unemotional as she told me.

"It's one of Jankovic's trademarks. He leaves a clue when he does a job so that those that matter know why the job was done. He asked me if I wanted anything and that's what I asked for. I thought that even when Ty Gwyn is a pile of rubble and Iris Jenkins is a pile of ashes I could look at that tree and know why it happened."

I was shocked as much by her lack of apparent remorse as by what she had tried to do. I had to ask.

"How did this all happen, Pauline?"

"It was Lucca Contemponi who started it," she said. "He's a vile man, he used to make my flesh creep but I found myself talking to him a lot when Beppo first came to us. I think he was trying to impress me. He was telling me how he could have a man killed at the click of his fingers. I think it was like a form of phone sex for him telling a woman how powerful he was. He even used to ask me if I wanted anyone taking care of. He seemed to get off on that."

"And you said you did?" I was incredulous. It's one thing to be offered the services of a plumber or a taxi driver by someone you happen to talk to on the phone but an assassin? What is the world coming to?

Rather surprisingly Pauline seemed offended by the suggestion.

"Not at the time," she said indignantly. I was hoping she wasn't going to follow that up with "what sort of person do you think I am?" because at that moment I had no idea how I would answer her. She clarified her remark.

"It was only when I caught MJ playing about with the trust fund that I began to think about taking Lucca up on what he'd said."

"You knew about the money?"

"Cher is not as stupid as everyone thinks," she said. "She told me about MJ and his sister and how that drippy bloke of hers was shooting his mouth off. I knew MJ didn't have a sister so I kept an eye on the bank account and I saw the money go out.

"By then I'd worked out what Iris had done from the file and what Terry had told me. I thought that if I could catch MJ with his hand in the till that would be the first step in getting my revenge for Debbie and no one would suspect that I was doing anything other than my duty as a loyal employee. I thought I'd deal with Iris later. I was watching MJ, waiting for the piece of evidence that could nail him when he started asking me for the IBAN number of the trust account. I knew he was lying about someone wanting to pay in. If it had been someone local he wouldn't have needed the IBAN number. I wasn't sure how he was going to do it but I thought he was going to steal some more. I waited till he had gone out of the room and left his jacket over the chair. He always walks round without his jacket in the office. I checked the pockets and found the piece of paper on which I'd put the IBAN number. I was going to photocopy it as evidence but when I saw the other piece of paper he had I realised it was not what I'd expected. I recognised the number of the bank account the stolen money had gone to and I realised that MJ wasn't planning to steal money from the trust but was going to pay it back. You know, Gareth, I was actually disappointed. He was honest after all. It was then Lucca rang quite by chance and that's what gave me the idea. If I got things right I could pay Iris back for what she'd done to Debbie and I could get MJ blamed for it. What could be better?"

I was about to say that maybe it would have been better to forget all ideas of hiring hit men to kill middle-aged women but before I could do so Pauline continued.

"I teased Lucca saying that I thought he was all hot air and didn't know any assassins at all. He got quite Italian about it. You'd think I'd insulted his manhood. He insisted he was an important man with killers on his payroll. I said that if this was true he should introduce me to one. I pretended that I wanted the thrill of talking to a killer on the phone. I could hear Lucca's breathing getting heavier when I said that, as if I was talking dirty to him. That's how, not twenty minutes later, I got a call from Jankovic. He must have got the shock of his life. He obviously thought he was calling to give a few cheap thrills to a naïve housewife and within five minutes I was telling him what I could afford to pay and taking down his bank details. Give him his due, he didn't show any shock. He was very professional about the arrangements. Just a pity he was so bloody amateur about doing the job. Don't suppose I'll get my money back."

To my horror Pauline seemed to be smiling as she completed the account. "You know the rest don't you? I switched the paper on which I'd written the trust account details with one on which I'd put Jankovic's details. They were both just a list of figures so I knew MJ wouldn't notice. Without knowing it MJ was transferring the money to Jankovic and not back to the trust. It was then just a question of waiting for Jankovic to do what he was paid for."

"But he didn't," I said displaying yet again my talent for stating the obvious.

"No," said Pauline, "he bungled it and when he bungled it I had to do it myself. By all accounts it looks like I've bungled it too. That Iris is like a cat, nine bloody lives she has."

Pauline had just told me how she had plotted a murder not once but twice and she's done it all in the same tone as she might have used if she were passing on the recipe for a particularly delicious cake. I'd asked her how it happened and she'd answered me literally. That wasn't exactly what I had meant.

"Why did you do all this, Pauline? Sam was the one screaming for revenge. You were always the pragmatic one, the one who preferred to be positive."

"That's just it," she said still in her cake recipe voice. "Sam will rant and rave and feel sorry for himself but you know and I know that he'd never do anything. That's the tragedy of Sam. He's let his own life be ruled by thoughts of revenge but he'll never take that revenge so he'll never get his life back. Rage never gets you anything but action does. You need to take action, decisive action when you can. When you've taken it you can get on with your life but until you can take it there's no point getting angry about it."

I thought of Rafa wielding his hammer in the cemetery as Pauline continued. "What do they say, Gareth? Revenge is a dish best served cold. They're right you know. Sam ranted and I waited. I kept myself busy, tried to be positive, kept patient and when my chance came I took it. Trouble is that I blew it and I don't suppose I'll get another chance."

Not for the first time this winter I realised that I didn't know someone whom I thought I'd been close to. I thought I knew Pauline and the way she thought but what I had never grasped was the depth of her feelings on her loss, the lengths those feelings would take her to and the way that the cool calculating unflappable brain that I had depended on for so long could be set the task of ruthlessly taking life. Now I didn't know whether to be appalled by her cold bloodedness or impressed by her dedication to the memory of her daughter.

"You did all this for Debbie? I understand all of that but surely you understand that nothing you do would bring her back. If you understand that why did you do it?"

"You don't understand do you, Gareth? It wasn't about bringing Debbie back. She's gone but Sam's still alive. He's the one I had to bring back. I hoped that when the initial excitement died down I could take him to where Ty Gwyn had been and show him the tree. He'd understand then even if he could tell nobody and he would know that his grieving could end. That's why I did it, Gareth, to get my husband back."

Pauline wiped a tear from her eye and reverted to the practical, efficient secretary I had known all these years.

"I realise what you have to do now, Gareth, don't feel bad about it," she said as if I were the one who needed sympathy. "Call Nev Powell and tell him to come for me. I'll not run away or anything. I just need to tidy my desk and leave a note for Lenny telling him where everything is. Meanwhile, if I can ask one thing of you, could you look after Sam for me? Tell him what's happened and make sure he's alright. Tell him not to worry about me, I'll be ok."

"I can do that for you, Pauline," I said. "I'll make it my business to keep an eye on Sam whenever I'm over here and I know Lenny will do the same while I'm away. I've already spoken to Nigel asking him to go round. He gets on well with Sam. Meanwhile you're going to need someone to look after you at the police station. I'll go along with you and then when you need someone who isn't past it to represent you, I and Lenny will sort that out too."

Pauline gripped my hand and smiled as she thanked me. I then left her alone while I went out to make the most difficult phone calls of my life.

I had only just switched my phone on after leaving the police station when it rang. It was Nigel but it didn't sound like the Nigel I knew. He explained briefly and I jumped in the car to meet him.

I found him standing on the mountainside staring out over the valley. Behind him was the bench that had been the focal point of Sam Hopkins' life for the last twenty years. At his feet was the memorial that Sam had tended for that same time.

As I approached Nigel I could see he was crying. The man who had an answer for everything and was fazed by nothing was crying. The human side of Nigel that had appeared so briefly when he had spoken of his Liverpool family and which had disappeared behind the shell again when he finished was now exposed naked to the elements.

"It's happened again," was all Nigel said as he looked down the mountainside to where smoke was rising from the black twisted metal that had once been a motor car.

"He was dead when they got to him," he said. "The car was on fire and when they put it out they found the body. There was nothing they could do."

"How did it happen?" I asked.

Nigel covered his face. "I failed again," he said between sobs. "I left Sam alone for five minutes while I went to buy some groceries for him and when I got back he was gone and so was his car. Somehow I knew this was where he'd be but I didn't expect this. It's my fault, Gareth. He just drove his car off the side and it's my fault."

I tried to console Nigel but he was not looking for consolation.

"I should have realised he'd do this to himself," Nigel kept repeating. "I should never have left him alone."

"You couldn't have stayed with him for ever, Nigel," I said. "You mustn't blame yourself. This would have happened whatever you did. Sam Hopkins was a dead man before you ever knew him. He died when he lost Debbie. He may have looked alive but he was like one of those people on a life support machine. One day that machine had to be switched off. Today was that day and nothing you could have done would have prevented the inevitable. Pauline was that life support machine and I was the one who switched it off. If anyone should feel responsible it should be me."

Even in his despair Nigel's urge to correct me surfaced. "You're wrong there, Gareth. It wasn't Pauline who was keeping him going. It was hate. That was his life support machine. As long as he could hate he had something to live for. Today he learned that he had wasted twenty years of hate for Terry Driscoll. It was too late to learn to hate someone else. He lost that hate and when he stopped hating he stopped living."

It was dark now and the rain was falling as Nigel and I stared silently down into the valley. In the distance we knew would be Ty Gwyn at the bottom of the coal encrusted slope on which the sheep would be silently chewing the sporadic tufts of wiry grass little knowing and little caring that once more they had witnessed a death in the valley.